BLACKMAILING BELLE

HOLLY ROBERDS

BOOKS BY HOLLY ROBERDS

<u>**VEGAS IMMORTALS**</u>

Death and the Last Vampire

Book 1 - Bitten by Death

Book 2 - Kissed by Death

Book 3 - Seduced by Death

The Beast & the Badass

Book 1 - Breaking the Beast

Book 2 - Claiming the Beast

<u>**DEMON KNIGHTS**</u>

Book 1 - One Savage Knight

Book 2 - One Bad Knight

<u>**LOST GIRLS SERIES**</u>

Book 1 - Tasting Red

Book 2 - Chasing Goldie

Book 3 - Igniting Cinder

Book 3.5 - Hooking Tink

Book 4 - Blackmailing Belle

Book 5 - Feeding Beauty

<u>**THE FIVE ORDERS**</u>

Book 0.5 – The Knight Watcher

Book 1 - Prophecy Girl

Book 2 - Soulless Son

Book 3 - Tear in the World

Book 4 – Into Darkness

Book 4.5 - Touch of Hell

Book 5 - End Game

* For recommended reading order, visit www.hollyroberds.com

For you sick fucks on TikTok who taught me about the barbed shifter penis thing.
Damn you.

CHAPTER I

A LAPFUL OF LEVERAGE
THE BEAST OF BOSTON

I thumb the edge of the file I have open, scanning the contents for the third time.

Twenty-eight years old. Owner of Chapter Three, Belle's Romance Bookstore.

"She's perfect." My words are low, bordering on a growl.

Hesitation swirls around the two men across from me like a physical cloud.

I close the file, moving it to the end of my antique walnut desk, reaped from the trees of Neverland itself. The heavy curtains are drawn, casting the room in enough darkness that Lucien and Tock can't get a good look at me, though I see both of them perfectly.

Long slivers of afternoon light manage to break through the velvet curtains and stretch across the floor. My lip curls as I cross the red antique rug, noting the claw marks scored into its fibers. Mrs. P has offered to fix it many times, but I always tell her to leave it. I need the reminder of what I am.

I'd only ruin the new carpets.

No, it's best to see, to be aware of the damage I do.

I pour two fingers of rum with my left hand. My human hand.

"Speak," I command.

The crystal glass grows lighter as I drink, the silence broken only by Lucien and Tock's urgent murmurs. They shift and fidget, elbowing each other forward until Lucien finally breaks.

"I don't think this will work." My enforcer runs a hand through his floppy blond hair.

Lucien's admission spurs Tock to gather his courage. The large, muscled man adjusts his round glasses. "What if she says no?"

Half my mouth curls back in a humorless smile.

"I don't pay you two to think," I address Lucien's concern, ignoring the impossibility of the second question.

The rest of my drink burns all the way down my throat, but not enough. It's too smooth. The harder life gets, the stronger I need my alcohol. That way I feel I have some power over the pain.

It doesn't control me if I choose it.

Instead of bowing, scraping, and scurrying away to fetch the girl for me, Tock sucks in a deep breath. "Dragging this young woman into this, we don't normally. . ."

A familiar sting and burn spirals through my muscles, spearing up into my brain. The glass shatters in my hand, shards slicing through my palm and fingers.

A roar erupts from me even as my vision turns red. Anger burns and boils me from the inside out.

Grabbing the entire bottle of 1902 Jolly Roger rum in my clawed paw, I hurl it against the wall between them. Both men flinch as it smashes in a spectacular spray of brown liquor and glass too close to their heads.

Tock instantly backs up several steps, bowing, avoiding

eye contact and submitting to my wrath. Lucien freezes in place.

Before I realize I've moved, I'm bearing over Lucien. Saliva dribbles out the corner of my mouth, my fangs elongating and contracting as a deep hunger for blood grips me.

His blood.

I hear it racing through his veins, begging me to tear into him like he's no more than a piece of meat. "What would you have me do?"

Fur sprouts on the backs of my hands before receding just as quickly.

"I'm running out of time." The words come out of me in a low, dangerous growl. My enforcer does his best to hold his ground, but Lucien reeks of fear.

His eyelids flutter as if he has to fight to keep them open to meet mine.

"Yes, boss." There's a tremor in his voice that makes me want to rip his throat out all the more.

I'm on the edge in a moment, balanced on the tipping point. It would be so easy to let go. To give in and tear out that bobbing Adam's apple.

Lucien knows better than to turn and run. That will only excite me more. He may be lanky and fast, but he's still just a human. He wouldn't stand a chance against my speed and power.

"I-I'll get her for you," Lucien says, his words wavering while the blood drains from his face, turning his skin waxy and pale.

"We'll bring her to you," Tock confirms. Sweat beads along his mahogany brown forehead.

Sense hammers into my violence-fueled brain. Turning my back on my men, I stalk to my desk.

"See that you do."

Only after I hear the click of the door close after him do I let out a heavy sigh. Exhaustion and disgust weigh me down.

I bare my teeth, stepping back from the edge. My men have always been unflinchingly loyal, but this is the first time I've seen them balk at a command. They're used to the production and selling of Thorns. They are often busy blunting the tiny sharp teeth of our rivals who think they can replace me or take over my business. Those mutts are becoming more bothersome by the day.

But this? Manipulating a girl who has no idea what she's worth? It's not the job my men know, and I can feel their unease.

Soon, our enemies will need to be dealt with permanently, but for now, we have another pawn to maneuver in our game of power and control.

What if she says no?

Lucien's question wasn't even worth a response.

No one says no to the Beast of Boston. I've made sure of that.

Everyone has a pressure point, a price. Luckily for me, Isabelle Lockhart's has fallen right into my lap.

I stare at the live security feed along the wall. A couple of the screens are cracked beyond repair, but they'll be replaced by tomorrow.

My leverage is currently sitting in a concrete cell in the basement. And that leverage guarantees me what I need.

Isabelle.

CHAPTER 2

MY FAVORITE CHAPTER

BELLE

I needed the panties gone. I needed Grim inside me, now. I needed him filling me until I couldn't think. The ache inside me was unbearable. He wasn't close enough and some part of me screamed I would be safe once he was inside. And I needed Grim to lose himself in me. I may have been the one restrained, but not for a second did I doubt the control I had over him.

"Mine," Grim snarled. My hips jerked as Grim ripped off my panties.

"This is disgusting." The sharp voice cuts through my reading haze, shattering my focus. "And I want my money back."

The need to scream builds in the back of my throat, but I muscle it back down, lowering the book I've got a white-knuckled grip on.

A woman wearing a camel hair coat that probably costs more than my monthly rent stands before me, brandishing a paperback like its evidence from a crime scene. The book's spine is cracked in multiple places, the pages suspiciously rippled as if it's been read in the bath. French-manicured nails drum against my counter in sharp, staccato beats, and her ash-blonde hair is pulled into a severe bun that makes my head hurt just looking at it.

It's not her fault that I've hardly been sleeping. My bloodshot eyes burn behind my glasses from spending days calling hospitals and police stations, searching for my mentally unstable father. My hair has escaped my bun in wild tendrils, and I know the cardigan I'm wearing over my *Happily Ever After or Bust* tee shirt has seen better days.

Floor-to-ceiling shelves create cozy nooks and crannies throughout my shop, each one carefully curated with twinkling lights and plush reading chairs. Romance covers in every shade imaginable line the walls—a rainbow of promises and passion that usually fills me with pride. The ancient hardwood floors creak beneath my feet as I set my book aside and take a steadying breath, the way I learned long ago when dealing with volatile individuals.

"I understand you're unhappy with your purchase," I say, keeping my voice firm but pleasant. "However, our return policy—"

"These should be banned," she cuts me off, volume rising. "Boston is a human city for a *reason*. We don't need shifter smut or mage romance or any other fae propaganda corrupting decent people. And you—" she gestures at me with disgust "—should be ashamed, pushing this monster-loving filth."

I maintain eye contact, my hands relaxed at my sides. The way she towers over the counter, trying to intimidate with her height and volume—I've seen it all before.

From people far more dangerous than an angry reader.

"All our books are clearly labeled with content warnings," I explain, the same steady tone I use when my dad is having an episode. "If you'd prefer, I can recommend something else from our collection."

"I want to speak to your manager."

A small smile tugs at my lips. "You're speaking to the owner."

Her face flushes an ugly red as she sweeps her critical eye over my form. "No wonder this place is a joke. Just wait until I post about this on—"

"Feel free to leave an honest review of your experience," I say, still calm and steady. "But I need to ask you to lower your voice or leave the store."

She opens her mouth, then closes it, thrown by my continued composure. It's a trick I learned young—the calmer you stay, the more foolish their rage appears.

"This isn't over," she snaps, but she's already backing away, her bluster deflating against my quiet certainty.

"Have a nice day," I call after her, though I doubt she'd be capable of enjoying it even if it were nice. The bell above the door chimes at her exit, its cheerful tinkle at odds with the tension she leaves in her wake. Only when she's gone do I let out a long breath, inhaling the familiar comfort of paper, coffee, and the lavender essential oil I use to combat anxiety.

Those few minutes of tense exchange sucked out what little emotional resilience I had left in me.

It doesn't help that I'm nearly sick with worry over my dad being out there in his addled state. Sometimes he comes home on his own, sometimes with a ride from the local police, but it looks like I'll have to resort to finding him myself, searching Boston block by block. Returning to places I'd rather never visit again, in case he thought to go to familiar territory even if we aren't welcome anymore.

I worked hard to leave our old life behind after dad's

incident, but it's difficult taking care of a man who forgets and goes back to what is familiar.

A snow plow noisily passes by outside, pushing fresh snow from the road. What I wouldn't give to forget all my problems and be at home in my threadbare reading chair, snuggled in a cozy blanket, drinking hot chocolate and tearing through the rest of this series.

I automatically open a drawer, reaching for a plastic-wrapped treat. Almost as soon as I pick it up, I put the Magic Morsel back down. As much as I want to eat a square of Magic Fairy Fudge, I do *not* want the fifteen minutes of telepathy that comes along with the magical sweet treat. Not today. I can barely handle my own thoughts.

The soft hum of conversation catches my ear. A group of women approach the counter, and my spirits rise. Their faces glow with the warmth of camaraderie and the many pots of vanilla rose tea. The last members of the romance book club, Lust & Lit, have packed up, and their arms are laden with books they couldn't resist buying after tonight's discussion.

I get to work checking out the books they've chosen for next week's meeting. They are ravenous readers.

"Isabelle, tonight was amazing," gushes Gingie, one of my regulars. "I mean, rereading *A Scandalous Arrangement* with the group? I forgot how much I loved it." Gingie has a penchant for Regency romances and enthusiasm in spades. "That moment in the carriage when Emma realizes he's actually a prince—it gives me chills every time."

"I'll never get over how perfect that is," Rachel Anne adds in agreement, sweeping her dark hair behind an ear. "It's your favorite for a reason, right? You even named the shop after that chapter? Chapter Three?"

I smile, the warmth of the memory bubbling up despite

my exhaustion. "I did. I'll never forget reading it for the first time. I couldn't stop thinking about it for weeks and reread the book *twelve* times that year."

They all laugh.

"Emma's such a strong character," Yanette says, one of the women who organizes the group. She rests her elbow on the counter. "She doesn't just see a prince—she sees the person behind the crown. It's not love at first sight, but once she sees him clearly, everything changes. I see so much of her in you."

I laugh softly, brushing off the compliment even as it stirs something bittersweet in my chest.

The new girl, Hannah, clutches *A Scandalous Arrangement* tighter to her chest. "This was my first romance, and I couldn't put it down. I didn't know books could make you feel so much."

"You never forget your first," I say warmly, handing her next week's read. "And this one is going to be even steamier."

Hannah giggles, her cheeks pink. "This is really raising the bar on the guys I date."

That earns a wave of sighs and playful nudges from the others, but my smile falters ever so slightly. "Good luck with that," I say with more sharpness than I intend. "In my experience, love is best kept between the pages of a book. Lucky for us, we've got plenty of them." I wave a hand to my many shelves.

While the other women laugh, Hannah's brows pinch like she's not sure whether I'm joking. Gingie elbows her gently. "Don't listen to her, hun. Belle gave up on love in real life a long time ago. Though I don't think it's given up on her." Gingie gives me a pointed look. "The right person will sweep you off your feet one day."

"He'll have to possess Herculean strength to pull that off," I say, waving a hand over my plus-size figure. The memory of camel coat's scathing, judgmental stare said everything her mouth didn't.

You're fat and worthless.

Not that I'm not used to it. What once cut like glass now only slides across my skin with the dull edge of a plastic knife. Not pleasant but expected.

It was a lifetime ago, but I grew up around people who taught me softness and vulnerability weren't just frowned upon—they were dangerous liabilities. I once read that sometimes our bodies adapt, creating shields where our minds can't. Maybe mine did just that, forging armor to protect me from the world I grew up in. If that's true, then I've made myself a soft place to land.

Sometimes, I wonder if one day I'll feel strong enough or safe enough to let the weight go.

Not that it's ever been for lack of trying. No crash diet or hours pounding the pavement ever even made a dent in my figure, so I stopped hating the body I live in and decided to appreciate it for what it is—mine.

The book club's joy is infectious, and I find myself waving them out with genuine warmth as they chatter about next month's pick.

As the door chimes behind them, a sense of calm settles over me. Moments like this make it all worth it—the long hours, the stress, the constant work to take care of my dad while running a business.

He'll turn up. He always does, I remind myself.

Knowing chapter three still resonates, that it sparked something in Hannah the way it once did in me. . .It's why I opened this bookstore. It's why I keep going, even when the world feels like it's closing in. The stories may be fiction, but the connections they bring? The main character energy it can inspire? The escapes it can provide from the unpleasant parts of life? That's as real as it gets.

The door chimes again, and two men enter. The lanky one, pale-skinned with floppy blonde hair, has a smile that could charm the spines off a hedgehog. Behind him is a behemoth of a man, bald with deep brown skin. His tweed jacket and scholarly glasses give him the air of someone who could teach an advanced college course on philosophy —perhaps right before or after picking up a person and breaking them into two equal pieces.

"Welcome to Chapter Three," I say warmly. "Are you looking for anything in particular?" I bite down on my desire to point out I have an excellent selection of Queer romance. It's rude to assume, but they'd make a striking pair.

The lanky one's lips twitch as he snaps open a metal lighter before clicking it closed in repeated succession. "We're not here for books, *mademoiselle*," he says with a slight French accent while sauntering over to my front display. Cajun French, if I'm not mistaken.

"I'm Tock and this is Lucien," the larger man says in a British accent.

Running his long fingers along the spine of a mage romance book, Lucien smiles up at me. "And our boss, the Beast of Boston, has something that belongs to you, *cher*."

"Your father," Tock clarifies.

Time slows. The sounds of my shop and background music become muffled in my ears.

Ice drips into my veins as panic pierces my already aching sleep-deprived brain.

The Beast of Boston.

The name alone makes my skin crawl. Even in a world

divided between humans, Mages, and fae, he's legendary—the mafia boss who rules Boston's underworld from the shadows. Worse yet, he deals in Thorns—the most powerful hexes and curses in any realm.

Some say he's an Ogre, others whisper he's something worse. But everyone agrees—what the Beast wants, he takes.

"You know where he is? My father?" The words barely scrape out of my suddenly dry throat.

"That we do, *mon cher*."

Tock rolls his shoulders back. "We'd like you to come with us. . .now." It isn't a request.

My insides twist like a wet rag until I can't breathe. I look between the men, trying to think of any way out of this. But they have my father, and it's my job to take care of him.

So I close up shop and allow the men to lead me outside to a black SUV that screams I'll never return alive.

CHAPTER 3

A TERRIFYING PROPOSAL

BELLE

The air inside the black SUV is thick with the scent of the bigger man's cologne. It's an oddly homey contrast to the chill clawing up my spine as the vehicle passes through massive iron gates. I have two books in my purse, but I haven't felt comfortable to take out either for the duration of the trip.

Tock opens the door the moment we stop. I step out and my gaze lifts to the looming brownstone fortress ahead. Not quite a castle, but it's close enough to make me feel as if I've crossed into a dark fairy tale.

Tock leads the way up the stairs, Lucien trailing behind me while continuing to flick his lighter on and off. They flank me as if to make sure I don't cut and run. I have no intention of leaving, not when my father is here.

The massive black doors are covered in ornate moldings —gothic swirls and floral designs that seem to swallow the winter's light. They swing open with a heavy creak, and I barely have time to register the dark, rich furnishings and antique rugs before I'm ushered down a hallway into a cavernous room. A study or office of sorts.

Despite the bright gray light of winter's day, the room is shrouded in near complete darkness. The faint aroma of smoke mingles with the smell of old wood and something spicy. Heavy curtains cover the windows and a lone candlestick in a corner flickers, barely penetrating the inky shadows.

I jump as the door slams shut behind me, sharp as a gunshot. Lucien and Tock have left me alone inside. Before I can call out to them, something shifts in the dark and my breathing turns harsh as I realize I'm not alone. My skin crawls and the fine hairs on the back of my neck rise.

"Who's there?" I demand, the roughness in my voice betraying my nerves. I need to hear it, to ground myself.

A looming figure too large to be human rises from behind the desk. I can't help but retreat a few steps, my heart thudding up into my throat.

The need to scream for help, to throw the door open and run grips me, but I force myself to root down through my feet.

"Who are you? What do you want?" I manage, the words scraped from a throat gone dry.

A low monstrous chuckle reverberates through the room, rattling my bones. Despite the laugh, there is no hint of humor in it. "Didn't they tell you?" a dangerous voice asks.

I take a steadying breath. "You're the Beast of Boston, and you have my father."

There is a pause from the mass behind the desk. "That I am, and that I do."

The Beast doesn't elaborate. The silence stretches between us with thick expectation. I squint into the shadows, trying to discern details. Is the Beast of Boston really an Ogre, like the rumors say? Though Ogres are usually considered to not be high functioning. They are more like big, thick-skinned himbos with violent tendencies.

Why didn't I pay more attention to the stories about his withdrawal from society?

Because you're too busy reading or peddling fantasy smut and ignoring the real world as much as possible.

Oh right. *That.*

"What do you want?" I ask finally. If he wants money, I don't have much. Not by his standards, anyway.

I can't see him, but I swear he grins in the dark. "*You,* Isabelle."

No one calls me by my full name, not even my dad. The words are spoken with such menace, such promise that I take another step back.

"Your father was found breaking into my property," the Beast says in a low growl. "You're lucky I'm not handing him over to the authorities. Breaking into my property alone would warrant jail time. Add my name to the report, and there's not a judge or jury in Boston who wouldn't make an example of him." Even as he says the words, a screen at the far end of the office lights up. showing an image of what looks like a jail cell containing my father.

My heart clenches painfully. He's safe. . .for now. The fraying mustard sweater I saw him in two days ago still hangs on his sparse frame. Tufts of white hair stick every which way from his balding head as if he's been running his hands through them. He paces back and forth in the cell, his mouth moving. He's talking to himself and gesturing wildly with his hands.

The constant ache born of worry drills through the center of my heart. Is he cold? Is he scared? Does he know what's going on? Have they been feeding him? He doesn't remember to eat. I always have to bully him into consuming enough calories to fuel his overactive brain. I had to do that even before the incident that unraveled his mind, but it's worse now.

"He was trying to steal from me." The Beast's words lash out with a venomous snap.

"I'm so sorry, but I'm sure he didn't really mean to. My father gets confused. He has a condition—"

"He tried to steal from me." The Beast's roar is sudden, a gust of wind that blows my hair back. My teeth click shut as I flinch. I clutch my hands together until my knuckles turn white, trying to hold steady. He's trying to scare me.

"Yelling at me won't accomplish anything," I shoot back. "I may be a woman you think you can bully, but I've dealt with my fair share of powerful, dangerous men. If you want to talk, do not raise your voice to me." My words snap out like a whip.

The shadow rears back slightly. Again, I sense more than see his surprise.

"I'm not like any man you've met before," he says in a low voice that trembles with barely restrained violence.

"Great. I'm not like any woman you've met before. Glad we cleared that up. Now, I'd appreciate it if you would let my father go and we'll be out of your hair."

When the Beast resumes speaking, his voice is calmer, colder. "I can't just let him go."

"Why not?" I manage to ask, my impatience rising as quickly as my frustration.

"I have a reputation to uphold."

"But no one even knows he—"

"A price must be paid," he interrupts, "and it will either be paid by him or. . .you." The Beast draws out the last word, a sinister purr. I can't tell if it's an invitation or a threat.

"What price?" I ask. He said he wants me, but I don't know what that means. The idea that I might have to pay for my father's freedom with my body passes my mind for a moment before disappearing into vapor. The Beast of Boston could and likely does, have any woman he wants.

Unless he's got a super specific kink for heavyset introverts who love to read smut, I'm safe.

The pause becomes heavy. I get the strange sense it's as if the Beast is loading a gun, before he's about to make a fatal shot.

"Your father's life or your hand in marriage."

Bang.

"And just so we're clear, should I decide to press charges, your father will spend the rest of his life behind bars. That's not a threat—it's a certainty."

I blink, my mind struggling to comprehend.

He doesn't want money or apologies. He wants. . .me?

Dear fae lord, did I actually hit on his kink?

Or does he know where I come from?

I shake off the thought. When I cut ties, I did it efficiently and completely. There's no reason to drag me into his life.

My thoughts spin out like a possessed clothes washing drum, but there is one thing I'm crystal clear on. This isn't a proposal. It's blackmail.

A cold, burning anger rises inside me, mixing with my fear. "I'm very sorry my father broke into your home, but this is not a proportionate response."

The massive figure leaps on top of the desk, sending papers, books, and items crashing to the floor. The distinct scrape of wood under claws sets my teeth on edge as my skin pulls back. Fear freezes my feet to the floor.

"You know who I am."

I nod.

"You know what I am capable of."

He doesn't need to say it outright. If I refuse him, my father loses everything—his freedom, his care, his fragile safety.

I know well enough the Beast of Boston could ruin me and my father with one phone call. Make my bookstore disappear, empty our bank accounts, have us held on murder charges for a crime the Beast himself committed, and all before lunch.

"Then you know I am deadly serious." A near-silken tone wraps around his harsh words. A deadly promise. "Either I put your father behind bars, or you leave your life and come live here with me as my wife. Effective immediately."

"My father's life or my hand in marriage." I say it aloud more for my own sake than his.

A grunt of assent lets me know that's exactly what's on the table.

It's insane. Ridiculous. Witchtitting bonkers. This is the insane plot of a romance book, a marriage of convenience or rather, inconvenience. A dark fae mafia lord takes a woman as his wife and prisoner, but this is the real world. Fae and humans don't mix. Not in Boston.

Not that I have a problem with interracial marriages. And it's not like I'm holding out for Mr. Right. Love isn't real. People just use each other for their own purposes and call it love.

I long ago gave up any romantic hopes for my life, but this certainly doesn't gel with the future I'd envisioned for myself.

I planned to take care of my father, run my dream business, and read books until I died an old, bookish cat lady with an insanely long unfinished TBR. I haven't gotten around to getting the cats, partly because I don't care for their judgmental stares. But still.

I focus on the screen now showing my father lying on his back on the small cot in the cell. He kicks his feet back and forth like a child, his mouth still moving a mile a minute. I can guess he is reciting chemistry equations. It's what he does when he's stressed out.

"Your time to decide is up." A mass of muscle shifts in the dark as the Beast snarls. "Which will you forgo, your father's future or your own? Make your choice."

As if on cue, Lucien appears on the screen. He stands at the cell bars, serious eyes turned up toward the camera, as if waiting for a signal. My father continues to babble to himself, arms thrown over his eyes. He has no idea he's in danger.

Panic grips me in a chokehold, nearly pulling me off my feet. My hands press into my heart to keep it from breaking through my ribcage.

My father is the only family I have. He's taken care of me my entire life. The man supplied me with more books than any girl could dream of. Before his mind unraveled, we had the greatest conversations about life, love, and what's possible.

I was twenty-two when he had his accident. The first few years of college had been a dream come true for me, and I knew I was exactly where I was supposed to be. But when my father needed extra care and support, I didn't hesitate to drop out of school and take care of him. It was because of him that I was able to open my dream business.

But he may be the same reason it's snatched away from me.

I swallow hard and steel my jangling nerves. "Come into the light."

The hulking mass goes deathly still.

"No."

I huff a sigh and push my hair from my face. "You want me to marry you? I want to properly meet who I'd be shackling myself to."

CHAPTER 4

A LITTLE MAN IN YOUR MONSTER

THE BEAST OF BOSTON

Come into the light.

The urge to roar at her again, to make her cower and submit, rises fiercely within me. But Isabelle's eyes stay locked on mine, her stance bold. There's a command there, unexpected and maddening. Yet I can't help but respect it.

One massive, clawed foot connects with the ground followed by the other, as I descend from the top of my desk. I slowly slink toward the warm glow of the candle, bringing me within six feet of the woman before me.

The candle's glow casts an inviting light on her creamy complexion. Mahogany hair is pulled back into an elegant ballerina bun at the base of her skull, though several harried tendrils have escaped it and cling to her face and neck. Long, thick lashes frame her dark eyes. A pair of glasses gives her the appearance of a severe yet sexy librarian. I can't help but notice how her pupils have expanded into dark pools as she hungrily searches the darkness. Her lips, pink and full, part slightly. Her fingers press tightly together as if bracing for impact.

And her scent. Warm and alive, with a sweetness that isn't cloying but pervasive. Filling the air around her like a shimmering aura. It doesn't just linger on her skin—it radiates, enveloping the space between us until it feels as if I'm breathing her in with every ragged inhale.

Isabelle is beautiful. Not just pretty but arresting in a way that both the man and the beast in me recognize. And that makes it all the harder to show her what I am.

I may be ruthless when it comes to business and getting what I want, but pride and vanity still riot in me, urging me to stay in the shadows.

The woman is all soft, round edges. The fabric of her shirt stretches over the generous swell of her breasts and hips. She isn't small or fragile, and that somehow makes her more desirable. Her body seems built for warmth, for holding, and there's a part of me that wants to feel her pressed against me.

I shove the thought away.

This transaction is about survival, not pleasure.

Don't let her see what you are. You'll only repulse her, the voice in my head hisses.

My claws scrape the wood floor as I step into the light, ignoring the desire to retreat. Knowing the monstrous visage I create, I straighten in the glow, allowing it to fully reveal me to her. I don't wear shoes—my massive, clawed feet make them impossible—and the black slacks and white half-opened shirt don't conceal the long streaks of fur lining my hard, corded muscles.

Had I known she would demand to see me, I would have fastened the shirt up to the neck.

Yet nothing can obscure the grotesque fusion that is my face.

Isabelle gasps softly, her breath catching in her throat, her lips parting further. Her eyes widen as she takes me in.

I grimace, knowing I look like the damn devil.

I let her take me in slowly.

From one side to the other, my face is a clash of human and beast, the man I was merging unnervingly with the creature I've become. My nose, once a proud arch, flattens into a lion's snout, the bridge roughened with a scar that stretches across my brow. Dark, tawny fur ripples over the left side of my cheek, spreading upward toward a pointed ear that twitches at her scrutiny. A single fang protrudes over the left side of my lip. The green of my right eye remains sharp and human, but the left is distinctly feline— slit-pupiled and gleaming with predatory intensity.

I brace myself. She might faint, run, or scream as other fae-fearing women have before. Isabelle might even leave her father to die in her fervor to escape my presence.

But I'm betting everything I have that she won't. I know what she's sacrificed for that old man in my cell, the depth of her loyalty to the old coot.

Knowing people's secrets is part of my business. Leverage is everything, and I'm leveraging Isabelle's love for her father to bind her to me.

"You're a Were," she stammers, her voice a mixture of disbelief and awe. There's hesitation but no obvious fear. "But you're..."

"Half-shifted," I confirm. My grimace morphs into a grin, knowing it presents an even more terrifying visage.

Am I trying to drive her away?

I can't help it. The fact I look like a monster only compels me to act more like one.

Isabelle doesn't retreat. She simply stands and studies

my distorted features. Her brow furrows, her gaze sharp with curiosity, maybe even something like fascination.

"Your name isn't really the Beast of Boston, is it?" she asks with plain open curiosity.

Why isn't she fearful?

Why isn't she recoiling?

A spring of surprise erupts in me. "No. It's. . .Dominic. Dominic Blackwell."

Suddenly, I find it maddening, the way she doesn't flinch, or turn away.

It's too much. Being in the light, exposed to her intense focus, makes me feel raw and vulnerable. I retreat into the shadows, letting the darkness close around me like a shroud. The familiar cloak of control returns. My breathing steadies, my heart rate slows, and the cold detachment I need reasserts itself.

If only I could get her scent out of my nose. It feels like she's inside me now, and I don't like it. Or perhaps I hate that I do like it.

"So what is your decision? Make it now," I snap.

"Why me?"

"What?"

"Why me? Why marry me?"

"Because you're perfect." I say the words quietly, before I know I've let them out.

"I'm not perfect," she says with a slight shake of the head, a line pulling between her brows.

My tone turns steely and business-like. "That is for me to decide, not you. Now I need your answer. Yes or no."

"Yes."

It's so soft I'm not sure I heard it.

"What was that?" I need to hear it. Her acquiescence. I

may know that everything and everyone has a price, but I don't tire of winning.

"I'll marry you," she says clearly this time, her voice tight but determined.

A twisted sense of triumph rises in me, though it's tempered by the cold reality of what I've forced her into. Isabelle's gaze has turned to the security cam of her father's cell, deep underground.

They call me the Beast of Boston for a reason, I remind myself, even as the tortured look in her eyes pierces something deep within me.

I keep my tone steady, formal. "Good. But understand this: you are to move into this house effective immediately and your father will remain in my custody until the ceremony is complete."

Isabelle blinks rapidly, fighting back tears before they can spill. Her expression shifts from horror to anger, raw and desperate. "You can't be serious. He's frail—He needs—"

"He will be cared for," I interrupt, my voice cutting. "He'll have food, warmth, and anything else he requires. But he will not be released until you are officially my wife. That is non-negotiable."

She draws in a shaky breath, her chest heaving, and I can see the conflict play out across her face—fear for her father battling with her desire to break free from my control. But I know I have the upper hand. The Beast of Boston always does.

Her pulse flutters in her neck, a rapid, enticing rhythm I can hear even from across the room. It sends my instincts into chaos—fight, claim, devour. I can't tell if I want to scare her or make her mine.

"Then I'll need to go home and pack my things," she

says quietly, her voice laced with an edge of bitter resignation.

"You have one hour," I say, unwilling to grant her more time than that. "Tock will take you back to gather your essentials but my staff will gather and transport the rest. I'll meet you back here to go over the contract before we close the deal and marry."

"The contract—" She pauses, clearly thrown. "You mean a prenup?"

I can't help that half-grimace, half-grin from sliding upward. "Not exactly. There will be no need for such a thing as the only way either of us will get out of this marriage is the old-fashioned way."

"Time travel through standing stones? I read enough historical romance to know how that ends."

Her retort is so matter-of-fact, I can't tell if she's joking or not. Or really *what* she is even talking about. Still, I can't help but be slightly amused.

"I meant death," I reply just as flatly.

"Oh." She nods as if unbothered by the terms. "Right."

"We will go over what is to be our marriage contract. The terms we've already discussed, plus a few more to ensure compliance," I reply smoothly. "You'll have the chance to review and sign it before the ceremony."

As she leaves my study, a strange sense of anticipation stirs within me.

I meant what I said. She's perfect. And hopefully, in a few hours, our marriage will bind us into a pack, and I'll be able to shift back fully into my human form.

I'll be me again.

Shrugging my shoulders back, I try to bury the guilt that threatens to rise. I remind myself that she's not a victim; she's a necessary means to an end.

I move to the window and part the heavy curtain, watching as Belle descends the front steps. The cold air outside seems to bite at her exposed cheeks, making her wince. She hesitates for a moment, her breath visible in the frigid air, before she heads toward the waiting SUV. Belle slips on the slick, snow-covered ground outside.

My body tenses, jerking forward involuntarily with a primal instinct to catch her. Tock grabs her elbow, steadying her before she can fall. A low growl rumbles in my chest, surprising me with its intensity.

I've already begun to view her as mine. My possession. My mate.

All to get what I want.

And I'll have ruined a woman's life to do it.

CHAPTER 5

A COMFY CAGE IS STILL A CAGE

BELLE

It's not a face a girl forgets.

The mix and mash of a man and lion's face stays imprinted behind my eyes the entire drive back to my apartment. The sky is the same cold bright expanse as when I closed my bookstore an hour ago, though everything's changed.

I can't deny being entranced by the way skin and fur wove into one tapestry of a fae being. No wonder the Beast of Boston drew away from the crowd's eye. The most powerful man in the city is secretly a shifter. One stuck between two phases.

Though admittedly, the human half of him clearly had all the makings for an attractive man. In that severe, dark way that I'd envision Mr. Rochester from Jane Eyre.

You're perfect.

He said it as if he was affirming it to himself. It's almost possessive, the way he says it. Like I'm. . .made for him.

I can't even begin to fathom what he means by that. But for the first time, something other than fear and anxiety rolls through me. It's a dark, aching want fluttering in my stomach.

Don't go there. Don't romanticize the Beast of Boston. For all you know, he eats babies for breakfast and kicks puppies before bedtime.

Annnnd that's the guy I'm going to marry.

Great. Fae-fucking fabulous.

It doesn't take long to pack my clothes and essentials, but even as I go about the task, ideas begin to formulate and harden.

When I'm done, Tock assures me the rest of my things will be packed and moved for me. I nod absently as he picks up my suitcase and duffle bag. "I don't have a wedding dress." The words come out automatically, an afterthought or my brain's attempt to organize the situation in some manner that is understandable.

Do I need a wedding dress? I'm getting married in a matter of hours.

Tock freezes like a deer caught in headlights. "Uhhh..."

Then, realizing what I've said out loud, I wave a hand in the air. "Never mind. Ignore me. Let's go."

Back at the gothic Boston mansion, I make my way up the freshly salted front stairs and am greeted by a thin woman with gray hair pulled up in a severe bun. Her cheeks are sallow, and her eyes are a heavy blue.

"I'm Agatha Potts, the housekeeper, though everyone calls me Mrs. P," she introduces herself with a firm shake of the hand. "Anything you need, I am here to see to it. We will have your things unpacked in no time. I'll have a light supper prepared for you to take between your meeting with the master and your...nuptials."

The idea of someone taking care of me, of preparing a

meal for me has my head spinning. That's usually my job. Maybe this won't be a hellish existence after all?

Free, prepared food. Any port in a storm, eh, Belle?

"Mrs. P," Tock greets her with a nod. She nods back. They exchange a grim look. I get the sense neither of them is thrilled with my being a new fixture in this place. Or maybe they are always this excited to attend a wedding. Again, the idea that this is my new home whirls around me like winds that never calm.

"I need to make sure my father is okay," I say, looking around and wondering how to get to that cell the Beast locked him away in.

Mrs. P grips my shoulders. "Your father is currently in the kitchen. I've been plying him with tea and a meaty stew. He's just fine."

"Can I have more cookies?" My father emerges from the kitchen, crumbs sticking to the white scruff on his face. He has the appearance of an old man and young child rolled into one.

My heart soars and a sob builds its way up my throat as I throw my arms around my dad.

"I'm so glad you're okay." I squeeze him tight and inhale his familiar scent of mothballs, and the slightly medicinal smell imprinted in his skin from those years mixing alchemical potions.

He's safe. The pinch in my heart intensifies before releasing.

I pull back, holding him by the shoulders. "I was so worried about you. But it's okay, everything is going to be okay now. You don't have to worry. I'm taking care of it."

Dad gives me a vacant smile, patting my arm. "I'm sorry, do I know you?"

My heart cracks along the familiar fissure from so many

breaks. I should expect this. It happens all the time. Yet logic cannot prevent the pain of being a stranger to my father.

He looks over my shoulder to Mrs. P. "Do you have any more cookies?" I release Dad so he can go to her.

Concern and pity are plainly etched into the housekeeper's face from our interaction. I try to cover up any evidence that I'm affected by his response.

"Hey, book girl," Lucien calls in a lazy drawl. He motions to me with a grin that doesn't meet his eyes. "Time to meet with the master."

I look back at my father, who is observing a suit of arms in the hallway with great interest.

"I'll take care of him," Mrs. P assures me again. "Is there anything you need right now, dear?" Despite her calm demeanor, Mrs. P tugs at her skirt with either nervousness or anxiety.

Heat floods my cheeks. "Not that I can think of."

It's not like she can supply some much-needed lucidity for my father. Or an escape route from the insanity that is this situation.

Agatha folds her hands together with another curt nod. "I'll bring you some tea."

Oh, tea. Now *that* I can get on board with.

"Let's go," Lucien prompts again.

This time I'm led to a grand dining hall. Heavy velvet drapes line the walls, muting the room in thick, near darkness, interrupted only by the flickering glow of a few candelabras. The air is warm and heady, carrying the faint, mouthwatering scent of something slow-cooked and savory coming from somewhere else in the house.

I step forward, my gaze locking on the figure seated at the head of the long table.

I can make out his face in the candlelight—I want to study the unsettling mix of roughened skin and fur, but he retracts further into the dark.

The Beast gestures to the seat beside him, where a contract is waiting on the table.

I settle into the chair, picking up the pen. The metal is cold against my fingers, but the sensation only sharpens my focus as I scan the words.

"Your wifely duty will primarily be to stay here on the grounds," he says.

I raise an eyebrow at the archaic demands. "To cook and clean for you?"

He snorts and the massive head shakes with disdain. "Of course not. There is staff for such things. Your duty will be to stay by my side."

I still don't understand. If it's not about service, it must be about sex. "What about. . .other marital duties?"

Is it sex? It has to be about sex.

I force my voice to stay level, but there's a betraying heat creeping up my neck. It has to be about sex. My mind tries to categorize this in a way that makes sense. This marriage is a transaction, not a love match. He's black-mailing me, but he's also... a man. A man I can't seem to stop noticing, even when I should be furious. Even when I *am* furious.

Another snort, but softer this time. "That won't be necessary. Your proximity is what's most important."

"So this isn't about sex?"

"No," he says, and I can hear the frown in his voice.

"Oh." For a minute I'm not sure if I'm disappointed, offended, or just confused. "So, are you gay? Do you need a wife for show? Like a beard?"

"No," he says louder this time, frustration seeping through.

"Not that there's anything wrong with that. I'd understand—"

His fist hits the table—the loud bang causing me to jump. "I'm not gay. I simply need you around."

"I have a business to run." The words sound faint to my own ears, barely more than a whisper. The weight of them is a desperate grasp at normalcy, at something that is still mine. But the truth of it is already unraveling, slipping through my fingers like sand.

"Not anymore. Not if you marry me. Then again, if you choose to be fatherless, you will have all the time in the world to do as you please."

Terror coils in my stomach, cold and nauseating. The idea of my father rotting away in a cold cell somewhere I can't take care of him is unbearable. More unbearable than walking willingly into a cage of my own. My life, my bookstore, everything I've fought to build—swallowed whole by this shifter before me.

He truly is a beast.

"I have friends, family who won't like this." I shoot out, desperate for any bit of reasoning to save me from the trap closing around me.

"You have few attachments, and no family outside your father."

"What about my boyfriend?" I'm testing the limits here.

"There is no other man in your life other than your father. Even if there was, it wouldn't matter." He says it so calmly. As if my life is a book he's read and knows front to back.

"And I won't abide you taking a lover." His voice drops to

an impossibly low, scary place. "I consider what's mine to be mine, Isabelle. If you were to even think I won't find out about a dalliance, you'll find out what a beast I can really be."

A shiver rattles its way through my bones. I can't get my mouth to work to tell him he won't need to worry about that. For all that I read romance, it's been years since anything had come between my legs other than my own hand. All I can do is nod.

His scary hulking form deflates ever so slightly.

"The terms are explicit," he says, a clawed finger pointing to the first line. "You must remain on the house grounds; we will rendezvous in a shared space for a minimum of six hours daily. Mandatory shared meals—breakfast and dinner. Two hours each evening together in the library or sitting room."

My throat tightens at each line. "And if I need to leave the grounds?"

"Then I accompany you." His tone brooks no argument.

"My bookshop—"

"Will be sold."

"Absolutely not." I straighten in my chair. "Chapter Three is mine. I won't give it up."

A low discontent rumbles from his chest. "Fine. You may spend one hour there. Daily. And I will escort you there and back personally."

"Eight hours," I counter. If he wants to negotiate, fine. "I'd think you'd understand the importance of a good business." We deal in very different products, but I'm trying to bring him to my level.

This man—this beast—has my father. And if he's dragging me into this life, I won't go without laying down my own terms.

His eyes flash. "Two hours."

"Six."

"Three," he snarls, "and that's final."

"I can't run a profitable business on three hours."

He waves his human hand, dismissing the thought. "We'll hire someone to run it for you. Delegation is easy."

"It's not easy when you don't have enough money to pay them."

He pauses a beat. "I thought you knew you were marrying into a great amount of money."

"*Your* money," I point out. "Not mine." It actually hadn't occurred to me.

"If you become my wife, any and all funds will be available for your use. And believe me when I say you will not find our accounts lacking."

He might as well have described his level of wealth as "comfortable." It's the code word for filthy rich. And even knowing the little I do about the Beast of Boston, I'm sure that money is, in fact, filthy.

I grip the pen tighter, studying Dominic's face. There's no give there, no room for further argument. And yet. . ."Fine. Three hours. But I choose which three hours."

A muscle ticks in his jaw. "Within reason."

"And I need my *staff* to be able to reach me if there's an emergency." I lather the word "staff" in honey. I have no idea how or who to hire, but I'll figure it out.

My gut twists with reluctance at allowing him to interfere in my business, but that's the least of my issues right now. My father may be sitting in the kitchen, comfortable and fed, but it doesn't mean his life isn't in danger.

"True emergencies only," Dominic emphasizes in reference to my request. "Not every time someone can't find a book."

"Agreed." I scan the rest of the contract. "The sleeping

arrangements. . ." I don't realize I've read the words out loud.

"Adjoining rooms with a connecting door." Dominic's tone suggests this isn't up for debate.

I narrow my eyes at a particular clause: *The wife shall agree to do whatever is deemed necessary for the benefit and success of the marriage.*

"What exactly does 'necessary' mean here?" I ask, my voice edged with skepticism as I glance up to meet his eerie, mismatched gaze.

He holds my stare, his expression unreadable. "It means I expect *flexibility*."

I narrow my eyes. "Flexibility? That's a convenient way to leave me open to anything you demand."

"Convenient, yes," he replies, a hint of dry humor curling his lip. "Necessary, even more so." He leans back, his focus shifting to the contract in a gesture of command. "But these terms are essential. Our proximity is paramount. There is much to your benefit here as well. This isn't an offer I'd extend to just anyone."

My attention lifts, locking onto his mismatched eyes, one human, the other gleaming with an unnatural intensity in the dim candlelight. "So you reserve this offer for women whose old, addled fathers you hold hostage?" The words are out before I can filter them, but I hold my ground.

His chuckle is a low rumble. "Your father was trespassing on my property, Isabelle," he replies, as though that explains everything. "I usually take payment in flesh. You are paying for him. A life for a life."

"And what of my father's life? I'm his caretaker. I won't have him sent off to some facility, not knowing if he's truly cared for."

Dominic lets out a heavy exhale. "Then he'll live here

with us. If he becomes cumbersome, we'll hire a caretaker. If he is troublesome beyond even their abilities, you will have to consider putting him in a place that can better handle his needs."

I blink rapidly as surprise grips me. I was expecting more pushback on that. Not many men would concede to having their father-in-law (or essentially a stranger with mental conditions) move into their home.

Then again, nothing about this is even remotely normal.

I look down at the contract, skimming over it again.

I can't help but be attracted to the simplicity of his proposal. No illusions, no pretense of romance. Just terms —something I can navigate, something concrete. I've never needed the promise of love to understand the value of loyalty and sacrifice. Love, after all, is just a construct, but duty. . .that's something real.

And taking care of my father is my duty. If this is how it has to be done. . .

Mrs. P enters the room with tea service on a silver tray. I thank her as she sets it down and pours me a cup. The delicious steam wafting off it carries the scent of bergamot and Earl Grey. My favorite. Before I can stop her, Mrs. P doctors my tea with a dollop of heavy cream and two sugar cubes.

Exactly how I do it for myself.

I open my mouth and shut it as the housekeeper makes her exit, struggling to mask my discomfort at how well they know my preferences. I stare at the perfect China cup of creamy tea as if it is poisoned.

The luxury of this gesture isn't lost on me. All the money I could want. I'll live in this beautiful, albeit slightly gloomy and dark mansion. Yet this all feels like a trap.

It is a trap, you idiot. A comfy cage is still a cage.

"I could call the police. Tell them you are holding my father."

Dominic gestures to an ornate rotary phone in the corner of the room. "Be my guest."

Would the police rescue me and my father from the Beast of Boston? I cross my arms over my chest. "It's probably for decoration and doesn't even work. Who even has a phone like that anymore?"

He doesn't answer, but his lip curls slightly in what is almost a smile.

The cold weight of the pen is heavy in my hand.

The Beast watches as I sign my name, his eyes—one sharp and human, the other an unblinking slit of green—fixed on me with unnerving intensity. His gaze holds until the last stroke of my name dries on the page, a strange and final sensation settling over me.

"Good," he says with a tone of dark satisfaction.

After that, everything turns into a whirlwind. I'm swept up to my new bedroom by Tock and Mrs. P.

It's far grander and nicer than my ant-infested apartment with uneven floors. There is a decidedly feminine touch to the room, with Tiffany blue and rose-colored damask curtains and a matching bedspread. The bed looks like a fluffy cloud of comfort I could sink into. My fingers find the warm carved wood of one of the four posters on the bed.

"Where *is* he?" Tock mutters to himself with open irritation, glancing at his expensive pocket watch for the twentieth time in only a few minutes. I can't even bring myself to ask who he's referring to.

Mrs. P sets down a dinner tray on the small marble table by the massive windows. My mouth instantly salivates from the amazing savory smell of the short ribs and what looks like butter carrots and cheesy potatoes.

"Where does. . .*he* sleep?" I can't bring myself to say his name.

"The master's room is adjoined by that door." She nods toward the door directly across from my bed.

Right. It was in the contract. But my head is still spinning with all the details we hammered out.

This all feels like a fever dream.

This is my bedroom.

This is where I'll live. Forever.

With my husband. In the next room.

The meaning behind the thoughts is slow and thick like molasses in my mind.

The door swings open and an out-of-breath Lucien stands there holding a garment bag. The man's face is bright red as he pants heavily, like he's been running for miles.

"At last," Tock chastises. "You are late."

"I think the words you are looking for are *thank you*," Lucien snipes back.

"Oh good, I thought you might not make it." Mrs. P snatches the garment bag from Lucien.

Still out of breath, Lucien shoots me two thumbs up with a grin before Tock pushes him out the door.

The housekeeper wastes no time hanging the garment bag and unzipping it to reveal a beautiful white dress.

I stand, my heart lurching into my throat. "What's that?"

Mrs. P smiles at me. "Your wedding dress, dear."

CHAPTER 6

MY BLOODY WEDDING DAY

THE BEAST OF BOSTON

I'm still uncertain why Tock and Lucien insisted I change until Belle enters the conservatory. She steps in, awash in the pink light of the setting sun streaming through the glass panes, and for a moment, I almost forget to breathe.

Her hair, once restrained, now cascades in loose waves, evoking the elegance of a 1940s starlet. White lace hugs her curves, flowing gracefully over her hips and sweeping down to pool around her feet in a delicate whisper of tulle and fabric. The neckline of her gown plunges daringly, framing her decolletage and accentuating the creamy swell of her skin. Off-the-shoulder straps rest just on the edge of her arms and a faint blush dusts her exposed shoulders, hinting at a tantalizing softness beneath.

Her eyes—warm honey-brown and unguarded, without the familiar shield of her glasses—meet mine, and I'm caught in them, spellbound. And yet my gaze can't help but travel to the inked lines that mark her skin. A half-finished sleeve of bookish tattoos adorns one arm. A testament to her passion for words, each design is a blend of delicate linework and vibrant color. Lines of text curve on the inside of her other arm, phrases from some hidden story etched forever into her flesh.

The sight of her—tattoos, bare skin, lace—strikes me with unexpected ferocity, stirring something deep within. I have the sudden, unbidden urge to pull her close, to press my face into the curve of her neck, to trace my tongue along the delicate dip between her collarbone and shoulder.

No. I will control myself. I'm not an animal who just takes anything he sees and wants.

And witchtitting fuck, do I want her right now.

This wasn't the plan. Not to want her like this.

My insistence that we move the brief ceremony to a mostly darkened corner of the house was ruled out by Mrs. P herself. She tutted and said the girl had already seen me and didn't run screaming. The least we could do is show the woman a little beauty on her wedding day. No place is better than the conservatory. Now, I'm glad I was too preoccupied to fight the request.

Isabelle deserves to be bathed in light, to be surrounded by the exotic plants curated from lands and realms far beyond here. She is as timeless and rare a beauty as any of the plants in here.

Guilt, gnarled and complex, strikes me in the chest. I'm essentially taking this woman as my captive. I truly am a beast.

Isabelle's fingers squeeze and release as if they don't know what to do. I turn and use my claws to cut a single pink rose that matches the color of her lips and hand it to her as she stands across from me. "Here," I say awkwardly, avoiding her gaze.

"Oh, thank you." She takes it from me, careful not to touch my paw.

Thank you? Did she really just thank me?

Tock clears his throat between us, ordained for just this purpose. Agatha and Lucien stand nearby as the witnesses who will sign the marriage certificate. Their expressions volley between admiration of my soon-to-be wife's beauty and tense, straight mouths of disapproval.

Tock runs through the cursory vows; nothing more than would be done at a courthouse. When he gets to the part about the rings, Lucien steps forward, handing each of us the predetermined jewelry.

I slip both the engagement and wedding rings onto Belle's finger.

"Oh," she says with surprise, eyes turning round. "It— it fits, and it's. . ." She doesn't finish the sentence, and I tell myself I don't care what she thinks of the choice I made. It's simply a status symbol meant to bind us together and show the strength of my power to any and all.

Yet the ring seems to be made for her. An elaborate jeweled rose with diamond thorns curving around the band. The opulent design is perfect on her hand, and I pride myself on choosing so well. My own is a black band, cheap and made of flexible materials for the ever-shifting tendons on my hands.

"I pronounce you man and wife," Tock concludes. "You may now kiss—"

"That won't be necessary," I say sharply. The room falls into an awkward silence.

I should have told him to cut that part before, but I expected Tock to assume the obvious.

How could anyone possibly kiss this grizzled face? I'd likely cut her with my protruding fang, but not before she vomited on my shoes from disgust.

Yes, I did manage to shove my clawed feet into some fashion of footwear, though it's rare I bother.

Belle shifts her stance, clinging to the rose I cut for her like her life depends on it. Needing this moment, this transaction to conclude, I stick out my human hand.

Belle's brows furrow as she looks down at it, then up into my face with confusion. Then she slips hers into mine. It's like electricity is sparking its way up my arm from the contact of her palm and fingers into mine before drilling into the center of my chest. She sucks in a breath, and I wonder if she feels it too.

Yet again, she meets my gaze head-on. There is no evidence of revulsion on her face. Only quiet, serious consternation. She makes me feel as though I am some kind of puzzle she is trying to work out. I don't want to let go of her hand.

The animal part of me flares. I want to draw her into me, breathe deeply of her scent, and run my lips along her skin until she's panting and flushed. The idea of rubbing my scent on her, of laving my tongue all over her and marking her, has my grip tightening around hers.

I *want* to press my mouth to hers, to claim her as my bride. I *want* to imprint on her in every way possible and taste the sweetness of her body, but I won't. Not with my gnarled half-human lip line. Kissing is not an option. No matter how much I'm tempted to feel her glossy ones.

The effort it takes to control my feral nature becomes more than a painful pinch. It feels like I'm cutting off circulation to my heart.

I drop her hand as if it scorches me and take a measured step away. There are no shadows to hide me here, but the urge to recede into the bushes and flower pots so as not to be seen anymore is strong.

With a deliberate movement, I create more distance, bracing myself for the shift.

Will it be like the roll of thunder, or will it come soft and easy to me? Will my form melt into one form or the other, or do I need to direct the energy?

When I feel nothing, I push some energy into the *Change*. I endeavor to become fully man again, but I'd settle for lion. Anything but this painful, half-melted form of two beings.

My muscles roil and stretch, and pangs of protest spiral through me with a piercing kind of agony. A growl escapes my throat, and everyone recoils.

My effort to shift suddenly ratchets up and out of my control. Claws lengthen and my human flesh turns tight, pulling around my bones. Fire streaks through my brain until my eyes nearly feel like they are bursting from my skull. The sound of fabric tearing is drowned out by my growls.

Isabelle lets out a surprised exclamation of pain before dropping the rose. The smell of her blood hits my nostrils and my mouth salivates as violence crashes over me.

A crimson droplet clings to one of the thorns on the downed flower.

"Get her out of here," I growl. Lucien is quick to respond, grabbing Isabelle's arm and dragging her away. Tock and Agatha hurry off as well. Those honeyed eyes meet mine even as she is pulled to safety.

Rage grips me and rampages through the conservatory. Pots shatter, dirt flies, and petals are demolished in my rage.

When I come back to my senses, darkness has fallen completely. The conservatory is smashed beyond recognition. It now resembles a graveyard more than a plant house.

Glass and my own blood smear the tile floor and the walls. The winter chill sweeps through the gaping holes where windows once stood, burning me with its freezing breath.

I have a wife. I've made a pack again. A new one.

I should be able to shift again. I should be me again.

Apparently, technicalities don't count. The natural laws of pack don't equate marriage as enough of a binding.

And if I don't create a new pack, Isabelle will be a widow all the sooner.

CHAPTER 7
THE ANGEL OF CROISSANTS IS A WITCH
BELLE

I sit next to my father, clutching a delicate China cup of Earl Grey that nearly rattles in my hands. The tea's warmth barely reaches me as the reality of this place —of this life I've been thrust into—sinks in.

"Belle," he nods with a lopsided smile. "You look so pretty today. Did you go to prom?"

Mrs. P meets my gaze over the large white marble kitchen island. Distress pulls at the tiny crow's feet at the corners of her sharp eyes.

The kitchen is a masterpiece of elegance, nearly overwhelming in its opulence. Black lacquered cabinets soar up to the high, vaulted ceiling, every panel and molding etched in gold, gleaming even under the dimmed chandelier that hangs like a crown above the marble island. The centerpiece, a massive marble-topped island, reflects the ambient light, its surface a swirl of creamy whites and gray veining, polished to perfection. Large, arched windows frame the falling snow outside, each flake drifting lazily through the night sky.

"Yes, I went to prom, and I had a wonderful time," I

reassure my dad absently, clinking the cup back on the saucer without even taking a sip. My fourth finger rubs gently along the bandage now wrapped around my thumb, covering the wound from where I drew blood on a rose spike.

When I first saw my father again I couldn't help but wrap my arms around him so tightly I never planned to let go. That was until he asked if I had any sweets for him, clearly still no idea who I was.

At least he's eating.

Now we sit in silence, drinking tea as I try to let it sink in that I'm married.

To the Beast of Boston.

My emotions have been a roller-coaster since the moment I woke up, fearful of my dad's whereabouts. Then my fear and fascination spiked as I was brought before the Beast of Boston, before I cut my feelings off altogether to make a life-altering decision. After a wedding that ended in glass and blood, now all I feel is a numbness permeating through me.

"Basil, why don't you come sit by the fire?" Mrs. P offers, coming around and taking my father by the shoulders and leading him to the adjoining room. "I'll bring you a fresh hot plate of croissants."

My father brightens at the mention of pastries. "Yes, please. Are you an angel? The angel of croissants?"

Mrs. P laughs a little though it's strained. "Yes, I suppose I am."

Mrs. P returns after escorting my dad to the fireside, her quiet footsteps barely echoing on the polished floor. With a flick of her wrist, the teapot on the table tips itself forward, gently pouring to top off my tea. The puffy tea cozy shimmers faintly, its vibrant splash of color standing out against the muted elegance around us as it fluffs itself into place.

"You're a Mage," I say stating the obvious.

Her thin lips quirk up in the corner. "Indeed."

I want to ask what level, but I don't want to risk being rude. There is an abundance of level one to two Mages in the world, but lesser still of three, four, and only a handful of level five Mages. The fact I happen to know a few of those most powerful magic wielders is more than a little unusual. Though, when I'll get to see my friends again is unclear.

Mrs. P turns toward the small oven on the counter, and as she opens the fridge, rolls of dough lift into the air on their own, arranging themselves in perfect rows on a baking sheet. Another flick of her fingers sends the sheet gliding into the oven, which hums warmly, its glow intensifying as if alive. It's not long before the warm smells of sugar weave through the room, the aroma wrapping around me like a soft embrace.

Mrs. P's eyes stay fixed on the oven. "Is that a problem?" There is no challenge in her question. She is merely trying to figure out where I stand. Mages are far more accepted by the human community than fae beings, even glamorized in the media at times, but Boston is still a human city. Some people, like that disgruntled woman who came into my store this morning—fae lords, was that really only this morning?—believe in the purity of mankind and value segregation.

"Not at all," I say with a shake of my head. "I'm surprised, though. I thought shifters found mages to uh. . ." I'm not sure how to say the next part without offending her.

"Stink to high heaven?" She finally meets my gaze with a raised eyebrow and a knowing look.

Blood rushes to my cheeks and I give a small nod, taking a sip of tea to cover up my embarrassment.

"Yes, well, Mr. Blackwell values a useful staff more than he cares about that. Though we do have some specialized sprays we use to help dull the effects to his sensitive olfactory system," she adds with that same tense, crooked smile.

Her mouth parts then closes twice as if she wants to say something but keeps changing her mind.

"You can ask me anything," I say. It's true. I've never been one for secrets. Too much stress to keep them. I'm an open book. Which is exactly how I like all my books.

"You run a romance bookstore, I understand," she starts hesitantly. "So I imagine you might be suffering a great deal of disappointment at ending up in a marriage that isn't a love match."

She rears back slightly when I laugh. Even I'm surprised any humor can break through the numbness pervading me.

"Sorry, I just. . ." I pause to figure out how to succinctly explain. "I don't believe in love."

Mrs. P blinks rapidly, struggling to comprehend.

"I know, I know. The irony of someone who doesn't believe in love running a romance bookstore is pointed out to me on a regular basis. But romance, true love, all that stuff is fantasy. I seek out that fantasy between the pages of a book, but I'm far too pragmatic to think that any of that can be found in real life."

Mrs. P studies me with an unerring focus that makes me wonder if her powers extend to being able to probe my mind. "You love your father. That much is clear."

I twist to look over my shoulder to where I can see a tiny sliver of my father cozied in a chair by the fire. "That's different. Loyalty, duty, companionship, and care are very real, and we call it love. But the out-of-control, passionate romantic love is nothing but layers of chemistry and biological attempts to create that bond. People use romantic love to get what they want."

"If the basis of love is manipulation, what are you using your father for then?" she challenges, leaning forward slightly.

"It's not the same thing," I say, gripping my cup tighter. "I didn't take from him—I made sure everything didn't fall apart. That's not manipulation. That's survival."

I drop my gaze to the amber liquid that's cooled in my cup. A rare surge of shame washes over me. "I used his money to start Chapter Three. He spoke of helping me make the dream come true when I was in college, but I refused. I planned to pay my way to my own dream without help. But then his mind. . .I had to drop out of college to take care of him. Eventually, I broke down and used his money to fulfill that dream. When he couldn't rightly consent to it anymore." It niggled at me. Though I'm not sure if it was because I knew I couldn't take care of him and realize my dreams independently or because I was afraid that I didn't fill my own cup somehow, I wouldn't be able to take care of my father. I'd grow resentful.

I never lied. Not even to myself.

And part of me is oddly relieved to be married to someone who isn't lying about why he's marrying me. It's purely transactional. Aside from the abruptness and physical threat to my father's life, this is oddly an ideal situation for a realist like me.

His reason for marrying is elusive, but he hasn't lied. And I'm slowly piecing together a reason all on my own.

"Sounds like you started a business to take care of both of you," the housekeeper says softly. "Sounds like a loving action to me." Then she leans over and lightly taps my China cup. Steam begins to rise from the once-cold tea.

I don't respond to that even as the tray of perfectly browned croissants floats out of the oven, doubling the sweetness in the air.

"The master's not so bad, not really," Mrs. P says in a low voice, though her eyes are still pinched with worry. They've been that way since the wedding ceremony began.

My wedding.

Nope. It still doesn't penetrate.

But something else has registered.

A girl could take it personally that her husband just lost his shit and destroyed a rather beautiful room of glass and plants promptly after our "I dos."

At first I wondered, was he angry he was bound to me? Even though this was his idea? His trap?

No.

In the depths of those mismatched green eyes sparked a torture I'm too new to inflict. First, it seemed like an internal spike of pain that seemed to plunge deeper into his physical being until he lost all sense.

"He's in pain, isn't he? Dominic," I clarify when lines of confusion deepen along her forehead.

Mrs. P's severe brows shoot up in open surprise.

"Being half-shifted. It's hurting him."

The housekeeper's lids lower. "It is," she says lowly. "More so with each passing day."

I scrub my fingers along my forehead before turning to look at my father through the hallway. Wrapped up in a blanket, he happily jabbers to himself about chemistry, wild dogs, and Thorns. His usual rhetoric. I don't think my father is in distress much, but when it hits, it's devastating.

"I'm sorry for that," I say plainly.

I turn to face the older woman when she sucks in a sharp breath.

"I believe the master is right. You are perfect." A wrinkled, cold hand covers mine for a moment before slipping away.

I don't know if she said that because I have a general sense of empathy or something else. I don't get to ask, as she has organized the fresh hot croissants on a plate and has whisked them away to my dad. She left one on a plate before me.

As I bite into the chewy, warm morsel, I allow its warmth and comfort to permeate through me. And try not to think about my wedding night in my new home.

CHAPTER 8

THE FUZZY ROBE OF SEDUCTION

THE BEAST OF BOSTON

There won't be any sleep on my wedding night and for all the wrong reasons.

Not because I'm buried deep in my bride, driving both of us to exhaustion with powerful strokes. No, it's the kind of restless energy that digs under the flesh, refusing to let go. The kind that burns when it should be spent.

The marriage didn't trigger my shift. Not like I thought it would. Not like I *hoped* it would.

Instead, I'm stuck here in this half-state, with claws too sharp, senses too keen, and frustration thrumming through me like a second heartbeat. My muscles coil and flex as if gearing up for a fight that isn't coming. I pace the west wing like a caged animal, my claws scraping faintly against the floor.

This energy—this simmering, gnawing frustration—has to go somewhere. I chalk it up to disappointment. The ritual didn't work. The shift remains just out of reach, like an itch I can't scratch.

Then I catch it.

A faint scent, sweet and unmistakably Isabelle, drifts toward me on the air. My restless energy latches onto it immediately, pulling me forward, compelling me to find her.

What is she doing out of bed?

The tension inside me sharpens, tightening like a noose as I follow the trail. Each step brings her scent closer until it wraps around me completely.

She rounds the corner, and for a moment, I stop in my tracks. Wrapped in a fluffy robe that emanates her clean and sweet scent with even more power, her dark hair is loose, spilling over her shoulders. She looks soft, tempting, and entirely out of place in these shadowed halls. She pushes her glasses up in an impossibly adorable gesture.

The frustration inside me flares hotter.

"You shouldn't be here," I say, stepping forward and filling the space between us. My voice is rough.

Isabelle's eyes widen with surprise as she steps back.

That's right. A beast lurks in these halls, *wife.*

But then her chin tilts up, her expression unfazed as her dark eyes meet mine. "I thought this was my house now too?" Her voice is steady, and it grates against the part of me that wants her to be afraid. She should be afraid.

"You know what I mean," I growl, my claws flexing again.

She crosses her arms, pushing up breasts I can't help but steal a glance at. "You're avoiding the question," she says, her tone light but her eyes sharp.

I grit my teeth, the tension in my jaw almost unbearable. "The west wing is off-limits," I say finally, the words coming out harsher and foreboding.

Her brow arches, and she leans closer, dropping to a

conspiratorial whisper. "Off-limits? What, are you hiding a secret, crazy wife in there?"

The reference catches me off guard, and despite the tension crackling between us, I find myself smirking. "I'm not Mr. Rochester. You are my only wife."

Her brows shoot up, arms dropping to her side, clearly surprised that I understood the reference.

"Yes, I also read," I add before she can say anything, my tone dry. But I don't let the moment linger. "Regardless, you are never to go in there. We are. . .dealing with an infestation."

"An infestation?" she repeats with curiosity, looking over my shoulder. "Bats? Or maybe something bigger?"

I studiously ignore the sound of flapping wings from the other side of the door.

My claws twitch at my sides, desperate to reach out, to drag her away from this room, this side of the house.

And then to the bedroom, or maybe my office. Where I can peel that robe off her body and lick and nip at her pretty pale flesh until it's bruised and marked. I would agitate the nerve endings of her full breasts until she's wet and ready, then drive into her pliant, willing body. I'd pleasure and abuse her from the inside out so she feels me even days later.

What are you thinking? This is not the deal. You are not to touch her even if she is your wife.

But fae fucking hell, she smells *sooo* fae fucking tempting.

"Enough." My nostrils flare as I snap against her curiosity and my own rising desire. "You're not to go in there."

Isabelle doesn't flinch, doesn't cower. Instead, she lifts

her chin, giving me a slow blink that's maddeningly unimpressed. "Of course, *husband*. I wouldn't dream of it."

My gaze catches on her shoulder. The robe has slipped, baring a stretch of creamy, unmarked skin. The faint flicker of light from the hall highlights the curve, the softness, the *invitation* of it.

Heat surges through me, sharp and all-consuming, like being caught in a storm I can't outrun. Every instinct screams to drag her closer, to taste that bare skin, to leave marks that wouldn't fade for days. Her scent wraps around me, sweet and heady, and when I glance at her face, those wide, honest brown eyes meet mine. They're usually so clear, like polished wood catching sunlight, but now—*now*—there's a glaze of something deeper, darker.

My hand moves on its own, a rough, hurried motion to pull the robe back into place before the temptation overpowers my control.

The sharp edge of my claw grazes her skin as I adjust the fabric, sealing it back over her. Her soft gasp hits me like a fist to the gut, the sound sharp and almost sweet, but my stomach twists.

What have I done?

The faint pink trail my claw left across her pale skin burns into my vision, an unintentional mark that feels more like a brand. My fingers linger on the velvet of her robe, the heat of her bare shoulder beneath it crawling up my arm like shame. I've hurt her.

The familiar loathing wells up, black and corrosive. My beast bristles inside me, torn between regret and the darker, more primal urge to make her mine completely.

I lift my gaze to her face, expecting a wince, fear, or anger—*something* to match the guilt surging through me.

But she doesn't flinch. She doesn't flee in abject terror.

Instead, her lips part, and her breath quickens.

The air thickens between us, heavy and charged, as I realize the truth: I didn't scare her. I didn't hurt her. If anything, the way she's looking at me now—with wide, dark eyes and flushed skin—tells me I did the opposite.

I drink in her expression, and the sight of her—unflinching, her eyes dark and defiant, yet somehow heated—sends a fresh wave of desire coursing through me. My body responds to it instantly, fiercely, like she's flipped a switch.

I'm the one who should terrify her. I'm the one who could break her, but the only thing in danger of breaking right now is the razor-thin line of my restraint.

"Are you afraid of me?" I ask in a soft growl.

Her answer comes without hesitation. "No."

"Why not?"

She tilts her head. "Because you married me. Which means you plan on keeping me around." I'm learning my wife speaks very matter-of-factly.

She licks her lips, the movement drawing my attention despite myself. "And because of what you said before," she adds.

I study her closely. What is she getting at?

"What I said?" My words are low, controlled, but inside, my instincts churn. "I'll have your father locked up if you don't marry me?" I prompt dryly.

A laugh bursts out of her, sharp and sudden, and I freeze. For a moment, the tension crackling between us lightens, just barely.

"No," she says finally, her voice softer now, more uncertain. She pauses, and I can see the debate flicker across her face, the way she's weighing whether to say the words at all.

"You said I was. . .perfect."

The word hangs between us, quiet but impossible to ignore.

Perfect.

Her brown eyes search mine, wide and unguarded, and I feel like I've been caught in the act of something I can't name.

I should deny it. Deflect. Say something to break this moment apart before it tightens around me like a snare. But I can't.

Because it's true.

"Because I'm nearing thirty and unattached? So I must be desperate—"

"No," I cut her off sharply. "Because..." I search her face for the right words.

The air between us crackles, the weight of everything unsaid pressing down on me.

I tell myself it's because she was unattached. No ties to anyone but her father, and that made it simpler. Clean. That kind of freedom was rare in my world.

She reads shifter romance. That was another reason. I'd hoped she wouldn't recoil at what I was—what I could be. It seemed logical.

And then there's her loyalty to her father. The lengths she'd go to for him reflect a quality I need in my corner. In my world, loyalty is everything.

"You just are," I say finally, the words rasping out before I can stop them. "Perfect."

Her breath catches, and I catch something crossing her face—confusion, vulnerability, surprise—that's gone too quickly for me to name.

I step back, putting space between us before I do some-thing reckless. "Never mind that now. Go to bed, Isabelle, before I throw you over my shoulder and take you back there myself."

"I mean, it *is* our wedding night," she suggests in a light, teasing tone.

Despite her levity, the words slam me with a jolt of heat, unexpected and searing. My body tenses against the surge of arousal and surprise.

Isabelle freezes, her shoulders stiffening as if she can't believe she let that slip out. Before I can react, she barrels on. "I mean, I'd expect nothing but rose petals and candlelight lovemaking after that proposal today. The hot air balloon ride? The acoustic guitar player? The heartfelt declarations of romance? How's a girl to say no to all of that?"

A scoff escapes me before I can stop it. For a fleeting second, amusement tugs at the corner of my mouth, almost a smile. But I shove it away, replacing it with the scowl I wear like armor. "Don't forget the doves."

She doesn't miss a beat. "Ah yes, the doves. How could I forget?"

Her lips twitch, and there's a glimmer of something on her face—dry humor, sharp and biting, yet somehow. . .charming. The way she speaks pulls me in despite myself.

I exhale slowly, the sound rumbling low in my chest, more growl than breath. "Go to bed, Isabelle," I say. The words are a rough, gritted out command to myself as much as to her.

I turn and disappear into the shadows, forcing myself to keep moving, to put distance between us. The way she looked at me, the way her breath caught, the faint flush that crept across her skin—it wasn't arousal. It couldn't be.

She simply smells. . .delicious. Too tempting, too fearless, too everything. My mind twists her scent and her lack of fear into something it isn't.

I grit my teeth, my claws flexing at my sides as I stalk down the hall.

Her scent saturates the space, coiling around me, an invisible chain I can't shake.

I absently wonder how many grooms end up jerking themselves off on their wedding night before I move on to the more pressing question. How many times will it take before I can get control of my senses and sleep again, knowing my wife will be sleeping in the room next to mine?

CHAPTER 9

WHO DOESN'T LOVE A LITTLE SMUT?

BELLE

The silence in this house isn't peaceful—it's oppressive like the air's been vacuumed out and replaced with something heavier. Even sitting at the most ornate dining table I've ever seen with a breakfast spread fit for royalty, I can't escape the strangeness of it all.

My lids are heavy with exhaustion as I read until dawn, only succumbing to a fitful sleep for an hour before Mrs. P knocked on my door, entering with a tray of coffee service. Hazelnut coffee. Sugar-free vanilla syrup and a dash of almond milk. Just how I like it.

I'd be freaked out about how much these people know about me if I weren't so damned grateful for the elixir of life.

Downing the deluxe caffeine is the only way I managed to crawl out of bed this morning and get myself to the dining room.

Dominic, my *husband*—the word feels surreal—sits at the far end of the table. I can barely make out his features through the silver candelabras, decorative fruit bowls, and fresh flowers that separate us.

I can just catch the shape of him shoveling food onto his fork with brisk efficiency. It's not messy, but there's an edge to the way he eats that's purposeful, predatory.

He doesn't glance my way, and I can't decide if I'm relieved or irritated.

I wrap my hands around my coffee cup—there might not be enough coffee for this day—the delicate China almost weightless against my fingers. But even the coffee's warmth doesn't reach me. My mind is a whirlwind of questions and worries, most of which I don't dare say aloud.

The Beast of Boston—Dominic—is a contradiction. On the one hand, he's this hulking, terrifying figure with a reputation to match. On the other, there's something more to him I can't quite put my finger on. Or maybe that's a side effect of reading too many romance novels, a lack of sleep, and an absolutely gripping attraction to my husband.

No two ways about that last one. I'm not in the habit of lying to myself, so there's no use denying that I find him fiercely captivating. Though with the way I was brought up, I can hardly be surprised to admit that I appreciate some monster in my man.

Well, not *my* man.

Or I guess he *is* kind of my man?

Sweet baby witchtits, my brain is going to end up dribbling out my ears if I think about this too long.

Still, I can't stop thinking about last night. Nothing says "newlyweds" like meeting your husband in a dark hallway, like strangers at a party. Yet I was held captive by his mismatched eyes. And I can't deny something decidedly base and feminine enjoys the fact he is so much bigger than me. My husband is broad and thick with the muscle of both man and beast.

This marriage might be official, but the stiff, stranger-like tension between us keeps reminding me of one inconvenient fact: I have no idea who this man is.

Though, finding out he is familiar with my favorite classic, *Jane Eyre*, by making a direct reference to it just about bowled me over. Then, he matched my dry humor, referencing the imaginary doves at our wedding.

But what barred me from sleep was the memory of his face as he affirmed I was *perfect*. His gaze softened then heated, like butter hitting a smoking skillet.

I take a sip of coffee to steady myself, but it's lukewarm now, the steam long gone. Across the table, Dominic abruptly pushes back his chair, the scrape of wood against the marble floor loud enough to make me flinch.

Without a word, he leaves the dining room.

A heavy sigh escapes me. I'm not even sure why or what for.

Relief?

Disappointment?

Either way, it doesn't matter. Today I intend to familiarize myself with my new routine. My new life.

After breakfast, I find Tock in one of the many hallways, adjusting the hands on a grandfather clock that ticks away, its pendulum swaying in perfect rhythm. He straightens, his tall, broad frame imposing even in the mundane act of fiddling with the clock. The tweed suit strains around all those round gym-built muscles.

"Tock," I call out, and he turns toward me, his expression neutral but his sharp gaze assessing.

"Mrs. Blackwell," he greets, his Oxbridge accent polished and precise. "What can I do for you?"

Isabelle Blackwell. *Witchtits*. I hadn't thought about changing my name, but I doubt the Beast of Boston would be amenable to my keeping my mother's surname.

"Please, call me Belle."

He smiles kindly. "Belle."

"I need to go to Chapter Three today," I say. The words come out more firmly than I intended, but I don't back down. "I have things to take care of at the shop. Orders, inventory, customers—"

Tock's brow furrows slightly, and he raises a hand to stop me. "I'm afraid that won't be possible today."

"Why not?" I demand.

"Mr. Blackwell has other. . .obligations," he says carefully. "He won't be able to accompany you."

"I don't need him to accompany me," I argue. "I'm perfectly capable of going alone."

Tock's lips press into a thin line. "That won't be happening, Mrs. Blackw—Belle. Tomorrow, perhaps. Today, however, you'll need to remain here."

Frustration rises with sharp pressure in my chest, but I force myself to exhale slowly.

He adjusts his glasses, his expression unreadable. "But if it puts you at ease, your new employee will be arriving at the house this afternoon." Before I can ask any other details, Tock whisks away.

New employee? So they just know someone who can sell romance books from off the street? Remembering the very specific, personalized tea and coffee service I've received, I know not to underestimate the level of detail around here.

I check on dad next.

He's settled in a spacious suite that's been outfitted with every comfort—plush armchairs, and a desk piled high with paper and pens. He's scribbling furiously, muttering to himself under his breath, and doesn't look up when I enter.

"Dad?" I call softly.

"Belle," he says brightly, glancing up for a moment before returning to his scribbling. "Did you know the structural integrity of a hex is multiplied by the—"

I freeze. He recognized me. Just like that. No hesitation, no vacant stare. The relief is quick and sharp, lodging itself somewhere deep, but I don't trust it to last. My dad also has no concept of what the last twenty-four hours have brought down on us though he is the cause. Not that I can justly blame him, so instead I take his lucidity as a temporary wedding gift. I smile tightly and settle into a chair across from him.

He seems content, his mind fully absorbed in whatever calculations he's concocting. I sit with him for a while, though he doesn't even notice when I leave and continues to ramble on.

I suppose there isn't much for me to do other than get to know my new home.

The house is a labyrinth, sprawling and winding, a warren of hallways and hidden doors. It's the kind of place that feels like it's lived a dozen lives before me, each one leaving its mark in some imperceptible way.

Room after room, hall after hall, all blending into one another with ornate decor and heavy atmosphere.

I hesitate at the top of the stairs, adjusting my glasses. The dim lighting and sheer vastness of the place make me oddly aware of how much I rely on them. Not that I'm blind without them, but enough that everything is a little softer at the edges, like a painting that's just slightly out of focus.

I push open a door to a sitting room lined with art so exquisite it takes my breath away. Museum-level pieces hang on the walls—imposing oil portraits, serene landscapes, and haunting abstracts that seem to follow me with their eyes. The light from the window catches on gilded frames, highlighting every brushstroke and whisper of genius.

Another door creaks open to reveal what must have once been a family parlor. The scent of aged wood and faint traces of lavender polish cling to the air, mingling with the melancholy smell of disuse. The room is large, with walls painted a deep emerald that must have once been vibrant but now looks dulled by time.

Sheets are draped over most of the furniture—plush sofas and armchairs arranged in an intimate circle around a grand, cold fireplace. The ghostly outlines stand as if waiting for a family gathering to begin. One corner holds a tall bookcase, its shelves filled with novels and games, the titles worn with love.

From Dominic's hands? No, probably not. Did other people used to live here with him? Did he buy the house with all the furniture and items included from someone who had a family and a love for gathering in this room?

On the mantel above the fireplace, a carved rose stands out, its petals intricate and lifelike, almost too perfect to be made of wood. I pause, frowning slightly. The detail is exquisite, far too intentional to be a random flourish.

The rose isn't just here. I've seen it elsewhere—woven into the iron of the stair railings, etched into the corners of the grand piano, and faintly carved into the frame of the door I just opened. It even sits on the fourth finger of my left hand.

Dominic's insignia, his calling card. It shows his owner-ship, and now I'm under his domain just like this house. I'm still not sure how I feel about being owned by the King of Thorns.

But. . .this house. These carvings. They're old. Too old to have been added by him.

The realization sends a chill through me. This wasn't just Dominic's empire—it didn't start with him. Whatever this is, it's bigger, deeper, and older than I'd thought.

A small side table sits uncovered near one of the chairs, its wood faded where countless cups must have been set over the years. There's a faint ring mark still visible, a little imperfection in the otherwise impeccable space.

I step further in, trailing my fingers over the edge of the table. The silence here feels heavier—not the grand, impersonal quiet of the rest of the house, but something deeper. This room wasn't just lived in—it was loved.

Most of the doors are locked. I jiggle a few handles but they don't budge, leaving me to wonder what secrets lie hidden behind them. The ones that do open reveal similar spaces—abandoned but not forgotten. Each room carries whispers of the lives that once filled them, their presence lingering in the little details: a forgotten chessboard midgame, a scarf draped over a chair back, a vase holding dried flowers that must have once been vibrant.

It feels like the house is holding its breath, waiting for life to return.

Had there been friends and family here? Maybe Dominic's pack?

Without saying a word, my husband has made it clear we are not to even come close to the topic of his pack. Though I suspect their absence is very much tied to his peculiar half-shifted state.

"Well," I say aloud, turning in a slow circle in what appears to be a music room, complete with a grand piano. The instrument gleams, its surface polished to perfection despite the layer of dust that clings to the corners of the room. "If we're going to spend a lot of time together, we might as well get to know each other."

The room doesn't answer, of course. I smile at my own foolishness but press on, trailing my fingers lightly along the polished wood of the piano as I speak. "I'm Isabelle. But you can call me Belle. Everyone does." *Except my husband.*

I pause, looking around the faded grandeur of the room, and a wry smile tugs at my lips. When I was growing up, a lot of people said I was odd, peculiar, a funny kind of girl—they were too scared to say anything worse. But I can't say they were wrong.

It's ridiculous, talking to the house, but somehow it feels less like I'm wandering aimlessly and more like I'm finding my place.

I pass through a grand hall with a double staircase spiraling up toward a high-vaulted ceiling painted with soft clouds and cherubs. Dust motes swirl in the shafts of light coming through tall windows. I pause and let out a low whistle, craning my neck to take it all in. "I'll admit, you've got quite the charm offensive going on. Bet you were stunning in your heyday."

My voice echoes faintly in the cavernous space, and I laugh under my breath. "Not that you're not stunning now, of course. But I'd wager you could use a little company, huh? You've been left to your own devices for far too long."

My curiosity has me turning toward the west wing, though I hesitate before going too far. The memory of Dominic barring my way is fresh in my mind, his fierce expression and warning growl still vivid.

I stop short of the wing, staring down the corridor. It's quiet now, but I swear I can still hear faint fluttering, like the sound of birds.

"Infestation," I murmur to myself.

What kind of infestation would make a man like Dominic so guarded? And why doesn't he have his staff take care of it? I'd think he'd have exterminators here in a snap.

I shake the thought away and turn back, deciding to explore elsewhere.

"You'll have to share your secrets with me another day," I tell the house, my voice soft. "For now, let's just be friends, alright? I'll be a good roommate and you. . .Well, you just keep being mysterious and intimidating, I guess. Deal?"

There's a faint creak from the floorboards beneath my feet, like a response. "I'll take that as a yes."

The house doesn't reply, but the faint tension in my chest eases all the same. As I continue on, I let myself feel the charm and mystery of the place, imagining it not as a cold, imposing mansion but as a place I could belong. A home.

Chip arrives mid-afternoon.

The first thing I notice is the hair—short and lavender, a sharp contrast against the muted tones of the house.

"I'm Chip, pronouns they/them," my future employee says in a warm, animated voice. The second thing I notice is half of Chip's front tooth is broken off. I'm guessing Chip is a nickname.

Where did Dominic find this kid? They're barely out of their teens and about as far from the thuggish enforcers I'd have expected Dominic to send.

"And I'm Belle," I reply, stepping forward to shake hands. Chip's thin fingers are chapped and cold, but their grip is firm.

"Mr. Blackwell says you have a job for me," they say, their tone light but with an edge like they're testing the waters. Chip is dressed in a sweater nearly three times too big for their skinny frame, along with a pair of rather large combat boots.

There's a skittishness in their body language. It's the kind of wary confidence you don't pick up in cushy jobs or safe neighborhoods. Chip looks like someone who's nice enough but isn't quick to trust—and probably has good reason for it.

"Um, yes. I own a romance bookstore, and seeing as I'm recently married, I don't have as much time to run my shop." The words come out forced and awkward, but I barrel forward. "Have you ever worked in retail?"

A strange smile twists the corner of their mouth but doesn't reach their eyes. "Sort of."

"Sort of?"

"As a kid I used to sell black market hexes," they say with a shrug. "So, you know—exchange of goods for money. Can't imagine books are that different."

I blink. "Oh."

"Not that I do that anymore," Chip rushes to clarify, their face tightening with something that looks uncomfortably close to regret. "I wouldn't touch that nasty stuff again if you paid me."

The sincerity in their voice is striking, but I still haven't decided whether that makes them more or less of a gamble.

"And you know my husband. . .how?" I ask.

Chip glances at the ornate chandelier overhead, buying themselves a moment. "From. . .around," they say vaguely, their tone light but evasive.

We fall silent for a moment, studying each other. Chip's expression is open but guarded like they're used to keeping people at arm's length until they decide otherwise. I have the distinct feeling we're both deciding whether the other is worth the trouble.

"How do you feel about romance books?" I ask finally, breaking the stalemate.

Their lips quirk into an easy grin. "Who doesn't love some good smut?"

I blink again, startled into a laugh. "Okay," I say, nodding slowly. "This might actually work."

Chip's grin widens as they relax a fraction, though their hands stay firmly in their pockets. "Guess we'll see."

CHAPTER 10

NO SKIN FOR YOU
THE BEAST OF BOSTON

Her skin.

The feel of it, the memory of touching her is a litany in my head that robbed me of sleep.

At dinner, we are worlds apart, separated by the long table and more ornate displays of decor and a generous spread of food. Yet I'm still in that corridor last night. The sight of her in that fuzzy robe was far more intoxicating than any lingerie. Maybe because it gives her an animal quality, like fur. Or because the item is drenched in her sweet scent, making me crazy with arousal.

It was all I could do to hold myself back, the animal side of me writhing, demanding I tear that cumbersome fabric from her body. My claws practically ached with the need, and even now, that pulse of heat lingers, waiting to flare if I let it.

But I won't let it.

Her skin.

The words circle my mind like a swirl of haunting ghosts. The thought pulses through my mind like a heart-beat, a steady, maddening refrain.

Her skin, her skin. Her skin.

Is not for you, I sternly remind myself.

As soon as I devour the slabs of steak on my plate, I practically flee the dining room to my study. There are two large sitting chairs by a fire that Mrs. P has already lit. No other lamps are turned on. Isabelle has seen me many times now, but I still dislike being so exposed. In here, I feel more comfortable. It's my business domain where I command my power. And I need all the power over my senses I can get right now.

So what if it's been an incredibly long time since I've had a woman? So what if it's been nearly two years? Even before the. . .event that led to my unfortunate current state, I rarely made time to indulge in carnal desire.

That must explain why the temptation of her flesh is driving me to near madness with the need to possess and claim.

So what if the knowledge that my wife is wandering the house under the same roof, mine to do as I please, threatens to make a bigger monster out of me?

Marriage does not equal sex in our case. I need to keep it that way.

The objective is to keep in close proximity until I am able to shift again. That is all.

The door creaks open, jerking me from my inappropriate thoughts.

Isabelle nearly backs out as if rethinking our arrangement. I catch sight of her bare feet first, toes painted dark purple. That surprises me—such a moody choice for my demure bookkeeper. She's changed since dinner into what I assume is her evening attire—a cream-colored sweater that drapes perfectly over her generous curves. The soft knit material clings and flows in all the right places, making her look utterly touchable. Her dark hair, freed from its earlier severe bun, tumbles in loose waves past her shoulders, and my claws itch with the urge to run through those silken strands.

"Sit." I command it, trying to distract myself from how inviting she looks.

"Please."

"What?"

"Please sit. The 'p' word is a powerful one." She still lingers at the door, shifting her weight from one bare foot to the other. The gesture is oddly vulnerable, domestic in a way that makes my chest tight.

"Put," I emphasize the 'p,' "your butt in that chair across from me," I say, ignoring her request and the way the firelight warms her creamy skin.

She snorts with displeasure before doing what I ask. Isabelle sits on the edge of the seat, not anywhere close to making herself comfortable. She sets a thick paperback on the side table. I wish she had set it down with the cover up so I could catch the title or picture and guess at the contents.

The fire crackles in the hearth as the scent of her—vanilla and something uniquely feminine—mingles with the burning wood, making my head spin.

"Now what?" she asks, tucking a wayward strand of hair behind her ear. The simple gesture draws attention to the softness of her features. Her cheeks are flushed from the fire's warmth.

"Now we sit in the same room together."

A brow quirks over her glasses. I'm still not sure if the sexy librarian effect is from the shape of her frames or her eyes themselves.

"And do what?"

"Just sit," I say, settling back in my chair. "Together." I grab my tablet off the table next to me and open it up, ready to catch up on emails. Production of Thorns has to be increased to deal with the interference of shipments. A rival gang, the Wolves, keeps intercepting my product. Frankly, it's pissing me off.

It's several minutes before I realize Isabelle is just watching me. Not glancing away when I shift or move like most do. Just. . .studying me with those warm brown eyes.

The way she's drawn her feet up beneath her, those purple toes peeking out beneath the hem of her black leggings, creates an image of casual intimacy that threatens to undo me.

"What?" The word comes out harsher than intended.

"Am I not allowed to look at you?"

"Not like that."

"Like what?" There's a hint of challenge in her voice.

"Like I'm a shifter specimen you are cataloging." My claws dig into the tablet's case. I continue on before she can respond. "Or is this morbid curiosity? Want to get a good look at the monster you married?"

She straightens in her chair. "I'm not going to avert my eyes like some blushing virgin every time—" She stops abruptly, color flooding her cheeks as the implications of her words sink in.

A surprised laugh rumbles out of me. "Blushing virgin? That's rich coming from the woman whose latest Instagram post recommended *Claimed by the Alpha* with the caption 'steamy enough to fog your reading glasses and ruin your panties.'"

Isabelle's flush deepens, but her chin lifts. "You've been stalking my social media?"

"Research," I correct, though the word sounds weak even to my ears. "Had to make sure you were. . .suitable."

"Suitable." She tests the word like she's tasting it. "Yesterday I was perfect, now I'm merely suitable. What do either of those mean?"

"We're not discussing this."

"No, of course not." She finally looks away to the fire, and I tell myself the relief I feel isn't tinged with disappointment. "You know so much about me. I don't know anything about you."

"We live together. What's left to know?"

"What you do for a living?" she suggests in a falsely light tone.

My scowl deepens. "That's irrelevant."

"Is it?"

"We're done talking about this, Isabelle," I say with a warning snarl, even as I put my tablet down on the table next to me so hard it cracks against the table.

Dammit.

The silence that follows is far from peaceful. She still doesn't pick up her book and I've just ruined my means to work and occupy my thoughts. I could send for another but it's late and my mind is fractured by the distraction Isabelle presents.

"What?" I demand again when I can't take her steady, judgmental gaze anymore.

"You can call me Belle," she says quietly.

Her change in subject takes me by surprise. Every time I think I know what she's going to say next, I'm proven wrong.

"I can, but I won't." I need to keep some amount of formality between us. Her full name is a reminder of the kind of arrangement we have.

"We're married now. . ." she begins hesitantly, and I get the sense her slow start is on my account, not hers.

"I know. I was there. Remember the doves?" I say flatly.

"That was the proposal," she corrects.

"Ah, yes." The banter bounces back and forth almost effortlessly. I try not to think too hard on it.

"You want me to be in the same room as you. You want me to spend time with you."

"Didn't I say that? It was in the contract."

She shifts in her seat. "Yes, but I think I'm only just now realizing why."

I hadn't planned on us talking. I don't like it. She's getting under my skin. "Don't you want to read a book? Do you not like the one you brought? We could send Mrs. Potts to get you another if you like. Then we can sit here in blissful silence." The last part comes out a growl.

"You're a Were."

"I'm aware." Annoyance flares, but I'm not sure if it's because I unintentionally rhymed or because she is still talking.

"Weres need a Pack to survive."

Uneasiness swirls in my chest. Pain begins to shift and stretch inside me. Fae fucking hell. If she keeps pushing, I'm going to end up exploding like I did yesterday. And I like this room.

"Don't ask me personal questions, Isabelle." There is a dark warning underlying my words.

Don't ask me what happened to my Pack.

Don't you fucking dare.

Pain of a different kind slices through me. One that will never heal no matter how much time has passed, no matter who or how many times I marry. The perpetual sword of anguish will forever be lodged in my chest.

"I'm not asking personal questions. I'm clarifying our. . .situation."

"Marriage?" I correct drolly.

Her pretty mouth flattens with open irritation. Good. If I should feel put out, so should she.

"You are trying to make me your Pack," she says flatly. "I'm assuming so you can shift again since you are stuck between two forms."

I sit back in my chair, a little gobsmacked, if I'm being honest. She keyed in on exactly what I was doing.

"You thought if we were married, it would count as Pack, but it didn't. So now we have to spend all of our time together because you think that's how it works." She adjusts her glasses. "Is it? Is that how it works?"

"I don't know," I confess. The words come out as a low rumble that emits from my chest even as I run a hand through my hair. The laws of Weres and their packs aren't so much a science as they are phenomena of nature.

Isabelle relaxes a fraction in her seat. "I think it makes sense. Time together creates bonds, and everyone knows Weres have to spend a lot of time with their Packs, because without them they could literally—" She stops speaking abruptly.

Die. Without a Pack, Weres literally die.

Her brown eyes flit to mine before looking away nervously.

"Not everyone knows that," I point out. "Just little bookshop keepers who read shifter romance."

An unladylike snort comes out of her. "I don't think anyone has ever called me little." Her fingers brush a stray strand of hair behind her ear, a flicker of uncertainty breaking through her usual composure. "But I think it may take more than time and proximity to create a Pack."

"Pray tell," I say, both wanting and not wanting her opinion.

Isabelle shrugs. "Well, it's about a connection, right? So to form connections, there also has to be communication."

"Nope." I'm off the chair like a shot.

"We can just start by sharing a couple small things each day," she rushes to say. "Like what our favorite color is, or our favorite songs, what you do for a living."

"Absolutely not."

"Right," she snorts, "because I'm supposed to pretend I didn't marry a mob boss who runs the largest criminal empire this side of the fae realms."

The audacity of her words strikes me silent for a moment, and then I laugh—a humorless sound that rumbles through the room. "A mob boss?" I repeat, letting the insult hang between us. Not that it's the first time I've been called that. "I'm a businessman."

Her brow lifts. "You sell Thorns—hexes and curses that wreck lives. How is that not—"

"Tools," I interrupt, my voice slicing through her words. "They're tools, not toys. And unlike the vermin scrambling in the gutters, I ensure those tools don't spiral out of control."

"Tools?" she says flatly. "You make it sound like a hammer or a wrench. A curse is a weapon, Dominic. A curse that can strip someone's voice, trap them in a mirror, or transform them into a lowly creature isn't a tool. Dress it up however you want, but at the end of the day, people use them to destroy."

It's the first time she's said my name apart from the vows. I like it too much. The way it slides off her tongue with familiarity. As if she knows me.

But she doesn't.

"It's not that simple," I snap, my agitation rising at my own insipidness over a name. "A Thorn is only a weapon if it's in the wrong hands. In the right hands, it's leverage. It's power. And at the end of the day, *I* am the equalizing force."

"How so?"

"Petals," I say with lofty knowing. "No Thorn is created without the antidote, a Petal. Thorns are not to be put out into the world without a means to reverse it. That's my rule."

Her brows knit together, her skepticism palpable. "So you sell destruction with a side of redemption?"

I lean forward now, letting her feel the weight of my presence. "I sell power, Isabelle. The power to take and the power to give back. Without control, without balance, it all falls apart."

"And you're the balance," she says, her voice laced with bitter irony.

"I'm the one who ensures the world doesn't go up in flames," I bite out. "My competitors? They deal in chaos. They sell irreversible hexes like candy, scorching the ground in their wake. That's not power—it's recklessness. And it's why they'll never be more than parasites." I rub my temples and add, muttering to myself, "They think brute force is all that matters."

Isabelle quirks a brow. "I mean, you're not exactly subtle either."

I shoot her a flat look. Subtlety and stupidity aren't the same thing.

She hums. "Oh, do go on. Enlighten me. "

I lean back, folding my arms. "Surely you know what happened to Senator Ryan Bicksbee. He got hit by a Thorn that wiped his mouth clean off his face. "

Her brows draw together, mouth tugging down in a

frown. "I remember. No lips, no teeth, just smooth skin where his mouth used to be." She shudders.

"And no Petal to fix it because my reckless rivals don't know how to garner true power. " I shake my head, jaw tightening. "They burned an opportunity. If I had done such a thing, I'd have had the Petal ready. It would have been an intimidation maneuver by which I would have fixed him up to put him entirely in my debt."

Isabelle tilts her head, watching me. "You think that's better?"

"I think it's smart," I correct. "Some take and destroy. I take and own."

She exhales, tapping her fingers against the armrest. "You know, I should probably be horrified by that."

I smirk. "And yet."

She shakes her head. "No wonder you thought you could buy me."

I shrug. "Everyone has a price, Isabelle."

She holds my gaze, her expression unreadable. If I didn't know any better, I'd think I caught a glimmer of respect in her eye. "And this makes you noble because you include an antidote to the poison you sell?"

Based on her critical question, I must have imagined the respect. Still, she debates without wrath or yelling.

"It makes me necessary," I growl. "People want Thorns, Isabelle. They'll find them one way or another. Better they find them through me than through someone who doesn't give a damn about what happens next."

The silence that follows is heavy, the crackling fire the only sound in the room.

"Necessary evil," she says finally, her tone quieter now, as if she's trying to make sense of it all.

Agitation rips through me. My muscles swell with pain,

a stretch that can never be fully realized. A permanent cramp grips my half-shifted body. It's not my wife's doing, though the tense discussion isn't helping. The physical stress ebbs and flows throughout the day.

The episodes are getting worse, lasting longer, the pain digging deeper into my bones. I push the thought away. I can't dwell on what it means. Not yet.

"Remember when I said I chose you because you were perfect?" I ask through gritted teeth.

"Yes," she responds slowly. There is an earnest gleam in her eye she tries and fails to hide. She still wants to know why I view her as perfect. And I'm about to give her the reason.

"I need someone who knows how to keep their own company in my presence. I know you are happiest reading in solitude. *Isabelle Lockhart, owner of Chapter Three believes every problem in life can be softened by a cozy chair, a steaming cup of something warm, and a really good book.*" I quote her bio from her website, not adding that I memorized the rest as well.

As the owner of a romance-only bookstore in Boston, Belle spends her days surrounded by shelves of happily-ever-afters and the intoxicating scent of fresh coffee and old pages.

I devoured every piece of information I could get on her after her father fell into my lap.

"And based on the stock of shifter romance you carry in your little store, I gambled that my grotesque form wouldn't be so. . .offensive to you. Therefore, we could sit in silence in close proximity for the rest of our days, *not* talking."

"Oh."

"Oh," I echo mockingly. "I did not pick you to be a

conversationalist, Isabelle. We can live separately but together."

A line forms between her brows as her lips pull in a downturn.

"What now?" I ask with open exasperation.

She gives a small shrug, her expression carefully neutral. "Nothing."

I pinch the bridge of my nose, feeling the familiar tension of a headache beginning. When a female says "nothing," she never means it.

Sinking into my wing-back chair, my sigh morphs into a little grumble. "Isabelle."

"No, really, you've got it all figured out," she says in that same unconvincing tone. Then she opens a book on her lap and stares down at the pages.

If a woman insists on pretending everything is alright, the gentlemanly thing to do is let her continue the farce. And, of course, allow the hundred tiny pinpricks of guilt and annoyance to torment him over what he's not even sure is wrong.

"*Isabelle*," I growl.

I'm no gentleman.

"Won't you please do me a kindness and let me know what is bouncing around that brain of yours?" The words are said through clenched teeth as I try to control my temper.

She stares at the pages on her lap a beat longer before she closes the book. "You're right about me. But..."

"What?"

"I still want more." Her warm brown eyes lift to meet mine.

"More?" I quirk a brow.

"There's more to me than just my being an introvert. There's my bookshop."

"What about it?" The words come out rougher than intended.

"You may have memorized my website bio." Her eyes meet mine, unflinching. "But it doesn't say how important it was for me to build something of my own. I want to get books into the hands of readers. I want to promote my favorite authors. I want to create a safe haven for readers where they can escape into fantasy and romance. Making that kind of sanctuary is important."

I lean back, lips curling. "Quite the ambitious little bookseller, aren't you?"

"That's not why you picked me, though. Not because I have dreams, but because you thought I'd be content to sit quietly in your haunted mansion forever, reading my little romance novels." She doesn't raise her voice, but there's steel in it.

I start at her use of the word *haunted*.

Does she know? Feel the presence of all those who used to live here? My skin itches at the thought. Thankfully she doesn't notice my reaction, but continues on.

"Because obviously, someone who reads shifter romance must be desperate enough to accept a life with a monster." Her face tenses. "I'm sorry. I didn't mean to refer to you as a monster."

I barely register the slight or her apology. I've been called worse, and I am a monster. I have no doubt about that.

But that's also the second time she's expressed the idea I view her as desperate. I don't like hearing it, but there's no use dispelling her of the idea, even if it's wrong. Especially since I did put her in a desperate situation, though it's not the kind of desperation she is referring to.

She's alluding to the idea she is seen as some kind of old maid who would take any husband. This isn't the 19th century, and for anyone to think the creature across from me is incomplete or wanting in any way is ridiculous.

"Isn't that exactly what you did?" I surge to my feet, my claws scraping against the arms of the chair. "You signed the contract. You took the deal."

She doesn't flinch at my movement. She just watches me with those steady brown eyes.

"I took the deal to save my dad. He's my only family left. Or he was. . .until yesterday."

Because we are married now. Family by law. But not pack.

"You're right—" she goes on. "I do love my quiet moments with books. But that's not all I am."

"So what?" I pace the room, my partially shifted form casting monstrous shadows in the dim light. "We can't all get what we want, Isabelle. You think I wanted this?" I gesture to my grotesque form. "You think I wanted to trap some bookshop owner in a loveless marriage just to survive?"

"No," she says simply. "But you're not the only one who's paying a price here."

The truth of her quiet words hits like a physical blow. I've robbed her of her future—of whatever dreams she had for herself and that little shop of hers. A chance at real love with a man who would adore her and romance her every day of her life.

"I don't—" I cut myself off, the rage and guilt warring inside me. "I can't—"

I storm toward the door, needing to get out before I lose

control completely. The wood splinters under my grip as I wrench it open.

"We still have three hours left," she calls after me, her voice steady despite everything. The firelight catches in her hair, turning the edges to molten copper, and I have to force myself to tear my gaze away.

"Consider yourself relieved of duty for the night," I growl, not daring to glance back at her curled in that armchair, looking so damnably perfect. "Consider it a honeymoon gift."

The door crashes shut behind me, the sound echoing through the mansion like thunder. But even as I stalk away, her presence lingers—the scent of her, the way she appeared in the firelight, the quiet strength in her words. Along with the uncomfortable knowledge that I've trapped us both—her in a cage of my making, and myself in the prison of what I've become.

And the worst part? She isn't wrong. About any of it.

CHAPTER II
A CHIP OF MISFORTUNE
BELLE

The next day begins with shouting.

Dominic's roar tears through the house, shaking the very walls. I'm halfway down the stairs when the sound stops me in my tracks. The air feels heavy, vibrating with barely contained rage. I grip the banister as the floor trembles beneath my feet, my heart pounding. Thankfully my father is still asleep and can snore his way through a train hurtling through his bedroom. Otherwise I'd worry all the upset would agitate him.

I hear Tock and Lucien in the hall below. Their voices are sharp, rapid-fire, each trying to deflect the blame on the other.

"For fae lord's sake, Lucien," Tock hisses, his clipped tone quivering with irritation. "If you'd followed the protocol, the Thorns and Petals wouldn't have been separated."

Lucien leans against the wall with no sign of his usual lazy grin. But there's the agitated flick of his lighter opening and closing in quick succession. "Protocol? That's rich coming from you. Didn't you swear up and down those crates were sealed tighter than a gator's jaws? How'd that work out for you, *mon cher?*"

"I'm not your 'cher,' and you're deflecting," Tock snaps, his words brittle. "You're security. It's your job to make sure nothing gets tampered with at the checkpoints."

Lucien's grin widens, but it doesn't reach his eyes. "And you're logistics. *L'homme* with the eidetic memory. You're *supposed* to know where everything is at all times. But now, half the shipment's out there without antidotes, which means it's just a bunch of dirty hexes, no better than what street dealers push."

Tock's mouth flaps open and close. "It's not like I personally packed them, you absolute cabbage." He pushes up his glasses with a trembling hand.

"Cabbage? That's a new one." Lucien's voice is mockingly light, though the clicks of metal double time. "You could write a manual on throwin' folks under the bus. You're like a cat. Always land on your feet, so nobody really trusts you."

"And you're like a dog," Tock shoots back, pushing up his glasses again in a show of exasperation. "All bark, no brains."

Lucien's grin widens. "Might be true, but who is *he* going to rip to shreds first? You, I think."

Tock's face turns ashen. "*You're* the one responsible for security, Lucien."

I edge past them carefully, not wanting to get caught in the crossfire. Their bickering fades behind me as I near the dining room.

Dominic sits at the head of the table, his massive form dwarfing the chair beneath him. He doesn't look up as I enter, his claws tapping a steady, ominous rhythm against the wood. Score marks from his claws mar the wooden surface around him. The sight sends a prickle of unease down my spine. His mismatched eyes are focused on a plate of untouched food, but the tension rolling off him is palpable. My husband is royally pissed.

I take my seat cautiously, keeping my movements slow and deliberate. The weight of his presence is suffocating, like the room is smaller with him in it.

"When are we going to Chapter Three today?" I ask, my voice steady despite the way my pulse hammers in my ears. I have to project for him to hear me all the way at the other end.

He doesn't look up. "Today isn't good."

I swallow the spark of irritation that flares in my chest. "I have responsibilities there. Chip is expecting me to show them how to run things. I've already lost a day and a half of business."

At last, he looks up, his expression sharp and unforgiving. "We're not going today."

The air grows heavier, the same kind of pressure I felt on our wedding day right before he exploded in a violence that decimated the beautiful plant laden conservatory. Though Mrs. P must have magicked it back together since it looks perfect now. My stomach knots, but I force myself to hold his stare.

"If you don't plan to honor the terms of our contract, perhaps I should consult someone who *will*," I say, my tone measured. "I hear there's a sea witch who is quite skilled with contracts."

His claws dig into the table, leaving more deep gouges in the polished surface. "You think threatening me is a wise move?"

"Not a threat," I say calmly, though my hands tighten on the napkin in my lap. "A logical measured action. You don't want *me* to act outside the boundaries of our agreement, do you?"

For a moment, I think he might snap—his muscles coil, and his eyes darken, his jaw tight as a spring.

Will he jump onto the table? Tear the room apart? Would he hurt me?

The thought sends a flicker of fear through me, but I don't let it show. I sit up straighter, my words firm. "Why did we sign the contract if you're going to ignore it?"

His mismatched eyes narrow, studying me like a predator sizing up its prey.

That's right husband. Call yourself a businessman. I'll make you prove it.

This is business and his claim last night reminded me that's all this is.

"*You think I wanted to trap some bookshop owner in a loveless marriage just to survive?*"

No matter that I find him attractive, or that I still shiver from the memory of his claw raking across my shoulder, this is a contractual agreement. That means I need to reap the benefits out of my side as much as possible.

Though my husband may blow his top and show me the true violent streak he continually warns me of...

Slowly, the tension eases from Dominic's frame. He settles in his chair, his claws withdrawing from the table. The shift is almost imperceptible, but I sense it—a small concession, a step back from the brink.

"We leave in an hour," he says tightly. "Be ready, or we won't be going today."

I'm not sure if the thrill that zips through me is from winning the battle or the anticipation of going to my favorite place in the world. Either way, I make sure I'm dressed in my *Vamp in the Sheets, Bloodsucker in the Streets* book quote shirt from the series I'm reading, waiting by the front door ten minutes early so Dominic doesn't have any excuse to renege on the plan.

The only thing that holds us up is the coat he insists I wear. I'm forced to trade out my purple puff jacket, which admittedly has gotten a bit thin through the years, for a long black trench coat with a hood. The fabric is decorated with ornate, embroidered pink roses and their thorny stems. It reminds me of my ring and of the carvings throughout this big house. It's another status symbol that shows I belong to the Beast of Boston.

As if I could forget.

Only when we are in the back of the black limousine and on the road do I allow myself to examine my husband a little closer. Dominic stares out the tinted car window, his massive frame dominating the space, his clawed hand tapping restlessly against his knee.

His scent fills the small space—dark, woodsy, with an undertone of something smoky. Warm, strangely comforting, and entirely unfair for someone who spends so much time trying to intimidate me.

"What was all that yelling about this morning?" I ask, keeping my tone light.

His gaze flicks to me, then to the window. "Just business."

"Business sounds. . .intense."

"It is."

His tone is clipped, a clear warning to drop it, but I press on.

"Someone is stealing from you?"

The air between us tightens as his head snaps toward me, suspicion flashing across his face. "How do you know about that?"

"We live in the same house. I overhear things."

"Well, stop it."

"You want me to stick my fingers in my ears whenever I think I *might* potentially hear something I shouldn't?"

"Yes," he huffs. Unreasonable man. "Also blindfold yourself if you think you might see anything as well."

I roll my eyes at his ridiculous yet serious suggestion.

"Well, that's not going to happen, so all your cloak-and-dagger attitudes are unnecessary."

For a moment, I think he's going to lash out again, but then he exhales sharply and looks away. "Some. . .rabid dogs have been causing trouble. That's all you need to know."

His words are vague, but the way his claws dig into the upholstery tells me there's more to the story.

Why am I even asking? I don't want anything to do with Thorns. I never have. Not that anyone cared about that when I was growing up. The bitter irony of ending up with someone just as obsessed with them as my father does not escape me.

Sometimes I wonder if my father really was as out of his mind as I believed when he broke into Dominic's. . .

Remembering I don't care about Dominic's personal ongoings—or I'm not supposed to anyway—I let it go. Afterall, I get to go to work for myself in my safe haven, which is all I've ever wanted.

WHEN WE PULL up to Chapter Three, a wave of comfort washes over me. My shop stands as a beacon of normalcy, its vibrant window displays filled with romance novels. Fairy lights twinkle along the awning and wrap around the doorframe, casting a soft, inviting glow. Even the cold gray frosting of snow on the building and streets only enhances its charm, making the warm interior stand out even more. Everything about it beckons—an unspoken invitation to step inside, sip a cup of tea, and snuggle up with a good book.

Lucien opens the limo door as I step out, his smirk as lazy as ever. "I'll be hanging around like a June bug in the heat today, *mon cher*. Keeping an eye on things."

"June bug in the heat?" I ask, even as my nose starts running from the bitter cold of the air.

Lucien simply winks.

I glance back at Dominic, who hasn't moved from his seat. He stares out the tinted window, his features unreadable.

"Aren't you coming in?" I ask.

"No." His voice is flat. "I'll wait here."

"Okay then," I say, wondering if he really plans to be in the car for the next three hours. Not that it isn't comfy and spacious. And maybe the intrigue of a limousine parked outside my shop will spike more foot traffic from sheer curiosity.

He'll be fine. I bet brooding in his limousine is his favorite pastime right after yelling at his staff, menacing old ladies, and sucking lemons for fun.

Inside Chapter Three, the heady scent of paper and ink envelops me, a warm, familiar embrace. I breathe it in deeply, like a junkie desperate for a fix, the nostalgic aroma settling something restless inside me.

My gaze sweeps over the packed shelves, each one a love letter to the genre—sweet small-town romances cozied up beside dark, steamy shifter tales. My fingers trail along a few spines as I move through the space, drawn to the carefully curated corners, each offering a sanctuary for readers looking to lose themselves in a story.

Chip greets me minutes later with bright energy, their lavender hair a perfect complement to the pastel tones of the shop. I texted them once I knew I would be coming here today.

"Morning, boss," they say with a grin. "Ready to put me to work?"

"Let's do it."

We spend the next few hours going over the basics—handling the register, managing inventory, and, most importantly, recommending books. Chip catches on quickly, their enthusiasm infectious. Lucien aimlessly wanders the store. He goes back and forth between his lazy pacing and picking up books to read their back matter.

When he starts to hit on some of my female customers, I move to stop him. I hold off when he flirts two women into buying twice the amount of books they intended to get by telling them they're "worth it." I get extra sales, and he gets some new phone numbers.

As long as he's not making anyone uncomfortable, it's a win-win situation. Though the second he's intrusive, I plan to kick his butt out into the cold, secret guard or not. Though, why I need a babysitter with Dominic just outside, I can't fathom. It's not like there was a marriage announcement on social media. No one likely knows the Beast of Boston has taken a bride. I vaguely wonder if anyone will.

Chip and I settle into a rhythm, and the knot of tension in my chest begins to unwind. This is where I belong—surrounded by stories, helping others find escape in the pages of a book. For the first time since Lucien and Tock walked through those doors, I feel that familiar glimmer of purpose.

Chip darts ahead of me, rearranging the book displays with an efficiency that borders on supernatural. I heft a stack of hardcovers onto the counter, watching them move like they're auditioning for the speed round of a game show.

"How do you do that so fast?" I ask, half-joking, half-amazed, as I set the books down with a huff.

Chip glances over their shoulder, grinning. "Years of practice."

I snort. "What did you do before all this? Before the Beast of Boston swept you up into his kingdom?" Chip mentioned selling hexes, but they made it seem like it was a long time ago.

The grin falters for a second, a flash of hesitation crossing their face. "Before this? I was. . .not much of anything. Just surviving."

The way they say it—casual, but not casual—makes me tread carefully. "Surviving where?"

Chip flips through a book, not looking at me. "On the streets. Boston's not exactly kind to people without a place to go, you know? Especially when you're carrying extra baggage."

"Baggage?" I press gently.

They tap their front tooth—the one with a sizable chip —and shrug. "Yeah. This bad boy earned me the nickname for a reason. For six years, I had a Thorn on me."

I freeze, the weight of their words hitting me like a freight train. "A Thorn? Like. . .like one of Dominic's?"

"No," Chip cuts me off, sharp and decisive. "Not Dominic's. I. . ." Their eyes dart off nervously. "When I was a kid, I took a job for some bad dudes selling dirty hexes. One day, when I went to pick up a package, those idiots decided I looked like a good test subject for their product.

They forced me to drink one to test it. A Thorn of Misfortune."

Oh.

Oh fae lords. I can't even imagine the pain and suffering—

My chest tightens, the parallel to my dad slicing through me like a blade. He was used too, a test subject for the Wolves' experiments. My nails bite into my palms, and I have to force myself to breathe.

"You ever feel like your body doesn't belong to you?" Chip asks with more than a little bit of self-consciousness. Their eyes flit over in Lucien's direction. One long leg is bent over the other as he turns another page of a dark mafia romance book called *Light Me Up.* He seems completely engrossed. If he's listening in, he doesn't show it.

Chip's question lands like a gut punch, and I can't stop my fingers from brushing against the edge of the counter, grounding myself. I nod slowly, swallowing hard. Not only because I relate on my father's behalf, but I also had the same sensation for most of my youth. I know what it's like to be forced to be someone you're not. Dissociation was such a regular habit, I made it into a business.

Chip nods back, like that's answer enough. "That's what it felt like. Every inch of me was wrong. My skin? Not mine. My hands? Not mine. It was like being a marionette on strings I couldn't see. And wherever I went, bad luck was glued to my ass. Losing my wallet from a hole in my pants, breaking bones every couple of months, always being in the wrong place at the wrong time. You ever get hit by a car and then mugged while you're trying to crawl off the street? Because I have. I barely ever had a place to sleep or anything to eat. There was no safety, just uncertainty every single day on a level I never knew was even possible."

They pause, staring down at the book in their hands as if it holds answers. "I lasted six years with that curse. Six years of trying to find someone who had a Petal even though I knew street Thorns didn't usually have antidotes. Somehow, I managed to keep this tiny little sliver of hope alive." Chip shrugs. "Or maybe it's just my body's stubborn refusal to ever give up."

"How did you...?" The words catch in my throat, but I push them out. "How did you get rid of it?"

Chip's grin returns as they lift a finger. "My one moment of good luck. Six months ago, after a particularly rough bout of bad luck and too many days without food, I collapsed outside one of Dominic's warehouses. I was half-dead and ready to be all-dead when they found me. They could've left me there. Would've been easier."

"But they didn't." Why is my heart beating so hard and heavy?

"No. I was hauled inside and asked what my deal was. I got the words out, not even realizing it was the Beast of Boston himself asking me the questions." Chip speaks of my husband with overt reverence. "Turns out, the Thorn I took had been from one of his stolen shipments. Which meant—"

"He had the Petal," I whisper.

"I didn't even know one existed, but he gave it to me. Woke up in a fancy bed with food at my side and a new lease on life. That day, Dominic earned my fealty for life. He asks me to jump? I'd go over the edge of a cliff." Chip's eyes glaze over with open worship at the mention of their savior. They mean every word of what they say.

Guess there is someone else who isn't afraid of him.

A strange pressure builds behind my sternum, a tangle of feelings I can't quite unravel. "He saved you."

Chip shrugs one shoulder, their expression unreadable. "Saved me, yeah. But more than that, he reminded me what it feels like to be taken care of." Chip's voice thickens with emotion. "Nobody gave a damn about me before that damn Thorn, and no one cared for those long six years. But Dominic, he actually gives a witchtit about me. Maybe even two."

That hits me in the chest with far too much weight. The idea of someone caring about me, taking care of me, holds some appeal if I'm being honest. In the last few days, I'd been waited on hand and foot with everything I could want by Mrs. P and the luxury of it still sends a delicious thrill through me.

I'd been on my own for a long time. Sure, I had my dad but he was out of his gourd most of the time. And my friend Rap, she helped me get set up in my new life and break ties cleanly with the old. But the idea of Dominic caring about this kid almost makes me. . .dear fae lords. . .jealous?

"Since then he's made sure I got a job, a place to stay, goals and shit." A wry explosive laugh escapes Chip. "There's like this whole thing about planning goals and setting your sights on something better. I remember when I only strove to see the next day. But Dom says I need to focus on my future. He checks in on me regularly, intent to help me figure out a way to build it. The guy is my hero."

I stare at them, their words ricocheting in my head. Dominic saved Chip. He used something priceless to help someone who had nothing to offer in return. And for what? Compassion? A sense of justice?

A necessary evil.

The realization slices through me. Dominic was a lot of things—Beast. Businessman. Dangerous. But this? This complicates things. And the parallels to my dad make my stomach churn. My family used my father just like some thugs on the street used Chip. Except there is no Petal for my father.

Only fractured pieces of him are left, but I'll care for those until one of us expires.

Chip moves on, rearranging another shelf like they didn't just crack my perception of my husband wide open. I grip on the counter, trying to push away the riotous emotions brewing inside me.

Dominic saved Chip to use them. My husband is methodical in tit for tat. Don't romanticize him. Though something niggles under my breastbone all the same.

Three hours come and go all too soon, and I climb back into the limo to join a dour, unresponsive Dominic.

"Thank you," I say with sincere gratitude.

He doesn't look up from his phone, just grunts.

"Seriously," I press.

Dominic finally lifts his head to meet my gaze.

I'm thanking him for more than allowing me to be at my shop. I'm thanking him for saving Chip, though I won't articulate that out loud.

"You're thanking me for something you already negotiated?" His brows rise with boredom, and it feels like a slap. "I keep my word. Don't expect more." His eyes flick downward. "Also you spilled coffee on yourself." Then he goes back to his phone.

Whatever flicker of warmth I felt earlier extinguishes.

Forget calling him a beast. My husband is a dick.

CHAPTER 12

KEEP A STRAIGHT FACE

BELLE

Dominic's study is unmistakably his. The walls are lined with dark wood paneling that absorbs the dancing firelight, while a massive desk dominates one corner like a throne. A bar cart stocked with crystal decanters gleams under the low glow of a brass lamp.

Every detail speaks of control and calculated power, from the precision of the seating arrangement—two imposing wingback chairs angled toward the fireplace—to the faint scent of cedar and smoke that clings to the air like an unspoken warning. This isn't a space meant to be shared; it's Dominic's lair. Yet here I am, trespassing nightly.

The next week continues in a routine. Three hours a day at my bookstore, some quality time with my dad, and each evening Dominic and I spend time in his study, respectively absorbed in our activities. He usually handles emails and business deals for a couple hours before following my example and cracking open a book. Usually, it's the history of some conquering war hero.

Dominic sits across from me, his massive form at ease yet unyielding in the chair. The firelight plays tricks with his features, deepening the sharp lines of his face and casting his eyes in an almost predatory gleam.

His clawed hand rests lazily on the armrest. In this room, he is more relaxed. Like the shadows here are old friends of his.

His mishmash features of man and beast shouldn't be sexy. Watching him work or read a book definitely shouldn't be sexy. But damn it, it is.

This should feel normal. The kind of predictable rhythm I've always craved. But it doesn't.

Because I think my half-shifted husband—who is most certainly a beast—is hot as sin.

I tug at my fuzzy robe, conscious of the rose-colored silk nightie underneath as I try to focus on my book—a well-loved shifter romance. It's one of my comfort reads, filled with all the usual tropes: overprotective alpha males, heated glances that turn into heated encounters, and plenty of detailed, pulse-pounding scenes.

The words blur together as warmth coils deep inside me. The alpha in my novel is commanding his mate, clawed hand around her throat and...

My body reacts to the familiar prose as if I've been conditioned for it, the slow build of tension settling low in my belly. I shift, hyper-aware of how close Dominic is.

My husband.

The kind of man who would throw me over his shoulder and growl something possessive. The kind of man who would—

I blink down at the page, startled to realize I've stopped reading altogether and started imagining Dominic. Heat spreads through my cheeks.

What is wrong with me?

Focus, Belle.

But the words in my book don't help. The scene has escalated: the alpha growling promises of pleasure, the heroine melting beneath him, gasping for more. I cross my legs, pressing them together in a futile attempt to dispel the ache building there. My eyes dart toward Dominic again, as if drawn by a magnet.

He's not helping. He shifts slightly, his thighs spreading wider, his jaw tight with concentration. Even the way he clicks his claws against the tablet has me imagining those same claws scraping down my back, leaving red marks as he—

Stop. Thinking. About. That.

"What are you reading?" he asks, his voice low and rough. Dominic's gaze locks onto mine.

My mouth goes dry. "What?"

"You seem to be enraptured by what you're reading. What's happening in the plot?" There is genuine curiosity in his question even as he wears his usual scowl.

I grip the book tighter. "Nothing's happening in the plot." Technically I'm not wrong. This is an action scene. Pure furious, frantic fucking. No plot in sight.

Dominic frowns.

Nope. Not happening. I shake my head and bury my face in the book, pretending to be engrossed.

But Dominic doesn't drop it. He leans forward slightly, his attention sharpening like a predator catching the scent of something intriguing.

The realization hits me like a freight train.

Oh no.

"You smell. . .different," he says, his head tilting as if to confirm it. "Sweet."

My stomach drops. "Excuse me?"

His nostrils flare, and he sets his tablet aside. "Your scent. It's stronger than usual."

I want to die. I want to crawl under the rug and never come out.

"I-It's probably the lotion I used," I stammer, desperate for any excuse.

His brow quirks. "Is it? Because it smells more like arousal."

There it is. The mortification. The earth might as well swallow me whole.

I need water. Or air. Or both.

"I think this is the part where I get up and leave," I mutter, my voice high and strained.

He growls in warning.

"I'll be right back," I wave him off even as I abandon the book and flee for the kitchen.

When I return, glass in hand, I freeze. My husband stands with my book open where I left my bookmark, scanning the words. Fear and something else—something hotter—twists in my core.

"What are you doing?" My words come out a squeak.

"I wanted to see what was happening in your book," he explains, his lips twitching.

I snatch the book from him. "Well, now you see I'm right. There is no plot." I hate the defensive edge in my voice.

I thought I rid myself of any shame long ago. For witchtit's sake, all I do is help other readers embrace reading the very same thing without shame, yet my face is as hot as a stovetop. I've reverted to my younger self, easily wounded by others' criticism over what I read. Though I swore I'd left that insecurity behind, the deep stab of my first beau making fun of me resurfaces with a vengeance.

Why do you read this trash? You don't think I give it to you good enough? You're so weird.

I wish Dominic would go back to his seat and give me space since I can't yet leave for another thirty minutes.

"I disagree," he says slowly. "There was quite a lot of action, and despite it being sexually driven, there is clearly an exchange of power happening, which is very much plot."

I stare at him, thrown by his literary analysis of shifter smut. Then he's directly in front of me, breathing in deeply.

"Though I'd say your shifter romance is missing something crucial when it comes to mating patterns," he goes on.

"Oh?" I ask in a strained tone, A line seems to connect us, reeling him in.

When his hand curls around my nape, I melt into his grip and my self-consciousness evaporates.

Dominic's nose brushes my cheek. He hesitates, but I tilt my head, offering more. Something dark and primal flashes in his eyes.

"Shifters have a thing about *biting* when they fuck." The crude words send electricity down my spine as he nips at my throat.

My book hits the floor. I don't care. He presses me back against the writing desk, his hard form pushing into my welcoming body. Every rational thought dissolves under his touch.

CHAPTER 13

YOU FUCK LIKE A GENTLE LAMB

THE BEAST OF BOSTON

I revel in Isabelle's skin, the feel, the smell, as I skim over the delicate shell of her ear before following down the line of her throat. My heart thuds in slow, steady beats as if drugged by lust, even as the tension in my groin continues to grow to a near-unbearable peak.

Oh fae lords, I can't stop. Not when she's so sweet and delectable.

Though I'm only guessing. I've never had a taste. I open my mouth to gently nip and lick at her column of throat.

Oh witchtits, she *is* fucking delectable.

A low rumble of pleasure rolls from her, encouraging me to press my body to hers until she's pinned against the writing desk. My hardness grinds into her welcoming curves, and my mouth goes dry from the sudden blast of desire.

I lick and suck at her neck with fervor. A dull thud signals she's dropped her book. I couldn't care less. All I can think of is more. I need more of her. I need all of her. I want to mark her, fuck her, make her forget her own name. I've pushed her back until she's half perched on the edge of the desk.

My claws slip beneath the edge of her robe and trail along the smooth silk of her nightgown. A groan rips out of my throat as I squeeze the generous swell of her breast, testing its firmness.

Belle's legs part on a gasp and I step between them, my hardness finding the hot dent between her thighs.

"I don't think that's all shifters," Belle counters.

For a moment, I don't comprehend the words. It's taking every ounce of control not to rip her clothes off, throw her on the ground and fuck her senseless.

"What?"

"I don't think all shifters bite when they. . .um. . .you know."

My lips curl. She can't get the words out which is beyond endearing considering she reads this content on a regular basis before selling it to others.

"When they *fuck*," I enunciate the word crudely, rocking between her thighs, wanting—needing to get closer.

"Yeah," she clears her throat even as her head drops back. "That may just be a *you* thing."

"No, it's all shifters. It's compulsive." My claws slip under her shirt. My hand hovers for a moment—this grotesque appendage shouldn't touch something so soft, so perfect. But when she arches into me, seeking more contact, my control splinters. I'm touching, sliding up until I find intricate lace.

"I don't know," she says. "When we made love on our wedding night, you were gentle as a lamb."

I pull away enough to glare at her at the resurgence of our make-believe game.

"Gentle as a lamb?" I repeat in disbelief.

Isabelle is flushed, her eyes dark inviting pools. She gives me a little nod. "Yes, you made sweet gentle love to me on a bed of rose petals. You even cried a tear of joy at the end."

Cried a what?

My claw roughly pushes the strap of her nightgown down, then yanks it further, baring her breast. She jerks in surprise. I find her taut nipple, running my thumb back and forth along it before kneading the full expanse around it and then tugging at the tip again. Her hips buck into mine with a strangled groan. I deny myself a look, though I'm desperate to know if the needy points are brown or pink. Instead, I dive deeper into those brown eyes that glaze as they fill with lust.

"I believe, *wife*, you are misremembering. Though there was that time I lapped between your legs softly for nearly two hours, not allowing you to come until you begged me, your alpha," my lips slide up to one side in a smirk, "to fuck you, and bite you until you came."

I notch my thigh between her legs so she can better rock her heat along my thick corded muscle. My mouth goes dry with the need to remove our clothing and feel all of her, but I'm unwilling to interrupt the glassy, almost pained look in her eye as she loses herself to the friction. The sounds escaping her throat keep moving upward in strained pitch.

Oh, I'm gonna make you come, wife.

Torn between the need to watch her succumb to pleasure and the urge to claim her throat again, I give in to both —letting my gaze devour her expressions before dragging my mouth back to her skin, only to repeat the cycle. My human hand has been holding her by the scruff of her neck this entire time, and a vision of gripping her by the throat as I fuck her mercilessly like in that book has me rubbing against her harder. Fuck, I'm so hard I could drill my dick through concrete. The speed in which blood has left my head leaves me dizzy.

"Now I want to know." My words come out as a rasp. "Do *you* have a strong desire to bite when you come? *Wife?*"

Her lids flutter open and I never want to look at anything else other than those deep brown depths. "Like me specifically, or humans in general?"

The fact she still has her reasoning ability tells me I'm not doing my job. So I drop down and catch one of those tight buds between my teeth, causing her to shriek and moan.

For fuck's sake. Her nipples are pink. They're candy pink.

Dear gods man, do not—I repeat—do NOT come in your pants.

"Oh," she coos in a tone that begs for more. Her nails dig into my shoulders as she pushes against my hardness with even more desperation.

The door creaks open, golden lamplight from the hallway spilling across us like an accusation. The sudden illumination catches the library's dark windows, transforming them into mirrors, and my gaze snaps to our reflection before I can stop myself. The sight steals the breath from my lungs.

My massive form looms over her like a nightmare—human hand gripping the back of her neck, fur bristling with savage need, fang gleaming in the new light. I'm a monster playing at being a man, and the evidence is damning. Belle looks so vulnerable beneath me, her lips swollen from my rough kisses, her clothes askew from my claws. What the hell am I thinking?

I stumble back, bile rising in my throat. The heat that

had been consuming me turns to ice in my veins. How could I have fooled myself into thinking I have the right to touch her?

"Dominic—" Belle reaches for me, her voice husky with lingering desire. The sound of it makes me want to weep. Or vomit. Or both.

"Your evening tea, dear," Mrs. P says from the doorway, either oblivious to or graciously ignoring the scene before her. The familiar routine of it feels like mockery.

"We're done here," I snarl, more beast than man, already retreating into the shadows where I belong. "Good night, wife."

The last thing I see is Isabelle's face—not twisted in disgust as it should be, but wearing something far worse: understanding. As if she knows exactly why I'm running, as if she can see right through every defense I've built.

I flee before she can voice that understanding, before she can offer words of absolution I don't deserve. The beast inside me howls at leaving her like this, at abandoning what we'd started. But better to leave her wanting than to let her see what kind of monster really lurks beneath my skin.

The sound of my claws gouging the hallway walls follows me all the way back to my chambers.

CHAPTER 14

ONCE, TWICE, MAYBE SPILL IT THRICE

THE BEAST OF BOSTON

Isabelle is delicious and I'm hard as hell licking up her slit. She bucks and moans as I feast on my wife's desire, digging my fingers into her thighs until they shake under my hold.

"Dom—" The rest of my name is strangled in her throat as Isabelle bucks, a scream building. So close, so close, almost there and—

I wake up, my hand around my very hard dick.

Fuck.

Time for a shower.

I'VE JERKED MYSELF OFF, and I *still* can't stop wanting Isabelle.

Our rooms are separated by a mere door. I find myself unable to do anything but pace back and forth as I try to think of anything but stripping my wife naked and slamming into her body until she is a screaming, orgasming mess.

Each inhale is saturated with her scent invading from the next room. It's sweet and maddening. It clings to me. It's embedded itself into my sheets though she's never laid on them. My pores are filled with her. No matter how many times I rake my claws through my hair or pace the length of the room, I can't escape it. Yet I don't want to.

The atmosphere shifts, heavy and humid with the unmistakable heat of arousal. But it's not mine this time.

I don't mean to move, but I find myself drawn toward the door, my mouth watering, my resolve crumbling.

The taste of her lingers on my tongue, maddening and addicting in a way that nothing else ever has been. It's ruined me. Just one taste, and I knew no one else would ever compare. Her warm skin beneath my mouth carried a flavor that felt like a secret—a whisper meant only for me.

As a man, I would've reveled in it, claimed her fully in my study until I left her trembling beneath me. Back then, I could wield my strength, my heightened senses, as a gift. Now, they're a curse, magnifying everything I want but cannot have.

The sound of Isabelle's movements filter through the connecting door, faint but unmistakable. The creak of her bed, the rustle of fabric, her breath—ragged and uneven. My steps falter. My body tenses.

I shouldn't.

But I do.

I still. I listen.

The sharp hitch of her breath is a shot of pure adrenaline, coursing straight to my groin. The broken, breathy noises she tries to stifle undo me.

In my mind's eye, I can see her. Her sounds paint a picture so vivid and inescapable that the door between us might as well not exist. Those wide, honest brown eyes, glazed with desire. Lips parted, teeth catching the corner of that plush lower lip. Her hair spills over her shoulders in waves, tumbling in rich ribbons over her pale skin. Sheets, tangled around her body, envy the warmth of her curves as her fingers press between her thighs.

A low hum fills the air. The muffled vibration jolts through me like a live wire. My wife is using more than her fingers. I shove my fist into my mouth, teeth clamping onto my knuckles to stifle the guttural sound clawing its way up my throat.

My abs tense as heat coils low in my body. My cock hardens further, straining against every ounce of control I'm trying to maintain.

The air thickens as her desire sharpens.

Oh, Isabelle.

My human hand drifts lower before I can stop myself, pushing my pants past my hips to wrap around my thick length. The first stroke is involuntary, a desperate attempt to ease the tension building to a fever pitch. But it doesn't help. Nothing will—not this, not anything. Not unless I'm inside her, making her cry out my name instead of biting back those maddening little sounds.

The beast inside me howls at the restraint, clawing at my control, desperate to claim what's already mine. To see her come undone under my hands. To leave her marked, ravaged.

Isabelle gasps—a high, breathless sound that spikes through me like lightning. My strokes match the rhythm of her breathing, the maddening tempo of her arousal.

My stomach tightens as I imagine her arching into the sensation, her supple body writhing, those curves shifting with every shiver of pleasure. Her breasts—round, perfect, and far too inviting—would rise and fall with her ragged breaths, her nipples pebbling in response to the chill of the night air. My claws twitch at the thought of cupping that softness, teasing those peaks with my tongue until her breathy moans turn to screams.

I stroke harder, faster.

And Isabelle. . .she wouldn't hide what she was doing. She's too straightforward, too unapologetically herself. She'd show me plainly, unabashed, with that same sultry power she wields effortlessly. Her eyes would meet mine, unwavering, and she'd say something maddening like, *"I figured you'd want to watch."*

My palm is nothing compared to the heat of her body, the slick warmth I know I'd find if I pushed through that door and pressed her into her mattress. The thought alone sends a fresh wave of arousal through me, and I stroke in time with her muffled noises, imagining the way her luscious thighs would tremble around my hips as I fill her.

But I can't. She's so close, and yet I can't touch her. The beast within me claws at my control, urging me to rip through the door and take what's mine. To claim her, to mark her, to show her that no one else will ever bring her to the brink like I can.

A low growl rumbles in my chest, unbidden. I fear she'll stop or notice but her gasps and moans continue in a steady and increasing pitch even as she tries to keep quiet. I sink my teeth into my bottom lip to stifle it. My grip tightens, my strokes rougher now, desperate. The friction burns, but it's nothing compared to the fire roaring in my veins.

And then, from the other side of the door, I hear it: a broken cry, muffled but unmistakable. Isabelle's release.

My knees threaten to give, and my control snaps like a brittle thread. The hunger inside me howls for release, for her, but I can't let it win. I tear away from the door, zipping up over my unsatisfied, pulsating hardness.

The mansion's hallways blur as I stalk through them, driven by pure instinct. The need to escape is primal, visceral, something feral thrashing beneath my skin. I don't bother with shoes or a coat as I shove past the heavy front doors. The cold, snowy night bites at my skin, but it isn't enough.

There is only one who can satisfy me, but I will never touch her. Never bed my own wife.

The icy wind cuts at my exposed skin, biting through the thin material of my pants, but I'm still an inferno. My claws extend as I shove off into the snow, my bare feet crunching over the frozen ground as I start to run.

My breaths fog the air as I bound through deserted streets, the sharp sound of my footfalls ricocheting off buildings. The beast takes over, my instincts sharpening as I leap onto a rooftop with inhuman grace, claws scraping against the slick, snow-covered surface.

A full-body cramp grips my muscles, but I force my way through it. I'm not free to fully shift, to run. My body fights itself, pushing and pulling with unrelenting pain. The confines of my condition only further aggravate my ire, and I push harder.

Above the city, I move like a shadow—swift, silent, and wild. My muscles burn with exertion, each stride pushing me farther from the mansion, farther from her. But no matter how fast or how far I run, Isabelle is right there in front of me. Her scent, her sounds, her taste—they're etched into me.

I leap from rooftop to rooftop, my breath coming in harsh gasps. The cold slashes at my throat and fills my lungs, but it's not enough. I need more—I need to be free of this need, this desire that's turning into an obsession.

I descend into the streets again, my claws scraping against brick as I drop into an alley. My body moves on instinct, navigating the twisting, snow-dusted pathways until the familiar scent of the docks reaches me. The salty tang of the harbor mingles with the acrid stink of diesel and rot, grounding me in its familiarity. I stop at the edge of a pier, my breath heaving. The water stretches out before me, dark and endless, an abyss that mirrors the one inside me.

I am, without a doubt, suffering the most horrendous case of blue balls in history. The unrelenting pain is not just physical—it's maddening, clawing at the edges of my control like an animal that refuses to be caged.

And Isabelle? She's the cause and cure of all of it.

Back when I was whole, women were about pleasure. Something fleeting and physical, easy to control and discard. But Isabelle? She's something else. Something I can't define, can't compartmentalize. She's unyielding, unapologetic, and somehow, without even trying, she's pushing past every wall I've built.

But Isabelle isn't just some woman.

She's so close, and yet impossibly out of reach. This was supposed to be transactional, a means to an end.

I think of all those times, glimpsing her through the window from the car as she worked. The way she runs her fingers over the spines of books with a kind of reverence. The way her lips twitch in dry humor at my expense. Her unflinching courage when she stands her ground against me. The loyalty and endless patience she shows her father, no matter how erratic he is. She's more than alluring— she's relentless. A force of nature I didn't anticipate.

It's maddening.

I can't help but remember another young woman who possessed the same fearless frankness. She also would say whatever came to her mind, without trepidation. Even when she was telling our father she didn't want to go to Europe for the summer. Instead, she planned to start an internship at a veterinary hospital. She delivered the news firmly, unfazed by the dark, drawn brows of our patriarch that had brought grown men to their knees, begging for forgiveness.

I close my eyes, remembering Lisette's confident, knowing smirk.

There she is, wearing a cable knit sweater and multicolored skirt with too many bracelets on that jangle irritatingly. The ghost of my sister seems to know what I'm thinking and cocks her hip, propping a hand on it with the clear message she doesn't care what I think, she's not taking them off.

With such a large age gap, I was never annoyed with her so much as fiercely protective. Where I fulfilled the duties of our family with unquestioning obedience, she was always far braver and independent.

A small, dark hole blooms in the center of Lisette's forehead, blood dripping in a slow, deliberate stream. Another hole appears, then another, spreading across Lisette's face and body as if invisible bullets are riddling her all over again, her now-light blue party dress soaking crimson with every phantom shot.

My memory twists into violent flashes of bullet-ridden flesh, of lakes of blood, and I choke on the acrid stench of bodies burning. The bodies of my family. My pack.

I open my eyes, but it's too late. Lisette's open, sightless gaze haunts me from where I found her unnaturally splayed over something else. Something that when I saw it made me turn and vomit instantly.

My gorge rises even as my muscles and tendons stretch and riot with unexpressed rage, continually trapped in this half-form. Pain ricochets through my bones, trembling with the fury and grief I can never release.

My body is a prison—the cursed in-between—and is slowly breaking me down. It's a constant reminder of what I've lost and what I failed to protect. I fall to my knees and claw at my own chest, trying to make the pain stop. I can't tell which is worse: the torment of my memories or the relentless, excruciating war inside my body that's tearing me apart piece by piece. Quite literally. I'm on borrowed time.

I shouldn't be here. I should've died with them.

But here I am, trying to start over, trying to survive. And my salvation has a name.

Isabelle.

Get it together, you fucking idiot. This is not a real marriage. This is about making pack.

But even as I think it, the words ring hollow. Isabelle isn't just some means to an end. She's...

The sea's icy wind slaps me in the face along with a realization.

That's it.

That *must* be it.

Isabelle's words return to me from the night she surmised why I shackled her into this marriage. *It may take more than time and proximity to create a Pack.*

It's about connection.

This transactional situation is keeping us separated from each other.

Scrubbing my clawed hand over my face, I realize if I want to form a pack, I have to change the rules.

To Isabelle's detriment.

I spend the rest of the night stalking the city with restless dread, knowing the conversation I need to have with her. Knowing it may be the most monstrous thing I've ever orchestrated—and as the crime lord who holds the strings of the largest Thorn syndicate in existence, that's no small claim.

CHAPTER 15
HEY, WANNA HAVE SEX?
THE BEAST OF BOSTON

I'm going to ask my wife to have sex with me. The Beast of Boston—who's bribed foreign diplomats with diamonds the size of walnuts, controlled entire supply chains with a single whisper, and fucked countless women, sometimes two at a time in his reckless youth—is absolutely scared shitless at the prospect of sharing a bed with his wife.

And I've been trying. *Fae help me*, I've been trying.

At breakfast, I sat across from her, the silence stretching as she read a book and drank her morning coffee. I opened my mouth twice, only to stuff another hunk of steak in instead. Who proposes adding sex to their marriage contract over eggs?

Later, I called Isabelle into my office—twice. The first time, I ended up asking if she had any preferences for dinner, which earned me a puzzled look and a shrug. The second time, I asked if the house was warm enough for her liking and sternly reminded her she has full control of the thermostat. She tilted her head like I'd grown a second one but didn't press me.

She knows. Fae lords, she knows I want to say something, but she's giving me the infuriating gift of patience and space. Space to hang myself on.

By the time I drove with her to Chapter Three, my brain was buzzing with idiotic ideas.

Should I text her? Write a note? How does one properly invite their wife to bed?

Dearest wife, fancy a shag tonight?

No. Absolutely not.

Isabelle had slid out of the car, her usual bag slung over her shoulder, and gave me a polite but pointed smile as if she didn't notice I was losing my mind.

Later at the house, the pending task fries my brain when I ask about the same shipment for the third time in fifteen minutes. Tock politely asks me if I'd like to take some Ginko Biloba, a helpful brain-boosting supplement.

Lucien interrupts my attempt to re-prioritize shipments for the third time. "Uh, boss, we handled that this morning," he says.

I scowl at him. "And we'll handle it again, won't we?" I fall back on a rather crude management technique of lashing out to cover my repeated mistakes.

Lucien raises his hands in surrender, whispering to Tock as he passes, "What's his deal today? He seems as nervous as a cat dangling over a pond."

"Female troubles, I'm guessing," Tock whispers back somewhat flatly.

"Man needs to get laid."

"Desperately."

I yell at them to get out. But they're not wrong.

Since Isabelle's arrival, my staff has been less on edge around me. It's infuriating. Like she's softened something in them—and maybe, *fae curse it*, in me.

By the time Isabelle and I retire to my office after dinner, my nerves are strung tighter than a bowstring. She sits across the room, reading a different book from this morning. She keeps pushing up those impossibly sexy librarian glasses perched on her nose, and I can't take it anymore.

"This isn't working," I blurt.

She looks up from her book. "What isn't working?"

"Us, spending time together."

A brow quirks over those impossibly sexy glasses. Then with a quiet sigh, she gets up and gathers her things—her book, blanket, and mug.

In the span of a second, I'm across the room. I rip the mug and blanket from her hands, the book hitting the ground with a thud. "Where are you going?" The question comes out harsh and guttural.

The line of befuddlement draws between Isabelle's eyebrows. "You said this isn't working, so I'm leaving."

"You will not be leaving me. *Not ever.*" The snarl erupts from a primal place, one that overflows with outrage at the notion that Isabelle could ever leave me.

She can't. Isabelle is *mine*. Mine to take care of. Mine to keep.

Some part of my brain logically wonders, with such strong emotions, how a pack bond has not been formed already?

Because you are a monster. She may tolerate you, but she can't love you. You are unlovable.

"Okay," Isabelle says softly, setting a hand on my arm. "I won't leave."

Her touch instantly soothes me, and my hackles fall. Keeping one hand on me, Isabelle sets the blanket and mug down to the side.

She pets and caresses my human arm in soothing strokes. In mere moments, I feel calmed by her touch.

"There. Now that you are calmer, use your big boy words and tell me what you mean."

I rear back as if she's slapped me. Despite my evident outrage, Isabelle doesn't seem to fear another outburst from me. She just continues to stroke my arm.

"My *big boy* words?" I repeat after her.

She gives a little shrug.

How can this woman insult me while endearing herself to me at the same time? Fae lords help me, I actually adore the mischievous little smirk that plays with the corners of her mouth. She knows exactly how to push and pull me in equal measure, so I am under her complete control.

I step back, untethering myself from the influence of her touch as I prepare to tell her what I require in "my big boy words."

"We haven't created a pack bond. Therefore, we must take things to the next level."

Isabelle settles into the reading chair again, gathering the blanket around her again as if preparing to digest my every word in earnest.

"And what exactly is 'the next level?'" she asks, that amused smile still pulling at her lips.

"Sex."

Poof. The smile and her mirth disappear in a magic puff of smoke.

Of course, she isn't happy about it. Who would be?

The memory of her arousal curling around me as I had her pinned against the desk beats into me. But that only happened because of what she was reading. I simply took advantage of her wound-up state. It wasn't for me or because of me.

Isabelle's smile vanishes, her face paling as she processes my blunt declaration. I can feel her hesitation radiating through the room, and it strikes a sour note in my gut, reinforcing the dark mantra that's been haunting me. The same one that reminds me, ceaselessly, that I am hideous—a monster she's forced to endure. But this isn't about indulgence or pleasure; this is about survival. This is what needs to happen.

I swallow the frustration and try to keep my tone steady, logical. "Isabelle, this. . . It's necessary." I force myself to keep my gaze on her, even though every instinct in me wants to look away, to avoid the disgust I'm sure I'll see.

"Necessary," she echoes, her voice faint.

I nod, folding my hands tightly behind my back. "It's clear proximity and shared meals have not created enough of a bond to merit pack, otherwise I would have been able to shift by now. So we are going to try the next step. Your idea, in fact."

Good gods man, way to put it on her, you worthless son of a bitch. Like this is really her idea.

Still, I barrel on. "A physical connection—intimacy—is essential to create the pack. Without it, the effect won't take hold. This was outlined in the contract, Isabelle. The clause about doing whatever is necessary for the success of this marriage? This is what it meant."

She blinks at me, her lips parting slightly in shock. For a moment, she looks almost dazed, as if trying to reconcile my words with the reality before her. Her hands grip the blanket so tightly that her knuckles turn white.

"So this is. . .a transactional requirement," she says softly, almost to herself. Her voice is carefully neutral.

"Yes," I reply, my tone clipped. Better to keep it clinical, detached. "It's not about desire or emotion. It's about fulfilling the terms of our arrangement."

She exhales sharply, steadying herself. "Have you had the birth control shot?"

My pause goes on too long. There hasn't been a need for so long. . . My words trail off as the heat of shame builds. She looks away at that as if going inward to process my words. I wait for her to reject my proposal, bracing for her anger or scorn. I wait for her to say she would rather die than have my baby. And then I'll have to bring up the clause again. I'll have to remind her of the promises she made. She'll despise me for it. And I'll have to live with the knowledge that I am, in fact, the kind of beast she sees me as.

When she studies me again, her expression flickers between calm resolve and something I can't quite place. Trepidation? Or is it fear? My stomach twists as I try to parse her reaction, but she doesn't look away.

"All right," she says at last, her voice barely more than a whisper.

All right? I echo, not sure I'm hearing her correctly.

I suppose having a baby could increase the chances of forming a pack bond, and I always wanted children.

Fae fucking hell. I hadn't been expecting this.

She begins to stand, letting the blanket slide from her lap as her hands move toward the buttons at the front of her blouse, fingers trembling.

The sight of her quiet willingness sets fire to something inside my chest. The thought of her undressing under my gaze, willingly making herself bare for me, fills me with a fierce, nearly overwhelming desire.

I want her.

I want to possess her, to claim her as my own, to run my

hands over every inch of her soft, perfect skin. The beast in me surges, hungry and aching.

But as her fingers fumble with the first button, something shifts inside me—a crack in the carefully controlled logic I've forced myself to maintain. Her hands shake as she works the fabric open, and in that trembling, I see more than hesitation. I see fear, not of me but of. . . something else. And it guts me.

"No." The word comes out harsher than I intend, and her hands freeze, her eyes wide as she looks up at me.

I rake a clawed hand through my hair, my breathing uneven. "Stop. This isn't. . . I didn't mean..." I trail off, searching for words that don't exist.

I step forward, reaching out with hands that tremble as much as hers. Gently, I close my fingers over hers, stopping her from continuing. "Not now." The words scrape out, raw and uneven. I can barely get the words out; every inch of me aches with the desire to touch her, to hold her, to make her mine in the way instinct screams I should. But it's too much. It's too soon, and I know if I give in now, I won't be able to stop.

"Dominic..." she breathes.

I release her hands and step back, clenching my fists to steady myself before turning to go.

"Relax for now," I say over my shoulder, voice rough. "Tonight. I'll come to your room later tonight."

With one last look at her—at the beautiful, infuriating, and surprisingly brave woman who is my wife—I turn and leave, retreating down the hall, my heart pounding and body thrumming with an energy I can barely contain. The beast roars within, angry at being denied, but I shove it down, forcing myself to breathe. This isn't the time to lose control.

Her gaze drills into my back as I leave, but I don't turn around. If I do, I'll stay. I'll either call the whole thing off or fall upon her like a starving wild beast.

This is a transaction—nothing more. Duty demands it, and I will keep it that way.

But the beast inside me is far too hungry. Worse still, the man is just as eager.

CHAPTER 16

A TEN-COURSE MEAL FOR A STARVING SHIFTER

THE BEAST OF BOSTON

I'm not nervous.

Argh. Who am I trying to fool?

Of course I'm nervous. For the first time in years, someone is going to see me—not the carefully curated shadows I live in, not the beastly exterior I allow when intimidation is required, but me.

Half-shifted. Half-human. All monstrous.

My claws flex involuntarily as I pace the length of my room, the candlelight flickering with each pass. The shadows comfort me, but they also remind me of what I can no longer hide. If this doesn't work, if this doesn't create the bond I so desperately need. . .

My wife will become a widow, freed by circumstance.

Unless a child seals the bond.

The thought is clinical at first—pack structure, legacy, survival. But it slams into something deeper, something primal.

I haven't bothered to get a birth control shot for longer than is necessary. There had been no reason to get it. But the idea of Isabelle, swollen with my child, curled by the fire evokes a fierce protective want I didn't even know I possessed.

Like she said, it might be the key to creating a pack bond.

Yes, Dominic because the smartest people fix tenuous relationships by having babies.

The resonant *dongs* of the grandfather clock filter up from downstairs.

It's time.

Breathing in deep, I exit my room and take the two steps to my wife's bedroom door. Isabelle's door. Using the connecting door seems too familiar, too intimate. I need formality and a little distance to keep my head about me.

For a moment, I stand outside, fists clenched at my sides, debating if I should run. But then her scent filters through the cracks—sweet, utterly tempting—and it grounds me. I lift my hand and knock.

Her door creaks open, and for a moment, all I see is her silhouette framed in the soft glow of her room. My gaze falls to the infernal fuzzy robe she's clutching tightly around herself, her knuckles white against the fabric. Her voice wavers slightly when she speaks. Did she change her hair? It falls in loose curls around her shoulders, reminding me of a classic movie star. Like on our wedding day.

"Would you like to come in?"

I should say yes. Step inside her room and take control of the situation. But I can't. Not here. Not where the light will strip me bare.

"I would prefer if we. . .continued this in my room." My voice comes out rougher than I intended, and her eyes glimmer with something I can't quite place. Hesitation? Annoyance? Disgust?

She nods and follows me without a word, the silence stretching taut between us. When we reach my room, I step aside to let her in first, keeping to the shadows like the coward I am.

Isabelle stops just inside the doorway, her gaze darting around the space.

It's not like her room, bright and airy with the scent of lavender and sunlight. My bedroom is dark, lined with heavy furniture and the faint smell of woodsmoke and leather. A place where power is commanded, not shared.

"You really don't like light, do you?" she says softly, almost to herself. The only illumination emanates from a candelabra on the farthest side of the room, keeping everything mostly dim or cloaked in shadow. Including me.

I grunt in response, my eyes following her as she takes tentative steps into my territory. Of course, I can see her near perfectly. Even when I was fully in my human form, my ability to see in the dark remained exceptional.

She hesitates near the bed, her fingers fiddling with the tie of her robe. Something about the motion stirs both longing and dread deep in my chest.

"You look beautiful," I say gruffly, the words scraping out before I can stop them. And she does. She glances up, startled, and for a moment, her expression cracks open just enough for me to catch something raw and vulnerable.

"I wasn't sure. . .what you wanted," she murmurs, her cheeks flushing. Her voice is steady, but there's uncertainty in her eyes.

What I want? I want to touch her, taste her, mark her until there's no question of who she belongs to. But I also want to turn away, to keep her from seeing what I am. To spare her this. But I can't.

I approach her slowly, my steps heavy on the floor. Her

scent grows stronger, intoxicating, but when I reach out to brush my fingers against her arm, she flinches.

The motion is small, almost imperceptible, but it guts me.

"You don't have to do this," I rasp, pulling back. "This is a bad idea—"

What was I thinking, making her have sex with me? I'm no better than a slaver if I force her, even if she is my wife.

"No." The word bursts out of her, sharp and quick, and she shakes her head. "That's not. . .I mean, it's not you. It's me. I'm just. . ." She gestures vaguely at herself, her cheeks flushing darker.

"Isabelle," I start, but she cuts me off.

"I'm not exactly in peak condition, okay? It's been years since I've done this and I've put on weight. And now here I am, standing in lingerie that looks like a cat's cradle, about to. . .I don't know. . .have business sex?" She waves her hands wildly, her voice rising with each word until she's practically vibrating with nervous energy.

For a moment, I just stare at her, her words sinking in. She's insecure. Self-conscious. The realization hits me like a freight train, and the tension in my chest loosens ever so slightly.

And what about lingerie and cat's cradle?

"Business sex?" I echo, and to my surprise, the corners of my mouth twitch. "That does sound. . .unappealing."

She huffs, crossing her arms. "Well, it's not exactly the most romantic setup."

"Would it help if I read to you?" The words tumble out before I can think better of them, and her head snaps up, eyes wide.

"Excuse me?"

"From your book," I clarify. "Perhaps you could read to me instead. Something steamy."

Her jaw drops. "You've lost your damn mind."

My lips quirk into a smirk. "Remember the last time you read to me? How you struggled to get the words out with me lapping at your sweet slit until you couldn't focus on the page anymore?"

Her eyes widen, her breath coming in short pants. The scent of her arousal blooms and I instantly begin to harden.

"No?" I step closer. "I remember it vividly. The way you tasted. The way you begged me not to stop. And the way you couldn't hold the book steady while I—"

"Okay, okay," she cuts in, her voice high and flustered. But there's a spark of interest in her eyes now, the tension between us breaking like a fever.

She reaches for the tied cloth belt, fiddling with it for a minute before loosening it and shrugging off the robe.

Oh.

Fuck.

Me.

I'm in trouble.

The entire world narrows to the criss-cross of red straps across her full, beautiful flesh. The sinful lingerie clings to every curve of Isabelle's body, and blood is drawn to my dick so fast I'm lightheaded.

My claws itch to tear it off her, like unwrapping a Christmas gift. I'm literally salivating, unsure where to even start. I want to start everywhere all at once.

I thought I could approach this with a relatively level head, but Isabelle is now a piece of bait I want to play with, bat at, lick up and toy with for hours.

I swallow hard, feeling the acute rise and fall of my Adam's apple.

She shifts under my gaze, her hands fidgeting with her glasses.

That only makes me harder.

I can't stop the low growl that rumbles in my chest as my eyes rake over her. Every predatory instinct screams to claim her, to mark her, to make her mine in every way that matters.

"Isabelle," I rasp, the word rough with need. "What do you think you are doing?"

Are you trying to make me lose my mind? Do you know how on the verge of losing control I am? I don't want to hurt you, but fae above I want to tear into you so badly my teeth hurt.

She freezes, her gaze flicking up to meet mine. "I thought you'd like it."

I open my mouth to answer.

"Like I said, I'm not in peak condition," she barrels on in a defensive rush while adjusting her glasses again. "I know that I look like a trussed-up ham, okay? It was a gift from one of my girlfriends. Not that it matters. You didn't marry me for this, but I thought the, uh. . ." she waves a hand over her body and the illicit strappy one piece, "might help."

"Help?" I choke on the word. Unable to look at her one second longer before I pounce on her, I turn and pace, squeezing my eyes shut, trying to access the man in me. The gentleman. Fuck, had I ever been a gentleman when it came to sex?

If not, I better figure it out quick.

I hear the rustle of clothes. Whipping around, I snatch the robe from Isabelle as she tries to pull it over an arm again.

"No," I snarl. Then I turn and roughly throw her up one of the spiral posters framing the bed. Her back arches, and she moans as I trap her wrists over her head. "Don't you dare put that thing back on. You think you are a trussed-up piece of meat, Isabelle? In fact, you are a whole mouthwatering five-course meal I want to devour twelve different ways over the span of what would feel like days. Because I am so very, *very* hungry."

I lean down and level my mouth to her ear. "And don't you dare try to leave or I will chase you down and hunt you like an animal. Then there will be no stopping me when I catch you." My voice trembles, half caught between the excitement of the idea and the terror of unleashing on my bride.

Her teeth snap together.

That scent. Oh fuck, she's fully turned on. It thickens and surrounds me, making me so hard I'm pretty sure my balls will burst if I don't get to pump, thrust, and blow inside her sweet fucking body.

"You like the idea of me chasing you down, my pet?" I purr, my animal side taking over.

"I doubt I'd get far," she says, turning slightly, her soft petal lips brushing against my cheek. I grit my teeth so hard, my fang cuts into my lower lip. The slide of my own blood over my tongue only heightens my senses and primal need to hunt.

"What if I gave you a head start?"

Am I really thinking of doing this? Chasing my wife down and fucking her?

This is wrong.

This is unconscionable.

I shake my head and break away. "I-I'm sorry, I—"

A whimper of disappointment escapes her and I freeze. Still holding her wrists, I meet her hooded, glazed eyes.

"I don't want to hurt you," I say in a moment of bald honesty.

She drags her tongue over her lips in deliberation, or maybe it's to help steady her ragged breathing.

"What if—What if I like it to hurt a little?"

Her confession simultaneously stops my heart as my blood rushes in my ears as loud as an entire raging ocean. I couldn't have heard that right.

That would mean she is beyond perfect. It would mean too much. This wasn't the plan. *She* wasn't the plan. Or she was but I didn't know we'd end up here, like this.

Logic and reason are crowded out by the sharp, demanding edge of my need.

I release her, taking a step back, regarding her coolly. Isabelle's arms fall as her brows draw with disappointment.

Every ounce of power I possess goes into controlling what I do next.

"I'll give you to the count of ten," I force through gritted teeth.

Those brown eyes fly wide.

"One." Pause. "Two." Oh fuck, if she doesn't move. . .

Oh fuck. If she *does*.

"Three."

Isabelle slips by me and out the door to the hallway, closing it behind her. The growl from my chest can't be contained as every muscle coils. As the need to chase her, to tackle her to the ground, to bite and fuck.

I haven't felt this alive, this excited, in I don't know how long.

"Six."

It won't last long. She can't hide from me. Not when she smells so damn good. Not when she leaves a trail of tangible warmth in her wake. Not when I want her so badly.

"Eight."

Don't hurt her. Whatever you do, you can't completely unleash.

What if I like it to hurt a little?

"Nine."

I can't wait any longer. I stalk to the door, throwing it open.

The thrill of a hunt tingles through me in a wash of energy and excitement.

Isabelle.

I'm coming for you.

And soon after, you'll be coming for me.

"Ten." I whisper it instead of shouting, the beast inside me surging forward.

My wife is about to learn exactly what it means to be hunted—and owned—by the Beast of Boston.

CHAPTER 17

A SNACK IS HIDING IN THE PANTRY

BELLE

The mansion is colder at night, its sprawling halls a labyrinth of shadows and quiet menace. Barefoot, clad only in the strappy lingerie I stupidly thought would help *make this easier*, I dart through the dark corridors, my breath sharp in my chest. My bare skin prickles with the chill in the air, and my nerves are alight with the knowledge that Dominic is somewhere behind me.

Hunting me. And gods help me, I *like* it.

The realization sends a flush of heat through my already overworked body. What is wrong with me? Why did I say that?

I like it to hurt a little.

Who says something like that?

But even as the thought crosses my mind, another follows close behind. It's not like it's a lie. I've had short flings, nights spent with men who liked it rough—men who left marks and bruises, the kind I didn't mind seeing in the mirror the next day. I even dabbled in the Dom/sub world for a while, thinking maybe that was my answer.

It wasn't. But what surprised me most wasn't the kink

itself—it was the part of me that came alive during it. The part that welcomed withstanding, absorbing all that power, taking it into me.

The part that Dominic seems to have unleashed without even trying.

It's absurd how quiet he is for someone his size. The mansion swallows sound, but even so, the soft scrape of claws against wood—the claws of his half-shifted lion feet —is barely perceptible. The anticipation sends a thrill coursing through me, equal parts fear and. . .something far more dangerous.

I round a corner, pressing myself flat to the wall, my chest rising and falling rapidly.

The faintest growl echoes through the hall, low and predatory. A shiver races down my spine. My breath catches, heart pounding in my chest as I push off the wall and take off again. My bare feet slap the cold floor, and the sound feels impossibly loud in the eerie silence of the house.

The mansion's heavy, locked doors that had frustrated me endlessly during my earlier explorations now serve as my salvation. I zigzag through the halls, twisting handles until one finally gives way, darting through and slamming it shut behind me. My fingers fumble with the lock just as the handle jerks violently from the other side.

A growl reverberates through the thick wood, shaking me to my core.

I step back, gasping for air, but I don't dare linger. He'll find another way in. Dominic knows this house better than I do, and I can't afford to be cornered.

Think, Belle. Think.

I scan the room—an unused sitting room with furniture covered in white sheets—before slipping through an adjoining door. The air here is colder, the hall beyond narrow and darker. My pulse thunders in my ears as I make my way through, locking the door behind me and continuing forward.

My feet carry me in random patterns, weaving through hallways and adjoining rooms, locking each door I pass to throw him off. Adrenaline thrills through me, making my senses acutely aware. I'm so aware of my breath, my skin, my state of undress, and the throbbing pulse at my center.

I risk a glance over my shoulder as I round another corner—and nearly scream. Two glowing green eyes cut through the darkness behind me, a feral gleam that's all predator.

A low growl builds, sending vibrations down the hall. I don't wait.

I bolt.

His heat closes in, his growls sharper now, like a lion stalking its prey. Each thud of his footsteps seems to match the rapid pounding of my heart. The walls blur around me and my breath burns in my lungs, but I push harder.

No one expects a girl my size to move this fast, but jogging with an audiobook has always been my escape. While it hasn't made me an athlete, it's enough to keep Dominic at bay—for now. The mansion works in my favor, its labyrinthine halls and countless rooms offering a chance to stay ahead.

I dart into another room—a formal parlor by the looks of it—slamming the door behind me and locking it. I barely have time to brace myself when the doorknob rattles again, followed by the unmistakable sound of claws scraping against the wood.

"Isabelle," he purrs through the wood. The way he says my name sends a shiver through me, causing my nipples to tighten in anticipation. "When I catch you, I'm going to eat you alive."

My knees weaken at the promise, but I steel myself and slip through another door, locking it behind me as I continue. My path becomes more erratic, weaving through hallways and rooms in no particular order. The sound of him grows faint, then disappears altogether, but I know better than to assume I've lost him.

I stumble into the kitchen, my feet sliding against the tile as rain pelts against the towering windows. The faint glow from the property lamps outside filters through the glass, casting fractured beams of light that only deepen the shadows. The massive space feels cavernous and unsettling, every corner cloaked in a dim, eerie stillness. My chest heaves as I scan for a hiding place, my eyes landing on the walk-in pantry.

Perfect.

I slip inside, closing the door as quietly as I can and pressing my back against the shelves. The smell of flour and spices fills my nose as I strain to hear any sign of him. My breath comes shallow, my heart pounding against my ribs.

For a moment, there's only silence.

Then, the soft click of claws against tile.

I press a hand to my mouth, stifling the sound of my breathing as the footsteps draw closer. He's here. The pantry door creaks open slightly, the dim light of the kitchen spilling in.

Then the door swings fully open, and there he is, his massive frame filling the doorway, his eyes glowing with hunger. His claws grip the edge of the door, and the sharp points of his teeth glint as he grins.

"Perfect place for a delicious thing like you to hide." His

voice is rough velvet, curling around me with dangerous intent.

Before I can answer, he scoops me into his arms as if I weigh nothing, carrying me effortlessly out of the pantry and into the kitchen. His claws scrape along my bare thighs as he sets me on the ice-cold marble island. A gasp escapes me, the chill of the surface's stark contrast to the heat pooling low in my belly.

"Dominic," I start, but the word dies on my lips as he steps between my legs, his massive frame eclipsing everything else. His hands grip my thighs, the rough pads of his palms grazing sensitive skin as he pulls me closer to the edge.

"I told you I was going to eat you up." The gravelly words vibrate through me in a way that's entirely unfair.

Despite the heat pooling in my belly, my defenses rise instinctively, shielding the sudden vulnerability creeping in. "Maybe the kitchen is closed."

The growl deepens, rumbling in his chest like a warning. He steps closer, pressing into me, and I can feel the dangerous heat radiating off him. "For everyone else, perhaps. Not for me."

I tilt my head, raising a brow. "And what makes you so special?"

His lips curl into a slow, dangerous smile, sharp teeth glinting in the faint light spilling in from the windows. "I take what I want, when I want it."

His shoulders loom over me, broad and unyielding, his hair thick and wild where it brushes my bare legs. The kitchen is dim, the fractured beams of light from the rain-soaked windows casting eerie shadows across his sharp, half-shifted features. His glowing green eyes lock on me, filled with a predatory hunger that makes my breath hitch.

My pulse spikes, but I refuse to let him see how his words affect me. But then he splits my legs apart so quick and hard I gasp. The strap of my lingerie barely hides anything from his gaze, and my center is already damp with my excitement.

When he lowers his head, I can feel his breath against me, hot and deliberate. My chest heaves, my nipples tight beneath the sheer fabric as I watch him, unable to look away.

It only now occurs to me how much my husband has been holding back his animal nature. It gleams from his eyes with predatory satisfaction, and I inspired it. The thought is too heady to absorb.

My breath cuts off abruptly. Dominic's thumb brushes over my barely covered cleft, slow and deliberate. His eyes flick up to meet mine, and a wicked smile curves his lips.

"So wet for me, wife."

He drags his thumb back and forth, rubbing the slickness through the thin material before lifting it to his mouth.

I can only watch, entranced, as his tongue curls over his thumb, licking it clean with a deliberate swipe. The way he does it—like he's savoring something rare and precious.

"So sweet," he murmurs, his voice a dangerous purr.

My heart flutters with anticipation. "All full yet?" I push a little more.

"You like being a brat?" he says in a low musing tone. A claw hooks under the strap, knuckles flush against my bare sex as he yanks it. I slide a couple inches to the edge of the island, then he jerks that thin bit of cloth to the side. Before I can register what he's doing, I jerk at the smack of his hand against my already bare neediness.

"Oh, that gasp was delicious, wife," he coos dangerously, though I can barely comprehend his words or register any sounds escaping me. "I think I'll have another." He spanks me again, a loud slapping sound against my wetness. I cry out in surprise.

"*Delicious*," he repeats.

He throws my legs over his broad shoulders, locking me in place, and dives in tongue first, licking and sucking me with a fervor that has my back arching off the counter.

Oh gods.

Oh fuck.

It's so good. It's out of this world good, and he has me bucking and begging for more even as he gives it.

His tongue moves like it has a mind of its own, curling and flicking, exploring every inch of me with unrelenting hunger. Its sheer length allows him to reach places I didn't even know existed, drawing cries from me that echo in the vast, empty kitchen.

I squirm beneath him, overwhelmed by the intensity of his assault, but his claws dig into my thighs, holding me steady. "Stay still," he growls, lifting his head just enough to shoot me a warning look. His lips glisten with my slickness, his sharp teeth peeking through as he smirks. "I'm eating here, wife. Don't interrupt my meal."

The way he calls me wife. It's the same every time. A slightly irreverent, ironic moniker, but always possessive. He says it the way he always does, but I know I'll never hear him call me that again without being transported directly back to this moment where he mocks and tortures me.

It stokes something rebellious inside me. I curve my back deliberately, rolling my hips forward just enough to break the contact between us. The shock on his face is fleeting, replaced almost instantly by something darker, more dangerous.

"I was just helping," I murmur, breathless but defiant. "Thought you might need a better angle."

Dominic's sharp teeth glint in the dim light as his lips pull back in a feral smile. "A better angle?" His voice is a purr.

Before I can respond, two fingers plunge inside me, filling me with a sudden, shocking heat. My head snaps back, a cry tearing from my throat as my body clenches around him. His digits curl, dragging along something deep inside me. Sparks explode behind my closed eyelids.

"Does that feel like I need your help?" he growls, his breath hot against my ear. His pace is relentless, each thrust precise, claiming me in a way that leaves no room for resistance. My body isn't striving for release—he's *taking* it from me, pulling it out with every pump of his hand, every flick of his thumb to my clit. He uses the beastly paw to push down on my lower stomach, intensifying the sensations.

"Dominic," I gasp. I'm near splintering as my hands scrabble over the counter for balance. My body trembles, every nerve alight with the intensity of his assault. I'm spiraling upward and I can't decide if it's too fast or not fast enough.

"Do you want to come, dear wife?" he asks, his tone mocking, daring. His thumb presses my clit, circling in slow, devastating strokes that have me teetering on the edge.

"Yes," I whimper, my words cracking as my body shakes. "Please."

His growl deepens, and he dips his head, his eyes glowing as they lock on mine. "Then you'll do exactly what I say." His words are dark. "Push those straps down. Show me those pretty pink nipples."

My hands tremble as I obey, the cool air brushing

against my flushed skin as I bare myself to him. My breasts are heavy and aching, the peaks tight and sensitive under his feral gaze.

"Good girl," he rasps, his clawed hand palms one breast, his thumb brushing over the hardened bud. The fingers inside me curl, dragging a broken cry from my lips. "Now come for me."

Then his mouth is on me again, his tongue flattens over my clit with a deliberate stroke. The texture of it—rough yet smooth, curling at the edges—sends me hurtling over the edge. My thighs clench around his head, my body locking as my orgasm crashes through me, violent and all-consuming.

Dominic doesn't stop. His fingers pump into me, his tongue teasing me through every wave of pleasure, until I'm a trembling, incoherent mess beneath him.

When I finally collapse on the counter, he pulls back, his chest heaving. His lips glisten with my release.

He lifts his fingers to his mouth, licking them clean with a deliberate, feline grace. His glowing eyes lock on mine as he smirks, his voice a dark purr. "That's merely the appetizer course."

My body shudders at his words, every nerve still alight with the aftermath of his dominance.

I'm trembling, my thighs still quivering from the force of my orgasm. This isn't over. Not even close.

CHAPTER 18

FUCK, FUCK, BITE, FUCK

BELLE

Dominic is already scooping me up again, his hands rough and unrelenting as he pulls me against his chest. His claws press just shy of breaking my skin, the sharpness a constant, thrilling reminder of the predator holding me.

"Dominic," I manage, my voice barely more than a shaky whisper, but he doesn't answer. He's moving, striding out of the kitchen with single-minded purpose, his heat searing into me even through his half-shifted form.

The shadows of the mansion blur around us as he takes me to his bedroom, the air growing heavier, darker, as though the house itself is holding its breath. By the time he kicks the door shut behind us, my pulse is racing again, my senses on high alert.

He sets me down on the edge of the bed, his eyes raking over me in the faint light filtering through the curtains. "You have no idea how hard it's been to hold back," he mutters, his voice rough, strained.

I barely have time to process his words before he takes a

step back and begins to strip. His shirt comes off first, revealing the broad, muscled expanse of his chest, the skin lined with jagged strips of fur. My breath hitches as I watch him, my gaze drawn to the claws that flex and curl at his sides, to the way his muscles ripple with barely restrained power.

But it's when he removes his pants that my heart stutters. His cock is impossibly large, ridged, and—dear gods—barbed.

Right. Every last bit of him is half-shifted.

I'd read enough shifter romance to know about knotting with canine based shifters, and that feline shifters have barbed penises. But I've never seen one, much less been about to be penetrated by one.

It should terrify me, but it doesn't. Instead, it sends a rush of heat straight between my thighs, and I can't stop myself from leaning forward, reaching for him.

"Isabelle," he growls, a warning that only makes me more determined. I want to touch him, to feel the weight of him in my hands, to know every inch of this man who's unraveling me piece by piece.

The ridges under my fingertips are firm but flexible, like molten steel wrapped in silk. He's so hard, yet the skin glides easily beneath my hand as I stroke him, the barbs flattening slightly with each motion, teasing my palm with their strange but not unpleasant texture. He shudders, a barely contained tremor that vibrates through my touch, and I grow bolder, my grip tightening.

My mouth waters with anticipation as I take him in, the heat of his length radiating through my palm. When I lay my tongue on him, tasting, engulfing his growl deepens, filling the room.

"Stop," he pants, his claws gripping my hair and pulling me back. His eyes burn into mine, a feral glow. "If you do that, I won't be able to control myself. And I have to be inside you."

There's something raw in his plea, an edge of desperation that sets my pulse racing. I nod as I let him push me back onto the bed. His hands slide down my body, claws scraping lightly over my skin as he grips my hips, positioning me beneath him.

I reach for him, my fingers brushing his jaw. "Kiss me," I whisper, the words trembling on my lips.

He freezes, his breath catching. "Isabelle." My name comes out rough and strained, his lips pulling tight, almost self-conscious. "You don't. . .You don't want that."

"Yes, I do." My fingers trace the line of his jaw. My heart pounds, but I don't look away. The hesitation in his glowing eyes is palpable, his gaze flicking to my mouth.

His lips meet mine, tentative at first, the unfamiliar shape of them skimming uncertainly over mine. But when I respond, gentle and insistent, his restraint crumbles.

The kiss deepens, and his mouth—half-shifted and foreign—becomes something I can't get enough of. His tongue glides over mine, the rough texture reminiscent of a jungle cat, launching a shockwave of sensation through me. He tastes like my own desire, mingled with the salt and musk of himself, a heady combination that drags a ragged moan from my lips.

His fangs graze my bottom lip, a teasing scrape that sparks a wicked jolt, making me clutch at him harder. The strangeness of his tongue, rough and deliberate, only heightens the intensity, a slow-burning ache spreading through my core.

My hands tangle in his hair, dragging him closer, our kiss turning wild and consuming. The slick, unrelenting stroke of our tongues, the way his mouth claims mine—desperate and searching—leaves me breathless, aching, and trembling.

When he finally breaks away, his breath drags through his lungs, chest rising in sharp, uneven pulls. His glowing eyes burn with an unguarded intensity. "Isabelle," he growls, the sound guttural and raw.

Slowly, he pushes forward, the thick ridges of his cock stretching me inch by torturous inch. My breath catches, my head drops back as I feel every contour of him—every pulse, every movement.

He thrusts once, burying himself completely, and my world tilts. *Oh gods—he's—* The friction, the fullness, the pulse of him inside me, it's too much. *How can this feel so good?* The barbs—soft, pliant, thrilling—catch and release with every inch he claims. Electric shocks of pleasure race through me. My body seizes as wave after wave of sensation floods me. *I'm coming.* The thought splinters through my mind, incredulous and raw, as my climax takes me by surprise, stealing my breath and tearing a cry from my lips. My thighs quiver, tightening around him instinctively, and I feel myself gripping him, my body trying to pull him deeper.

"Isabelle." His claws dig into my hips as if my release undoes him as much as it unravels me. The pleasure crests again, leaving me trembling, gasping, unable to think, unable to do anything but feel. *Too much, too good*—I don't know where I end, and he begins.

"Do you remember what I told you about Weres, Isabelle?" he murmurs, his voice a low growl as he pumps into me steadily, driving me out of my mind.

My breath catches as his lips skim over my neck, his touch calling forth a trail of goosebumps. I feel like I'm flying.

"We bite," he continues, his teeth grazing the sensitive curve of my shoulder. "When we want something, when we need it, when we take it."

I shiver beneath him, my body arching instinctively as his claws slip beneath the straps of my lingerie, tugging them tight across my skin before slicing through them. "And gods help me, Belle, I can't help myself." His voice turns strained and taut.

The admission ignites a rush of pleasure, but before I can respond, his teeth sink into the curve of my shoulder. The pain is sharp, but it's eclipsed almost instantly by the wave of pleasure that follows as he increases the pace of our joining.

The ridges of his cock stroking deep inside me, combined with his bite, is a sensation so exquisitely over-whelming that it shatters me all over again. Pleasure deto-nates inside me, violent and raw, a scream torn from my throat as I clutch at his shoulders, my nails biting into his flesh.

"Mine," he rasps into my shoulder. "You're mine, Isabelle. Every inch of you. Always."

Dominic's movements grow erratic, as he fractures into raw, desperate sounds. When he finally surges deep inside me, his roar shakes the air, his release violent and all-consuming. I feel it—the searing heat of him filling me, the way his body molds to mine, trembling with the force of his climax.

His teeth remain embedded in my shoulder as his hips jerk buck in a final, shuddering thrust, a hoarse sound breaking from his throat. It's not just pleasure; it's anguish, possession, and need all tangled together. He's giving me everything, and I feel it in every quiver of his muscles, in the way he clings to me as though he will never let go.

When he finally stills, his body trembling with the aftershocks, his eyes glowing in the darkness, I realize there's no going back.

CHAPTER 19

FALLING OFF LADDERS

BELLE

My arm finds nothing but empty mattress where Dominic was all night long.

I blink up at the elaborate canopy overhead and can't help but think I'm ruined. Absolutely ruined.

He wasn't kidding about having me as a five-course meal, or rather, ten.

After absolutely driving me to insanity, pounding into me relentlessly, teasing me, claiming me, licking me, biting me like I'm only the sustenance a starving shifter needs, he held me all night long.

Normally I'm not much of a cuddler, but somehow every part of me fit perfectly to his ridges and gaps. Like our bodies were two puzzle pieces that click in together with absolute precision. The amount of oxytocin it released into my body had to be near criminal amounts. I didn't even know my body could produce that much.

That may be even more dangerously addictive than sex with Dominic.

Then I remember the unexpected friction and havoc

those barbs and ridges exacted on me and how he wrapped a clawed hand around my throat while saying he needs his gorgeous wife all over his cock just one more time.

Yeah, the sex has pretty much ruined me for all time. Which works fine since I'm a married woman and he *forbade* me from taking a lover. Now, how do I break the news to my sex toys that they'll never cut it again?

A lingering ache reminds me just how thoroughly my husband took me. And maybe—just maybe—how much he left behind.

My stomach tightens. I meant what I said when I agreed to this. If a child helps form the pack bond, then it's logical. Sensible. That's what this arrangement is about.

But a secret part of me—a part I don't indulge—knows it's more than that. I've always wanted a little one to read to, to share stories with, to pass down the things I love. But I buried that desire years ago. A child without a partner, while balancing the weight of my father's care? That dream had never been practical.

Yet now. . .I stretch and soreness makes itself known with the movement, pulling a moan out of me.

The feeling of awe and happiness ebbs quickly when I realize I'm alone in Dominic's room. I sit up, pulling the covers around my naked body. Suddenly, this feels like one-night stand territory, which I'm not unfamiliar with. But this part still isn't my favorite.

I get up, tie on my robe, and grab the remaining tatters of that string bodysuit.

Thank you, Goldie. That girl deserves a card or something to show my appreciation.

How quickly I went from feeling like a ridiculous prop from a failed boudoir photoshoot to Dominic's delicious dish.

Calm down Belle, he was just doing it to create a Pack. This is all a transactional situation. Don't get carried away. Enjoy the fact you had excellent sex (incredible sex, mind blowing, world altering sex) and get out.

I open the door and nearly shriek when I find Dominic on the other side. I drop the heap of broken straps in surprise. He's showered and fully dressed..

Dominic raises an eyebrow before dipping down and hooking a claw under the destroyed lingerie, holding it up. "Where do you think you're going?"

For once I struggle to find my composure and the proper words. "W-well we were done, and you were done because you were gone, and I thought I should get out and we'd get on with our day." I find myself stammering as my fingers dig into the fabric of my robe.

His gaze slowly scans my body, quietly assessing, making me feel like he's preparing to pounce.

"First of all," he says, pocketing last night's outfit, "This is mine now. Secondly—"

He trails off as if in deep thought. Meanwhile, I'm clutching the neck of my robe trying not to think at all. I certainly won't ask him to do what he did last night again. And I certainly will not reach up and kiss him, running my hands through his hair and mane.

He steps back, giving me room to pass. I can't deny the disappointment that fills me, though I don't let it show on my face.

"I won't be joining you for meals today. I have. . .business," he grimaces.

"Oh, okay," I say, making my way past him, feeling more than ever like a fling who is now in the way.

His hand circles my arm, stopping me and pulling me back so we are side by side, facing opposite directions. Dom dips his head to inhale me deeply with such animal satisfaction that it vibrates from his chest when he exhales. I shut my eyes, feeling it too.

Suddenly the self-consciousness peels away as I realize this one moment is far better than any reassurance like, "thanks for the wild bang last night, top marks to you."

I *feel* his deep appreciation thrumming through my body and bones. There is no falseness in it, only pure possessive emotion and it curls my toes into the lush carpet of the hallway.

"I regret not being able to see you until this evening, but I have a surprise for you. 'Til then."

Then Dominic lets me go and I open my eyes again, the space he previously occupied now terribly empty. And the heat in my belly competes with a wild fluttering of anticipation.

A surprise?

Should I be afraid, or excited?

Or maybe just very, *very* turned on.

CHIP CLAIMS NOT to mind working the shop from opening to close today since Dominic can't escort me to Chapter Three. They text me that they realize what a sweet gig I have since the shop is pretty easy to keep in order and they enjoy the extra time either chatting with the customers or devouring books. They found their new favorite genre which is cozy Orc romance and have been cruising through volumes while trying to get other customers on the big green cozy train.

I feel Dominic's absence through the day more keenly than I'd like. But because he's away, I take meals with Mrs.

P and my father in the kitchen. The housekeeper keeps glancing at me with a secretive knowing smile that makes me more than a little uncomfortable.

Does she know how I spent my night?

She does live onsite but in a house out back on the property. Surely she didn't hear us?

My father happily jabbers away to her about being the angel of croissants and chemistry equations. He's been reciting them more and talking about "the dogs," which tells me he's winding up again. At least if he has a half-lucid, half-manic episode I know there are more people around he's familiar with to help calm him down.

When I leave them both to head toward the study, Mrs. P calls after me, "Have a lovely night, dear." Again there is some kind of knowing in her voice that makes me feel not a little uncomfortable.

Dominic and I didn't talk about having sex again this evening. Though surely if the goal is to create a pack, we will need to continue having intercourse. Is it to be expected every evening? Should I ask Goldie to get me some more outfits? It might help me to wear some armor in these situations to make me feel more in control before I forget. . .

Before I forget this isn't about love.

I swipe my face hard with my hand and try to erase the thought. Love isn't real. Relationships are built simply on chemistry and necessity, and I can't let myself forget that. Not for a second.

I change into my comfy reading clothes and grab my book. When I make my way to Dominic's study for our nightly routine, I find my husband leaning casually against the doorframe. His broad shoulders make the heavy wood look fragile by comparison.

Though there's tension in his stance that's impossible

to miss, a spark gleams from his eye. It's muted, like he's trying to tamp it down, but if I didn't know any better, I'd say he was. . .excited.

And honestly? He looks so good like this—rumpled and brooding—that I briefly forget how to breathe. It's almost criminal, the effect this man has on me. I might need CPR, and I'm not sure if I'm hoping he'd be the one to save me or finish me off.

"Evening," I say, aiming for nonchalance. My voice comes out a little shaky as if my body hasn't entirely recovered from last night's marathon of pleasure and destruction. Which it hasn't. Though I try to hide it, seeing him spikes a bottomless hunger that doesn't care if I should take some downtime.

He straightens when I speak, his gaze sharpening with a focus that makes my stomach tighten. "Come with me," he says simply, extending a hand.

I hesitate, caught off guard by his abruptness. "Uh, okay?" I place my hand in his, the warmth of his palm engulfing mine. His grip is firm, steady, and. . .far too thrilling for something as simple as hand holding.

Without another word, he leads me down a corridor I've never explored. The air here feels quiet, secretive, as though we're walking into the heart of something private. Anticipation winds tighter within me with every step, and my mind races. *What is he up to?* My free hand fiddles with the hem of my sweater, my nerves buzzing.

We stop in front of a pair of arched double doors, intricately carved with ivy and roses, their craftsmanship exquisite. Dominic pauses, still holding my hand, and glances at me. For a moment, his expression softens, his usual guarded demeanor giving way to something. . .warmer. Vulnerable.

"There's something I want to show you," he says, his voice rough. "Something I've kept locked away for far too long."

My breath catches, his words doing something dangerous to my chest. *Oh no. Don't fall for this. Don't let yourself feel things.* But the intensity in his expression—half challenge, half offering—makes my knees weak.

With a deliberate motion, he pushes open the doors, and my jaw drops.

The library is breathtaking. Towering shelves stretch up two stories, their dark wood polished to a warm glow in the flickering firelight. Frost rims the enormous windows, distorting the icy night beyond, while the golden glow of the fireplace casts dancing shadows across the room. A marble hearth dominates one wall, its mantel intricately carved with roaring lions and blooming roses locked in an eternal battle of strength and beauty. It's a sanctuary of stories and warmth. The space feels alive, defying the frozen stillness outside.

It's..." My voice falters as I step inside, turning in a slow circle. "Dominic, this is incredible."

He stays back near the doorway, his hands buried in his pockets. "Mrs. P refreshed it for you today," he says gruffly. "I thought you might appreciate it."

"Appreciate it?" I laugh softly, brushing my fingers over the spines of nearby books. "This is a dream, Dominic. It's perfect."

He nods once, but tension lingers in his posture.

I stop, turning to him. "Why keep it closed up before now? It's beautiful."

His jaw flexes, and for a moment, I think he won't answer. But then he exhales. "This was my mother's favorite room," he admits quietly. "She loved it. Spent her days here. After she died, I locked it up."

"Oh." My voice comes out small, my chest tightening at the weight of his words.

His mother is dead. I suspected but didn't know. I try not to assume anything, and he gives me so little help to fill in the gaps.

"Since you are so enamored by books," he continues, his gaze falling to the floor so as not to meet mine. "I realized you might appreciate it like she did."

The vulnerability in his voice punches through my defenses, nearly forcing me to reach for a chair to sit down. I push through the urge.

Before I can stop myself, I cross the room toward one of the tall shelves. My hand hovers over the ladder affixed to the shelf, needing something to anchor myself. "It's. . .Thank you," I manage. "This is the most incredible gift anyone's ever given me."

"It's not exactly a gift," he grumbles.

I climb a few rungs, my fingers brushing along spines, soaking in the beauty of this space.

"It was always here," he points out.

A strange lightness rushes through my head, and the shelves sway—no, I sway. My grip falters. My stomach dips as the world spins, and before I can catch myself, I'm falling.

Two strong hands catch me, and I'm pulled tight against Dominic's chest.

My heart races, his arms like a fortress around me. For a moment we're frozen, his breath hot against my neck. The heat of him seeps through my clothes, and my pulse drums in my ears. His arms grip me like he's afraid to let go.

I lick my lips, turning my face slowly to the side to see his.

The need to kiss him is so strong, my lips tingle. I want to tangle my fingers in his hair, to lose myself in the intensity of this moment. We could strip naked and have at each other again right here. For pack, right?

Dominic steps back, breaking the contact, leaving me on shaky legs. When I turn, his expression is unreadable, shuttered.

Suddenly I feel ashamed for wanting him again.

Contract sex shouldn't be spontaneous. We should be sending each other calendar invites on our phones. It's methodical and for a purpose.

Which means no slamming his cock down my throat in the library to show him how grateful I am for the gesture and how much I enjoy the way he takes what he wants, even when I shouldn't.

"I, uh, figured we could move our evenings to in here." He grabs his tablet off a side table and settles into a wing-back chair as if it's no different from any other night.

The dismissal stings more than it should, and the air between us feels charged and awkward. My mind spins with questions as I steady myself.

Was last night really just another duty for him? Does he have any intention of repeating the act with me? Should I ask?

The idea of voicing my insecurities out loud only glues my lips more tightly together.

The moment passes, but the weight of it lingers, leaving me breathless and aching in its wake.

Dominic may have been inside me. He may have pulled my body apart in twenty different directions before slamming me back together again, but the truth is we still don't know each other. Not really. Not when my husband hides so much of himself, of his past, of his business.

To be fair, I've also cut my past out of my life, but it isn't dogging my present like it clearly is with him.

Maybe that's why I don't unravel when men like Dominic change the rules. My uncle always said the only way to survive in our world was to keep moving—never linger, never look back. Kindness is just a detour on the way to disappointment, and only fools believe otherwise.

So I make my way to the lounge chair across from him and settle in with my book, pretending that everything is as it should be. That I don't want him and that I don't care what he's thinking.

Dominic might have given me this room, this sanctuary, but it's clear he's still keeping the most important parts of himself locked away.

CHAPTER 20
CORNERING THE LOST GIRL

BELLE

I want to fuck my husband.

Since that night, neither of us has brought up the subject of sex again.

Some deep, dark scary part of me fears he thought I was bad. But then I remember the things he said, the way he kept coming back to me for more, until we'd come countless times and were beyond dehydrated. How he commandeered the ruined red strappy lingerie and shoved it in his back pocket. How he held me all through the night.

I didn't make up any of that. He could have sent me back to my bedroom after we were done, but he wrapped himself around me, nuzzling the back of my neck, occasionally kissing or nibbling my shoulder or ear.

Now we are back to our routine. Safe, reliable routine.

It should feel normal. The kind of predictable rhythm I've always craved. But it doesn't. Not after what happened between us.

I sit across from Dominic in the library, often pretending to read, pretending that the memory of that sweaty, vigorous, impossibly unforgettable night isn't burning me alive. But it is. My body betrays me with every flicker of firelight that catches the sharp edge of his jaw, every rasp of his clawed fingers against his tablet.

How does he sit there so composed every night, like nothing happened? Like I didn't fall apart on him or under him about a dozen times? Like I didn't lick and suck him until he grabbed my hair to thrust brutally deep before he'd finally spent? Like it wasn't worth repeating?

I cross my legs tightly, forcing myself to focus on the book in my lap. But the words blur, and my pulse hammers, every part of me hyper-aware of my husband mere feet away from me.

I just need to keep my distance, stick to our arrangement, and focus on what matters: taking care of my father and Chapter Three. The rest of this—the heat, the pull, the way my thoughts always circle back to the feel of his thigh between my legs—it's just noise.

And I've gotten very good at tuning out noise.

That's what I tell myself while pretending that I'm not using far too much of my energy to keep from climbing into his lap to do it all again.

But I keep my distance, and life marches on.

At Chapter Three, Chip has learned the ropes faster than I expected, and I can't help but wonder why I didn't hire help sooner.

With a little more glee than is probably appropriate, I flip the sign to *Closed* and lock the door behind me.

The limousine is still parked at the curb, Dominic inside, waiting. Watching, no doubt.

I let the laughter of my Lust & Lit friends draw me across the street to the Poison Apple. Sometimes, the book club takes the party over to the neighboring bar, and on those nights, I close early to join them—and catch up with my friends who work there, the Lost Girls. I still have an hour before I have to go back to that massive house of sexual frustration and tense silence with my husband.

Early in the week, it's a quieter vibe—perfect for sliding into one of the massive velvet booths and discussing all things fantasy romance. Later in the week, the Lost Girls are up on the bar, shaking cocktails with flair and entertaining the crowd, but tonight feels perfect for something low-key.

Inside Poison Apple, I'm welcomed by the warm, low lighting that gleams off its signature black and gold accents. It smells like smoked leather and fresh apples, the kind of place where secrets are whispered over espresso martinis, and everyone walks out looking guiltier than when they walked in. The sultry music by the Fae Wanderers pumping into the room is as heady as opium.

I immediately spot the owner, Rap, behind the bar.

The tough-as-nails woman is hard to miss with her banana blonde hair. She let her mohawk grow out so she could line one side of her head with viking-style braids. Her eyelids are always heavy with smoky black shadow that dares anyone to cross her. The leather cuffs wrapped around either wrist give her even more of a punk rock look. The band tee she wears looks home cut into a crop to show off her impressively lean torso.

To have a body like that, I muse with envy and appreciation.

"Belle," Rap beams. "Look at you, book queen. I've missed you. You look different. Something you did with your hair?"

I look down at my outfit. Instead of one of my graphic tees, I'm wearing a cozy black sweater dress. The turtleneck and the high boots make up for the length hitting my knees in such cold weather. I am wearing the black hooded cloak with roses embroidered on it.

Nothing much has changed here except the coat. Maybe she's talking about my having a husband now? Though surely that doesn't show on my face. And I'm careful to pocket the ring when I'm at work. I'm not ready for the questions.

"Oh thank the fae lords, you're here Belle," a familiar sweet and perky voice calls. Goldie—one of Raps bartender's—beelines it for me sporting her usual pink and black leather, blonde hair falling over her bare shoulders.

"I'm *dying* for your professional romantic opinion," Goldie says, sauntering up next to Rap, who has a knowing smirk on her face.

I barely open my mouth before the Lost Girl barrels on, procuring a giant wedding binder from behind the bar and opening it in front of me. "What do you think about this for the reception centerpieces? Ted thinks using old books is a great idea, but he says yes to everything, which basically makes his opinion useless." She waves a hand dismissively with an eye roll.

I work to cover up my smile. Goldie is part sunshine, part sass, and all pink froth, which is the total opposite of her grumpy lumberjack-shaped fiancé. But he'd get her the moon if she only asked.

It strikes me then—maybe I should bring up the fact we are both attached to shifters. Granted, Ted is a bear shifter with a pack, and my husband is a half-shifted mob boss running an illegal syndicate of curses in the city.

I keep my mouth shut.

"Okay," Goldie says, flipping rabidly through the pages of her brick of a planner. "And you know the struggles of being a voluptuous girlie like me. What do you think of this sweetheart neckline versus this straight-edged corset?"

The plus-size bartender has made multiple attempts to convince me to squeeze myself into her clothes since we are close to the same size. While I love Goldie's confidence and style, I have to admit that I prefer my graphic tees and a more understated style. Though that didn't keep her from gifting me that rather risqué lingerie bodysuit last Christmas.

I tried to tell her I don't typically dress up for my "alone time." She dead-eyed me and said maybe I should start.

But who knew I'd have a husband to show it off for?

A bitter taste floods my mouth. Not that my husband has seemed interested in seeing if I own any other fancy underthings since then.

Rap grins and slides my usual across the bar before I even ask—a small demitasse of espresso and a champagne stem filled with prosecco.

It's the perfect pairing. An upper and a downer that always makes me feel like I'm celebrating the day, while still able to up and read past my bedtime. The book club is already claiming one of the booths in the corner, giggling like they're back in high school and giving Snow, another bartender, their order. She's another Lost Girl like Goldie. That's what Rap calls the girls she hires to work the bar. Though she calls me her original Lost Girl. Rap was the one to help me cut ties with my past. We're business owners and friends.

"Can I take a picture?" a voice interrupts.

I turn to find a girl with impossibly long copper hair in a wheelchair. She's thin with a smattering of freckles under her big aquamarine eyes. and is holding up a camera. "It's for the Poison Apple socials. I like your aesthetic."

"This is Ariel," Rap introduces, cleaning nozzles under the bar. I sometimes suspect if Rap ever stopped working, she'd drop dead on the spot. "She's our new social media manager. One of my new Lost Girls."

I nod, and Ariel surprises me when she asks if I'd pose with the drinks. We take a few shots, and I'm so impressed that I ask for her info. I'd love to hire her to take promotional pictures for Chapter Three's social media pages. Then I grab my drinks and head to the booth and grab one of the chairs on the outside of the table.

I lose track of time as we discuss the possibility of the author's speculation that the Realm of Roses is populated by succubi and incubi. Magic realms that have seceded from the Common World are filled with secrets they don't care to share.

"The Midnight fae are literal blood drinking vampires," Misty points out. "It makes perfect sense that the Realm of Roses would be populated with sexual vampires." She waggles her eyebrows over this month's signature cocktail, the Sleeping Death.

"If they do, I propose we all take a spring break vacation there," Gingie says, lifting her glass in solidarity.

"For science," Rachel Anne agrees.

"For research," Yannette adds.

"It's honestly charity, isn't it, if they need sex to survive?" another one of my favorites, Nikki, points out.

The buzzy warmth in my chest shifts when the bar door slams open.

It doesn't just open—it explodes, the hinges groaning as it hits the wall hard enough to rattle the hanging liquor shelves. The laughter stops. Even the music quiets.

I feel him before I see him.

Dominic.

He stands at the entrance like a storm given flesh—a nightmare of man and beast. His green-gold eyes blaze under the dim lights, the telltale shadow of fur creeping up his jaw and neck. He doesn't look at anyone—he only looks at me, as if he can't see past his tunnel vision.

My breath catches in my throat as I tense. A half-shifted violent looking man just broke down the door. All hell is about to break loose.

The rest of the bar stares, but not the way I expect.

No screams. No running. Just a low buzz of curiosity and fascination. Someone mutters something about "shifters on the edge being sexy," and Rap snorts from behind the bar.

Poison Apple used to be a strict humans-only bar, a reflection of the city itself. But after everything that's happened—the growing fae and mage presence—it's become impossible to keep up that illusion. Now, the clientele has changed. Adapted. No one's enforcing the old rules anymore.

As I take in the un-terrorized bar, I secretly hope my reading material across the street also had something to do with that.

Dominic's gaze flicks all around, his lip curling back in what I'm almost certain is a snarl. But then his claws twitch, his fists clench, and—without another word—he closes the distance between us.

Annnnnd my husband is about to ruin the hard-won fae reputation around here if I don't do something.

"You left," he half growls, half shouts. The women recoil in the booth around me. Embarrassment sweeps through me.

"I just went across the street," I keep my tone as even as possible, refusing to blink. "This is one of Chapter Three's regular book clubs, Lust & Lit. I often shut down early for them to come over here."

"You left, and I didn't know where you were," he snarls again, but lower. I've forced him down several notches by holding my volume and composure. "Come with me," he growls, low and sharp, his voice barely human.

I blink. "What?"

He doesn't wait for me to process. His clawed hand wraps around my wrist—not painfully, but firm—and I barely have time to snatch my purse before he's pulling me up.

"Belle, do you know this guy?" a hard voice asks from nearby.

I turn to find Rap and Snow flanking, shoulders tense and eyes sharp. Snow's blue eyes are two flashing ice chips against her deep, dark brown skin. She's already pulled her white hair up into a ponytail as if preparing for a brawl. She's petite, but I have no doubt she can hold her own.

Even Goldie stands behind the counter and not-so-subtly sets a baseball bat on the bar top.

The security bouncers also creep closer from either side. Though if anyone were to forcibly move my husband, they wouldn't succeed at budging so much as a pinky.

"Yes," I nod to Rap who asked the question. "This is. . .This is my husband."

A collective gasp ripples between the book club members as well as Snow and Goldie. Rap's expression only hardens.

"Is that so?" she says in a deceivingly light tone. "Why didn't I receive an invitation? I would have got you a wedding present." Uh, oh. Pending danger ripples through my tummy. I've seen the bar owner be as formidable as my hot-headed husband.

Rap doesn't care about attending a wedding. She thinks I'm in danger.

But right now, I'm *certain* she's threatening Dominic who still refuses to take his eyes or his grip off me.

I adjust my purse over my shoulder. "We eloped. It all happened so fast." I force a smile, but Rap isn't buying it.

"Belle?"

There's a question underneath my name. Am I good? Because if I even hint I'm not, I have no doubt Rap will step in and do everything within her power to help me.

And I know never to underestimate a Lost Girl, least of all the original one.

I wrap my arm through Dominic's, and his body ceases shaking with barely restrained violence. I stroke his bicep with the other hand and give Rap a steady look. "Thank you for the drinks. Put it on my tab. I'll see you next week." I make sure there is no doubt, fear, or uncertainty in my voice.

I say goodbye to the women from the book club who wave back with expressions torn between uncertainty and incredulity. As soon as I pull Dominic toward the door, they explode into barely restrained whispers behind me.

A wave of heat and then cold washes over me as we step out onto the dark, snowy street. Despite being much smaller than Dominic, I'm the one practically dragging him along. Except I don't go to the car. I pull out my keys and unlock Chapter Three, forcing him into the quiet dark of my shop.

The bell tinkles inappropriately as I slam it shut, the

sound far too cheerful for the storm brewing between us. The familiar scent of books wraps around me like a balm, but even my beloved bookstore feels stifling under Dominic's suffocating presence.

"Are you out of your mind?" Dominic snarls, his claws raking through his disheveled hair and fur as he spins to face me. His muscles flex under his heavy trench coat, every inch of him coiled tight like he might explode.

"It was just a drink, Dominic." I jerk my arm back, my nails digging into my own palm. "*Relax.*"

"Relax?" The word lashes through the air, sharp and cutting, and for a second, the animal inside him bleeds through. A sharp inhale flares his nostrils, and his eyes flash gold, bright and dangerous. "You disappeared, Isabelle. I didn't know where you were."

"You were parked right outside," I counter, forcing an even tone even as his rage hums through the air like static.

"I didn't know where you were," he says, the words strained, tight with an edge of something deeper.

I throw my hands up, exasperated. "I walked across the street, Dominic. Across the street."

Dominic looms near the entrance, his massive frame casting shadows against the bright streetlights filtering into my dark store. His chest still heaves as though he's been holding back a tidal wave of rage. Snow clings to our boots, melting into puddles.

"You embarrassed me in front of my friends." My fists clench at my sides as I step deeper into the dim space. "Do you realize how that looked? Storming in there like some—some feral beast. They probably think I'm trapped in an abusive relationship." I scrub a hand over my face. This man is beyond agitating. It takes a lot to make me lose my cool, and he's pushed me to the brink more than once already.

"You didn't think to text? To call?" My frustration is fully bubbling over. "You came in like a hurricane, Dominic. Do you even realize how controlling that looks?"

He finally looks at me, his green-gold eyes blazing in the dim light. "I don't care what they think," he growls. "I care that I didn't know where you were. You just disappeared."

He's talking in circles.

A wash of exhaustion overcomes me. I lean back against the counter, gripping the edge for stability. "You're acting like I'm going to run away. I have no intention of running away, Dominic."

The truth of my words settles over me as I say them. Despite the chaos he's brought into my life, I realize I've come to rely on the routines we've built. I've grown used to the quiet comfort of the mansion, Mrs. P's kind but firm presence and tea service, the way my father seems calmer in our new home. And Dominic—despite his stormy moods and overbearing nature—has become a constant I hadn't realized I needed. Even if we never have mind-blowing sex again.

"I—" He cuts himself off, as he struggles to find the words. "I thought—" He stops again, turning away from me as if the words are too painful to say.

"You thought what?" I press, softening despite myself.

"You don't understand," he growls, stepping closer.

"Then *make* me understand," I say, my frustration rising again to meet his.

"You could have been anywhere," he spits, his tone rough, serrated with frustration. His pacing stops, and his gaze pierces mine. "Do you know what I thought when you didn't come out? When I didn't know where you were? *That you were gone.*"

His raw edge catches me off guard, but I don't let it show. "I wasn't going anywhere," I reply evenly. "You've made it abundantly clear you own me."

He actually has the audacity to roll his eyes. An inferno lights up inside of me.

"It's not about ownership," he says.

"Then what is it about?" I yell, losing my cool. All my feelings are bubbling over, and I can't stop them anymore. "Because from where I'm standing, it looks like you're trying to keep me at arm's length while also keeping tabs on every move I make. We have sex because it is 'necessary,'" I even throw up finger quotes for his stupid contract, "and now after nine days you're barely able to even bring yourself to look at me. So why the hell do you think you can tell me you care?"

Dominic looks away, his claws flexing. His tone sinks to a near whisper, so quiet I almost miss it. "I'm trying to keep you safe."

"Safe from what?"

"From me."

The admission hangs in the air like a lead weight. My chest tightens as the pieces begin to fall into place—the distance, the avoidance, the barely restrained violence in his actions. "You're afraid."

His gaze snaps back to mine, sharp and defensive. "I'm not afraid of you," he growls, stepping closer, the heat of him washing over me.

"No," I agree, my pulse racing as he crowds into my space. "You're afraid of yourself. Of losing control. Of me seeing something you're trying to hide." When he doesn't answer, I round back to the original issue. "You're acting like I ran off to sell state secrets. I still planned to be done at our arranged time. I had ten minutes left; I hadn't forgotten. I was across the street with my friends. It's not a big deal."

"It *is* a big deal," Dominic snarls. His hands flex, claws sliding in and out. He's pacing now, too restless, too furious. "You don't get to just disappear, Isabelle. I won't lose you—"

CHAPTER 21

BE AFRAID. BE VERY AFRAID

THE BEAST OF BOSTON

The words leave my mouth before I can stop them.

I won't lose you.

I turn away, the line echoing in the silence, harsher than I intended but no less true. I drag in a breath, but it's shallow, unsteady. My pulse is a relentless drum in my ears as I wrestle with the fear clawing at the edges of my control.

She doesn't understand.

"What are you afraid of?" she asks, her voice soft but cutting, piercing straight through my armor.

Afraid.

The word cuts through me, jagged as broken glass. I'm the Beast of Boston. I'm not afraid of anything. Everyone fears me.

My hands curl into fists, but it does nothing to stop the trembling in my muscles.

I swing back toward her in two steps, the distance between us disappearing as my hand finds her jaw, tilting her face up toward mine. Her scent is maddening—warm and familiar yet charged with a defiance that makes my blood burn.

"I'm not afraid," I bite out, my tone edged with raw defiance.

Her breath skims my lips, but she doesn't flinch. She stands there, staring up at me with those wide, unyielding eyes, and it unravels something deep inside me.

My grip tightens, claws grazing her skin—not enough to hurt, but enough to remind her of what I am. "Everyone fears me, Isabelle. Everyone. But you?" I lower my head, letting the warning coil in my throat as I lean in, my breath curling against her lips. "You don't know fear. And that's your problem."

Her hands fly up, gripping my forearm, her nails digging in—not in fear, but in challenge. "If you think I'll cower because you're throwing a tantrum, think again."

I cage her in, both hands braced on the counter behind her now, my body swallowing the space between us. The weight of her scent—something soft and floral, overlaid with the salt tang of her skin—crashes over me, tightening my control to a thin thread.

"You don't understand," I bite out, my words tight and clipped.

"Then make me understand," she fires back, her eyes blazing with the kind of fury I should crush beneath my heel—but I don't.

I hesitate. Just for a moment.

I don't want to tell her how I thought she'd been taken. That when I realized she wasn't in the shop, a cold terror swept through me, dragging me into the darkest depths of my mind. That the image of her broken and bleeding in an alley, her life traded for one of my rival's twisted games, is burned into my brain like a brand.

The people who want to destroy me would have no hesitation in using her to do it.

"You just disappeared," I say instead, my words rough with the echoes of everything I can't say. "I didn't know where you were."

"I went across the street." Her shoulders tense as her big brown eyes drill into me. "That's it, Dominic. Across the street."

Her tone fuels my rage, but it's not her I'm angry with. It's myself. For letting this happen. For not being able to keep her safe.

"They're watching," I hiss, leaning closer. "You don't understand what that means. Every step you take, every place you go, they see it. They wait for the opportunity to strike. To hurt you because of me."

Her eyes widen, and I see the first flicker of realization in her gaze, but it only lasts a moment before her defiance returns.

"I'm not a damsel," she says firmly. "You don't need to treat me like I'm some fragile thing."

"You don't know how fragile you are." The tension in my jaw aches as the words rip free. "You think you're untouchable because no one's laid a hand on you. Yet."

The word hangs between us, heavy and sharp.

I step back, needing distance, needing space to breathe. My claws retract as I press my hands to my thighs, trying to calm the storm raging in my chest.

It's been like this since that night.

Since I made her mine in every way I swore I wouldn't.

The distance I've forced between us is supposed to protect her. From me. From the part of me that wants to possess her completely, that wants to keep her locked away where no one—not my rivals, not the world—can touch her.

And yet, here I am, letting her pull me into another storm, her fire fueling mine in a way I can't escape.

A slow, dark realization settles in my gut. "You're trembling." My eyes drop to her hands, clenched at her sides, her breathing uneven. "Maybe you're not as fearless as you claim."

She narrows her eyes with open resentment. "That's not fear. That's frustration."

Her breath catches, and her heart slams against her ribs. I can feel it—feel her heat, her need—and it's too much.

Frustration doesn't begin to cover it.

I've been going out of my fucking mind. Every time I see her, smell her, hear her. . .Every second I'm near her and I can't touch her again is torture. She has no idea how badly I want to ruin her all over again.

Then why haven't you?

It's the question that's dogged me every moment since that night I chased her down and fucked us both blind.

Because I'm a coward. Because I don't trust myself. Because I can't bear the thought of getting in too deep and dragging her down with me.

I don't say any of that. Instead, my hips roll forward, pressing harder into her.

"Is this what you're frustrated about, wife?" I rasp, my voice dropping into a growl. The tension between us tightens like a noose, and I can't stop myself from teasing her, forcing her to acknowledge the fire I know is consuming her, too.

Her moan escapes, low and drawn out, and I freeze. My body locks, every nerve taut as a live wire. *Fuck.* She's not just matching me—she's surrendering to me, feeding this insatiable hunger.

I'm already hard, thick, and aching, my arousal straining against the confines of my pants. I've been like this every night since that first time. Unable to think of anything but her. The way she looked beneath me, the sounds she made, the way her body wrapped around mine, pulling me deeper. The memory drives me mad, but the fear. . .The fear keeps me in check.

I should stop. Pull back. Regain control. But the sounds she makes, the way her body arches toward mine, the way she whispers, "No. I'm not afraid of you, Dominic. And I never will be," undoes me.

Her defiance is a dagger, slicing through the last shreds of my restraint. My hands move on their own, gripping her hips and pulling her closer. Her body molds to mine, soft and yielding, but still holding her strength, her challenge. It makes me want her more.

I press her harder into the counter, the edge digging into her lower back. My body radiates heat, and I know she feels it—my need, my frustration. She's the only thing that can quell it, and yet I've been forcing myself to stay away. Every instinct tells me I should walk away now, but I can't. Not anymore.

Her mouth opens as my thumb grazes her lips, and before I can think better of it, I slip it inside. She sucks lightly, her tongue flicking over the pad of my thumb, and my control snaps. My pupils blow wide, a guttural sound ripping from my chest.

I yank her dress up, shoving her panties to the side. My fingers slide into her heat.

"Fuck," I hiss. She's so tight, so ready. I'm on the brink of losing myself, of forgetting every reason I've stayed away.

Every thrust of my fingers feels like a claim, a brand, and I don't want to stop.

The cry that tears from her throat is a symphony. Her body clenches around my fingers, her hips rolling instinctively to meet my movements. I curve my fingers, finding the spot that makes her gasp, and I press harder, stroking until her moans rise in pitch.

"You are a pain in my ass, wife." Heat simmers beneath each syllable, my brutality taking over. "I should finger-fuck you until you're right on the edge, right on the precipice of screaming my name and breaking your spine on the orgasm I've built up in you. And then I should leave you there. Hanging. Insane with want."

I thrust harder, deeper, her cries driving me to the edge. "And then maybe you'd have something to be afraid of. Because you won't be able to give yourself the relief I could. And then you'll learn to be afraid of wanting me as much as I want you."

Her nails dig into my shoulders, her body arching as her moans reach a crescendo. She's close, so close, and I know I should push her over the edge, claim her completely. But something holds me back. A thread of hesitation, of fear, that I can't quite untangle.

I'm losing control, and she's unraveling me piece by piece.

Her hands grip me, one trembling as it slides lower, toward my waistband. I know what she's doing, and I should stop her. I should put an end to this before we cross a line I can't come back from. But I don't. I let her touch me. Let her find the hard, ridged length of me.

The words come out as much for me as for her, a desperate attempt to regain some shred of control, to remind myself that I'm the one who holds the power here.

But the way she arches into my hand, the heat radiating from her, tells me I'm failing. She's dismantling me, brick by goddamn brick.

Her whimper cuts through the haze of lust and frustration, and I freeze. It's a needy sound, vibrating with an undercurrent of surrender. It punches through me, obliterating the walls I've spent the last week desperately trying to keep intact.

I can feel her unraveling, her body trembling beneath my hands. My grip on her throat tightens, and when she drops her head, the soft groan that escapes her lips shatters something primal inside me. It vibrates through me, sharp and electric, feeding the animal clawing its way to the surface.

Her nipples strain against the fabric of her dress, begging for my touch, but I don't dare let go of her throat. My hand moves, sliding another finger into her drenched heat. Her walls clench around me, pulling me deeper, her slickness coating my skin in a way that sends my own need spiraling.

I hear myself mutter, "So wet for me already," the words rough and jagged, as if they've been dragged from the deepest part of me. It's not just her I'm convincing—it's myself. I need to believe that I can do this, that I can take her apart and put her back together without losing myself in the process. She's pushing me too far, too fast, and I can't stop it.

Her hand presses lower, fumbling at the waistband of my pants. My breath hitches as her fingers slip beneath, her movements unsure but determined.

"Isabelle." Her name is warning and a plea all at once. But she doesn't stop. Her fingers explore further, stroking my hardness. Teasing. Pressing. Like she's searching for a reaction—and fuck, she gets one.

Her fingers slide over my ridges, brushing against the textured barbs that mark me as something not entirely human. My breath catches, the sensation shooting through me. The edges of my vision blur, tunneling to only her, only this—the tentative press of her palm, the wicked drag of her nails, the way she tilts her head, watching me unravel.

"Don't," I bite out. My restraint unravels further with every stroke of her hand. But she doesn't stop. She explores further, her touch tentative but insistent, and the sound that rumbles from my chest is more animal than man.

And then I snap.

My mouth crashes down on hers, the kiss fierce, unrelenting. My teeth scrape her lips as I devour her, pouring every ounce of my frustration, my need, my fear into the contact.

I drag her closer still, my clawed hand sliding up to cradle her jaw. I tilt her face to deepen the kiss, my tongue sweeping into her mouth, demanding everything she has to give. Her taste floods my senses, sweet and intoxicating, and I know I'm done for.

My fingers drive deeper, coaxing desperate reactions from her trembling body. Her gasp pours into my mouth, a fractured sound that sparks along my spine. I barely register my own restraint crumbling, too focused on her—on how she arches into me, on the way she tightens, unfurls, yields.

She melts against me, fingers clutching my arms, grasping like I'm the only thing anchoring her. I can feel her unraveling, the tension in her body winding tighter with every stroke of my fingers. She's close, so close, and I know I should give her what she needs, but I hesitate.

"More," she begs. Her nails dig into me, hips bucking against my hand. "Please, fuck. Ungh, Dominic, don't stop."

A dark laugh escapes me, strained and vibrating with the last vestiges of control I'm clinging to. "You think you can tell me what to do, wife?" I taunt. I withdraw my fingers, just enough to make her whimper. Then I thrust them back inside, harder, deeper, savoring the way her cries spike. "You don't command me. I take what's mine."

Her walls clamp down on my fingers, her moans rising in pitch, each sound dragging me further into madness. She's so fucking close. I feel it in the way her thighs quiver, in the way her breathing fractures, in the way her body writhes against me.

She comes undone, her release wet and messy, soaking my hand as her cries echo through the space around us. The sheer force of it, the way her body clenches and spasms, pulls a guttural curse from me. My chest heaves as I hold her, watching her shatter under my touch, her pleasure radiating through me like a drug.

But it's not enough.

"Please, fuck me." Her raw need destroys the last thread of restraint I'd been holding on to.

I haul her onto the counter, my movements rough, unrelenting. Her thighs spread beneath my hands, and my pants are gone in a blur. The blunt, ridged head of my cock presses against her soaked entrance, and the heat is almost unbearable.

"You think you can just disappear on me?" The words tear from my throat, raw and jagged. I thrust forward, the stretch overwhelming both of us, her sharp cry mingling with the guttural growl that escapes me. "Do you know what that did to me? What I thought?"

I need her around me desperately. Every gasp she emits

reminds me she's here. She's real. She's alive. My fear wraps around her in greedy tendrils demanding more, more, more.

"I didn't disappear." She clutches my shoulders, trying to steady herself even as I pound in her body.

"You were gone." My voice cracks as I thrust harder, burying myself to the hilt. She takes me, her body wrapping around me so tightly it's almost too much. Almost. "I thought I'd lost you. Again."

Her breath catches, and she echoes the word back at me, soft and confused. "Again?"

Shit. The word slams into me like a wrecking ball, and I feel the weight of my mistake. A slip I hadn't meant to make. The past surges forward, a tidal wave I can't stop. The image of her lifeless, broken, traded away by my enemies tangles with another—darker, more painful. My family. Their screams. Their blood. The unbearable void they left behind.

My movements have come to a halt, and I feel frozen from the inside out.

The confusion in her eyes cuts deeper than it should, and for a moment, I'm drowning. Panic wars with grief, twisting my insides, and I don't know how to make it stop.

"Dominic?"

No. I won't drown in my past, in my fears.

I drive into Isabelle again, my thrusts hard and desperate, the need to silence my own thoughts consuming me. Her cries rise with every movement, her nails raking down my back as she clings to me. I feel her unraveling again, her body tightening around me as she builds toward another peak.

Her release hits like a violent surge, wet and raw and visceral, pulling me over the edge. When I finally come, it's with a roar that rips through me, shredding my soul along the way. My teeth sink into her neck, and the satisfaction of pouring everything I have into her intensifies from my balls to the base of my brain.

The silence afterward is deafening. My forehead presses against hers, our breaths mingling.

For a moment, I let myself feel her, the hum of her body matching the chaos in mine. But it's too much. Too real. Too dangerous.

I pull away abruptly, stumbling back like I've been burned. My breathing is harsh, my hands shake as I adjust my pants. The distance feels like a knife to the chest, but it's necessary. I can't let her see how deep this goes, how much she's already undone me.

"Dominic—" she starts, her voice soft and vulnerable, but I cut her off with a sharp shake of my head. I can't do this. Not here. Not now.

"We're going home." My instructions are cold and final. It's the only way to end this, to regain some semblance of control. I don't wait for her response, don't let myself look back. I stride out of the shop and into the limo, a weak attempt to escape the chaos inside me.

The door slams shut, and the inside of the car is suffocating. My hands clench into fists as I try to steady my breathing, to push down the emotions threatening to consume me.

I thought I'd lost her tonight. And the truth is, it hurt far more than it should have. Far more than I want to admit.

For the first time, I realize marrying Isabelle may be the second biggest mistake I've ever made.

CHAPTER 22

A NOT SO SILENT PARTNER

THE BEAST OF BOSTON

I'm an absolute bastard.

No. I'm a beast. The Beast of Boston.

And that means I take what I want, when I want, and instill fear in everyone to do so if necessary.

Yet I can't stop berating myself for yesterday, for coming down on Isabelle so hard. For what I did next...

I may be in the business of orchestrating illegal hexes and curses, of maiming or killing others to get what I want, but I have *never* been the sexual predator I acted like last night. I tried to scare her, intimidate her, then took her forcibly.

She did seem to enjoy it, but that doesn't excuse what I did.

I'd been a messy spiral of fear, unable to stop the past from dragging into my present. Though that may be an indication that my body is breaking down, taking my mind with it.

The massive oak table stretches before me, set meticulously with silver and porcelain, gleaming in the muted morning light. An array of breakfast dishes covers the table

—steaming plates of eggs, crisped bacon, buttery croissants, fresh-cut fruit, all surrounded by delicate pots of coffee and cream. The rich scents drift into the air, warm and inviting, though I have no intention of touching any of it.

Somewhere upstairs, the faint squeak of a marker against the wall drifts down, barely audible over the quiet clink of dishes. Basil must already be deep into his morning equations, filling another blank canvas with numbers that only make sense to him. Mrs. P will clear them off by evening, only for him to start over again tomorrow.

At least he stays in his damn room where he belongs.

His daughter, on the other hand, is a fae fucking menace.

Going off without telling me and then making me answer to her. I was out of my mind with the fear something had happened to her. Something in me broke, and I turned feral.

And there she was in Chapter Three smelling delectable, acting like she wasn't the problem, and accusing me of embarrassing her in front of her friends. I had to make her feel something. Anything to even the score between her ire and my raging emotions. I kept pushing and pushing until there I was, pushing between her thighs and sinking my teeth into her.

My heart thunders despite myself. Isabelle steps into the dining room wearing what should be an utterly unremarkable outfit: a romance book graphic tee tucked into soft, stretchy pants that cling to her every curve like a whispered secret. Over it, she's thrown on a cardigan that she's pushed up at the sleeves, revealing the delicate bookish tattoo twirling down her forearms. Her hair is up in a neat bun, parted at the center like a ballerina's, her glasses perched on her nose, lending her a scholarly allure that borders on maddening.

And there. The imprint of my teeth on her neck.

The sight of it gets me hard. I want to make her mine all over again.

My instincts scream at me to claim her, to mark her more, to bind her to me in every way that matters. Because that's how a pack is formed—with proximity, with connection, with sex. But being near her is tearing me apart.

She takes her seat gracefully, unfolding a napkin and laying it across her lap with practiced ease. She looks almost regal.

How dare she?

She might as well have sauntered in here wearing nothing at all, announcing she'd like to be fucked for breakfast.

How dare she flaunt her scent, her softness, her skin in a way that is so *deliberate*—taunting.

How dare she sit there, composed and unaffected, while I'm unraveling? Every second I spend around her feels like a test I'm failing. She's supposed to make me stronger, to stabilize me, to give me the pack I need to survive.

"Good morning," she finally says, voice calm, eyes meeting mine without a hint of fear or hesitation.

She doesn't hold last night against me. She should.

That blend of vanilla and wild roses wraps around me even from across the room, tightening the noose I've been trying to escape since this marriage began. I can't help but close my eyes and inhale deeply.

I picked her out to be my wife based on her background and that little bio on her website, but I hadn't anticipated that absolute drugging heaven that emanates from her skin.

What's next? She'll come to breakfast wearing that delectable fuzzy robe that now gets me hard every time I see it? When she wears that damn thing during our evenings in the library, I have to hold my breath and keep my tablet up in front of my face to block her out of my senses.

It drives me wild.

Well, more wild than she already makes me. She often pushes me to the brink.

I grip the edge of the table, forcing the beast within me to quiet. It's a constant battle—keeping myself in check, restraining the urge to close the distance between us. I hate it. Hate how she stirs something primal in me, something that isn't soothed by the reminders of what I am, what I've become.

She takes a delicate bite of her toast, chewing slowly, savoring it. I hate how effortlessly comfortable she seems, as if my presence doesn't rattle her in the slightest.

I can barely look away, even as a stab of self-revulsion twists in my gut. She has no idea how monstrous I feel under her touch, how grotesque I must seem compared to her grace. Her softness and warmth, the utter human ease with which she occupies the space—it's both a balm and a torment.

We sit in silence, but I feel the tension thickening in the air. The silence is ripped in half as her phone buzzes loudly from her pocket. She pulls it out and answers.

After making only a few displeased sounds, she hangs up. Isabelle clears her throat. "I'll be leaving shortly. My bookshop has a burst pipe, and I need to handle it."

I whip my gaze to her, incredulous. "No. Absolutely not. Someone else will handle it."

She raises an eyebrow, completely unfazed. "It's my bookshop. I'll be the one taking care of it."

"No, you won't." The words come out sharper than intended, a command more than a request. "This. . .situation means you stay here. Out of danger. I have people who can handle whatever problems arise with your shop."

I'm still rattled by her disappearing act yesterday, but I refuse to admit it.

The idea of finding her drenched in blood, limp on the ground, turns me cold. The scent of burning flesh hits my nose out of my memories. That moment remains so real, so close, I might as well be standing there in the middle of the conflagration, bodies piled around me right here in this dining room.

"Dominic," she says, my name falling from her lips with a calm certainty that makes my blood burn. "I appreciate the concern, but I'm not some delicate flower who needs to be coddled. I've been managing that bookshop on my own for years. I will go, and you can either come with me or. . .not." She takes another sip of her coffee, entirely at ease, as if she's just stated a fact, not issued a challenge.

"Isabelle, I am not some. . .lapdog you can order around."

She simply looks at me, her stare unwavering, serene as ever. "I'm not ordering you around. I'm telling you what I'm going to do. If you want to follow, that's your choice." She gives me a soft smile, her calm infuriatingly unshakable. "Besides, I thought we were supposed to spend time together."

There is a glint of something ice cold in her eyes and I realize she isn't so wholly unaffected. My wife is pissed. Pissed off at me to be exact. And she's not afraid to yank my chain when the opportunity arises.

She tilts her head, studying me with those steady eyes, and it takes everything in me not to reach for her, not to pull her close and see if I can melt that chilly disposition. Instead, I bite back my frustration. "Why can't you be like everyone else and cower before my awesome power?" Even I can hear that I sound more like a sulky child than a formidable businessman with senators in his pocket and an empire at his feet.

"Because I know the difference between bark and bite."

"Tell that to your neck," I shoot back on reflex.

She rolls her eyes. "You're not as bad as you think. You're just in pain."

There's a sincerity that I wasn't expecting. Her words cut directly to my core, slicing straight through all my many defenses. "And I think. . .I think if you were truly a monster, you wouldn't care so much about protecting me," she adds softly.

The words settle between us, heavy and charged, and for a moment, I can't look away from her, caught in her gaze like she's somehow the one holding me captive.

I let out a long, ragged breath, finally tearing my gaze away. "Fine," I growl. "I'll accompany you to the shop. But I expect you to follow my lead."

She simply nods, a small, knowing smile tugging at her lips as she rises from the table.

My wife wins yet again.

Dammit.

～

THE MOMENT we enter Chapter Three, I stick to the shadows, instinctively moving away from the front windows.

Yesterday, I hadn't thought. I hadn't cared. I'd stormed

into Poison Apple without a second's hesitation because I'd thought Isabelle was in danger, and nothing else had mattered. But now, with the urgency gone, I still can't force myself to stay in the car. I need to stay close. No matter how uncomfortable being out in the open makes me feel.

Isabelle is surprised when I follow her in.

"I don't need your help. This is *my* business, not yours." She stresses that last part before her eyes flit to the counter I had her trapped against last night. Where we'd felt each other up like a couple of randy teenagers. I swallow hard at the memory and force myself to focus on the present.

I lift my hands. "I'm just here to observe. Like a silent business partner."

Isabelle casts me a warning glare before going about business. Chip is already there.

They were the one to catch the leak in action, informing my wife of the issue.

"Mr. Blackwell." Chip greets me formally but I can practically see them vibrate with energy at seeing me.

I nod at the kid in approval. "You've put on weight. That's good."

Isabelle first regards me and Chip. "Put *on* weight?" she asks in disbelief.

"You want that tooth fixed yet?" I ask Chip, not acknowledging my wife's comment. "Like I said before, just say the word and we'll get dental on it in a heartbeat."

Chips shakes their head. "No sir, it, uh," they tap the tooth with their forefinger, "it reminds me where I came from."

I give another sharp dip of the chin. I understand that.

It's still strange that someone gets so excited to see me. Most of my crew don't even know what I look like, but Chip was one of the first to see me in my half-shifted twisted form. Little did they know, I'd been in that warehouse torturing one of the men responsible for my condition—my pain, my tragedy—when I found them outside, near death.

Chip barely reacted, so beaten down by life by that damn stolen Thorn. When I offered salvation, Chip saw past my physical state and hero-worshipped me, something I'm not always comfortable with. And if we'd taken better care of our product, Chip would have never been subjected to it. It's part of the reason the recent months have been so infuriating. The Wolves, as they stupidly call their little human crew, have been stealing from me with more frequency.

Blinds draw up with a sharp rattle as Isabelle sheds more light on the store.

It's been years since I've been out in the open in light like this. The sensation is disorienting, the brightness harsher than I remembered. Isabelle moves through the store with a practiced ease. The space smells like fresh paperbacks, lavender, and *her*. I want to bottle it up and huff it whenever I need a hit of something heady.

She pauses in the center of the room, hands on her hips as she surveys the water damage creeping across the ceiling. A thin trickle seeps through a crack, hitting a stack of ruined hardcovers with a damp thud. Her mouth sets into a grim line as she assesses the destruction.

The plumber arrives minutes later, strolling in with the swagger of someone ready to overcharge a clueless customer. I stalk down a different aisle so he doesn't see me, but where I can watch the two of them.

"These old places are a nightmare to fix, you know?" His tone is dismissive, almost bored, as he glances at the ceiling and sniffs. "Gonna cost you at least fifteen hundred, probably more once I start tearing things out."

Isabelle's polite smile falters just a little. "Could you look over the entire space first? I'd like to know the full scope before making any decisions."

He snorts, waving her off. "Look, lady, it's not rocket science. You've got leaks, you've got damage. It's gonna be expensive no matter what."

The words are barely out of his mouth before I step forward, emerging from the shadows with enough force to make him stumble back. I let the dim light catch on my jagged teeth, let my hulking form cast a terrifying shadow over him. His face drains of color.

"What. . .What the—?"

I don't even need to growl to make him flinch. "You'll treat her with respect, or you'll find money to be the least of your troubles. And you'll give a fair price. No games."

He stammers, nodding frantically. "Y-Yes. Of course. I didn't mean any disrespect. I'll, uh, check everything properly."

As he scrambles to get to work, Isabelle sets her hands on her hips. When the plumber disappears into the back to "reassess," she turns to me, eyebrows raised.

"So much for silent partner, huh?"

"I won't stand by while you're disrespected. That was never part of our agreement."

She studies me, her expression softening in a way that makes my chest tighten. There's a flicker of surprise in her eyes, like she's seeing something new. I force myself to look away, focusing on the cracked ceiling instead.

After a beat, she crosses her arms, mirroring my stance. "So, I assume you'll just scare everyone into giving me a good deal from now on?"

"If that's what it takes," I say, only half-serious. Her lips twist as she does everything to fight the smile from forming on her face. Her reluctant pleasure hits something deep within me, a warm pulse I push down, focusing instead on my next steps. This place is hers, but it's also. . .mine to protect now.

When the plumber reappears with a revised, considerably lower quote, Isabelle hands over a deposit, her face unreadable. But as he leaves, I pull out my phone and quickly dial Tock.

"Dominic," she says sharply, catching my attention. "What are you doing?"

Ignoring her, I wait for Tock to pick up. "Tock, get a crew to Chapter Three today," I say into the phone. "Top of the line, efficient. No delays."

She lets out a frustrated huff, her arms crossed tighter now. "I told you, I can handle this on my own."

"This isn't negotiable." I meet her gaze, letting her see the resolve in my eyes. "This place is important to you, Isabelle, so it's important to me."

Her mouth parts in surprise, the protest dying on her lips. She blinks, momentarily caught off guard by my words, and I feel a faint pulse of satisfaction. There's a softness there, a vulnerability I wasn't expecting, and it makes the need to protect her burn even hotter.

She clears her throat, recovering quickly. "Well. . .thank you," she murmurs, clearly unsure how to respond.

I shrug, pretending it's nothing, but I feel the weight of those words settle between us, creating a new understanding. She's more than a partner in a transaction; she's mine to protect, my pack—even if the fae lords won't acknowledge it and grace me with shifting powers again. And anyone who dares cross her will have to answer to me.

As Isabelle and I stand in the quiet aftermath, she shoots me a sidelong glance, her lips quirking into a small, reluctant smile. "I don't know how to tell you this, but you're not the monster you'd like me to believe, Dominic."

I grunt, dismissing the idea with a wave of my hand, though I can't deny the warmth her words bring. But as we lock eyes, the air between us shifts, a pull that's both unnerving and undeniable.

"Monsters protect what's theirs," I murmur, almost to myself.

And Isabelle, for better or worse, is mine.

CHAPTER 23

UNEXPECTED COMPANY

THE BEAST OF BOSTON

Before I even enter the house after coming home from dealing with the plumber, I know there are unwanted entities inside.

The scent hits me the moment I stepped out of the car.

"Stay here." Commanding Belle to remain just outside the door, I wonder where the hell Lucien and Tock are. "We're not alone."

Her brows knit up in confusion, but she does as I say.

Mrs. P is there to greet me. "You have visitors."

"Who are they?" I ask, with not a little bit of menace.

Mrs. P raises her eyebrows at me, silently pointing out I don't usually take that tone with her. "I didn't mean for you, Mr. Blackwell. They are here for *Mrs*. Blackwell."

Belle crosses the threshold at hearing that. We look at each other, but her expression reveals she's just as mystified. But she walks past me, only pausing to hang up her coat of roses. I don't let her go in there by herself, though.

Four figures await us in the sitting room.

The distinct odor of strong magic emanates from the blonde one wearing pink and black, though it's not nearly as offensive as I am used to encountering. She's perched casually on the arm of the sofa, her legs crossed and her sharp eyes already appraising me. Next to her, a lumberjack-sized man stands stiffly, his broad shoulders and towering frame exuding an unspoken threat. His scent is unmistakable—bear shifter. I'd caught it from the car, the earthy musk of something powerful invading my territory.

My gaze moves to the others. A petite Black woman with hair pure white sits with her legs spread wide, looking overly comfortable. Her pale blue eyes are steady but piercing. She's quiet but watchful, like she's the one I should really be worried about. Then there's the woman with the colorful viking braids. She stands when I enter, her green eyes locking onto mine with an intensity that sharpens the air.

They've made themselves quite at home, their postures unconcerned, the firelight casting their shadows like they belong here. They don't.

"Can I help you?" I ask, my voice a low growl as I take another step into the room. My muscles coil, every instinct demanding I assert control.

The blonde one tilts her head, her lips curving in a way that's both amused and unimpressed. "We're Belle's friends."

Friends. That one word lands like a challenge.

A hand presses on my arm. Belle's subtle message to relax. Isabelle goes on. "This is Rap, Snow, Goldie, and her fiancé, Ted."

I glance at the shifter, who stands behind the blonde one like a silent enforcer. His presence isn't overtly threatening, but it's enough to make my hands curl into fists at my sides. Ted gives me a slight nod.

"We're here to congratulate you both on your marriage," Rap states, her voice even but edged with steel.

The hell they are. This is a wellness check.

Isabelle catches my eye with a knowing look. I read her nonmoving lips perfectly. *See? They think I'm in an abusive relationship and are here to check on me. If you hadn't acted like a brute, they wouldn't be here.*

As much as I want to argue the point that it was her fault, there is no use.

I let my gaze sweep over the group again. "It's a pleasure to meet you all. Welcome to our home."

Oh, that felt more than a little weird. Too normal for the circumstances of our marriage, our relationship. Though in another world this could be a joyous occasion for Isabelle to introduce her friends to her husband. A pang of guilt goes through me. That's not the life I've given her.

"Could you please go ask Mrs. P to bring us some tea?" Isabelle asks me with a smile. Again, I read her unspoken thoughts. *Give us a minute alone so I can assure them I'm not your unwilling prisoner.*

"Of course," I answer stiffly.

I turn on my heel, leaving them in the living room. Their scents cling to the air behind me, and for the first time in years, I feel the weight of intruders in my home.

In the kitchen, I find not only Mrs. P but also Lucien settled over in the breakfast nook, drinking coffee.

"You couldn't have warned me?" I practically snarl at both of them.

Lucien takes another sip as he continues to read something on his phone. "They're the mademoiselle's friends. You did not say she is forbidden from having any," he says in an almost bored tone.

Mrs. P keeps moving about the kitchen, unbothered as

well. Another testament to how Isabelle has softened them to my power. "Of course, she is allowed to have friends. I'm assuming they'd like some tea?" She is already at work magicking together some croissants and a tray of China cups.

"I walked into an ambush. They were ready to tear me apart if need be," I accuse the two wildly unconcerned members of my staff.

Lucien snorts. "I doubt they could get the drop on you, boss."

"And all you needed to do was show up and be polite. It's the least you can do for Belle after all she's done for you."

Tock strides in next. "Could I get a cuppa as well?" he asks Mrs. P, settling in next to Lucien. Then, as if noting my decided tension, he asks, "Is everything alright?"

"Belle's friends do not care for the boss," Lucien says again in that infuriatingly flat tone.

"She's assuring them in the next room she's not a hostage," Mrs. P says as she manually opens a tin of loose leaf tea, "and that Mr. Blackwell is not really the beast he seems."

"Oh." Tock nods as if in understanding.

"I am standing right here," I say in a raised voice that is more than a little strained.

They all look up at that. A pause.

"And since you are here," Mrs. P says, "how are things progressing with Mrs. Blackwell?" Her tone is tight, reminding me she hasn't approved of this from the get-go.

"Can't be going too well if you are still in this state," Tock gives me a hard, studious look while adjusting his glasses as if searching for signs of my ability to shift.

"They spend a lot of time together. What else can they

do?" Lucien says, pulling out his lighter and clicking it open and closed.

I open my mouth to stop this speculation.

"Sex."

My teeth clack against each other the moment it's out of Mrs. P's mouth. Even Tock and Lucien stare at her, as if startled as well.

"What?" she asks as golden croissants float from a hot tray out of the oven to fill a cloth-lined basket. "Sex is a powerful method of creating intimacy and connection. If Mr. P were still alive, fae lords rest his soul, he'd agree with me. They should be having sex, lots of it. Heaps of it."

I drag a claw over my pained expression.

Tock and Lucien are now watching me, their expressions somewhat crumpled as if they are trying to fight back laughter.

The urge to rip their faces clean off swells inside of me. The basket of croissants is pushed into my hands before I can make a move to do so.

"Now go out there, take this, lead everyone to the library for tea, and be hospitable to your wife's friends."

The urge to push back rises but just as quickly deflates as my housekeeper gives me a sharp look. I turn and take the basket back into the living room, wondering when I lost control of my household.

Mrs. P follows me into the sitting room shortly after with a full rolling cart of teacups and a pot of tea. Goldie and Snow are openly and vocally delighted about Mrs. P's abilities as the cups fly and fill themselves before everyone. Mrs.

P seems more than a little pleased by the fuss made on her account.

Meanwhile, Rap's cutting gaze remains glued to me, making it difficult to stay calm. I'm not used to being looked at, and my hackles rise under the scrutiny. Thankfully, Isabelle is always sure to have a hand on me, whether on my arm or leg, while we sit next to each other on the couch. While I'm not sure if she's solely doing it to put on a show for her friends, it calms me nonetheless.

Rap finally eases up as the second pot of tea is near empty. There are half a dozen empty plates and little buttery flakes of croissants all over the coffee table and even a bit on the floor, but everyone seems to have relaxed a bit, including me. Though I could chalk that up to the glasses of rare cognac that have been distributed. Only Belle and Goldie passed on the apéritif while Snow boldly downed the first like a cheap shot. Now she sips the second glass more leisurely, her petite frame practically melted into the chair. Occasionally, a tiny hiccup escapes, a faint reminder of her earlier enthusiasm.

"I remember after Ted and I formed a pack bond," Goldie says. "We were attached at the hip, or me and my Teddy Bear would feel real physical pain at the distance."

"Goldie," Ted addresses his fiancée with more than a little exasperation. She pats him on the chest and leans up to drop a placating kiss on the cheek. Then she leans forward to grab the last little piece of croissant left on her plate. "He hates when I call him that," she says in a mock whisper.

Ted's eyes roll up as if praying to the heavens above for strength, even though his arm remains fused around her body. I have to admit I don't mind the bear shifter so much.

He owns a construction company and says little but enough.

"Is that what it's like for you too?" Despite languidly swirling the glass of cognac, Rap has all the subtlety of a shark scenting blood.

I'm not sure what information Isabelle conveyed about our marriage. Did she tell them it was a love match?

If she conveyed that I blackmailed her into marrying me after using her father as leverage, I bet the tone of the room would be wildly different.

Looking at Isabelle, I decide to let her take the lead. If she wanted to set them upon me like an angry, vengeful mob on her half, I think she'd have already done it. She looks at me and those big brown eyes seem to be at a loss, trying to determine the right thing to say in my gaze. The arm that rests along the back of the couch moves so my fingers can find the back of her neck. It's both a possessive gesture, and one meant to reassure as I knead the muscles there.

"Um. . ." she starts, still looking into my eyes. Suddenly I wish we were the only two in this room. Sex and intimacy. That's how to make a pack, says my level three mage housekeeper.

"Of course it is," Goldie answers for her. "Pack is paramount for shifters. Ted can only be away from his two brothers for longer periods because they've established that bond for so long. Of course, Dominic would be out of his mind if he didn't know where Belle was. I shudder to think what Ted would do if he didn't know where I was."

The man's jaw tightens, his broad shoulders going rigid. For a moment, his expression goes blank—not vacant, but controlled, as though he's shuttering something dangerous just beneath the surface. The muscle in his temple twitches almost imperceptibly, his fingers curling tighter around his glass, the faintest crack of tension in his grip.

I know the feeling.

"I am sorry for alarming you or any of your patrons." I direct this at Rap with sincerity, rolling the glass in my hand.

I am, after all, a businessman. I created a disruption at Poison Apple that was unwanted. Not to mention I seemed to be negatively affecting one of Rap's people—though Isabelle is mine. It's understandable she'd come check things out. It's what I would do in her shoes.

Those green eyes settle on me for several heartbeats, but I don't look away.

Again, I can't help but note the smell of the woman is strange, undefinable. Rap isn't wholly human, but I've no idea what her deal is. If I had cared to spare the resources, I could find out.

Finally, she nods, and I know we are fine. . .for now.

Isabelle shifts under my touch. The way she looks at Goldie and Ted, I can only guess at what she's thinking.

Is that what it's supposed to feel like? Is that how we are supposed to be?

Of course those must be Isabelle's thoughts. Not mine.

The only thing I need to gauge whether things work or not is by my ability to shift, which means we need to continue to stay close.

Yet again, Mrs. P words come back to slam into the side of my head.

The mental image of fucking Isabelle all over the house, on every surface, as often as possible sends my blood south. I shift on the couch to relieve the sudden pressure.

"Can we go now?" The question comes from Snow,

followed by another hiccup. Her legs are now draped over the leg of her chair.

Rap dead-eyes me. "Yeah, we're good here."

They all stand.

"Thank you so much for having us," Goldie says, stepping forward as if about to give me a hug. Both Ted and I tense. She instantly reels back and sticks a handout.

The wisest move between two over-territorial shifters.

I shake it and thank her for coming. Ted also gives me a firm shake before following the other women out. I pretend I don't hear Rap whisper to Isabelle as they hug, "If you are ever even remotely uncomfortable or scared, you come to me."

Isabelle gives her a quiet thank you and we wave to the groups as Ted drives them off in a truck that can easily handle the nasty slick streets this late at night.

We shut the door, and suddenly it's just Isabelle and me. She's standing far too close, looking up at me through those thick eyelashes behind her glasses.

Everything about her is sultry and inviting.

The need to take her, fuck her right against the front door, is so intense I bite down on my tongue. And based on the scent of her and the way she licks her lips, she wouldn't mind in the least.

I step back. Not far, just enough to give myself room to think.

Her friends' voices still echo in my head, sharp and lingering. Rap's pointed questions, Goldie's too-perfect anecdotes about her "pack bond," and the watchful silence of Snow—they all stick to me, scratching at the edges of my control. I'd felt their judgment in every glance, every subtle shift of their postures. They didn't have to say it outright— I'm not good enough for her. I'm a force of chaos in her ordered world, a threat to the lightness they want to protect.

My hand finds the back of my neck, claws curling into my skin as I look past her, the polished grain of the front door catching the dim light. "I have some work to finish," I say, voice low, too casual, already turning away.

The truth is, I'm suffocating. Her friends' comments about pack bonds, the expectation that I'd already forged something deeper with Isabelle, sit like stones on my chest. The pressure to be more, to give her something I'm not sure I'm capable of, builds with every step I take down the hall. If I don't find a way to clear my head, I'll lose the fragile threads of control I've been clinging to.

My footsteps echo in the quiet, heavy and deliberate, carrying me away from her pull. The beast in me snarls at the retreat, but I ignore it, shoving down the instinct to go back, to claim her, to drown myself in her scent. I won't let myself unravel. Not here. Not now. If I can't sort through this, I may need to go for a run in the freezing Boston night just to get my head on straight. Anything to keep the chaos inside me from spilling over.

Only one thought repeats over and over in my mind. *Coward.*

THE FORBIDDEN WEST WING

BELLE

I've officially become a gothic romance heroine, roaming around the mansion in my fuzzy robe, unable to sleep. Even after getting myself off multiple times, there is still an ache, a need pulsating in me, demanding I do something about it.

It demands I go to the door separating my husband's bedroom from mine, knock on it, and ask Dominic to shove me onto his bed and fuck me until there's nothing left of this awkward tension that keeps cropping up between us.

It became such a strong intrusive thought that the only way to keep my hand from rapping against the wood or curving around the handle was to put some space between us. So here I am, a lonely, horny waif avoiding that damn door.

Even as my bare feet pad down the cold, dimly lit hallways, my body wants more. It wants Dominic's heat, his weight. It wants the unexpected pleasure of hands I can't anticipate, that aren't my own.

The irony of vowing never to be seriously romantically entangled again, only to find myself bound to a temperamental half-shifter I find devastatingly sexy, is not lost on me.

How dare he come with me to my bookstore and defend me to that plumber and get the place back in perfect shape in record time. He even kept straightening book displays here and there. He picked up entire shelves and stacks of books, moving them to safety away from the leak. My insides inexplicably melted and then swelled up like a bubble until I felt my chest might burst.

Probably heartburn, right?

I mean, it's nothing. Just several nice gestures in a row that make me feel cared for in between some very intense, sexy, panty-melting encounters.

It's not like I'm falling in love with him or anything.

I've seen the cost of believing in love. My parents were proof enough of that. My mother wanted grand gestures, sweeping declarations, a love she could show off to the world. My father? He didn't believe in performing emotions for an audience—or anyone, really. He loved his work, his duty, and he loved us in his own quiet way.

When she finally left, he barely blinked. He didn't fall apart or even stumble. He just kept working, kept caring for me like nothing had changed. And eventually, I learned to do the same. Pretend it didn't matter. Pretend we didn't need her until it was true.

But it wasn't just them.

Adrian taught me the rest. He was my first everything— my first kiss, my first love, my first mistake. I believed him when he said I was special, that I mattered. I let myself get swept up in the fantasy, thinking I'd found something real.

I hadn't.

Adrian didn't love me. He loved what I could give him— a means to an end, nothing more. He thought it was better to give me a beautiful lie. But I'd rather have the cold, hard truth than be made a fool of.

Wandering these dark halls, I try to outrun the ache in my chest, the heat simmering low in my belly. But my body refuses to listen.

It remembers too much. The way Dominic's hard frame pushed me against his desk, the way his sharp green eyes watched me like I was the only thing in the room. And then there was the fear of losing me, like he'd lose his mind if something happened. The weight of his presence, the brush of his claws—these moments replay in my mind, dragging me under.

The way he picked up my book and read it because it caught my interest. Even those tiny glimpses of his sense of humor slip under my skin like silken claws, hooking me from the center of my chest.

No.

Romantic love doesn't exist. What does exist is chemistry, companionship, and mutual need. Relationships are transactions, and this marriage is no different.

Dominic needs a pack. I need protection and stability for my father. That's it. That's all.

The way he looked at me when he thought I didn't notice, possessive and raw, doesn't mean anything. Helping Chip doesn't make him a good guy. Coming to my shop and shouting down the plumber for disrespecting me didn't make me feel taken care of or like I was special.

I stop and sigh.

No matter how hard I try to logic my way out of it, I can't lie to myself.

I've never wanted anyone the way I want my husband.

And that terrifies me.

A fluttering sound echoes around me as I near the west

wing. The odd, insistent sound that sends shivers racing up my arms. The hallway stretches endlessly before me, its dim light swallowed by shadows that cling to the edges of the walls. My feet carry me forward as though under some spell, my fingers brushing against the polished wood of the railings as I go.

I stop in front of the door. The heavy oak is just as forbidding as it was the first time Dominic barred me from entering. But there's still that sound—a soft, rhythmic thrum—emanating from behind it, like dozens of fans going.

I press my hand to the door, feeling a peculiar warmth radiating through the grain. Curiosity wars with caution, but the compulsion to know what lies beyond is too strong.

My fingers curl around the handle.

"Isabelle, no," Dominic's voice roars behind me, and I jump, spinning toward him just as the door gives way.

An explosion of fur and wings bursts from the room, a chaotic flurry that swarms into the hallway in a cacophony of chirps and frantic flapping. I duck instinctively, throwing my arms over my head as the creatures rush past me.

When I finally dare to look, I blink in utter disbelief.

"Are those..." I murmur, staring at the winged rabbits as they hover, swoop, and flutter around the hall. Most are jet black, their fur gleaming like obsidian, but a few are lighter shades—grays and snowy whites with patches of golden brown. A small pair of horns protrude from the tops of their heads.

One particularly bold rabbit flits close to me, its translucent bat-like wings edged in black with iridescent silver. Its nose wiggles as it regards me with wide, curious eyes before darting away with an almost mischievous chirp.

"What the hell have you done?" Dominic growls, storming toward me, his eyes flashing with rage.

Dominic is bare to the waist, exposed. The hard planes of muscle ripple beneath his skin, a fascinating interplay of smooth flesh and coarse patches of fur. My fingers ache with the temptation to reach out, to trace the contrast, to feel the give of muscle under my touch. His skin is flushed, tinged red from the bite of cold, as if he's been outside in the freezing air. He smells of the ocean—raw, untamed, and alive. The scent clings to him, blending with the faint musk of his sweat, a telltale sign of exertion. It's utterly intoxicating.

The flying fuzz bombs dart and dive through the hallway, their tiny wings beating furiously as they perch on sconces, banisters, and even on Dominic. One particularly audacious creature perches on the edge of his shoulder, its claws gripping skin as it sniffs at his hair with a curious wiggle of its nose.

I bite my lip to stifle a laugh, but it escapes anyway—a helpless, breathless sound that bubbles out of me. The sight of this towering, half-feral man, glowering as he's bedecked by winged rabbits, is too much.

The secret of the west wing is out.

The only question now is why is he keeping these creatures locked away?

CHAPTER 25

GHOSTS LOVE FLUTTERBUNS

BELLE

"They're...adorable." Cute aggression is becoming a very real problem as the flying rabbits with tiny horns fly around me, and I have to fold my hands into my stomach to keep from catching and squeezing the bajeezus out of all of them at once.

"They're a disaster," Dominic snaps, his voice tight with irritation as he reaches up to shoo a particularly bold bunny-like animal off his shoulder. "And now they're everywhere."

The creature chirps indignantly before flapping off, its wings brushing his cheek.

I cover my mouth, but it doesn't help to suppress the giggle that escapes me. "What are they?"

Dominic glares at me, his jaw tightening, but there's a flicker of something softer in his eyes as he watches me try to compose myself. He swipes at the one on his shoulder but it swoops out of reach, letting out an indignant chirp before darting to a nearby bookshelf. "They are called flutterbuns."

One of the lighter-colored animals lands on my arm, its

tiny claws tickling my skin. I lift it closer, marveling at the softness of its fur and the delicate veins that thread through its wings. It nuzzles against my cheek, and my heart squeezes to the point of pain.

"You've got to be joking," I murmur, stroking its tiny head. I might have dissolved into uncontrollable laughter at hearing that ridiculous word slide out of my husband's mouth if I weren't being so careful not to startle my new friend.

"I assure you, I'm not. They are creatures from the Midnight Realm." Dominic exhales sharply, the sound more resigned than angry now. "They weren't supposed to get out."

"How could you possibly keep these little babies locked up?"

He pinches the bridge of his nose. "Because they breed like. . .well, rabbits. They are illegal to have in this realm, and now that they've been released so unceremoniously, they will chew, claw, and nest in every little crevice of the house. Fae lords help us if they escape to the outside." Then he mutters something under his breath before striding toward the open door. "Help me get them back inside before they get the notion they own the entire house."

It takes longer than I expect with the flutterbuns fluttering just out of reach as if playing a game. Eventually, most of them settle back into the room, their tiny bodies clustering on shelves and ledges like living ornaments. Though I saw several of them swoop down the stairs and out of sight.

Hope that's not a problem like Dominic predicts. . .

Dominic ushers a few stragglers through the door with a low growl, and I can't help but notice how careful he is not to hurt them, despite his irritation.

Once the hallway is finally clear, Dominic pushes the door shut behind us with a decisive click, locking us inside. He drinks in the room with a pained expression as if it hurts to be in here.

It's a bedroom, or it was once. The walls are painted a soft lavender, faded now with age. The furniture is delicate, feminine—a canopy bed with sheer curtains, a vanity cluttered with dust-covered trinkets, a bookshelf crammed with old, well-loved volumes. Many of the titles are YA romances I recognize.

The flutterbuns flit around the room like tiny guardians, their presence somehow less chaotic here. Tons of cat towers have been brought in as perches and the little holes are clearly the little animals' favorite nesting spots.

Dominic sinks onto the edge of the bed, his shoulders sagging under a weight I can't see. Little chirps precede an explosion of three flutterbuns escaping from under the bed.

"This was my sister's room," he says quietly, his voice rough.

My laughter at the indignant creatures from under the bed dies in my throat as I step closer.

"Lisette wanted to be a veterinarian," Dominic continues, his gaze fixed on the floor. "She was always bringing home injured animals—birds, groundhogs, even a wild turkey once." He shudders at the memory. I can't imagine the kind of girl who thinks bringing one of those thuggish birds indoors is a good idea.

"She had this. . .fierce need to save things. Nobody could stop her when she was determined to nurse a little creature back to health. She was a lot like you," he adds, finally looking up at me. "Stubborn. Opinionated. Impossible to control."

I glance around at the swarm of flutterbuns perched on ledges and furniture.

"Thank you," I say sincerely, taking a few steps to close the space between us and sit on the bed next to him. I'm barely settled before one of the flying rabbit-like creatures lands in my lap. I stroke the impossibly soft fur, and the flutterbun settles into a little loaf-like posture of relaxation, wings folded on its back.

"Did she bring these little guys home too?"

He pauses for so long, I wonder if he plans to answer at all. "No," he finally answers. "I was the one who found them—on the black market—injured and malnourished. The moment I saw that cramped cage with them shoved inside, I knew my baby sister would love and care for them like no other."

I want to ask where his sister is, though the abandoned room, the way Dominic regards these walls—as if they were haunted—and the slow icy drip in my stomach tells me the answer is far from a happy one.

Lisette is not away at college or on vacation as much as I'd love to believe that.

"So I've been keeping them contained in her room," he continues, as if trying to regain his composure, "feeding them, trying to keep them a secret. If anyone found out. . ." He trails off, his expression hardening.

"If anyone found out, what?"

"They'd destroy them," he says flatly. "They're considered pests in the Midnight Realm. Dangerous pests."

I look down at the flutterbun on my arm, its tiny fangs peeking out as it nibbles on the edge of my sleeve. "They don't seem very dangerous." The pad of my finger follows the curve of the tiny horn to its pointy end before stroking the fuzzy ear. I suppose the fangs and horns could do a fair bit of damage, but when a second flutterbun creeps up on the other side of me, nudging me with its tiny nose, I think whatever destruction they cause would have to be instantly forgiven.

"They're not," he admits. His gaze drops to the creature in his hands. "Not really. But they're illegal, and that's all the justification some people need."

Another flutterbun lands on Dominic's knee, its wings folding neatly as it snuggles into the fabric of his pants. He strokes its head absently, the motion tender despite his earlier irritation.

"She would have loved these little terrors," he says, his lips quirking into a small, sad smile.

Loved. Past tense.

The tenderness in his voice is startling, a stark contrast to the gruff, irritable man I've come to know. I swallow the lump in my throat, unsure of what to say. I want to ask so badly but I muscle down the question. "I mean, we just met, but it's hard not to instantly love them."

For a moment, we sit in silence, surrounded by the quiet rustle of wings and the ghosts I can almost feel brush against my skin in here. When I can't take it any longer, the question building, an unstoppable bubble, I stand. The flutterbun on my lap flies off as I cross to the other side of the room.

My fingers trail over the delicate carvings of a young woman's vanity.

"What. . .happened to Lisette?" *To your pack?*

I expect anger, rage, wrath, and all associated emotions that would have him avoid telling me. Still, I couldn't stop myself.

"I was late, *again*," he begins to my surprise, his tone brittle and raw. "Flying in from New Avalon after conducting business. Lisette hated waiting, especially on her birthday. Seventeen."

"I was going to make it up to her. I got her something special." He closes his paw and human hand around the fawn-colored flutterbun, lifting it up. The creature snuggled into his massive palms with all the trust in the world. It makes me wonder if they are naturally friendly or if it's been Dominic up here, socializing them.

My husband always seems so unmovable, so unstoppable. Yet there's a fragile edge to him now, like the weight of the memory is too much even for him to carry.

With a little toss, the flutterbun catches air, flapping up and up to the ledge of molding that borders the entire ceiling.

"But I was late." His throat bobs as he swallows hard. "When I got to the restaurant, I left the cage of neglected animals in the car. The building was on fire."

The words hit me like a punch to the gut. My breath catches, but I stay silent, waiting for him to go on.

"My whole family was there," Dominic says, his words cracking. "Cousins, uncles, aunts—a massive celebration." He stops, his jaw clenching so tightly I hear his teeth grind. "I felt it before I even landed, like my body was tearing apart. Molecule by molecule. Something was wrong, and I ignored it because I thought it couldn't be that bad. But when I got there. . . ."

He was too late.

I have to remind myself to breathe. Even the creatures around us seem to have stilled in deference to what he's sharing.

"I ran into the wreckage. Flames, smoke—I didn't care. I thought maybe. . .maybe I could save someone." His fingers flex like they want to rip something apart—his own skin, the past, anything. "But it was too late. They were all gone."

My feet are rooted to the spot, my body tense with his pain.

"Anti-Were zealots," he snarls, his glowing eyes meeting mine for a moment before darting away. "They left their fae hate scrawled on the walls. *Mongrels don't deserve mercy. Animals belong in cages, not in cities.*"

I wince at the horrible sentiments. Though it's not the first time I'dve heard some of those words said, though certainly not from anyone I associate with. Even where I come from, power is power, no matter what shape it takes. There was a begrudging respect for fae creatures at the very least.

"When I found Lisette, she was riddled with silver bullets." He stares past me, past the room, eyes unfocused as if still seeing the bloodstained walls. "Her blue birthday dress was soaked in blood. And she was. . .arched over something. Our little cousin. He was five." He swallows hard, his chest heaving. "She tried to shield him, but the bullets that killed her went through her and directly into him."

A gasp of horror escapes me even as my hand flies to my mouth. The backs of my eyes sting as my eyes blur, hot tears escaping down my cheeks.

His raw agony seeps into my bones, lodging there like a splinter I can't remove. I want to say something, anything, to bridge the gaping chasm between us, but my throat constricts around the words. I've faced cruelty, seen pain, but this? It's a grief so profound it's almost a living thing wrapping around him, suffocating us both.

Dominic continues to stare up at the flutterbuns overhead, eyes glazed over and distant.

"She never even got to see them," he murmurs, his voice soft but bitter. "But I kept them, nursed them to health ,and they multiplied. She would've loved that."

I don't know what to say. The flutterbuns seem to sense his anguish has reached a peak. They flutter around the room, their wings stirring the air with little flaps. One lands on his shoulder, nuzzling against his neck as if to comfort him, but he doesn't react.

"I moved my bedroom across the house after that," he says. "Away from *their* rooms. Their ghosts are still here. Their laughter. Their voices. Their silence. Every damn day."

Dominic lifts his gaze to meet mine then, his expression dark, his animal eye glowing fiercely in the dim light.

"But I hunted all of those bastards down." He rises slowly, a panther uncoiling from the underbrush. There's something final in the way he moves, something that says the past is still bleeding under his nails. "Every last one of them. The men who did it. They begged for mercy." He rises to his feet, stalking toward me in steady strides. "They tried to escape, offered me money, even their own family members, in exchange for their miserable, worthless lives. One tried to claim someone else hired them to do it. But I ignored their lies and manipulations as I tore their cowardly spines out of their throats."

Yet again. He wants me to be afraid. I can feel it in the way he looms over me, the way his claws flex at his sides.

But I'm not.

I hold his gaze, my pulse racing. His grief is palpable, but so is his rage, his hatred—for those who hurt his family, for himself, maybe even at me, standing here and witnessing it all.

"You avenged your family," I say quietly, refusing to

break eye contact. "You didn't just let it go. That doesn't make you a bad man, Dominic. It makes you human."

This I understand. While I don't agree with most of the things instilled in me from childhood, this one I understood. I may read romance. I may be independent and run my own business, and as much as I rise above the nasty comments I've had to endure about my weight or the disgruntled customers who take out their unhappy lives on me—there is a point where nothing less than an eye for an eye will do.

His expression twists into something between anger and disbelief. "I'm not human," he spits. "As I stood among the corpses of my family, I transformed into this." Even as he says it, his fangs lengthen, muscles stretch and swell, fur and hair bristle. The sound of creaking and cracking bones is audible. The flutterbuns explode up in the air in a flurry of wings, retreating to the farthest corner of the room as if sensing danger is near.

"And now here I am, everyone dead but trying to start over with you. Trying to make a new pack with a woman I forced into marriage, yet still I am this." His fervor rises as his body continues to contort and stretch in ways that sounds and look painful. "Perhaps I'm damned. Who could ever form an attachment to a beast like me?" As he says it, the words dip and grate as if he's turning into a monster before my eyes.

My feet are glued to the spot. I'm pinned by his story, his pain, and his loneliness.

"I'm so sorry, Dominic. And I'm here," I say as I reach for his hand. I don't know what else to say. I don't know why we aren't making a pack, why our time together hasn't been enough to let him shift back.

Before I can touch him, he jerks back. "Don't," he warns.

Like the night at our wedding, I can see he's on the precipice. Pain, both internal and external, is pushing him to the edge. Would he hurt me? Hurt the flutterbuns? Destroy his sister's room?

Strangely, I'm more worried about him than me. If he loses control in here, I already know he'll regret it.

Instead, he steps back toward the door.

"I'll see you at breakfast," he mutters, his mismatched eyes flicking to mine for the briefest moment before he turns away.

The door swings shut behind him, its final click like a gavel striking judgment. The air feels heavier, charged with his past, his pain. I sink onto the edge of Lisette's bed, my fingers digging into the thick comforter.

What kind of man carries that much grief and still finds the strength to try again?

And what kind of woman would I be to refuse him the chance?

A terrifying thought occurs to me.

To make a pack, does he need someone to love him?

Because of all the things I'd do for my father, for Dominic, I don't think I can give him that.

CHAPTER 26

RUNNING WITH WOLVES

BELLE

A roar shakes the entire house as I make my way down the stairs, the sheer volume of it rattling the picture frames on the walls. Lucien darts past me, muttering something about checking the cars, though we both know hiding in the garage is only a temporary reprieve. Mrs. P scurries toward the kitchen, mumbling anxiously about making sure dessert is perfect, her hands trembling as she passes.

Another guttural cry tears through the mansion, raw and animalistic. Even from across the house, I feel the rage rolling off Dominic, thick and potent, filling the hallways like a dense fog. The impulse to flee seizes me, but I fight it, my heart pounding as I continue down the stairs.

I turn toward the source of the noise, tracking the path of destruction—an overturned chair, a smashed vase, splintered wood where something was thrown against the wall. I step through the chaos, finding Dominic in the dimly lit study, his chest heaving with anger, his eyes blazing green in the shadows.

"What's wrong?" I sound steadier than I feel.

He whips around, and the intensity of his gaze nearly makes me rear back. "What's wrong?" he repeats, with barely restrained wrath. "What's wrong is your father. I found him in my basement. The man is completely unhinged and should be locked up."

Any fear I felt for my safety dissipates, replaced by a sharp, protective anger. "I will not put him in an institution, Dominic. He needs family, not to be cast aside like some criminal."

"He needs to be kept in a padded cell," he snaps. "The man broke into a laboratory—*my* laboratory. How he got in my locked basement a second time, I can't account for it. He was in there, tampering with materials that could kill him." He gestures toward the door with a clenched fist, his entire body tense. "He's unstable, Isabelle. I caught him mixing things, throwing ingredients together like he knew what he was doing. He nearly destroyed months' worth of work on Thorns."

The words hit me like a slap.

"Thorns," I say slowly, realization hitting me like a freight train.

I didn't know. I didn't know he kept that stuff *in the house.*

You didn't want to know, part of me whispers.

It's true. I do my best to ignore my husband's dealings.

But now everything clicks into place. Why my father broke into Dominic's home in the first place. His mind may be scrambled, but there was always a method to his madness.

An invisible force clamps around my heart and then my throat, and I have to shut my eyes to ground myself.

"Is he okay?" I ask, trying to keep calm despite the wild surges of fear rocketing through me.

Dominic's mouth twists in frustration. "He bolted before I could stop him, muttering nonsense. That's twice now he's gone into that lab and run amok. He's uncontrollable, Isabelle. *Dangerous.*"

"You yelled at him, didn't you?" I accuse. "You must have terrified him half to death."

His eyes flash. "He should be terrified. There are volatile compounds down there, hexes and curses, things I've worked hard to contain. If he takes the wrong one—"

"Enough," I cut him off, turning on my heel. His rage won't help my father, and I'm certain he's out there somewhere, frightened and confused. "I have to find him."

"Isabelle, wait—" Dominic's words follows me, rough and frustrated, but I don't stop. I reach the front corridor just in time to see the door standing wide open, cold night air pouring in.

"Oh no," I whisper. When he's scared or anxious, my father runs—and he's had at least twenty minutes to get a head start. I slip into my boots, grab my long coat from the rack, and shrug it on. Pulling the heavy fabric tight around me, my fingers already shake with cold and dread. My shoes crunch on the snow-covered threshold as I run out into the night, calling out for him.

I take off down the steps, my heart pounding as I scan the snowy landscape for any sign of him. Fresh tracks lead through the garden and down the front path, but thick flakes are already falling, obscuring his footsteps.

Despite the heavy coat that falls to my ankles, the cold night air seeps through it and into my bones. I should have grabbed a hat. Dad went out the back gates and onto the streets. I follow the distinct tread of his boots, but it gets harder when he reaches the city sidewalk. The snow melts almost instantly as it hits the salted street, so I can barely make out which direction he's headed.

When I can no longer follow his path, I realize I don't need them anymore. I know exactly what direction he's headed, and the thought chills me more than the winter air biting at my skin.

Please fae lords, let me catch him before he gets there.

It makes me speed up until I'm in a half jog. My breath puffs in front of my face. The streets are oddly quiet for this time of night. My own beating heart thunders in my ears as sweat gathers and then chills along my skin and under my clothes. I'm not sure if I'm hot or cold anymore. All I know is pure panic.

I step onto a quiet side street. Laundromats, coffee shops, and clothes retailers have all closed for the night. I pick up my father's distinctive tracks again. I learned to buy him boots with special tread for moments like this.

"Don't do this. Please don't do this," I beg my dad, though he's not here to listen.

Despite my burning lungs and being covered in a cold sweat, I push myself to go faster. A solid, dark figure emerges from the shadows. I nearly slip and fall backward but catch myself at the last minute. A man about my age wearing all gray, hands in his pockets, advances slowly on me, forcing me to back up.

"A woman like you shouldn't be out this late."

"Please, I'm looking for my dad, he's—"

A second figure joins him, circling behind me. He's got a buzz cut that makes him look short and round, but the glint in his eye is just as dangerous as his companion's. "I don't know, Curt," he says with a grin, giving my coat a slow once over. "Maybe she's looking for something. . .else."

A woman with scarred cheeks and an unfriendly smirk

moves closer, her eyes narrowing. "Trouble, maybe. Definitely looks like trouble." Her gaze lingers on my coat. "I like that coat. Looks expensive."

Fear coils in my stomach, but I refuse to let it show. "I don't want trouble," I say evenly. "I just need to find my dad."

I recognize the gang affiliation of the Wolves from their gray outfits almost instantly. Despite their name, these thugs are purely human.

Curt closes in on me, a mocking smile twisting his lips. "Maybe we can help you find him. . .for a price."

I take a step back, only to find the woman blocking my path. Her expression darkens as she reaches for my arm, her fingers curling around my sleeve. "Or maybe we'll just take what we want."

"Please," I say, as calmly as I can manage. "You don't know who you are messing with."

The one called Curt laughs, a low, mocking sound. "Pretty girl like you shouldn't be wandering around in Wolf territory alone, especially not in that coat." He reaches out, fingers brushing against the fabric of my sleeve. I jerk my arm away, but his grip tightens, holding me in place.

My heart pounds as I try to pull free, but his fingers dig painfully into my arm, and his face twists with an ugly sneer. "What's wrong, sweetheart? Don't you want to play with the Wolves?"

I open my mouth to explain exactly why I don't want to and why they should leave me alone when someone pushes me from behind. I slam into the ground. Snow and salt scrape then burn my bare palms.

The sting from the snow and salt is nothing compared to the sharp surge of fear as I struggle to push myself up, only to feel a boot pressing down on my shoulder, pinning me in place. Panic flares, clawing up my throat, but I bite it back, forcing myself to keep a calm façade even as they close in.

"Oh, we're gonna have fun playing with you," one of the men sneers, his gaze glinting with a feral hunger. More shadows emerge, solidifying in a pack of Wolves.

The moment the boot lifts, I scramble away, but there's nowhere to go, the tight circle of Wolves hemming me in on all sides. The air feels suffocating, thick with their anticipation.

"Dibs on her coat," the woman claims.

"Belle?" a voice calls, hesitant. The Wolves all snap their heads around, homing in on my father. Dad stands there, in a sweater too thin for these temperatures. His nose is bright red from the cold and his eyes are unfocused and unsure as he looks at the gang members surrounding me. He clutches the leather pouch at his side tightly. "I-I brought the Thorns. Can I come home now? Can we come home now?"

"Wait," says the short Wolf with the buzz cut, looking first at my dad and then back at me. Recognition flickers in his eyes. "Aren't they—"

A deep, guttural growl that rips through the night, a sound so fierce and primal, it cuts like a blade. The air shifts, charged with an almost electric menace, and for a heartbeat, everything goes still.

Then, like a dark storm, Dominic bursts onto the scene.

He moves with a terrifying speed, his silhouette massive and wild, green eyes gleaming with unrestrained fury. The first man he reaches barely has time to turn before Dominic's fist slams into his jaw with a sickening crack, sending him sprawling across the ground.

"Never touch my wife," he snarls.

A flurry of blows, arms, and kicks ensues. Dominic is

ferocious and wild, but there are six of them on him. The glint of steel catches my eye before it plunges into Dominic's shoulder.

I cry out. "No, don't hurt him!" The words are stupid, useless, falling harmlessly to the ground along with the snowflakes even as Dominic cries out in pain. I slip as I try to get to my feet, but I don't have a weapon to help. I look around for a rock, tree branch, hell, anything.

Two of the Wolves go flying, hitting the side of the brick buildings with painful harrumphs.

Something sharp kisses my neck at the same time a body presses to my back. "That's enough," the woman with scarred cheeks hisses. "Back off, fucker, or I slit wifey's throat."

The flurry freezes as everyone turns to us.

"You hurt her," Dominic says in a low threat, "and I'll rip you open from belly button to throat."

She scoffs in my ear with a hot breath that makes me cringe. "Yeah, I don't think so. But pray tell, what's a badass shifter like yourself doing here?"

There is a bit of awe as she asks.

"You don't know who I am?" Dominic says in a cold, suddenly controlled tone. "Well, little pup, I'm the Beast of Boston."

I feel rather than see her falter behind me.

"Don't hurt her," the Wolf with the buzz cut calls out, struggling to get to his feet. An angry red mark on his round face indicates the blow he's taken from my husband will turn into a nasty bruise later.

"Why not?" the female Wolf asks, though her weight shifts back and forth nervously. I wince as the blade slices my skin.

Dominic's shoulders tense. He's about to lunge.

"Because she's a Wolf," the man says. "They both are." He gestures to my father as well.

"We are not Wolves." I should keep my mouth shut, but the words shoot out of me on instinct.

Another scoff from my captor. "Don't fuck with me, Levi."

"I'm not. That's Roman's cousin," Levi says, staring me straight in the eyes.

"Don't be an idiot," the female says. "I heard she was dead."

"I assure you," I say calmly. "She isn't."

CHAPTER 27
THE FAMILY WE ARE BORN TO
THE BEAST OF BOSTON

The world pulses red, the edges of my vision narrowing, closing in like the jaws of a trap. My focus is razor-sharp, locked on the blade pressed against my wife's perfect throat.

Roman Valentine. The name alone scrapes against my mind like claws on stone. He's the leader of the Wolves—the rival gang tearing through my territory, the one I've been fighting tooth and claw to destroy. The halfwits stealing my product or distributing Thorns that don't have petals.

And by her own admission, Isabelle is his cousin. Which makes her father Roman Valentine's uncle.

This can't be right.

The muddled old man who's been skulking around my estate, trying to steal Thorns from me, is tied to the Wolves? How in all the cursed realms did I not see this?

My chest tightens, fury roaring to life, but I can't afford to focus on that revelation now. Not with that knife glinting against Isabelle's skin.

"Let my wife go," I growl.

"Do it," Levi, the Wolf who recognized Isabelle, agrees.

The woman's lip curls as she shifts uneasily. The knife presses closer, the blade nicking Isabelle's neck.

A thin line of blood blooms against her pale skin, and the scent of it—her blood—ignites everything animal inside me. The tension in the air snaps like a live wire.

I move before I think, before the Wolves have time to react.

The woman gasps as my claws close around her throat. I lift her off the ground, her feet kicking uselessly, her knife falling to the snow.

"I was going to let you all walk away tonight. But now? You die," I snarl, shaking with rage. "You touched her. You hurt her. You think you can spill her blood and walk away?"

The Wolf's hands claw futilely at my arm, her breath rasping in desperate gasps. "I—It was an accident—"

Despite the Wolves' namesake, there is but a delicate human neck in my hand. She doesn't stand a chance.

"Accidents don't matter." My grip tightens, the sharp points of my claws biting into her skin. "Not when it comes to my wife."

Her breath catches, her lips moving as though she wants to plead, but no sound escapes.

I slam her to the ground with enough force to crack the ice beneath her. Her eyes widen in shock, her lips moving soundlessly, but there's no mercy left in me. My claws drive into her chest, silencing her forever.

When I rise and twist, the Wolves continue to stand there in silence. Levi raises his hands slowly. A silent message. *The kill was yours to take.*

I huff, a cloud puffing from my nose as I relax a fraction.

The Wolves slink back, each one glancing uneasily between me and Isabelle, leaving their dead at my feet. Levi nods at Isabelle—a subtle acknowledgment, an under-standing passing between them.

Silence descends, broken only by Isabelle's sharp inhale as she touches her neck.

I'm at her side in an instant, my bloodstained claws carefully retracting as I lift her chin. "Let me see," I murmur, tilting her head to the light. My thumb brushes lightly against the edge of the wound, and she flinches again.

Isabelle's skin is cold beneath my fingers, but her pulse thrums fast and strong. The cut is shallow, barely more than a scratch, but the sight of it enrages me all over again.

"It's fine," she whispers, her voice shaky but calm.

I exhale slowly, forcing the fury down. "It's not fine." I'd strike down anyone who even looks at Isabelle wrong, so the fact she's bleeding is beyond my limits of control. The entirety of Boston should shake in the echo of the rage inside of me.

Her hand covers mine, her touch warm despite the cold. "I'm okay," she says again, more firmly this time.

I catch my breath, grounding myself in her steady gaze. There's a calm determination in her eyes, the fire of defi-ance that I've come to admire—even if it drives me mad.

"Dad," Isabelle says gently, reaching out to the man who doesn't seem to notice he's shivering. "You're coming home with us."

Basil hesitates, his eyes flicking to the darkness where the Wolves vanished. "They. . .They need me. Said I could help. I have the Thorns. They need these."

"No," she replies, voice firm but soft, taking his hand. "They don't need you. *I* need you, Dad. Come home with me." She gently pries the pouch from his fingers, passing it over to me without hesitation.

I take it, even as I still inwardly reel.

Basil blinks at me, confusion clouding his face, and then he focuses on the pouch in my hand as though just realizing it's gone. "The Thorns..." he murmurs, lost again. "I got the Thorns so they would take me back. I could create again."

"Basil." I wait to go on until the man's glazed over eyes meet mine. "I apologize for losing my temper earlier. Can you forgive me?"

Basil looks down at his empty hands. I suspect he is looking for the bag of Thorns but may not even realize what he's missing.

"How about we get you home and by the fire with some of Mrs. P's fresh, hot croissants?" I suggest.

That penetrates. Basil's chapped red face breaks into a smile. "Scones? With jam and curd?" I pull my own coat off and put it around his shaking shoulders.

"And clotted cream," I add.

When our eyes meet, I see her relief—her gratitude.

Taking care of her father means everything to her.

But not fear. Not disgust. Not the kind of shock I'd expect from a woman who just watched her husband rip someone apart. Then again, it turns out my wife had a much different upbringing from what I supposed.

Despite her appreciation, I'm unmoved. We have a lot to discuss. Namely, how in the hell I married a woman related to the Wolf gang and why the fuck I didn't know. Her smile falters. She knows as well as I, it's going to be a long night.

~

IN THE LIBRARY, Lucien stitches up my knife wounds.

I insisted he take care of Isabelle's cut first, though.

They both wanted to argue since I was bleeding everywhere from multiple stab wounds, but one look had them both submitting to my demand. A bandage covers the thin cut on her neck now, which is why I've finally submitted to his attentions.

Basil is seated in the kitchen being doted on by Mrs. P with a fresh batch of croissants and tea as promised. Isabelle sits across from me, curled up in a chair, staring into the fire with a distant look in her eyes.

"You shouldn't have run after your father like that."

"You shouldn't have yelled at him and scared him off."

"Yeah, well. . .he needs to be controlled."

"He needs to be loved and taken care of."

"Enough," I growl at Lucien, pushing him away.

"They still need more cleaning and to be bandaged," Lucien points out.

I snort.

"I've got it," Isabelle says, rising and crossing to take Lucien's place.

He shoots her a thankful look before beating a hasty retreat and shutting the door behind him.

"Talk," I say brusquely.

Those big brown eyes lift to meet mine even as she grabs the disinfectant. "What's there to say? I'm Roman Valentine's cousin."

"And you didn't think to tell me? You didn't think to disclose that you are the cousin to the leader of the Wolf gang?"

Again, how this got by me and my people is mind boggling. We did thorough background checks, even learned how Isabelle took her tea, but we missed this?

Her lips thin. "I didn't think it mattered."

"Of course it matters." My words start as a snarl but

turn into a yelp as the sting of the antiseptic hits with a little too much pressure from her cloth.

"You lied."

"I didn't lie, I. . ." She pauses. "I dissociated. It's kind of my thing." Isabelle's mouth parts then closes. "Sorry." I'm not sure what she's apologizing for. Not disclosing her relations or for being too rough with me.

"We did background on you. You didn't have any other family other than your father."

Isabelle nods, still not meeting my eye. "I worked very hard to make it like that. And I had some. . .help."

Without even saying a word, I know she means Rap. The woman is formidable. I caught that from the first.

I don't fill in the rolling silence between us as she bandages me. Despite every fiber of my being shouting to shake her by the shoulders until she tells me everything, I wait. To explain how this could have happened. Whose fault it is and whose blood should be spilled over it.

Finishing up, she stands back and walks over to the lit fireplace with a heavy sigh. "The Wolves. . ." She starts and then stops as if struggling with what to say next. "It's a family business. My uncle ran it, his father before that, and now my cousin." A knuckle taps the bottom of her chin as she stares at the fire. "My father worked as their potions man. He's brilliant, or. . .he was. I don't think my dad ever thought much about the consequences of putting hexes or curses on the street. It was never about hurting anyone with him. He's a deep intellectual with a hyperfixation. His first loves in life are chemistry and magic." She shoots me a lopsided smile. "But I'm a close second."

Something in my chest squeezes.

"My uncle let him have a lot of leeway with what he wanted to work on, but when my uncle died of a heart attack, my cousin Roman took over. Roman had an agenda. And he pushed that on my dad. A new Thorn. Something special, something terrible. Before you ask, I don't know what it was for. I was in college when I got the call. My dad had ingested a Thorn, and it fractured his mind. He basically poisoned himself, and to this day, I have no idea if he drank it voluntarily or if Roman stood over him and forced his hand. Either way, my bastard cousin was responsible for my father being under too much pressure. That was the day I decided to cut ties. A family that uses and experiments on their own like lab rats isn't a family at all. I went to Roman and told him in no uncertain terms my father and I were out. That we want nothing to do with the Wolves or the family. No more birthdays, Christmas gatherings or Sunday night dinners."

A low growl builds in my throat, but I choke it back, my claws digging into my thighs to keep myself grounded.

Roman Valentine.

That name is already poison, already tied to the chaos I've been cleaning up for years. And now it's tied to Isabelle.

I rake a hand through my hair, the firelight catching on the tips of my claws. My voice comes out low, a rough growl. "He simply let you go?"

Her shrug is nonchalant, but there's a tension in her frame that betrays the effort it took to say those words. "His top alchemist had destroyed his own brain, and I served no useful purpose to the family business. I'd never been interested in pursuing a place there and had gone away to college." She pauses, her eyes drifting toward the door as if she can see her father resting in the other room. "If I'm being honest, I think Roman felt guilty."

Her words don't soothe the rage coiling in my chest. Guilt. Roman Valentine and guilt are two concepts I can't reconcile. Not when he's flooding the city with hexes that leave nothing but destruction in their wake.

"My father is not a bad man," she says quietly, but the conviction in her tone makes it feel like a challenge. "He made hexes and curses for the family, but it was never about the effects of the potions. He loved the work itself. He's brilliant. And if he'd been tasked with curing a disease instead, he would've been just as devoted. But the family you're born into has a gravitational pull that can be impossible to get away from."

Her words hang in the air, but my gaze stays fixed on her. The way her shoulders slump under the weight of everything she's carried. The quiet pain she exudes as she defends her father, even knowing the damage he's caused.

I can't stop myself. "And you think I'm terrible for dealing Thorns?"

She simply sighs, covering her face. "It doesn't matter."

"Of course it matters." This situation is so interwoven, it's a fucking bag of witchtits.

"You could have said no."

Her irritation flares, a flush creeping up her neck as she rises to her feet. "You mean condemn my father to death instead of marrying you? No." The words are clipped, her temper simmering just beneath the surface. "My family, or what's left of it, is the most important thing to me."

The Wolves aren't her family, she insists. She practically vibrates with frustration as she repeats it, as if saying it enough times will make it true.

"Family doesn't use you for their own gain," she says firmly, crossing her arms.

My gaze narrows. "Sure they do," I counter. "They use you for validation. For support. For love."

She glares at me, her fingers raking through her hair.

"Not my idea of family. Maybe it's all those books I read, but I somehow got it in my head that family shouldn't treat their own like trash."

Her words slice through the space between us, but I hold my ground. "I'm not like the Wolves, Isabelle."

"I don't want to talk about this." She starts toward the door, but I step directly in her way.

"They're releasing hexes and curses into circulation with no antidote. My Thorns always have one."

She scoffs, her frustration boiling over. "Are you trying to tell me this makes you better? If so, I really don't want to hear it."

The air between us crackles with tension as I tower over her, forcing her to meet my gaze.

"I'm not saying I'm a good man, Isabelle," I continue, my voice dropping into a quiet, dangerous cadence. Her scent, warm and uniquely hers, mixes with the faint burn of the fire, grounding me in the moment even as the confession burns on my tongue. "But I'm not like them. You probably think I'm just another version of Roman—a man profiting off misery, playing god with people's lives. But you'd be wrong."

My wife's silence doesn't unsettle me. I know she's taking this in, processing every word. It's written in the way her arms cross defensively, the way her breath catches but doesn't falter.

"Enlighten me, then," she snaps. "How are you different?" She straightens, lifting her chin in a challenge that I can't help but admire.

The corner of my mouth twitches, but it's not amusement that stirs in me—it's the razor-thin line between fury and desire. "Because, like I've told you, I don't let chaos run wild," I say, the words slipping between clenched teeth. I step even closer, our faces mere inches apart. "I don't release destruction without control. Every Thorn I sell comes with an antidote. Every curse I create has a counter-measure. The Wolves? They don't care who their hexes hurt or how many lives they destroy. They'd flood the streets with poison and sit back, counting their money while the city burns."

Her glare sharpens, and the firelight dances in her eyes, making them flash with defiance. "That doesn't make you a saint. You're still profiting off pain."

I've heard those words before—felt their sting—but not from her. Somehow, from her, they cut deeper. My jaw tightens, and I feel the muscles in my temple tick as I force myself to keep my tone steady. "I never said I was a saint. I'm not here to save the world, Isabelle. But if there's going to be blood spilled, I make damn sure it's not without reason. This world is a battlefield, and if someone's going to arm themselves, I make sure they know the cost. I provide the weapon, but I also provide the cure."

She's shaking her head before I even finish, her frustration rolling off her in waves. "That's just a justification."

"It's survival." My volume rises with an edge I can't hold back. My hands clench at my sides as I step closer again, invading her space because I can't stand the distance, not when she's standing there like a storm I can't control. "You don't survive in this world without getting your hands dirty. You should know that better than anyone, considering where you came from."

Her flinch is subtle, but I catch it. My words land harder than I intended, and something in me twists as I see the flicker of pain in her eyes. For a moment, I soften. "I'm not like your cousin."

The silence stretches between us, her attention flickering away before she looks back, her lips parting as if she's searching for the right words.

"I don't *use* my people," I press on, my tone quiet but fierce. "My business is ugly, yes, but it's controlled. I deal in shadows, but I don't let the darkness consume everything. And whether you like it or not, Isabelle, that makes me better than the Wolves."

She doesn't answer right away, her arms tightening around her as she holds my stare. The tension between us thickens, the weight of my confession hanging in the air like a storm cloud. Her doubt is tangible, but so is her reluctance to outright condemn me. She doesn't want to admit it, but there's truth in what I'm saying.

"You're mine," My words are a dangerous whisper. "And I protect what's mine. Always."

The fire crackles, filling the silence that stretches between us, but my focus is entirely on her. The bandage covering the slice on her neck, draws my attention like a beacon. The memory of it—her blood, her injury—ignites something primal in me.

"That cut," I growl, my hand rising but stopping just short of touching her. My claws curl as I fight the urge to trace the line, to erase the evidence of her pain. "That shouldn't be there. It should never have happened."

I grip the edge of the desk instead, my claws biting into the wood as the fury courses through me. "You shouldn't have gone after him. Running into the night, putting yourself in their hands. . .Do you know what it did to me, seeing you like that? Knowing I might not get to you in time?"

Her eyes widen, startled by the force of my words, but she doesn't retreat. "I had to—" she begins.

"You didn't," I cut her off, stepping even closer until my shadow engulfs her. "I don't care what you think your duty is, Isabelle. You don't risk yourself like that. Not for anyone."

I don't give her time to respond. My hands find her hips, pulling her to me with a force that's as much desperation as it is control. She's mine—*my wife*—and I'll be damned if I let anyone take her from me.

Her breath hitches as my mouth claims hers, my kiss searing, bruising, a brand that stakes my claim as much as it releases the fury inside me. My hands tighten on her hips, lifting her onto the desk effortlessly as I step between her legs, crowding her with the intensity of my presence.

"This isn't about love," I growl against her lips, my breath ragged. "This is about what's mine."

"Okay," she breathes.

CHAPTER 28
A WOLF IN BELLE'S CLOTHING

BELLE

The room seems to hold its breath in the silence that follows, the crackle of the fire the only sound as he pulls back just enough to look at me. His mismatched eyes search mine, fierce and unyielding, and for a moment, I see it—the raw vulnerability beneath the layers of control and fury.

And then he moves, his hands sliding up my thighs, his touch firm and deliberate. My heart leaps, my breath hitching as anticipation coils low in my belly, but there's no hesitation in his movements, no second-guessing as he pulls my shirt off, then my bra. Soon I'm without clothes, laying on the couch warmed by the dancing firelight.

I groan and tug at his clothes until he divests them as well.

"I won't let anything happen to you," he murmurs, his voice softer now, though no less intense, as he covers my body on the couch "Not ever."

When his lips capture mine once more, I realize there's no place I'd rather be—no one else I'd trust to hold me, claim me, protect me. Dominic Blackwell may be a monster, but in this moment, he's my monster.

Though it's hard to nod as he pistons two fingers inside me, putting me in a frenzy. My stomach tightens, rising up higher, higher to new heights.

"You are a Blackwell now. My wife. And anyone who so much as looks at you wrong. . ." He loses his voice as if overcome by a sudden bout of violence that has robbed him of words. "I'll fucking rip out their throat and feed it to them, Isabelle. I'll fucking do anything for you. I'll make the world bow at your feet."

I open my mouth to reply, but it's a wail that escapes me as my inner muscles clamp down and my hips buck, my orgasm hitting me full force. I scrabble at the couch and dig my fingers in Dominic's hair.

Then his fingers are replaced by a long, dexterous tongue licking as his fingers move to rubbing hard and fast along my clit. I choke and then scream as a second intense orgasm somehow collides with the first.

"That's it. Come for me, Isabelle. You taste so fucking good." My body and brain spin and time blurs and constricts before releasing.

When I finally catch my breath, I vaguely hear the unmistakable sound of a zipper being released. "I can't fucking wait any longer," he growls, agony tightening the words.

Anticipation sends my heart shooting up to lodge in my throat. He covers my body with his, and his hardness nudges at my wet, still quivering sex.

I grab his shoulders, holding on even as he pushes up without warning. A yelp escapes me as he fills me. Dominic freezes.

"Don't stop," I practically sob, as I rock my hips trying

to get him further in. It's too much, but my body aches for more. "Please. Please, Dominic."

A strangled sound escapes him as he continues to slide in but at a slower rate. My back arches and I throw my head back. "Ah, oh fae lords. It's so good." His length is deliciously different from any normal man's, and I don't think I'll ever get enough of it. If he hadn't just brought me to a frenzy of several orgasms I might be crying in pain but my body is desperate for him. I am desperate for him if I'm being honest.

Dominic rocks gently but insistently, his teeth bared, eyes flashing.

Dominic's claws dig into my thighs as he pulls me impossibly closer, pushing my knees up to better drive into me. His breath is ragged and hot against my ear. "You're mine, Isabelle." His words vibrate through my entire body. "This body is mine to touch, to taste, to fuck. No one else will ever have you. No one else deserves to."

I should bristle at the possessiveness in his tone, at the way he speaks as though I'm his property. But his voice drips with a dark hunger that stirs something deep inside me, something I can't deny no matter how much I want to.

I matter to him. My absence would cause him pain. Even my bare nick of a wound outraged him. And fae lords help me it hits me on a visceral level I didn't even know was possible.

His fingers find my clit again, circling it with a relentless precision that has me crying out, my body arching against his.

"These sounds," he murmurs, his lips brushing my jaw. "These are mine too. All of them. Every gasp, every moan. Every time you come, it's for me."

"Dominic," I pant, my nails clawing at his back,

desperate to ground myself against the tidal wave of sensation he's unleashing.

"Say it," he commands, his voice rough. His free hand cups my breast through the thin fabric of my lingerie, squeezing possessively. "Say you're mine."

"I'm yours," I gasp, the words spilling from my lips unbidden. "Gods, I'm yours, Dominic."

He groans in satisfaction, his hand sliding to grip my hip with bruising force as he thrusts into me again, the ridges of his length dragging against my inner walls in a way that has me spiraling toward another climax.

Then he claims my mouth like he has my body. I'm drowning. The way our tongues meet and dance only pushes my desire higher and tighter.

The couch beneath us creaks under his sheer size, the strain of his movements making the frame groan ominously. Dominic snarls low in his throat, pulling out just long enough to scoop me up as though I weigh nothing. His lips crash against mine, feral and demanding, as he lowers us to the floor. The plush rug cushions my back, but the heat of his body consumes me entirely.

"This is better," he mutters against my mouth, his hands gripping my thighs again to spread me wide beneath him. His green eyes burn with a dark intensity as he looks down at me, his expression one of raw, unbridled need. "Now I can fuck you like you deserve to be fucked."

A shiver runs through me at the vulgar promise in his words, and I realize with startling clarity that I don't care about his possessiveness. I don't care if he treats me like his to use, to claim, to ruin. If he keeps touching me like this, if he keeps looking at me like I'm the only thing he wants in the world, I'll gladly let him.

He rises to his knees, holding mine up to my shoulders. "You'll take everything I give you. Because you're mine. And I don't share," he growls, pounding into me again and again at an angle that makes my brain fuzz over. The barbs glide and grate in a manner that has me panting and sweating. "Each orgasm I force out of you is me staking my claim, Isabelle. Each shuddering pussy melting orgasm is my imprint on you and you will take them until I've drilled into the marrow of your bones."

The pressure builds impossibly high and I cry out, the sensation shattering me completely. Another orgasm rips through me, leaving me trembling and gasping beneath him.

Dominic doesn't stop. "You're going to take all of me, Isabelle," he murmurs, his voice rough with barely restrained control. "Every inch. Every fucking ridge. You're going to feel me for days."

"Fuck," he groans, his forehead dropping to mine. "You feel so perfect. So tight. Like you were made for me."

I whimper in response, the sensation of him so deep inside me overwhelming. He doesn't give me time to adjust, his hips pulling back only to slam forward again with a force that steals my breath.

"Mine," he growls, his pace punishing and relentless. "This cunt is mine. This body is mine. Every fucking part of you belongs to me."

"Dominic," I cry out, my nails raking down his back as he pounds into me, the heat and friction building again with every thrust. The air is thick with the scent of sex and sweat, the sound of skin slapping against skin filling the room.

His teeth graze the curve of my shoulder, his breath hot

against my skin. "You know what Weres do when they claim what's theirs, don't you?" he murmurs, his voice low and teasing despite the ferocity of his movements.

"Dominic," I gasp, the thought sending a fresh wave of heat through me.

He chuckles darkly, his tongue flicking out to trace the curve of my throat.

The pressure inside me builds to an impossible peak.

Suddenly I need it. I need him to bite me so desperately I'll lose my mind if he doesn't.

I cry out, unable to articulate my true needs.

Fangs sink into the top of my breast. Heat spikes and sears straight to where we are joined.

I shatter completely. My climax rips through me, dragging him over the edge with me. His roar fills the room as he spills inside me, his body trembling with the force of his release.

Dominic shudders above me, his release spilling into me, and the heat of it sends a final shiver of pleasure through my body. He collapses onto his forearms, careful not to crush me, his breath hot and ragged against my neck.

The world fades, the intensity of the moment leaving me utterly spent. Dominic's weight presses down on me, grounding me, his breath warm against my neck as we lay tangled together on the floor.

For a long moment, there's only silence, broken by the sound of our ragged breathing. His hand brushes over my hair, his touch surprisingly gentle as he cradles me against him.

"You're mine," he murmurs again, his voice soft now but no less possessive.

And for the first time, I realize I don't mind.

As the tremors of release subside, I expect Dominic to retreat. It's what he does—builds walls as quickly as he lets them down, pulls away just when I think I might be able to reach him. I brace myself for that familiar ache, for the cold distance to settle in.

But this time, he doesn't pull away.

His weight shifts, and I feel the ripple of tension in his body, but instead of letting go, he cups my face in his large hands. His mismatched eyes lock onto mine, their intensity piercing through the haze of exhaustion. For a moment, he looks torn, his jaw tight with unspoken words.

"Come to bed with me," he says finally. "I can't stand being apart from you."

Before I can respond, he scoops me into his arms. The firelight flickers across his face as he carries me effortlessly out of the library, the heat of his naked body seeping into mine. I don't question him, too stunned by the change in him, by the vulnerability I can feel radiating off him in waves.

The journey to his bedroom is a blur, the dim light of the hallway casting long shadows. When we cross the threshold, the space feels intimate and private. The room is bathed in silvery moonlight, its simplicity a stark contrast to the intensity of the man who sets me down on the edge of the massive bed.

His hands linger on my hips as he steps back, his gaze raking over me as though committing every inch of me to memory. "I almost lost you," he says, his voice rough with emotion.

"Dominic. . ." I whisper, but it seems to anchor him, pulling his attention back to me.

He shakes his head, a flicker of frustration crossing his

face. "No, Isabelle. I've spent so long keeping you at arm's length, convincing myself it was for your own good. That if I kept the monster in me caged, I'd somehow protect you from what I am. But tonight—seeing you, hearing you—I can't do it anymore."

His words hang in the air, and I can feel the weight of his confession pressing against my chest. Before I can find the words to respond, he lowers himself onto his knees before me, his hands sliding up my thighs with deliberate slowness.

"I'm not letting you go," he murmurs, his lips brushing the inside of my knee. "Not now. Not ever. I lied to you when I told you why you were perfect."

I open my mouth, but he goes on. "You were unattached, all alone except for your father, someone who might not be so disgusted or fearful of my form based on your reading material, but the truth is—" His words break off as if it's a struggle to keep going. "The truth is," he says, finding the words he needs. "Since I saw that picture of you on your website, I wanted you." His claw caresses my jawline, and suddenly it's hard to focus on him, my eyes have gone blurry with unshed tears. "I wanted this to be methodical, easily compartmentalized, but you are so much more than anything I could have planned on. I'm obsessed with you." The last words are a pained hiss through his teeth.

He pushes me back onto the bed, his body following as he settles between my legs. The intensity in his gaze steals my breath, and when he leans down to claim my mouth, there's nothing hesitant or reserved about it. His kiss is deep, consuming, a promise that he's done holding back.

This time, there's no rush, no frantic edge. Every touch, every kiss feels like a vow, like he's making up for every moment he's kept himself from me. His hands explore my body with a reverence that sends shivers racing across my skin, his lips trailing fire down my neck and shoulders.

The world narrows to the heat of his body, the steady rhythm of his movements as he claims me again, and the quiet, whispered promises that slip from his lips like prayers. When we both shatter, it's not just physical—it's something deeper, something that leaves me trembling in his arms.

He doesn't let me go. As the haze of pleasure fades, Dominic gathers me against his chest, pulling the covers over us. His hand trails through my hair, soothing and steady, as though grounding himself in my presence.

My body feels wrecked, branded. And somewhere in the haze, a thought unfurls like a seed planted deep—a baby with Dominic's green eyes curled against my chest, my voice lulling them to sleep with bedtime stories. A tiny hand gripping my finger, impossibly small but wholly ours.

My throat tightens, my fingers flexing against his skin as the longing takes root.

"I've been a coward," he admits quietly, his voice raw. "Pushing you away, pretending I could keep you safe by keeping you at a distance. But I can't anymore. I won't."

My throat tightens at the vulnerability in his tone, and I press a hand to his chest, feeling the steady thrum of his heartbeat beneath my palm. "Okay."

His arms tighten around me, his breath warm against my temple. "I mean it, Isabelle. You're mine. And I'll spend the rest of my life proving to you that you're safe with me."

The words sink into me, filling spaces I didn't know were hollow. Dominic isn't just holding me—he's letting me in.

As sleep pulls me under, the warmth of his body and

the steady rhythm of his breathing lulls me into a peace I haven't felt in years. And for the first time, I let myself believe that maybe, just maybe, Dominic Blackwell isn't just a monster.

He's *my* monster.

CHAPTER 29

A SHAKESPEAREAN KIND OF REVENGE

THE BEAST OF BOSTON

The air reeks of salt and gasoline, heavy with the promise of a storm. Rain drizzles steadily from a gray sky, coating the snow-covered docks in a thin sheen of ice. The murky waters of Boston Harbor lap at the pylons below, their rhythmic slap the only sound aside from the low rumble of a distant boat engine.

I stand with Tock and Lucien at my back, my claws twitching at my sides.

It was mere hours after the encounter with the Wolves in the alleyway that we received a message. A request to meet. On neutral territory of course.

I don't like it, but I did kill one of their people. And married their leader's cousin, though that was unbeknownst to me.

Tossing a quick look to the car where Isabelle sits in safety, I can't help but think how I don't like this. I don't like it one bit.

But circumstances demand a meeting.

Roman's men emerge from the fog, their silhouettes sharp against the horizon. At least six of them, but my focus narrows on the figure leading the pack, his stride loose and cocky. Roman Valentine.

Behind him is another man. Tall, lanky, and dressed too clean for the docks, his slicked-back blond hair and tailored coat stand out against the gray.

"Dominic," Roman greets, his grin wide and wolfish. "I almost thought you wouldn't show." His features are sharp, his nose beak-like under a pair of beady, constantly assessing eyes. I search for the resemblance between him and Isabelle but I find none.

Despite the cloudy day, I've relegated myself to the only kind of cover I could find. I keep to the long shadow cast by the building behind us.

I don't respond. Silence unsettles men like him more than words.

Roman is nothing more than a child, poking me with a stick.

Roman chuckles, a low, grating sound that puts my teeth on edge. "No need to be aloof and silent, I know all about the Beast of Boston now. Hiding in the shadows there, my guy, isn't going to change a thing. I know your dirty secret."

I pause, not because I'm surprised or put off, but because I don't care to take one step closer to this man's proximity.

"Isn't this a funny situation? For a long time now, I've been wanting to meet the Beast of Boston face to face, man to—well. . ." He trails off with a smirk.

Lucien shifts behind me. I flex my hand, a signal for the enforcer to hold though I know he'd gladly set every last one of these bastards on fire.

Roman's insults slide off me like the rain. Let him think he has the upper hand. The truth is I've already won. I own this city, among others. I possess the power he so hungrily seeks. And more than that, I possess Isabelle. His flesh and blood.

"And now that we are finally meeting, I find out we're practically family." Roman claps his hands then opens his arms wide, as if he's welcoming me as a brother.

"I assume this meeting is in regards to the Wolf I killed," I say, my voice steady, even. "You should have trained them better."

Roman's grin falters, but he recovers quickly, tilting his head like he's sizing me up. Dark bangs fall into his eyes. There is something about the way he drinks in my half-shifted face that is different from most. There is a hungry kind of fascination flickering in his dark eyes. Then whatever he's thinking is chased away by his false devil-may-care attitude.

"On any other day, killing one of my soldiers might have started a war between us," he rubs his chin with exaggerated thoughtfulness. "But no, I didn't drag myself out here just to scold you for taking out one of my pups. She was out of line." The last sentence snaps out with true disdain.

I wonder if it's because he doesn't approve of his cousin being collateral damage or because she didn't listen to her superior, who tried to call her off. Roman has rules about the chain of command in his crew. The Wolf alpha structure is taken quite seriously.

"No, I think you know why we are here," he says in that deceivingly light tone as he puts his hands in his coat and rocks forward on his feet. He cranes his neck and looks around. "Where is my dear cousin anyway?"

There's something about the taller blonde man who's been scanning the area, as if he's been specifically looking for my wife. It irks me more than even Roman's abrasive words.

I hoped his chattiness would carry on so we could leave Isabelle out of this, but Roman lays his flat gaze on me and waits.

The message is clear. We won't continue until we've dragged his cousin out onto the chopping block. I suppress another growl, which makes my nose wrinkle.

My left claw twitches.

Tock moves to open the back door of the black SUV. Isabelle steps out. The black coat sweeps down around her legs, the hood pulled up but not covering her features. In the dreary gray day, Isabelle's face brings a contrast of warmth and color. Her mahogany hair falls in those classic Hollywood waves. She's also lined her deep brown eyes in charcoal, which makes them luminous and add an edge of danger I never noticed about her.

I almost sense she is bringing an energy, a version of herself she had shelved—quite literally—and is accessing a part of her only her family can inspire.

Her expression is implacable, and for the first time I realize another predator has entered our midst. A quiet, patient predator who has no need to roar or slash claws to establish dominance. My wife exudes a quiet kind of power, the kind Roman could never understand because it's real, unassuming.

All the comments she's made about having to handle people more dangerous than me, being able to discern bark from bite all click into focus. This is the world she came from and managed quite well until she cut her and her father off from it entirely. Even that was done with expert precision.

A ripple of pride goes through me, and my slacks

tighten slightly against a sudden blooming arousal. I want to fuck her right here on this dock, show everyone she is mine. Set her back against the cold, damp wood slates and worship her in every way possible.

I force myself to look away and turn my attention back to Roman. I'm on edge enough as it is from the last twenty-four hours. It would take too little to unravel me, and I can't afford that right now.

Roman's eyes narrow as he focuses on the embroidered roses on Isabelle's coat. They are a brand, wrapped around what's mine. My wife. Just like the massive rose ring on her finger. This time a rumble of satisfaction ripples through me.

That's right, you bastard. Look at what you lost with your own stupidity.

"Hey there, Belly," he greets tightly with a smile that's too sharp. Though I detect some genuine distress, maybe even regret, pass over his eyes.

Belly? What kind of fucked up nickname is that? The need to claw his tongue out causes tension to shoot through each one of my fingers.

A soft, "Don't," hits my ears. It's firm but low enough that only I can hear Tock's warning to hold despite my rising ire. I hear the click of Lucien's lighter. He's also agitated by the nickname. My men have become quite attached to my wife, and it doesn't settle easy for her to be disrespected.

Isabelle gives her cousin an implacable nod back. "Roman."

Family dynamics are complicated and as old as time. Doesn't mean I have to like it.

Roman's second in command, the tall blond, is no longer warily eyeing my crew. He stares at my wife as if refamiliarizing himself with her. There is an eagerness, a hunger that sparks in his eyes I don't like.

After a few moments of his intense scrutiny, Isabelle meets his eye and gives him a curt nod. The second in command acknowledges her with a lazy, lopsided smile. It contains that patented Wolf arrogance but something more.

They know each other.

My chest tightens, heat licking up my spine. I don't know his name, but I instantly despise him.

"How you been?" Roman asks his cousin.

Isabelle doesn't even blink. "Good."

The dialogue is simple yet loaded with years of familial history.

"Married apparently," Roman says, his voice breaking a bit. A half-hinged laugh escapes him. "To the enemy." Then he breaks into full peals of laughter, bending over as his eyes water from the uncontrollable spasms of humor wracking him.

I meet Isabelle's gaze. She stands between both sides. The Wolves and the Roses. I lift my chin ever so slightly, a silent command. Or maybe it's a question. She's softened me so much in a matter of weeks that I'm treating her with a deference I've never given anyone before.

Something in her eye heats, then melts. She strides over to stand by my side. However, Isabelle positions herself just a step behind me. My heart swells and strains in my chest.

Roman's humor dries up like the Sahara.

The move is as overt as an earthquake. My little book lover understands power plays, and in that simple move she has reinforced, not only that she has chosen me over her cousin, but also that she trusts me to lead.

"I have to admit," Roman says, his face taut with

displeasure now. "I didn't see this coming. Marrying my cousin as an act of revenge. It's got a kind of poetry, I admit. This is some Shakespeare shit." A dry laugh comes out of him as he brushes his nose with his thumb.

Revenge?

Roman's minuscule kingdom is admittedly annoying, but it's certainly not damaging enough to my business to warrant anything even close to revenge. The little man thinks so very highly of himself.

Isabelle snorts. "Like you've ever read Shakespeare in your life, cousin."

The sharpness of her tone draws his attention, and for a moment, his mask slips. An ugly, power-hungry child lays under all his false ease.

Then he smiles, slow and oily. "Ah, cousin, always the wit. Tell me, does he treat you well? Or has he tortured you into submission? Taking from our family because we took his?"

"What are you talking about?" Isabelle asks, her words coming out stiff. She asks so I don't have to, but an icy tremor of something foreboding shivers up my spine. I feel Lucien and Tock tense behind me.

"Don't tell me you didn't know," Roman presses with that light laughter even as his attention volleys between the four of us, drinking in our tension. "Surely you took Isabelle because we were the ones who had your family killed."

His words drop like a bomb, echoing in the freezing air.

Time freezes the blood in my veins as my mind blanks.

Beside me, Isabelle sucks in a sharp breath. I stay perfectly still, my mind reeling. Then my vitals heat, and speed up. My blood rises to a simmer before it begins to boil in my veins, burning me from the inside out.

"Really?" Roman says, his tone shifting to incredulous amusement. "You didn't know? And here I thought this was some grand revenge plot. Marry my cousin, make her yours, then torture her, keep her, kill her eventually, perhaps. A beast of your wrath, I expected more. This feels so. . .calculated."

For a moment, the world narrows to just him. Roman Valentine. The pebble in my shoe. A man I completely underestimated.

This can't be right. It was anti-shifter zealots who burned down the building, who pumped my entire family with silver bullets. And I hunted each one and killed them all. Yet just as quickly, the puzzle pieces swirl in pandemonium before clicking rapidly into place.

One of them had screamed and cried as I went about ripping them from belly button to throat, that they were paid off. Hired to make the hit. I wrote it off as a desperate attempt to play me and stay among the living for at least a little while longer. I'd tasted their blood and was deaf to their claims, only hungry for their screams.

But Roman had been the architect of my family's demise. Of my current cursed state. Of agony and grief that will forever tear me inside and out. The torturous half-life I'm trapped in.

"Dominic?" Isabelle's voice reaches my ears, but I can't look at her. I can't move. If I do, I may see Roman in her face and be compelled to tear it off from her skull.

I shut my eyes, trying to get a grip, but behind my eyelids I only find the bloody bodies of my pack. Piles of them amidst the balloons and streamers. Lisette's bullet riddled body covering our younger cousin, her blue eyes turned up, sightless. A frozen expression of horror in the open "o" of her mouth.

"This meeting is over," I hear Tock say with tight, firm authority from some faraway place. The blood boils in my ears.

"See you soon, Beast of Boston." Roman's final words are full of awe.

We've both been surprised by this interlude.

I barely register the shuffle of retreating feet as the scent of Roman and his men fade.

"Dominic?" Isabelle calls to me.

I don't answer. I can't. My chest burns with a fury I haven't felt in years. The storm is coming, and I need to release the fire before it consumes me whole.

"Move away from him, *cher*," Lucien gives the command in a steely tone. "Slowly."

He knows what's about to happen.

The rage I've been holding back surges forward like a tidal wave. My fists clench, my claws extending fully as all my rage consumes my mind and body.

There is no one, nothing, but the storm howling for release.

And nothing can stop it.

GOING FERAL

BELLE

Dominic's claws glint like steel, fully extended. His breaths come in short, sharp growls. The space around him seems to darken, his rage a palpable force that ripples outward, heavier than the rain-soaked air.

Inside me, fear curls low and sharp, but it's not for myself. It's for him—this man, this beast, undone by the grief that my own flesh and blood is responsible for. My chest tightens, and the weight of what Roman revealed crushes me anew. My cousin murdered his family. I thought I knew the extent of pain my family could dish out, but this is different. This is more than grief-soaked resentment; it's a blade. And it's cutting me apart piece by piece.

"Move, *cher*," Lucien orders again, his body now angled protectively in front of me.

"No," I whisper, my voice thin but steady. I can't leave him like this.

I watch as his body trembles, the muscles under his shirt rippling unnaturally. His shoulders broaden, the fabric straining before tearing as if his skin itself is rebelling against him. His face contorts, a snarl revealing longer, sharper canines. He's not fully a lion, not wholly human—he's something monstrous and in between, and the sight of him sends an involuntary shiver down my spine.

Tock steps closer to me, his usually easy demeanor replaced with razor-sharp focus. "You don't understand, Belle. He's not human right now. He's barely Dominic. He's—"

"Feral," Lucien finishes grimly.

Dominic's head snaps toward the sound of his name, his green eyes blazing. They're not the warm, teasing shade that sometimes catches me off guard in the quiet moments when we're alone. No, these are sharp, more predator than man.

His growl reverberates through the air, low and guttural, and my pulse spikes. He can't hear Tock. He can't hear any of us. He's lost, consumed, and I can see that the enormity of his pain has swallowed him whole.

My family did this. Not to me this time, but to him. I knew they destroyed lives, twisted everything they touched, but to bring down someone like Dominic—to rob him of his family, his foundation—it's monstrous. Worse, I don't know how anyone survives that kind of loss.

Tock curses under his breath. "We need to get you out of here before—"

The moment Tock moves toward me, Dominic's head snaps toward him. His lips curl back in a feral snarl, revealing sharp, gleaming canines that are far too large for a human mouth.

He's magnificent and terrifying in the same breath, but it's the kind of terror that doesn't scare me. It hurts me. Every growl, every swipe of his claws—it's grief spilling out of him in the only way it can. I can't hate him for it, and I sure as hell can't leave him alone in it.

"Stop," I say sharply, surprising even myself. "Don't touch me." Dominic is possessive, controlling, and Tock touching me is just going to make things worse. Whether Dominic views me as something to claim or kill in this moment, it doesn't matter. I'm his.

"I'm not going to let him hurt you. It would kill him," Tock says.

My heart lodges its way into my throat. "No."

But Tock grabs for me.

Dominic lunges.

It happens so fast I barely register the blur of movement before Dominic slams into Tock, sending him sprawling into a stack of crates. The wood splinters on impact, the sound loud and sharp against the rain.

The violence of it is breathtaking, raw and unrestrained, but it's not blind. Not quite. He could have killed Tock with a single blow, but he didn't. That restraint—the shred of humanity still clinging to him—tightens something inside me. He's fighting it, even now.

My family didn't just take his pack away—they took his control, his sense of self. And now he's left with this: half man, half beast, his grief so consuming it's physically tearing him apart.

"*Merde,*" Lucien curses, stepping between me and Dominic as Tock groans from the ground, clutching his ribs. There's the click of his lighter, but then both his hands go up in flames. He holds them up in warning.

Holy witchtits, Lucien is a fire mage. And he's going to get himself killed.

"Dominic, stop," I yell, but my voice is swallowed by the next guttural growl that tears from his throat.

Lucien moves to intercept him, fire blazing from his fists, but Dominic swats him away like he's nothing more than an annoyance. There is a splash as Lucien stumbles right over the pier.

So much for fire.

But Tock is up and headed toward me even as he bleeds from his head.

"Don't!" I shout at everyone. My heart pounds as I raise my hands, palms out, trying to project calm even as my knees threaten to buckle.

Dominic's head swivels toward me, his nostrils flaring. His claws twitch again, scraping the air as his gaze locks on mine. His chest heaves, his breath coming in sharp, animalistic pants.

I can feel the rage radiating off him in waves, a heat that seeps into my skin and sets my nerves on edge. He's wild, a dangerous predator on the edge of losing control entirely.

"Dominic." I force my voice to stay steady despite the terror clawing at my insides. "It's me. It's Isabelle."

He growls, a sound that's more animal than human, his lips pulling back in a snarl. His claws flex, digging into the wood of the dock, and I swear I hear it groan under the pressure.

"You can't reach him, *cher*," Lucien warns, climbing up the side ladder of the pier, soaked to the bone. His voice is tight with pain. "Not like this. He's too far gone."

"I have to try," I whisper, the words trembling on my lips. Because if I don't, I'm no better than Roman. No better than the family I left behind for their ability to wreak this kind of havoc.

But it's not just about what my family has done. It's about what Dominic needs. Someone to face the fire with him, to hold steady when the world has burned to ash around him.

Dominic closes the distance, his movements slow and deliberate, like a predator stalking its prey. My breath catches as his massive frame towers over me, his claws twitching at his sides, his eyes locked on mine.

"Dominic," I whisper again.

His head tilts slightly as he stares at me. I think I've reached him.

Then his claws flash, slashing through the air, and I barely have time to duck before they rip through the space where I'd been standing.

"Move, Isabelle!" Lucien shouts, panicked.

"No," I snap, spinning to face him and Tock. "Stay back."

They hesitate, their instincts warring with their concern.

I turn back to Dominic, my heart pounding in my chest as I inch closer. His growl deepens, a warning that rumbles through the air, but I don't stop.

"You need this, don't you? You need to let it out."

His claws flex, his lips pull back in another snarl, but he doesn't move.

He's not just angry—he's drowning in his pain. And somehow, I have to be the lifeline.

I take a small step forward, my hands shaking but my resolve solid. He could kill me. I know that. But I also know he won't. Not because he can't—he's stronger, faster, more dangerous than anyone I've ever met. But because deep down, I know he still knows me.

"Take it out on me," I say, my words barely more than a whisper. "I can take it."

For a moment, he freezes, his eyes narrowing as he

stares at me. Then, with a growl that shakes the air around us, he moves.

He doesn't attack me, not exactly. His claws close around me, firm but not crushing, and he lifts me as if I weigh nothing. The world tilts as he bounds away, his massive form moving with a speed and grace that shouldn't be possible for something so large.

CHAPTER 31

ABSORBING THE PAIN

BELLE

All I can hear is the rushing wind and Dominic's ragged breaths. Ice cold rain drops drill into my exposed face until I turn into his chest, my fingers find his thick soft fur. His body is so hot as if it is radiating the heat of hell itself.

Wood splinters and cracks as Dominic slams his shoulder into the door of a boathouse, forcing it open with a ferocity that vibrates through my sternum. He doesn't pause to check the damage—just barrels inside and lets the warped door swing half-shut behind us.

Inside, the air is thick and damp, and the musty scent of salt and decay fills my nostrils. Shadows twist across the warped floorboards, thrown by the light broken through the single, jagged window. An overturned table lies in one corner, its rusted legs tangled with a rotted tarp. The remnants of some forgotten fishing gear—hooks, nets, a warped metal bucket—are scattered across the space.

Dominic drops me to my feet but doesn't let me go. His breath is hot and ragged against my skin. The tattered remains of his shirt cling to his shoulders, the fabric torn and stretched over his thick, rippling muscles. His eyes burn with feral intensity, and the growl rumbling in his throat is more animal than man.

"Take it out on me," I whisper again. "I'm yours, Dominic. Give it all to me. I can handle it." I reach up and slide my fingers into equal amounts of damp hair and fur.

His cheekbones seem sharper as if his human features can barely contain the animal beneath. The golden-green glow of his eyes pierces me, and I can't look away from the raw, feral beauty of him.

A growl rumbles, reverberating through the space like thunder. His lips curl back, exposing those too-sharp canines, and for a moment, I brace myself for pain. Instead, his mouth crashes into mine, the kiss a collision of teeth and tongues, raw and desperate.

Dominic's claws tear at my coat, ripping through the embroidered fabric as if it were paper. The sound of tearing cloth echoes in the empty space, and the coat falls in pieces around me.

His claws hook under the hem of my sweater dress, dragging it up over my thighs in one rough motion. The damp chill of the boathouse prickles over my skin, but it's swallowed by the blistering heat radiating from his body. He doesn't hesitate, shredding my leggings and panties in a flurry of impatient swipes. The fabric falls away in tatters, leaving me exposed to his gaze.

And I want this. Fae lords help me, I *want this*.

It's fitting, isn't it? For him to take his pound of flesh from me. My family took everything from him—his loved ones, his sense of self, his peace. I don't deserve to escape unscathed, and some part of me doesn't want to. Maybe it's because I *like* it. The bruises he'll leave, the bite marks, the pain—they'll mark me as his. And maybe, just maybe, it means I'm more like Roman than I want to admit. That thought twists inside me, ugly and thrilling all at once.

Every scrape of his claws against my skin, is another piece of the agony he's shedding. He's using me to pour his grief into, to carve out the weight that's crushing him. And I welcome it. I deserve it. For what my family took from him. For what I am to him. I don't know how or why I can take it all, but I was made for this. For him.

The tattered remnants of his shirt hang from his shoulders, and he rips it away with a single swipe of his claws, revealing every ridge and ripple of his broad chest. The buttons of his pants strain against his arousal, but he doesn't bother with finesse—just yanks at the waistband until it gives, the fabric falling to the floor alongside my ruined clothes.

The fur running down his forearms catches the fractured light from the window, each strand glistening like spun gold. His claws flex, black and gleaming, almost elegant if not for the destruction they're capable of. His body is massive, so much bigger than mine, every muscle corded with tension that makes my breath catch in awe and fear.

The floorboards creak as he backs me against a wall, his massive frame pressing into mine. Splinters bite into my shoulders, but I barely notice. His claws grip my hips, hard enough to bruise, and his mouth drops to my neck, his fangs scraping over my skin.

His urgency should scare me. It should turn me off, but I find myself panting and ready. I want him. I always want him. The animal side of him thrills me even though it shouldn't.

I push off the remains of my coat and pull my dress over my head. As soon as my skin is bared, Dominic lets out a roar of victory before he drops his head. Fangs sink into my shoulder, breaking skin. My nipples wrench up into painfully tight buds as liquid lava melts at the apex of my thighs. An unlikely flood of endorphins rushes to the spot where he's biting me, but he keeps it shallow. He's not there to render flesh away from bone, he's penetrating me, marking me, lodging himself in where no one else is allowed.

His cock is monstrous—thick, ridged, and barbed like the predator he is. It glistens in the low light, and my mouth goes dry at the sight of it, every instinct screaming that I should fear him. But I don't. I ache for him.

There's no warning when he thrusts into me, a single, brutal stroke that has me crying out. The stretch is overwhelming, the ridges along his shaft dragging against my inner walls in a way that steals the breath from my lungs. My nails dig into his bare shoulders, the pain grounding me as he claims me in every possible way.

"Dominic," I gasp, my voice cracking. Each thrust sends pleasure and pain crashing through me, the two indistinguishable from each other. His growls mix with my cries, the sound of skin slapping against skin echoing in the small, abandoned space.

His claws grip my thighs, bruising, biting into my flesh as he pulls me closer. My back scrapes against the wall, and my head knocks against the wooden boards behind me, but I don't care. I was *made for this*.

For him.

It might make me sick in the head, but no one else could take this. No one else would let him be this unrestrained. And no one else would revel in it the way I do.

He pulls me away from the wall, spinning us until my back hits the cold, splintered surface of the overturned table. The wood creaks under our weight, but Dominic doesn't pause. He spreads me wide as he drives into me so hard stars explode in my vision.

When I glance down, I see it—his cock sliding into me, glistening with my arousal and smeared with streaks of red. It's obscene, beautiful, terrifying, and I love it. I love the way he fills me, the way he breaks me open and puts me back together all at once.

"Mine," he snarls, his teeth grazing the curve of my neck. His movements grow faster, more frantic, his breath hot and heavy against my skin.

"Yes," I whisper, my voice quaking. "Yours."

His teeth find the top of my breast this time. My body arches into him, and I let go of everything—my shame, my guilt, my fear. I am a vessel for his rage, his sorrow, his grief. Every bite, every brutal thrust, feels like it's carving pieces out of me, but I don't break. I absorb it, revel in it, because the harder he pushes, the more I feel like I'm anchoring him, pulling him back from the abyss.

I become something else, someone else. Not a benevolent goddess, but a maelstrom, a force of nature built to take him, to match him blow for blow, thrust for thrust.

His claws dig into my hips, anchoring me as he drives me higher, his movements growing faster, more erratic. I feel the grief radiating off him with every rough motion, every growl. He's not just claiming me—he's punishing me, purging his rage and sorrow in a storm that leaves no part of me untouched. The pain is sharp, radiant, and I rise to meet it, to meet him, because if this is what he needs to survive, I'll give it to him. Every broken piece of him can shatter me, and I'll take it willingly.

I'm lost to him, to this. To the overwhelming force of him. My body is his to claim, his to use, and I give it willingly, meeting each of his thrusts with a desperate hunger of my own.

He roars as he finds his release, his body shuddering against mine as he fills me completely. I shatter with him. My eyes fly wide though I am sightless. The pleasure is blinding, searing through every nerve, every inch of me, until I'm nothing but sensation and sound.

Dominic pulls out of my body and a whine of disappointment escapes me. The room swims, the weightlessness of my head makes it difficult to think.

But he's not done. Dominic drops to his knees, dragging me down with him until my back hits the floorboards. His mouth is on me before I can catch my breath, his tongue lapping at my folds, lapping at our mingled desire with a desperation that borders on madness.

Pain blooms under where his fingers grip my thighs and I know there will be bruises later. I don't care. I buck, chasing the pleasure he's pulling from me with every flick of his tongue, every rough suck.

I moan his name over and over, knowing he needs to hear it.

Even as he pushes me to orgasm two more times, until the shake in my thigh travels up and out to rock my entire body, Dominic never lets up.

It's not enough. It will never be enough.

When he flips me onto my stomach, pressing my chest into the table and dragging me back onto him, I scream his name. Wet wood and splinters bite into my skin as he pushes his hard dick into my softened, greedy center. The air pounds out of me with every stroke, my body pliant, greedy for him.

He hits deeper than before, driving my mind straight out the top of my head. When he finally explodes again, I'm incoherent, tears streaming down my face from the pleasure and pain he's wrung out of my body.

For a long moment, there's nothing but the sound of our ragged breaths and the rain pounding against the roof. His body trembles against mine, his claws still biting into my hips, his teeth grazing my shoulder as he struggles to come back to himself.

His breaths are shaky now, less animal, more human, and I feel his grief softening into something quieter, something broken. The violence he poured into me wasn't just rage—it was release, a purging of everything that's been rotting inside him. I can still feel the imprint of his teeth, the burn of his claws, and I know that I've taken it. I've taken his pain, his punishment, and given him a moment of peace.

A fierce stinging attacks the back of my eyes as I can't help but think my cousin is right. This twisted, fucked up situation does feel like a Shakespearean tragedy. A tear leaks out of my eye, trailing hotly down my cheek as I try not to think of myself as a Capulet and Dominic as a Montague, both of us destined to die horribly.

CHAPTER 32

WOLF IN THE LION'S DEN

THE BEAST OF BOSTON

Isabelle doesn't wake when I get up and go outside to call Tock.

"Send a car back to the docks, use my GPS location."

"Is she alright?" Tock's voice is tense, disapproving, and conflicted as he asks after Isabelle's wellbeing.

He's seen me rip the heads off of those who have betrayed or inconvenienced me, and his loyalty has always been unwavering, until this moment.

Tock's fealty goes to my wife first now. Disgust rises in me.

Despite the fact that her family is the one that slaughtered mine. Tock wants to know if *she's* okay.

"She's fine. Send the car," I practically spit in the phone before hanging up so hard the phone crunches in my human hand.

Everything hurts, in some of the old ways and some new. I furiously fucked my wife until my body was sore yet depleted. The old grief that has haunted me has torn me open anew in a bloody wash of violence that makes it hard to think or see straight.

Standing naked on the dock in the rolling cold of sunrise, I plant my feet more firmly into the wet wood underneath me.

I don't want to go back inside. I don't want to look at the wolf in my den.

She didn't kill your family. Isabelle shunned and denied them. She wasn't even with them when your family was killed.

Because of my exhausted state, logic gets its chance to make its case.

Still, it doesn't erase the rage, the insanity of choosing this woman as my wife. Perhaps someone would call it some kind of poetic fucking irony. But all I can think yet again is that I must have karmically brought down this hell on myself somehow.

My keen senses pick up the hum of an engine, the approach of a car. It's still a distance away but I need to go back inside and get Isabelle.

The anvil in my chest grows heavier.

I can't be with her. Not anymore. Not after this. I close my eyes, resolving that I don't give a fuck if I don't create a pack again. I don't care if my half-shifted state kills me anymore. The only thing I need to do before I die is take out the Wolves. They will all die painful, bloody deaths, and then afterward I can lay down too and join my family. There's nothing else for me but vengeance.

The freezing air only turns my internal calm even colder and more resolute.

I'm done with Isabelle, and I plan to send her away. Far away. I have the ability to move her bookstore across the country, or maybe even to one of the fae realms. All I know is I never want to see her again after today.

Because seeing her will always be a reminder of what her family has done to mine. Of finding my mother crumpled on the dance floor in a pool of blood. Of my father, who was barely recognizable. As if they had targeted him specifically or maybe stood over his already dead corpse continuing to release rounds of bullets into his body and face to make a point, or just for the fun of it. *Of Lisette.*

I walk back inside the shack and find Isabelle still sleeping on the floor. One of us must have found some blankets in the night, I'm not sure who, and she is wrapped up in them though they don't cover her body entirely.

In the cold, dark shack, she is yet again a spot of color and warmth. Her mahogany hair rolls over her outstretched arm. I expect to feel disgust when I set my eyes upon her, but shock slices through it all.

Isabelle's body is a map of my wrath. Purple, red, even some yellow and green has bloomed over her arms, her shoulders, her breasts. They intersect or are interrupted by teeth marks that are caked with blood. I bit her breasts, her neck, and though the blanket covers it, I know I sunk my jaws into her inner thighs and along her back as I fucked her over and over again. Even at her hairline, sweat and blood has dried.

My once cold resolve sloshes in a twisting spire of nausea.

I took out all my pain, all my anger and grief on my wife's body, and she took it. She welcomed it.

Give it to me. I can handle all of it.

Her words were sincere and full of compassion.

I want to look away, but I refuse to allow myself to. I was an absolute animal to her. But then again. . .so was she.

She never once said stop. Not that I'm sure I would have been able to control myself and abide by such a request.

The thought sickens me. But Isabelle begged for more, screamed my name in pleasure until she was hoarse. I touch my abs where she grazed thin red lines across my flesh. I run the pads of my fingers over my shoulder. She bit into me too, muffling her screams, marking me like I do to her.

They hurt her too. Logic speaks up louder this time. *Isabelle isn't one of them. Roman and her entire family betrayed her. They hurt her father and forced her to change her entire life, leaving everything she knew because she was a victim.*

No. Isabelle isn't a victim. She's too strong-willed to take on that identity, and I know my wife well enough now that she would be irritated to ever hear me call her that. But they hurt her deeply, irrevocably, and she wouldn't stand for it, breaking off all ties with the money, the power, and her family.

And now she's my family. I made her that way. I didn't look enough into her past. It doesn't matter. The pile of reasons I gathered made her perfect to be my wife, and they are no less perfect now. Though the reasons she's perfect have multiplied by a factor of thousands. From the way she reads a book, to how she speaks with Mrs. Potts, to how she looks at me seductively from underneath those dark lashes and glasses. To her fuzzy robe and all the romance book-themed tee shirts she wears. My wife is far more than the blood relation to those fuckers who took my pack from me.

And I refuse to let them take her from me too.

The crunch of tires comes to a halt, and the sound of the ocean and caw of morning birds is drowned out by the idling engine.

I scoop Isabelle up into my arms, keeping the blanket around her. She hums but doesn't wake. She turns into my chest, her fingers finding and curling into a patch of fur.

Protectiveness and an emotion I can't name spread through me with a fierce yawn.

I drop a kiss onto her forehead as I walk outside, taking her to the warm car.

They can't take her away from me. I won't let them.

CHAPTER 33

AN APOLOGY IN BUBBLES

BELLE

How can waking up feeling like you've been hit by a Mack Truck also feel so satisfying and wonderful? I'm sore between my legs in a way I've never known I could be, yet under all the bruising and bites, endorphins still steadily course through my veins. Satisfaction at being taken and claimed and fucked thoroughly for countless hours is indelibly imprinted on my mind and body forever.

Again, I might be shocked by how willing I am to lean into sex with such a violent side, but like I've told hundreds of women who read things that "aren't right," we like what we like. Don't make yourself wrong for enjoying your fantasy and the itch it scratches. Though I can't say I've ever had such fulfillment in a real-life scenario. That is definitely throwing me.

I stretch my limbs against the soft sheets and weight of the heavy comforter, but only when I inhale deeply do I realize this doesn't smell like my room. The scent is layered and drenched in the spice and musk of Dominic. Forcing my eyes open—which is no small feat with the sleep gluing them together—I find myself in his room, in his bed, with his darkened figure sitting at the edge of it.

"Dominic?" My voice is scratchy, hoarse, and absolutely ruined.

"I'm sorry."

I extend my hand toward him, but he's just out of reach. I scooch on the massive bed so I can run my hands along the complicated textures of his muscular back.

Sorry? Why is he sorry?

The flood of endorphins comes to an abrupt halt.

Roman, my own cousin, confessed to orchestrating the horrific murder of Dominic's family, and my husband is telling *me* he's sorry?

"For what?" I ask, my voice still a wreck of concrete pieces and razors.

He turns at that. Green eyes glow with anguish as they meet mine. "I hurt you. I took out all my rage on. . ." A claw brushes over the bite marks on my shoulder. A shiver rolls through me at the memory of how I got it, but he stills.

Unable to properly use my words after a night of screaming in the cold, wet sea air, I grab his paw and bring it to my lips, dropping a kiss on it before meeting his gaze again. In that look, I try to convey everything I feel. That I regret nothing. That I'm sorry for what my family has done to him and his. That I understand he needed to let loose. That I was there with him. That I'm still not afraid.

His nose twitches, and then he gets up.

A pitiful moan escapes me as he steps out of reach. Dominic flashes me a half-smile. "I'll be right back. Stay here."

He disappears into the adjoining bathroom, and I hear the bathtub faucet turn on. I roll onto my back at the same time my stomach rumbles and rolls. The pain starts to radiate through my entire body a bit more intensely now, but I refuse to let it dampen my satisfaction.

Dominic comes back after a few minutes. He pulls the bedding away from my body, leaving me cold for only a moment before he lifts me up. Even if I lived as long as a fairy, I would never get used to the fact Dominic can make me feel small and light.

He sets me gently on my feet in front of a massive, sunken tub, recessed into a marble platform. Steam rises from the water, curling like phantom hands, and piles of bubbles shimmer beneath the soft, golden light of the chandelier.

My husband firmly but gently presses my lower back, directing me to it. I suck in a breath knowing the hot water is going to sting like hell when it hits all my broken skin, but I step forward. My body is definitely covered in grime and dust from the shack, not to mention I'm covered in sweat and smell like sex.

I appreciate the two shallow steps it takes before I can get into the tub. The big claw-footed tub in my bathroom is lovely, but it's awkward for me to climb in and out of. Here, I only need to step down into it.

Half gasp, half sigh escapes me as I immerse myself in the deep pool. It has to be big enough to accommodate my husband's massive form so I have plenty of room and even a lip to sit on.

Surprisingly, it doesn't hurt. I lift a handful of bubbles and give Dominic a questioning look where he sits on the edge of the tub.

"Mrs. P is also very proficient at creating or procuring—I'm not really sure which—salves and potions that soothe the skin and help healing." I nod in understanding. Then I sink down further until I've soaked all of my hair before coming back up. Its dripping weight is heavy along my back.

Dominic sucks in a breath, but when I open my eyes again, he's made himself busy dousing a loofah in soap until it's more suds than mesh. I moan when he gently begins to run it along my skin. He only disappears for a moment to return with a beautifully laid tray of tea and one of my favorite blue and white China cups. Watching my massive, half shifted husband pour tea is another strange sight I will always keep filed away to be pulled out whenever I need a moment of ridiculousness and cozy loveliness. He passes it to me, and I sip the Earl Grey with honey. I don't usually take it with honey, but the concoction instantly soothes my throat as it slides down.

Long, luxurious moments of Dominic washing me as I sip tea like a queen have me questioning everything about my life. I lift my legs so he can wash my thighs and knees. It's like some kind of fairytale. A sexy, slightly violent fairytale, making it all the better.

When the loofah slides into the water down my inner thigh to gently scrape across my raw bits, I bite my lip to try and keep the moan at bay. The touch is both pleasure and pain, reminding me of last night all over again. I can't help but set the teacup back in its saucer a little harder than I intended, the clink resounding through the room.

The sound of harsh breathing has me opening my eyes again, even as that loofah continues to slide along my slit. Dominic studies me with such intensity my breath catches in my throat.

Then the loofah disappears, replaced by his human fingers. This time, I can't keep the needy moan from escaping. I don't know how it's possible for arousal to start dropping in my stomach until it's tightening my groin after all we did last night. I should be completely wrung out, yet I can't seem to get enough of him. Dominic is careful to keep his touch light and teasing, as his fingers caress up and down, and up and down, my abused sex.

More whimpers emanate from my throat as my hands wrap around the edge of the tub, and I sink in further. Then his digit splits my lips for a quick dip that turns my brain fuzzy. Then he moves up to circle one finger so very gently over my raw clit. He attacked my clit so many times last night, at one point I absurdly wondered if it would fall off when he was done with me.

But there it is, responding and swelling all over again.

"Your poor, pretty pussy," he finally says in a low growl. "I was too hard on you." His words break slightly, and I realize he's still experiencing remorse for what happened.

"No." It's easier to speak after the tea and honey, but I'm breathy from what he's doing. "I wanted it. You needed it."

His face tightens momentarily with some internal pain. He never ceases stroking me, never goes harder or speeds up, yet my need is slowly, lazily rising.

"I'm so sorry, Isabelle."

I open my mouth to tell him he doesn't need to say that, but then I realize we both hurt each other. Intentionally or not. Relations or not.

"I'm sorry too." My throat thickens with emotion. "I'm sorry about your family."

He gives me a brief, wry smile. "I'm sorry about yours too."

Usually, the water can turn things a bit raw, but whatever is in the water helps with the smooth glide of his fingers. I wriggle a bit as I start to need more.

Even with the smallest gesture or sound, Dom recognizes what I need and slips a finger inside me. I cry out. It's as intense as when he thrust his massive barbed cock into me last night.

"So tight," he whispers, and I know he's hard as nails. To prove it to myself, I force myself to open my eyes and look down at him. The tent of his black silk boxers confirms just that.

"Please," I moan, wanting him all over again.

"No, baby." It's the first time he's ever used a pet name, and it absolutely undoes something inside of me. "You're too raw for me to fuck you again. I'm just going to bring you off nice and easy like this." He removes his finger to rub my clit again in gentle circles before dropping again to slide his middle digit inside me.

I gasp, that coil growing tighter, hotter, brighter the longer he coaxes my body.

"But you—"

"Came harder than I ever have in my life last night, multiple times," he says, cutting me off. "This is about you and making up for abusing your gorgeous body."

There's things we need to talk about. My family. His family. How he feels. What he's going to do next. No. What *we're* going to do next.

But I can't think straight as he slides and penetrates while reverently grazing my clit with perfect, patient rhythm. My head falls back again, my fingers digging into the cold porcelain as it builds and builds inside me.

"That's it, baby. There's no rush. Just let yourself feel good. Let me pleasure you. Just relax as I tease your tight, abused little cunt."

His words wrap around my nipples like a string being yanked taut and they pebble, hard despite all the delicate work going on below the bubbles.

When I come, it's like tumbling over a waterfall, the descent lasting far longer than the tension that built before it. The release isn't sharp or frantic but soothing, a slow, rolling wave that cascades through me. Satisfaction spreads outward, reaching the tips of my fingers, toes, and even the bridge of my nose, leaving me utterly weightless and completely at peace.

I drift off to sleep again for a bit, my head supported on the lip of the tub. I doze in and out even as Dominic gets up and moves around. I barely register the knock at the bedroom door or him disappearing.

A feral roar explodes from our bedroom followed by a loud crack. I sit up fast. The water sloshes hard over the lip, knocking the teacup over.

Despite every painful protest of my body—though the bath did help soothe me quite a bit—I step out of the tub and grab a heavy midnight blue robe that I have to pick off the floor to keep from tripping on as I make my way to the bedroom.

Dominic stands there, clutching the now splintered side of the door. Mrs. P and Tock stand at the door with tight expressions. The tell-tale flick and click of Lucien's lighter tell me he's just behind them.

"What is it?" I ask, feeling their gaze fall too heavily on me.

Mrs. P swallows hard, struggling to maintain eye contact with Dominic but continually coming back to meet my gaze. "It's your father, dear. He's—" She swallows yet again.

"He's been taken," Dominic growls.

CHAPTER 34

A FORMAL AFFAIR
THE BEAST OF BOSTON

’m going to kill Roman. I’m going to tear him limb from limb.

Though I’m not sure which reason I’ll cite first—slaughtering my pack, abducting my wife’s father, or making me don a suit in my awkward half-shifted state. I look as ridiculous as I do monstrous.

Thank fae for Mrs. P’s abilities; she helped tailor one of my best suits to fit my bulky, unusual frame. The dress shoes, too, are sufficient to cover my half-morphed feet.

As Tock adjusts the necktie around my throat, making me feel like I’m being fitted for a noose, I’m even more determined to claw Roman’s heart from his chest.

Not tonight, though. Not while we are on neutral territory per the arrangement explicitly stated in the email Tock received.

The Wolves have Basil and they are willing to give him back in exchange for. . .Well, what they want, they haven’t made clear yet. They simply said they’d explain their terms in person.

There was also a bunch of crap in the email about

wanting to properly celebrate my and Isabelle's union. It's a load of witchtits.

Fae lords, I may not possess the strength it takes to keep from ripping off both of Roman's arms and beating him to death with them.

Not only was Basil snatched at the edges of my property, I now have to show up in a public place with this face.

Confining my pain and my monstrousness at home has been my choice over the last year. The fact I even left the car to track down Isabelle in the Poison Apple, or to discuss the plumbing issues with the contractor, are two anomalies caused by one very strong-willed wife.

Who is currently sick with worry about her father.

And who is currently gliding down the stairs in a yellow satin dress that climbs over one shoulder and falls over her body with lethal beauty. Her hair is pulled back into a complex bun of some kind, with tendrils of hair caressing her shoulders. Her lashes are longer, and she's glowing. The dark bruises and bite marks have been covered and concealed with makeup, but I know just where to look to find traces of the havoc I've wreaked on her. Something she assures me is fine, but I still can't forgive myself for.

There's something different about my wife now. Not just the fact she's dressed like an elegant bombshell, but also the way she descends the stairs. Her face, her posture, reminds me of when we ran into the Wolves in the alleyway and then again on the pier. She has donned her emotional armor, and there is a command about her.

Like she wouldn't hesitate to ask anyone to do her bidding if she saw fit. Surprise ripples through me. This is a woman who grew up among people with power and learned how to wield it.

Isabelle reaches the bottom of the steps, her eyes hard and lips pursed.

I want to tell her she's beautiful. A goddess worth worship from any and all beings. That I don't feel worthy to lay a single finger on her while also desperately wanting to touch her everywhere at once. But from her expression, I can tell she doesn't need or want platitudes. That's not what this is about now. This is about getting her father back and facing her past.

I may be the Beast of Boston, but she is my queen and every bit as formidable as royalty.

I hold out a hand. "Are you ready?"

Isabelle gives a short nod, slipping a manicured hand into mine. "Let's go."

ALL TOO SOON, the limousine pulls up to the aquarium. Lucien exits the front passenger seat and rushes around to open the door leading to the turquoise blue carpet entrance of the gala. As light fills the back of the cab, I instinctually rear back, my lips curling up in a defensive snarl. Nerves volley up and down my stomach with a vengeance.

A hand falls on my arm. "Remember the last gala we attended?" Isabelle says. "How everyone was shocked to find out you were a half-shifter for the first five, ten minutes, and then nobody cared anymore?"

I swallow down hard against the unsteady riot inside of me. "I only remember that the shrimp was subpar and that no one could keep their eyes off you."

Turning, I meet Isabelle's gaze. She smiles. "Which is why you danced with me not once, but twice, even after claiming you would never."

The imaginary memory takes shape in my mind, calming me in a way that shouldn't be possible. But Isabelle does that. We have our own inside jokes, and I feel bonded to her in a way that makes me feel—fae lords help me—safe.

So why haven't we formed a pack? Why can't I faefucking shift?

I push aside the questions that will get me nowhere and focus on what is. "It's impossible to resist wanting to show you off, especially when you look like this." It's only then that I allow my gaze to turn hot as I scan her satin-clad figure.

"I know the feeling," she says, squeezing my arm and appraising me just as openly. I can't help the surge of confidence as she runs a hand along my jawline with a sultry look in her eye. I didn't realize until now how much it matters that she approves of how I look. I could stand being monstrous to the rest of the world and in pain for the rest of my days, and none of it would matter if she only continued to look at me like this. Like I was some kind of devastatingly attractive creature she couldn't keep her hands off of.

With that I slide out of the car and onto the bright blue carpet to be blinded by countless camera flashes and the dull roar mixed with gasps of surprise from the press.

The idea of stepping into the spotlight, hideously disfigured as I am, always seemed to be a pain worse than death.

I put all my focus on helping Isabelle out of the car. The massive ring on her finger glints under the flashing bulbs with near-blinding brilliance. It says she's mine, in no uncertain terms. I drop a kiss on the back of her hand, cementing that in front of the cameras.

With Isabelle on my arm, there is no shame or regret

even as the exclamations ripple through the crowd on either side. It doesn't matter what I am or how people see me as long as my wife wants me. Though I remain perfectly aware I'm not deserving of her admiration or affection, not even a little bit.

And I certainly don't deserve her heart, though it's now all I want.

We follow the line of attendees through the massive aquarium entrance, glowing in ethereal blues and greens from the towering tanks inside. The space smells of saltwater, clean glass, and wealth—polished, ostentatious, and deeply calculated. The clinking of the champagne glasses and murmured voices of Boston's elite fill the air. The media cameras remain at the doors, held at bay by security as we step into the hushed opulence of the gala. Some charity for ocean conservation.

My arm tightens around Isabelle's as we approach the heart of the event. She moves with purpose, her chin high, her body language commanding in a way that makes my chest ache with pride—and unease. She's transformed herself tonight, the edges of her vulnerability hidden behind a poised mask. It reminds me how much I don't know about the woman I married.

The crowd parts subtly as we walk through. It's impossible to miss the stares—the gasps—as people take in my half-shifted form. I catch snippets of hushed voices.

"The Beast of Boston..."

"He's a Were?"

"Who is that with him?"

A woman over six feet tall with generous curves and a shark-like smile intercepts us.

Morgana—a vision in deep teal silk—is flanked by two tall, dark-haired men. Her light gray hair is swept back into a sleek chignon highlighted by lavender streaks. Her eyes flash with a confidence that veers dangerously close to arrogance. She's every inch the power player tonight, with her twin mages flanking her like dark sentinels.

Zephyr and Surge, identical in their tall, lanky forms and sardonic smirks, are dressed in tailored black suits that fit them like shadows. Their mage scent—a mix of bitter herbs, burning wood, and a faint, acrid chemical tang—hits me like a punch to the gut. My stomach clenches, but I don't flinch. I never do.

"Dominic," she greets in a sultry contralto that carries a gravelly edge, hinting at a past she's never tried to hide. The transgender woman is the essence of femininity—her gown draped to perfection, her makeup flawless—there's a proud defiance in the way she carries herself, as if daring anyone to question what she's built herself to become. "Brave of you to come out like this. But then again, boldness has always been your signature, hasn't it?"

"Morgana," I greet, "May I introduce my wife, Isabelle Blackwell. Isabelle, this is our host. Morgana Delmare is the most ruthless and sought after lawyer in the city."

"The east coast," she corrects me with a sharp tone.

Morgana's smile widens as her gaze flicks to Isabelle. "Aren't you a gorgeous thing?"

Isabelle hesitates for only a fraction of a second before taking Morgana's hand, her grip firm. "Likewise."

Morgana's smile widens as her attention shifts to Isabelle. "And here I thought Dominic didn't believe in partnerships. You must have worked some magic to change his mind."

Isabelle returns the smile, her tone measured. "I wouldn't call it magic. Just an agreement that benefits us both."

Morgana's brows lift, clearly intrigued. "A pragmatist. How refreshing. I imagine that serves you well, being married to someone like Dominic."

"It does," Isabelle replies smoothly. "Though I like to think we balance each other out."

Morgana laughs softly, a sound both amused and knowing. "Balance. Now that's a word I rarely hear in Dominic's orbit." She turns back to me, sharp as ever. "But perhaps that's why I've always found you so fascinating."

"Well," Morgana says, her tone light but her eyes sharp, "we'll have to catch up later. It's been too long since you and I have danced on the edges of legality, Dominic."

"I look forward to it," I say with a tight smile. While we sit on either side of the law—and are keenly aware of it— our interests have yet to come into conflict. Though I don't look forward to the day when that comes about.

The twins linger a moment longer then turn and follow Morgana into the crowd.

As the trio disappears, Isabelle lets out a breath she must have been holding. "She's. . .intense."

"She's a shark," I mutter, leading us toward the open bar. "And she's dangerous. But she's also one of the few who understands the rules of leverage. Keep that in mind tonight."

"I'm not the one you need to worry about," Isabelle says quietly.

We reach the bar, and before I can call for the bartender, Isabelle turns to face me. Her eyes are steady, her voice low but firm. "Dominic, I need you to let me talk with Roman alone first."

I blink at her, the words sending an immediate ripple of tension through my body. "Absolutely not."

"Listen to me," she says, stepping closer, her tone calm

yet unyielding. "I know my cousin. He may be a bastard, but he still has some loyalty to his blood. I can appeal to that better than you can—especially without you looming over my shoulder reminding him I married his enemy."

A growl rumbles deep in my chest. "Isabelle, you have no idea what he's capable of. If you think for one second—"

"I'm not asking," she interrupts, lifting her chin. There's a fire in her eyes, one I've rarely seen but can't look away from. "I'm telling you. He has my father, and I've got to get him back safely. Let me handle this."

I hate the sound of those words. Every instinct I have rebels against the idea of her stepping out of my shadow, even if it's only across the room. Roman is dangerous—a predator circling the edges of a kill—and the thought of Isabelle anywhere near him without me sends rage boiling under my skin.

"You're my wife. That makes you my responsibility."

"Dominic, I've been taking care of myself my entire life. I don't need anyone's protection. Not even yours."

I clench my fists, trying to hold on to the argument forming in my mind, but the determination in her eyes disarms me. She's resolved, and I know there's no stopping her without making a scene. My pulse thunders as I grit my teeth and force the words out. "Fine. But if he so much as looks at you wrong—"

"I'll be fine," she says, her voice softening just enough to show a flicker of gratitude. "Thank you."

Before I can stop her, she turns and glides away from me, moving through the crowd with a confidence I've never seen before. It's not just the dress that transforms her, though the way it clings to her every curve would tempt a saint. It's the way she carries herself now—poised, commanding, as she steps back into a skin she hasn't worn in years but still fits her perfectly.

I watch as she crosses the room, her every step deliberate, her head held high. She's heading straight for Roman, who stands surrounded by his men near the other side of the gala floor. My muscles tense as I catch the flicker of surprise in his expression when he notices her approach.

My hand flexes at my side, itching to follow her, to rip Roman apart before he can say a word. But I force myself to stay rooted in place, every nerve in my body straining as I track her progress. My ire rises when I catch the tall blonde man smiling at Isabelle.

I should rip off his face for even looking at my wife, much less with that smug knowing.

She doesn't falter, doesn't glance back at me for reassurance. This is a side of Isabelle I've never seen before—sharp-edged and utterly in control.

The woman who, at this moment, is showing me just how formidable she can be.

Tock sidles up next to me. Lucien is elsewhere seeing to his own special task.

"Shall I stay near her?" Tock asks, keeping his own level gaze on the Wolves. He may be human, but between his eidetic memory and diplomacy, he might as well be supernatural.

I give a sharp nod and my man peels off.

We are merely biding our time. What Isabelle doesn't know but can likely guess is the moment we have Basil secure, I intend to wipe out this pittance of a wolf pack. And nothing she can say will change my mind.

CHAPTER 35

BOINKING?

BELLE

The room feels too bright, too polished, as if all the glamour and glitter are trying to smother the raw tension crackling just beneath the surface. My heels click softly against the floor as I weave through the clusters of people, my every movement measured and deliberate. I don't need to look back to know Dominic's eyes are pinned on me, his restraint undoubtedly fighting against every protective instinct.

But this is my family. This is my fight.

Roman notices me before I reach him, his sharp eyes lighting up with that trademark smile—a mask of charm stretched over something far more dangerous. He steps away from his entourage, raising a champagne flute in mock greeting. His tailored suit fits perfectly, as always, and his easy confidence makes my stomach churn.

"Hey there, Belly," he says smoothly, his voice rich and warm like the predator he is.

I hate that nickname. I've always hated it.

"Or should I say Mrs. Dominic Blackwell? I can't decide

whether to congratulate you or send flowers to your funeral."

"Where is he, Roman?" I cut straight to the point, ignoring his grin. "Where's my dad?"

He laughs, low and dismissive as if I've just asked him where he misplaced his wallet. "Basil? Oh, he's quite comfortable, I assure you. More than comfortable, actually. It's almost like he never left."

His casual tone, the smug curl of his lips—it all sends a fresh wave of anger rolling through me. But I don't let it show. Not here. Not now.

"You don't need to drag him into this. Haven't you done enough to him?"

Roman observes me almost as if bored. "And you didn't need to marry the enemy, but here we are, Belly." He sweeps an arm out.

"Why does it matter?" I say in a harsh whisper. "Why does any of this matter?"

I never wanted to be in the middle of a turf war for Thorns. I left my family and everything I knew behind just to try and escape exactly this.

I didn't plan to marry the Beast of Boston. I didn't want to be part of their crimes or their politics, but that's the hand I'd been dealt. Apparently, fate couldn't allow me to escape this world. At the end of the day, I was just a girl trying to take care of her father. I wanted to read and sell romance books. I didn't mind my small life as long as it was mine, but standing here in front of Roman with my father on the line it's like I never left.

Because of Dominic.

I try to swat the idea away, but it blooms before I can pluck it.

Roman's face finally hardens. "It matters because *family* has always mattered."

My nostrils flare as I try to keep calm and collected but my cousin gets me as raging as a bull faster than anyone else. "Is that what you told yourself when you had my dad swallow the toxic contents of that Thorn? When you used him as a human guinea pig?"

His expression cools again. "Your father understood what we were trying to achieve. Unlike you, he was committed to our goals, our vision. Though ironically, you are the one to come closest to getting what I've been trying so hard to give to our own Pack." His eyes cut across the room. I follow his gaze to my husband. Lucien is speaking to him, but Dominic's focus is completely directed at me and Roman. If I give him the slightest signal something is wrong, he'll come over and rip my cousin's head off, neutral territory or not.

I turn back to my cousin. "Our Pack," I repeat dismissively. "We are not Shifters. Your obsession with brute strength has always mystified me."

"And yet you're the one boinking a Were, dear cousin."

My brows screw up so fast, they threaten to collide and fly off my face. "Boinking?"

He shrugs nonchalantly before patting my shoulder, passing me by. "Don't worry, cuz, Basil's nice and comfy and I think your *husband*," he stresses the word with both mocking and annoyance somehow, "is open to playing nice tonight."

My nails bite into my palm as my feet root into the ground. Roman is as infuriating as ever.

"You really shouldn't," a smooth voice reaches me. "Worry, that is. Roman has things under control."

I meet Adrian's familiar blue eyes. My ex and Roman's

best friend is as handsome as ever. Hair falls over his forehead in that way I used to find devastatingly attractive. He holds up his empty champagne flute. "But I think we both need something strong to get through tonight."

"I don't think you're wrong," I murmur, following him to one of the bars.

"I always knew you'd surprise us all in the end," Adrian says with a chuckle.

If you had told me four weeks ago, I'd be standing at a bar with Adrian, being subjected to his roguish charm again my heart might have stopped. Not because I loved him—love isn't real, so I never could have—but because of what he taught me.

Though now, while he still has the pretty face, he seems so much. . .smaller. Softer. He once crushed my heart in his bare palms, but now. . .I realize he has no power over me whatsoever.

"You were the one who surprised me." The words come out flippant and dismissive.

He sets the champagne glass on the bar, sagging his shoulders as he sighs. "I suppose I deserve that." Then holding up a hand to the bartender, "One bourbon and one gin and tonic. Make the G&T a double."

Five years later, and Adrian still remembers my drink. At one time I would have been touched by the thoughtfulness, but I know that Adrian files things away to use against others.

Just like Dominic did, leveraging your father to force you into marriage.

I mentally swat the idea away again. Dominic isn't like my family. He isn't like Adrian.

My attempt to convince myself feels feeble.

"You still selling those sex books?" he asks.

I suppress the urge to roll my eyes, but it comes out as rapid blinking instead. "Romance books," I correct flatly. "And yes. My bookshop is doing very well."

He snorts softly but doesn't go on.

That is a big difference between Dominic and Adrian. Where Adrian used to constantly inform me that I was reading trash and he found it embarrassing if we were going to be together, Dominic actually picked up the book that captured my interest. My skin heats at the memory of what came next.

Adrian takes the drinks from the bartender before turning to hand me mine. As my hand is about to close on the glass, a clawed hand intercepts.

Dominic places the gin and tonic back on the bar with deliberate force. His golden eyes lock onto Adrian, unblinking and burning with warning. "I don't know who you are," he says, his voice low and rough, "but you're standing too close to something that belongs to me."

Adrian's smirk falters, but Dominic doesn't stop, leaning in just enough to make the air between them crackle with tension. "I suggest you remember that before you try to hand her anything again."

Dominic's hand slides to my lower back, pulling me into his side as he steers me away. The growl in his chest doesn't fade as we walk, his body tense and radiating heat. I let out a bitter laugh, shaking my head. "You think he wants me? Dominic, you don't know the half of it."

His grip loosens just slightly, his eyes narrowing with suspicion as he waits for me to continue.

"There was a day I overheard him with some of the other Wolves," I begin, the words bitter on my tongue. "I stayed out of sight, listening like some stupid girl hoping to hear something sweet. But what I heard. . ." I trail off, my throat tightening as the memory claws its way back.

I force myself to meet Dominic's intense gaze, grounding myself in the present. "He said I was useful. That keeping me 'wrapped around his finger' gave him access to my family, to power. He talked about me like a tool, something to be used. And love?" I laugh again, the sound sharp and raw. "He said love wasn't real. That I was just part of his plan to rise in the ranks. Apparently, I'd make a decent wife, and he 'could get skinnier tail on the side.'" That was a direct quote that lives like a permanent dagger under my ribs.

Dominic's lips curl into a snarl, his claws grazing my skin. "He said that about you?"

I nod. "I learned my lesson that day. People don't love, Dominic. They use. My parents did it. Adrian did it. It's all just. . .utility and convenience."

Dominic doesn't speak, his sharp gaze pinning me in place, but I feel the weight of his focus urging me to continue.

"My mother used to complain about my father constantly. She'd sigh and say he didn't love her the way a husband should. That he cared more about the Wolves, about chemistry equations, and work than about her. And then one day, she just. . .left."

I glance away, but Dominic's grip keeps me grounded, his claws trailing lightly over my skin. "And my father? He didn't fight for her. Didn't beg her to stay. He just carried on like she'd never existed. If that was love, then it was brittle. Hollow. A myth people tell themselves to make life bearable."

Dominic's growl rumbles low in his chest, his claws flexing against my skin, pulling me back to the present. "So now you don't believe in love at all." It's somehow both a statement and a question.

I shake my head. "But isn't that what makes me perfect? For you? For our arrangement?"

An internal battle seems to be taking place behind his eyes.

"And you don't love Adrian anymore?" His lip curls almost involuntarily as he says the name. "You say you don't believe in love, but he was your first. Firsts usually have weight, a hold that is impossible to dislodge."

I shrug and shake my head. "I never did. I was just under the illusion I did for a little while. It evaporated when I found out he was using me."

My tongue feels tied even as I say the words. Why is it difficult to denounce love to my husband? We have a contract marriage. Well, I suppose it's not entirely limited to the confines of paper anymore.

Dominic's teeth flash in a dangerous snarl. "Then you won't mind if I make sure he knows exactly what happens when he covets what doesn't belong to him."

A shiver races down my spine at the possessive fire in his tone. "Dominic—"

"You're wrong, Isabelle."

I blink up at him, trying to keep my voice steady despite the sudden intensity radiating off him. "About what?"

"About him." His thumb brushes the curve of my jaw, forcing me to meet his smoldering green gaze. "I can scent his arousal. His desire. He *wants* you." His words are clipped, filled with barely restrained fury. "But he can't have you."

"Dominic—"

"You're mine," he cuts me off. "Say it."

A flash of heat rises in me, clashing with the tension in my chest. "I'm yours."

"He touched you once, but he won't again. Not when every inch of you belongs to me now."

His grip on my throat loosens, not in retreat but in preparation. Before I can catch my breath, he spins me sharply, pressing me forward until I'm bent over the railing.

The cool metal bites into my hips, the sensation grounding me as his claws trail down my sides. Behind the glass, the glowing jellyfish pulse in ghostly blues and greens, casting shifting light over us as his body presses firmly against mine.

His claws hook the hem of my gown, lifting it slowly, deliberately, baring me to him. The chill of the air makes my skin prickle, but it's nothing compared to the heat of his touch as his hand slides between my thighs.

"You're not even wearing anything under this," he growls, with dark approval. His fingers find my slick heat, tracing slow, deliberate strokes that send shockwaves through my body. "Did you know I'd do this? Did you want me to?"

A gasp escapes me as he presses closer, his breath hot against the back of my neck. My mind swims, tangled in the weight of his words and the molten ache pooling low in my belly.

"Dominic," I whisper, clutching the railing as my knees weaken beneath his relentless touch.

He leans down, his lips brushing the curve of my ear as his fingers delve deeper, stroking with maddening precision. "You're mine, Isabelle," he commands. "And I won't let you back in there until you are full of my cum. I want you to feel it sliding down your thighs with every step you take, reminding you who you are here with and who you belong to."

CHAPTER 36

DRIPPING DOWN HER THIGHS

THE BEAST OF BOSTON

drian.

Just the thought of his name sends a fresh wave of fury rolling through me. He stood there, *smiling.* Like he had any right to breathe the same air as Isabelle. Like he hadn't discarded her as if she were something replaceable. *Mine.* She's mine now, and I'll tear him apart for daring to look at her like he still has a claim.

My claws flex as I grip her hips, her silky yellow dress already hiked up around her waist. The contrast between the smooth fabric and her bare skin beneath my hands sends a jolt of heat through me, sharpening the edge of my fury.

She doesn't believe in love. Told me as much with that dismissive edge in her voice. I chose her because she wasn't supposed to need it—because I wasn't supposed to need it. But hearing it from her lips was like a slap, as if love, her love, was something I'd never be worthy of. Something she gave away to a bastard like Adrian, even for a moment. I'd do anything to touch it, to taste it.

I bet her love feels like standing in an endless ray of sunshine, warm enough to burn away the cold of any winter.

I undo my slacks and free my hard length that practically vibrates with need.

Without another word, I position myself at her entrance, the heat of her drawing me in as I thrust forward in one swift, powerful motion. She cries out, her hands gripping the railing for support as I fill her completely. The tight, wet heat of her squeezes me like a vice, and I can't hold back the growl that rumbles from deep in my chest.

"I wanted to rip his head off," I growl, my voice low and guttural. My claws grip her hips harder as I thrust deeper, the slick glide of her pulling me closer to the edge. "Do you know what it took not to end him right there? To not drag him out by his throat and leave his blood on the carpet? Just for looking at you."

Her breath comes in gasps, her body trembling beneath mine as I move.

Every thrust sends a ripple of sensation through both of us, the barbs of my length catching just enough to heighten the friction without breaking the rhythm. She moans louder, her body writhing, and I grip her hips harder, knowing that I'm overwhelming her.

The rhythmic slap of my hips against hers echoes in the quiet, broken only by her moans and the harsh rasp of my breathing.

"You let him touch you once," I repeat the words in a snarl, pulling back before driving into her, harder this time, "but he'll never touch you again. Not when every inch of you belongs to me now."

She can't answer, her voice lost to the shuddering sounds spilling from her lips. Her body says enough, though, the way she meets every thrust, the way she clenches around me as I drive into her again and again.

"You think love isn't real, Isabelle? Fine. But this—what I'm doing to you—this is real. The way your body responds to mine, the way you give yourself over to me like no one else could. I own this, every part of it. And no one, not Adrian, not anyone, will ever take it from me."

I wrap my hand around her neck, forcing her to arch back so my teeth can graze the delicate skin of her ear. "You're dripping for me, Isabelle. Your body knows who it belongs to."

As I pound into her, her gasps turn into cries that send a thrill through me.

"Come for me," I command, my voice rough with need.

Her body tightens around me as she shatters, her cry echoing through the room. The feel of her pulsing around me pulls me under, and I follow her over the edge, spilling into her in hot, relentless waves.

But it's not enough. I have to see it. I have to see the proof of what we've just done.

I drop to my knees, gripping her hips as I pull apart the perfect globes of her ass to reveal that glistening pussy. She clenches and trembles, our mingled desire spilling from her in shimmering streaks. The sight is enough to set my blood on fire all over again.

"Fuck," I growl, the word ripped from my chest as hunger consumes me. I lean forward, burying my face between her legs, my tongue sweeping through the slick mess of her and me combined. The taste is irresistible, the heat of her quivering sex only fueling my need. She's still trembling, her body wracked with aftershocks, but I can't stop.

She gasps, her fingers scrabbling for purchase on the

railing as I devour her, licking and nipping like a predator savoring the spoils of a hard-won hunt. Her scent—ripe, raw, wholly mine—floods my senses, pushing my restraint past its limits. She smells like sex, like us, and it fills every corner of my being with a deep, primal satisfaction.

My growl deepens as I press closer, my tongue dragging over her, slow and deliberate, like I'm branding her from the inside out.

She's mine in every way that matters. Her body tells me what her words won't, what she doesn't even believe in. Love might not be real to her, but this connection between us—it's undeniable. It's fire, scorching and inescapable, and if it's all I'll ever get, it will have to be enough.

Something inside me bucks at that. Something that wants more. Wants all of her. Her soul, her heart, her love.

Her moans rise again, breathless and ragged, and my cock aches with the need to fill her once more. Every instinct in me demands I leave no part of her untouched, unclaimed—not just her body but her scent, her soul. To make her mine in ways no one can ever undo.

I'm on my feet, driving right back into her. Isabelle grips the railing as if her life depends on it.

"I can't," she gasps, her voice breaking, her legs trembling.

"You can," I snarl, gripping her hips tighter and angling my thrusts to hit that spot again, the one that had her crying out just moments ago. "You will. You're mine, Isabelle, and I'll make sure you remember who owns this perfect little body."

Her moans become desperate, her thighs quivering as I drive into her with relentless precision.

"Dominic," she chokes out, the sound broken, pleading. "There—oh gods, right there. Please, don't stop."

Isabelle's body clenches around me. Her hands clutch the railing so hard her knuckles turn white, her head dropping forward as sweat beads along the back of her neck.

I obey, slamming into her at that same angle, over and over. Her cries grow louder, incoherent, and the way her body tightens around me tells me she's close.

"That's it. Look at you falling apart for me. My wife. My greedy little cum slut who can't get enough."

Her response is a strangled scream, her entire body shuddering as I drive her over the edge. She's vise-tight around me, her release drenching my cock as her voice rises in a ragged cry. I slam into her one last time, burying myself deep as my own release crashes through me, hot and consuming, marking her all over again.

Her body slumps against the railing, trembling and spent, and I keep her there, locked in place as I catch my breath. My hand slides up her back, soothing, as I press my lips to her damp shoulder.

"You did so well, baby," I murmur, my voice low, satisfied. She reaches a hand back to run her fingers through my hair. I use the angle to drop tender kisses along her neck.

Isabelle doesn't see it yet, but she's more mine than she'll ever admit. And as much as my wife rejects love, the irony isn't lost on me—because for her, I think I might burn the whole world down just to see if I could make her believe in it again.

"You're mine," I murmur, the words a vow and a promise. "And no one will ever take you from me."

~

THE AIR inside the main hall feels cooler against my skin as we step back into the crowd. The faint smell of seawater and expensive perfume lingers, the low murmur of voices and clinking glasses buzzing around us. My hand stays at the back of Isabelle's neck, my thumb tracing circles over her skin. She's radiant, her cheeks flushed, her lips swollen, and her golden dress slightly askew in a way that screams satisfaction. She looks gorgeously, beautifully fucked, and I can't help but smirk as my gaze locks with Adrian's across the room.

He stiffens, his jaw tightening, and I give him a slow, deliberate smile—the cat who got the cream—and then some.

Tock is waiting near the edge of the hall by the archway leading back to the private area we'd just left. He's acted as a subtle, silent guard to our. . .activities. He takes his place trailing behind Isabelle as we pass by.

I'm ready to finish this, get my wife's father back, and get home.

It doesn't take long to find Roman; he's holding court near the large tank housing the sharks. Roman's expression sharpens the second he sees me approaching, his ever-present air of casual arrogance shifting into something more calculating. Adrian sidles up to him, hands shoved in his pockets. There's a dark surliness to his expression that I'm more than happy to take credit for.

"Dominic," he greets, his tone slick as oil. "It's time we discuss our future, don't you think?"

Roman's eyes flick between us, his smile widening just enough to reveal a hint of teeth. "Seeing as we're family now, it seems best that we all leave the past behind us and move forward a united front."

"Family," I echo, letting the word drip with disdain as I step closer. "What exactly are you proposing, Roman?"

He spreads his hands, the picture of faux sincerity. "It only makes sense, doesn't it? Family should work together. Combine forces. Share territory. Product? Think of the possibilities."

I let out a low chuckle, the sound dark and humorless. "You mean I should let you help yourself to what's mine? That's not how this works."

Roman's smile falters before he recovers, his eyes narrowing. "I'm talking about strength, Dominic. The kind that only comes from unity. We have just as much to offer you."

I force him to tilt his head up slightly to maintain eye contact. "Here's my counteroffer," I say, my words edged with steel. "You return Basil without a single hair harmed, and I won't light up every warehouse you've got on Dry Dock Avenue, Tide Street, or the stretch you're hiding on Marginal Road."

Roman's expression tightens, his jaw clenching as he processes the threat. I lean in, my tone turning almost conversational. "Since we're *family*, I'll even let your Wolves live to reinvent themselves. Find a new trade, something that doesn't involve dirty hexes. Hell, if it's worthwhile, I might even invest."

The lie slips from my tongue effortlessly, but Roman isn't fooled. His smile sharpens as it stretches back into place. All teeth and no warmth. "How generous of you."

"Isn't it?" I counter, meeting his gaze unflinchingly.

Roman's eyes flicks to Isabelle, then back to me, his smile turning sharper, more deliberate. "It's no wonder you've managed to claw your way to the top, Dominic. A shifter leading this city—it makes sense. The strength, the instinct, the. . .savagery. It's in your blood, isn't it?"

The air between us thickens, the insinuation in his words hanging like a blade ready to drop.

I let the comment sit for a beat, long enough for the silence to stretch uncomfortably, then close the already small distance between us. "You're right about one thing, Roman. It is in my blood. And it's exactly why you'll never beat me."

Roman's smile falters, and I savor the flicker of unabashed hate in his eyes before it vanishes behind his mask of control.

He looks down into his champagne glass. "We'll have Basil delivered to Chapter Three tomorrow."

That's when Tock approaches. He whispers in my ear the words I've been waiting to hear all night.

I flash a grin at Roman. "No need. We sent someone to pick him up."

Even Isabelle looks at me in question. Roman looks uneasy while Adrian is outright scowling.

"What?" Isabelle asks.

"I just got word that Lucien is driving him home right now. He's no worse for wear." I face Roman. "You know, to save you the trouble."

An intense blast of hatred emits from him, and I expect the fire alarms to trigger.

Roman nods at Adrian. His second, who's been sipping on a glass of brown liquor, holds out the glass of champagne in his other hand, extending it to me.

Roman raises his own glass in a mock toast, the gesture dripping with condescension. "Then here's to family, Dominic. May we continue to. . .coexist."

I don't reach for the glass. Instead, I give Roman my best bored stare. I'm not playing into his theatrics anymore.

This isn't a game, and this fuck is not long for this world. Not if I can help it.

Isabelle takes the glass from Adrian, clinking it to Roman's. "I'll drink to that."

My wife tips it back and swallows. Roman frowns at her, and I wonder if it's because he's pissed he has no leverage over either of us, or if the open scorn is over her marrying the enemy.

"We'll be seeing you," I promise before taking Isabelle's arm and turning to go.

The Wolves cut off in the opposite direction. Likely running to see if what I said was true, if I really do have Basil.

Fools.

But before we've gone far, Isabelle's grip on my arm tightens, her nails digging in just enough to draw my attention. Her pace falters, her breath hitching. I glance down sharply. "Isabelle?"

Her brow knits, her face suddenly ashen, the flush of earlier pleasure replaced by a startling pallor. Her breath comes in shallow, uneven gasps. "I. . .I feel. . ." Her voice fades, unsteady, the words trailing into silence.

"Isabelle?" My voice hardens with alarm as the unease clawing at my gut sharpens into dread. Something's wrong —deeply wrong. Her body sways against mine, unnaturally limp, her breathing erratic.

The glass slips from her hand, tumbling in agonizing slow motion.

It hits the marble with a sharp, crystalline crack, shattering into jagged shards that scatter across the floor.

I catch her before she hits the ground.

A tight band of panic closes in around my windpipe.

I call her name again, but she doesn't respond.

A single shard of glass spins in a slow, wobbly circle before stilling, and in that frozen second, dread floods my system.

Her face turns ashen.

"Isabelle!" I bellow.

CHAPTER 37

DOCTORS SUCK

BELLE

Broken glass glitters at my feet. It blurs and sparkles. A trickle of blood runs from a cut on my ankle, but I don't feel it.

"Isabelle? Isabelle. What's wrong?" Dominic's voice is controlled but on edge.

I blink. Blink again.

The words seep through my brain like molasses. I rearrange them in my head, but I can't make sense of them.

A bitter taste floods my mouth as pain squeezes the blood vessels in my body like a vengeful python. Then my legs give out. Instead of hitting the cold floor, I'm caught in a pair of strong arms.

"Isabelle," Dominic cries out. Not in fury. No, the way his eyes flash, I can tell he's terrified.

I lift a hand to his face, though it's blurry and shiny, like the glass on the floor. I open my mouth, wanting to tell him it's okay.

But then a sharp pain slices through my middle, and I whimper in pain.

"Fae fucking witchtits," he curses crudely even as he

picks me up entirely. "Move, get out of my way!" he bellows, making his way through the crowd. I feel as though I'm floating on a cloud while my insides are being shredded with a cheese grater.

One moment, Dominic's voice bellows through the crowd, rough and desperate. The next, shadows creep into the edges of my vision, swallowing everything whole.

When I open my eyes again, the brightness of a hospital room sears into me, but it feels distant, unreal, like a dream I can't quite wake from. I blink, trying to focus, but the room blurs, melting into blackness once more.

The void comes and goes, swallowing swaths of time, and I can't hold onto anything except the faint echo of Dominic's voice, raw and pleading, calling my name.

Snippets of conversation reach my ears. I follow the trail to the two men in the corner. Dominic bears over another man in a white doctor's coat with a stethoscope draped around his neck.

"I'm telling you, it's her weight. Probably too much exertion at this party."

Inwardly, I cringe. I'm remembering why I hate doctors so much. Turning my head away, embarrassment flares in me. It's always the same line. Whether it's stabbing stomach pain or a cold, the culprit is always my weight.

And listening to a doctor painstakingly explain it to my husband is a level of humiliation I don't think I can endure.

"You're telling me, my wife walked around a party, spoke to people, sipped champagne, and then collapsed because of her weight?"

I swallow over the thick ball suddenly lodged in my throat. Dominic's tone is steady and even.

"Yes, Mr. Blackwell. We see it all the time—ACK!"

When I force my eyes to open again. I find the doctor

pinned to the wall, his feet dangling like a rag doll off the floor. Dom holds him up, bearing his half human teeth, half fangs right in the doctor's face.

"I brought my wife here because she is unwell."

As if my body wished to prove his point a jabbing pain pierces through me with such force that I jolt and cry out.

"Did you hear that, you arrogant hack? She's in pain, she is ill or hurt, and all you can do is stick your nose up and refuse to help my wife? Is it sheer laziness or perhaps just arrogance that has you unwilling to do your job?"

The doctor stammers, his feet kicking from a foot off the ground.

Another stabbing lance of agony jerks my entire body. I whimper, digging my fingers into the mattress below me as sweat covers my body. I can't tell if I'm hot or cold.

The doctor hits the floor in a clatter of limbs, and Dominic is by my side. He runs a calloused palm over my forehead. "It's okay, I'm here."

"You treat her with all the seriousness of a heart attack or send a doctor in who will," Dominic barks over his shoulder. "And so help me, if I hear one more imbecilic word from you about her pain being a result of her weight, I will rip your skin off your body and make a rug out of it. Do you understand me?"

I don't register what the doctor replies over the blood pounding in my ears, but when I open my eyes again, he's gone.

"But it won't match with our decor." My voice comes out raspy and hoarse.

"What's that?" Dominic asks, eyes searching mine.

"The shade of his skin is all wrong. We can't put his skin rug in the sitting room. I much prefer the burgundy oriental carpet. And I don't think it will work in any of the guest bedrooms."

Dominic smiles though it doesn't reach his eyes. A brief reprieve from pain that comes in the form of flutters. "What about pinned to a wall then, my wife?"

I shake my head even as pulsing aches spiral through my body. "No," I grunt. "It will compete with the current aesthetic."

He gives a mock sigh. "So true. What would I do without you?"

A laugh escapes halfway before my lungs seize around it, cutting it off and turning it into another moan and whimper.

Dominic's fingers brush back my hair in a soothing motion. "You're going to be okay."

I give him a weak smile. I don't believe him.

Six hours later, my body is wrung out from tests and medications, but the pain subsides enough for me to finally sleep.

When I wake up, I'm surprised to find a Black woman in a light blue sequined suit standing beside my bed. The sequins shimmer with every tiny movement, like the rippling surface of a crystal-clear pool.

"It's just what you thought, honey. No doubt about it," she says, her voice smooth and commanding, as if she's holding court.

"Kiki?" The word barely makes it past my dry lips.

She turns with a flourish, and Dominic follows, his expression as sharp as ever. Kiki's dark eyes sparkle as her glossy lips curve into a knowing smile.

"There she is," Kiki says, waltzing over with the kind of swagger only she can pull off. Hips swaying, confidence radiating.

Dame Kiki Eleganza, Boston's finest drag queen and unofficial Fairy Godmother, is standing in my hospital room. Whether Kiki's dripping in diamonds and stilettos or strutting in a suit like this one, she flows between pronouns like sequins and satin. She once told me she doesn't care what anyone calls her—so long as she gets what she wants. Today, her pate gleams bald and proud under the fluorescent lights, understated makeup accentuating her high cheekbones and deep, expressive eyes.

"I haven't seen you since we were downing prosecco at Goldie's wedding shower," Kiki says, sidling up to the bedside and picking up my hand as though it's the most natural thing in the world. "And, baby, you look exactly how I felt the morning after."

I try to chuckle, but a sharp spike of pain cuts through me, and I wince instead.

Kiki's expression shifts, softening instantly. She takes a seat at my side, her voice low and comforting. "Your hubby here called me to come take a peek at what's going on in that gorgeous body of yours."

"She's a level four healing mage," Dominic adds, his voice tight. He stands near the foot of the bed, his arms crossed over his chest like he's physically holding back his worry. I want to reach out to reassure him, but the weight of my exhaustion keeps me pinned.

I glance at Kiki, who grins. "I know, I know," she says, flicking her wrist dismissively. "You thought my superpower was being a fabulous queen, didn't you? But surprise!"

A tiny smile tugs at my lips despite everything. "I thought your superpower was making people feel seen."

Tenderness lights her eyes. "Okay, hush now, honey," she says, patting my hand. "I'm about to go fishing in that hot little bod of yours and see what's got you so worked up."

Her warm, dry hand presses gently against my forehead. The touch is soothing, almost hypnotic, and I let my lashes flutter closed, trusting her entirely.

"Hmm," Kiki says thoughtfully. She continues to hem and haw as if having an interior conversation.

I can practically feel the energy vibrating off Dominic as he paces behind her, his steps clip-clopping back and forth.

"Be still," she finally snaps at him. Dominic freezes. I daresay he's afraid to even breathe at that command.

Kiki's palm rests on my head again, sending a strange tingling sensation cascading through me. It's not painful, but it's. . .invasive. Like invisible threads of her energy are weaving their way inside me, searching for the problem. My muscles twitch involuntarily, and I suck in a sharp breath.

"Got it," Kiki mutters, her usually smooth voice taut with effort. "I usually only deal with wounds and sickness, but this is a hex. Not just a hex—it's dirty work. Something layered. Sticky." She clicks her tongue like a disapproving school teacher. "Dominic, baby, you weren't exaggerating when you said this was ugly."

Dominic's pacing halts abruptly. "Can you fix it?" There's an undercurrent of desperation he doesn't bother hiding.

"Fix? Yes. Entirely? No. It's not my specialty, and this thing is tangled deep. But I can neutralize it enough to stop the damage." She glances at him, her usual confidence dimmed by concentration. "Give me space, beastie, and let me do my job."

Dominic steps back reluctantly, arms crossing tightly over his chest. "Just help her."

I feel a pulse—hot and cold all at once—spreading from Kiki's hand through my body. The sensation is. . .strange. Like someone unraveling a tightly knotted rope inside me. My stomach churns, and I moan softly.

"There it is," Kiki mutters. The air around us feels charged, thick. She hums under her breath, the sound a rhythmic vibration that makes the tension in the room rise and fall in waves. Sweat beads on her brow, the sequins on her suit catching the fluorescent light in a fractured rainbow. She's usually unflappable, but now there's strain in every line of her body.

I try to focus on her face, on the calm determination in her eyes, but another pulse of energy sends me reeling. My vision wavers and Dominic's voice reaches me like it's underwater. "Kiki—"

"Quiet," she snaps, not looking at him. "Almost done."

The tingling sensation surges one last time, then dissipates. Kiki exhales sharply, her hand sliding from my forehead to my shoulder. Her energy pulls back, leaving me feeling hollowed out but. . .lighter. My muscles relax and I take my first deep, steady breath in what feels like hours.

"That'll hold," Kiki says, her voice hoarse. "But you're not out of the woods yet, sugar. Whatever this thing is, it wasn't designed to kill outright. It was meant to rot you from the inside out—slowly. Nasty stuff."

"Rot?" I croak, my throat raw.

Kiki nods grimly. "That's right, baby. It's a hex laced with decay magic. Meant to wear you down, not take you out in one go. Whoever made this. . . well, they're a petty son of a bitch."

Dominic growls low in his throat, and I catch the flicker of his claws before he clenches his fists. "I'm going to kill Roman."

Kiki steps back, wiping her forehead with a sequined sleeve. "Let's save the vengeance for later, darling. Right now, she needs calories. Lots of them. Healing burns through energy like a house fire through kindling."

"Calories?" I echo weakly.

"Food, sugar. And plenty of it. I don't care if it's pizza, cake, or a steak the size of your head. You're ravenous, aren't you?"

Now that she mentions it, the gnawing hunger in my stomach is undeniable. I nod shakily.

"Thought so." Kiki straightens, her dazzling confidence returning. "You're gonna be fine, sweetie. But don't skip meals, or I'll know. And if I have to come back here because you're stubborn, there won't be enough glitter in the world to soothe my irritation."

She goes to speak to Dominic, and I drift back into the darkness, but this time it's from deep relief and exhaustion.

CHAPTER 38

BRINGING BACK BASIL
THE BEAST OF BOSTON

Belle has been in and out of consciousness for the better part of a day. At least she's at home, tucked into bed in my bedroom. *Our* bedroom.

A pair of flutterbuns hover near the headboard, their iridescent wings catching the soft light filtering through the curtains. I knew we didn't get them all contained once she let them out. Though I can't say I care much about their escape.

One flits closer to her as if curious, while the other bobs lazily in the air as though keeping watch. No matter what I do, they refuse to leave her side.

Whenever she rouses, I'm right there. Mrs. P brings in steaming plates of food, everything from steak with a side of lobster, mashed potatoes, and green beans to a mountain of chocolate chip pancakes with scrambled eggs and bacon. The more she eats, the more color comes back to her face. She fusses at me when I keep urging her to eat more, telling me she knows when she's full and not to push.

"Why don't you come over here?"

I jerk up from where my chin is settled on my chest. I'd

fallen asleep in a chair. Isabelle pats the bed, and I'm there in a heartbeat. Wrapping an arm around her, she snuggles into my chest.

"How are you feeling?" I ask, trying not to be so anxious about the answer.

"Much better but still weak," she confesses. Then she tenses in my arms. "Is my dad okay, really?"

"Yes," I assure her, running my claws through her hair. "He's been here, spoiled by Mrs. P's baking and back to writing on the walls of his room with permanent marker. Guess I should have noticed all his equations were for making Thorns. Now that I'm listening to him, I'm not sure how I missed it." And since I've been examining those walls and listening to his babbling, I've been picking up some interesting ideas.

The way I stroke Isabelle's hair evokes a happy humming sound from her. This may be my new favorite sound. Though I don't deserve to hear it or to have her pressed against me like this. If it weren't for me, she wouldn't have drank that hex.

"How long have I been out?"

"Just over a day."

"Ugh." She wrinkles her nose. "I must smell terrible."

"You smell like you," I say, dropping a kiss on her head before inhaling deeply. It's true, and I'm addicted to her in any and all states. My heart wrenches inside my chest. "I'm sorry this happened. It should have been me."

She cuddles deeper into me, shaking her head. "It's not your fault. It's Roman's," she adds darkly. "He and Adrian meant to poison you with that champagne."

Roman. I swear to all the fae lords I will rip his spine out through his throat.

"He knew," she says quietly. "He watched me drink it,

and he still turned around and walked away, not saying a thing. My cousin truly doesn't care what happens to me or my father."

My insides twist with pain. She sounds so dejected.

"I would never hurt you like that." I need her to know that I am nothing like her old family.

"I know," she says quietly.

Isabelle drifts off again, her breathing soft and even against my chest. The weight of her in my arms feels grounding, anchoring me in a way I don't deserve. As much as I want to stay here, to soak in the quiet reassurance of her presence, I can't shake the gnawing guilt churning in my gut.

The champagne wasn't meant for her—it was meant for me. And now, because of me, she nearly died. If Roman thinks he'll walk away from this unscathed, he's more of a fool than I ever imagined.

But Isabelle is right about one thing: her father deserves more than the scraps of a life he's been given. She's sacrificed so much to care for him. Maybe I can finally do something that doesn't end with me breaking everything I touch. If Basil's equations hold the key to fixing his mind. . .and if they might help Isabelle one day. . .

I ease out of bed, tucking the blanket around her carefully. Her brow furrows slightly, but she doesn't wake. One flutterbun lands lightly on the pillow beside her head, while the other circles lazily above, its wings shimmering faintly. They stay behind, a small, silent guard, as I step out of the room, closing the door behind me.

The air in Basil's room is charged, humming with a manic energy that matches the scrawled equations covering the walls. He doesn't look up when I enter, his attention locked on a cluster of symbols he's circling furiously.

"Basil," I say, keeping my tone low but firm. "Why don't you show me what you've been working on."

He doesn't respond, not at first. But as I move closer, scanning the walls, the pieces start clicking into place. If I look and listen between the nonsense, it's clear what he's been trying to do. Basil has been trying to make a Petal for his own condition.

I should be upstairs, next to Isabelle as she heals. She's my priority. But if I can pull even a thread of Basil's mind back into place—maybe I can fix one thing to make up for the mess I've dragged her into.

THE METALLIC TANG of potions brewing fills the basement, sharp and acrid, crawling up the back of my throat. The low hum of the equipment merges with Basil's muttering as his pencil scratches furiously across the paper. I can almost follow the rhythm of his thoughts now, the way he layers concepts like bricks in a wall, each one tenuously holding the next.

"You're trying to bind it tighter, aren't you?" I say, pointing to a cluster of equations on the paper. "If the bond holds, it'll mimic the structure of a Petal."

He freezes, his pencil hovering over the paper. Then he looks at me, his eyes narrowing with suspicion. "You—You see it?" he mutters, almost accusing.

"I see enough," I say. "Enough to know you're close."

His shoulders sag slightly and he exhales, a wheezing sound that feels as much relief as exhaustion. I glance back at the plate and make a mental note to bring more food soon, maybe something easier to eat. He doesn't notice the way his hands tremble, but I do.

It's less than thirty minutes later when I'm examining the vial in my hand, its contents glowing faintly, volatile and dangerous. This isn't just for Basil—I need to understand every part of this. For him. For Isabelle.

"You sure about this?" I murmur to the old man.

Basil's head bobs up and down enthusiastically without looking up. I hold it out to him, and his wrinkled fingers curl around the glass.

The shuffle of slippers against concrete snaps me out of my focus. My head jerks toward the door just as Isabelle steps into the room.

She looks pale and fragile, her robe clinging to her frame and her hair loose around her face. She shouldn't be out of bed. She shouldn't be here.

Her eyes connects with the vial in my hand. Then to the stack of papers on the desk. To the scribbled equations covering the walls, her father's looping, frenzied script crammed into every inch of space. I see the exact moment it clicks—the way her breathing changes, the tremor in her fingers.

Her gaze snaps back to me, wide and dark with something between disbelief and betrayal.

"Wh—What are you doing?" Her voice breaks the uneasy rhythm of the space, sharp and raw, cutting straight through me.

I set the vial down carefully, turning toward her, hands raised in what I hope is a calming gesture. "Isabelle," I start, my voice steady but soft. "This isn't what you think."

"This isn't what I think?" I can hear the chords of her voice strangling the panic rising in her. "It looks like you are experimenting on my father."

Shit. It's exactly what she thinks.

"Isabelle," I say her name, trying to keep that calm even keel she does even when I'm raging. "I'm trying to help your father. I think I can heal his mind. I think I can bring him back."

From the wild whites of her eyes, even as she shakes her head, I know I'm fighting a losing battle. "You—You are just like Roman." The airy disbelief drops, and she rushes forward, grabbing the vile out of Basil's hand. He's in his own world, not even aware of what's being said around him. She pulls him to his feet and ushers him across the room.

"Isabelle, please—"

She rears around to face me, even as Basil meanders up the stairs oblivious to our fight. "What is this? Some sick attempt to make your pack bigger? If you can pull me, then maybe you can pull my father, and then two of us can help you escape your damned situation?"

Her fury crackles through the air like a live wire. Hands tremble—not with fear, but with barely restrained rage—as she clenches the vial against her palm. Fire burns in her eyes, wild and untamed, the same defiance that made me fall for her now turned against me like a blade.

She's yelling. Completely unleashed, and she's a force to be reckoned with.

"No, that's not it at all." I do my best to keep that even tone, but the desire to shout to be heard is strong. Still, I throw a rope over that and yank as hard as I can to keep it controlled. "I'm trying to help him. I'm doing this for you."

Shock registers on her expression as violently as if she'd been slapped across the face, and I know I've made a grievous mistake. Perhaps even a fatal one.

"You didn't do this for me." The words come out in a

harsh whisper as her chest heaves like she'd been running for miles. Worst of all is the betrayal burning in her expression. "If you had, you would have asked me. You would have told me what you planned to do."

"You would have said no," I say calmly. As soon as it's out, I realize I've made another misstep. Each thing I say is yanking me down further into the quicksand pit of my own making.

"You're fae fucking right I would have said no. Treating him like an experiment is what hurt him in the first place.

"Isabelle," I start, my voice strained but steady. "You have to understand—I'm trying to help him, not hurt him. I've seen what Roman did, and this isn't that."

Her eyes blaze with betrayal, but I force myself to hold her gaze. "Roman weaponized Thorns. He created monsters. I'm trying to do the opposite. Your father. . .He's already been affected by them. The damage is done. But I think I can reverse it. I think I can bring him back."

Her voice cracks as she shouts, "By making him a lab rat? By doing the very thing that ruined him in the first place? How is that helping him, Dominic? How is that different?"

I take a step closer, forcing my claws to retract before I hurt something—someone. "Because I'm not doing this for power, Isabelle. I'm doing it for him. For you. To make sure no one can ever use something like this against you again."

Her lips tremble, but she shakes her head violently. "You didn't tell me. You didn't even ask. You decided this was your choice to make."

Her words slice deep, but I can't let them stop me. "You're right. I made a choice because I couldn't risk wasting time. I watched you nearly die, Isabelle. If it happens again—if someone uses something like that hex—

I need to be ready. For you. For him. The only way he can get better is if we do something about this."

"He doesn't *need* to get better. He needs to be taken care of. To be loved. He doesn't need more poison shoved down his throat." She's crying now. My wife is gripped by pure, unadulterated terror. I want to go to her, pull her into my arms, and tell her everything's okay.

"That's not what this is," I insist, my voice desperate. "This isn't poison—it's a way to reverse the damage. To heal. If there's even a chance that it could bring him back for you, how could I not try?"

I step toward her, my hands instinctively reaching out, but she recoils, flinching as if I might strike her.

Cold floods through me, sharp and suffocating. Isabelle is afraid of me.

The realization hits like a blade, sinking deep, twisting. Despite all the times I've tried to intimidate her, to push her away, to keep her at arm's length with growls and threats—this is different. This isn't the fear of a powerful man she refuses to back down from. It's the fear of someone betrayed, someone who doesn't know if they can trust me anymore.

I wanted her to be afraid of me once. Didn't I? I thought fear would keep her safe, make her stay out of my war, my world. But now, seeing her look at me like this—with pure, unadulterated terror—it's not triumph I feel. It's devastation.

My chest tightens, and for a moment, I can't breathe. I thought I could protect her. I thought I could keep her safe by being the Beast she needed, by making decisions for her when she wouldn't make them for herself. But now, I see how wrong I was.

I've succeeded in the one thing I only hours ago swore

I'd never do: I've hurt her. And worse, I've proven her right. I've become exactly what she feared all along.

The weight of it crashes over me, a cannonball through my center, leaving me hollow and raw. I want to pull her into my arms, to tell her it's okay, to fix everything I've just broken. But the space between us feels insurmountable, and for the first time, I'm terrified she won't let me cross it.

"Uh, boss?" Lucien interrupts. Tock is next to him at the top of the stairs. Their faces are as set as stones.

"Not now," I snap.

"You'll both want to see this," Tock continues despite my feral warning. There's something in his tone that pulls not only my attention but Isabelle's. When she meets his gaze, his large brown eyes are filled with sympathy as he fiddles with his buttons. "It's Chapter Three. There— There's been a fire."

CHAPTER 39

A CONTRACTUAL END

BELLE

Snow falls in fat, lazy flakes, dusting the ruins of my bookstore like a mockery of something soft and beautiful. I can see my reflection in the soot-blackened glass of what used to be my front door, but the image is warped. I look as broken as I feel—covered in ash, my hands scraped and shaking. The air smells like burnt wood and wet cement, acrid and cold.

Dominic is beside me, his towering presence strangely subdued.

I'm still burned by seeing him in the basement when I close my eyes—the vials, the equations, and his hands, steady and sure as if he believed he had every right to play god with my father.

I'm used to his growling commands, cutting through the space around him like he's always on the brink of violence. But now, he's silent, still as stone, watching me pick through the wreckage.

"This was my dream," I whisper, my voice raw and cracking.

I clutch what's left of my favorite sign—a hand-painted wood carving that read *Romance Lives Here*—now charred and splintered in two. I press the broken pieces to my chest like they're all that's holding me together.

At least no one was in the bookstore when it went up in flames. Chip was here earlier, but I sent them home after the fire had been fully put out. Even when Chip tried to stay, I insisted there was nothing they could do tonight. And I need space to grieve.

Dominic exhales through his nose, the sound sharp against the quiet snowfall. "I'll rebuild it," he says. "Better than before. Whatever you need. It'll be yours again."

I turn to him, the bitterness bubbling up so fast I can't stop it. "You think this is just about money?" My voice rises, shaking with every word. "You can't rebuild *this*, Dominic. You can't buy back what it meant to me. And you can't erase what you did. Not to my father, not to me. You can't rebuild trust the way you build walls."

He doesn't flinch, but his jaw tightens. "I can try."

"No, you can't," I snap. "This shop wasn't just a building It was my *freedom*. It was the one thing I built that wasn't tied to the Wolves, to my family, to any of this violence. And now—" My breath hitches as the reality slams into me again. I toss the splintered sign onto the rubble. "Now it's gone. And why? Because of you? Because of them? I don't even know anymore!"

They did it to punish Dominic. To punish me. Without even knowing or caring what this place meant to me.

The snow keeps falling, blurring the edges of the world, softening everything but the burning ache in my chest. I rake my hands through my hair, shaking my head. "I don't want to be part of this war, Dominic. I don't want to be caught between two sides I never wanted to be part of in the first place."

He doesn't speak for a long moment, and when he finally does, his voice is unnervingly calm. "You're right."

I blink, thrown by the sudden flatness in his tone. "What?"

He's not looking at me anymore. His gaze is distant, his green eyes shadowed and cold. "You're right. This isn't your war. You don't belong in it." His words are deliberate, each one delivered like a nail in a coffin.

"Dominic—"

"Consider our contract terminated."

The air seems to thicken around me, the snowfall slowing as my brain tries to catch up. "You mean. . .our marriage?"

"Yes." The word is clipped, devoid of any warmth. He's not Dominic anymore—he's the Beast of Boston, sharp and unreadable, a man made of steel. He looks past me at the rubble, his expression carved from ice. "I'll make arrangements. You'll be safe. Your father will be cared for."

He starts to turn, his coat brushing against my arm.

"Wait." My voice cracks, but he doesn't stop. "You can't just—"

"I can." He cuts me off without looking back. "And I will. You deserve better than this. It's clear the only way to make up for this is to remove you from the situation entirely."

My brain can't comprehend what's happening, but my gut sinks all the way to the dirty ash-streaked snow.

"I'll have Basil move in with Mrs. P until you can find accommodations if it makes you feel better. Of course, Tock will help arrange anything you need."

I didn't know words could blur together but they're

melding and stretching incoherently in my ears. Dominic's hands are in his pockets and he speaks so calmly, so decisively, so cold.

"I'm sorry this situation has caused you so much distress, Belle."

Belle.

The word lands like a blade, clean and merciless.

Dominic has only ever called me Isabelle. It was a tether, a claim, a quiet promise wrapped in syllables no one else had ever bothered to give me. But now? Now he strips those syllables away, sharp and impersonal, like he's cutting the last thread between us.

His boots crunch over the snow-dusted rubble as he walks away, his broad shoulders disappearing into the white haze.

I'm frozen, my breath clouding in the air, watching him leave. I should feel relieved, shouldn't I? He's giving me an out. He's letting me go. But all I feel is the jagged, unbearable pain of loss.

The snow keeps falling, and I sink to my knees in the ashes of my life, wondering how it's possible to lose the same thing twice.

THE WARMTH of Poison Apple hits me like a tidal wave as I step through the door, and the low hum of conversation buzzes in my ears. My coat drips melting snow onto the floor, but I barely notice. The roses on it and the weight of my matching ring make me feel even more hollowed out.

"Belle," Rap's voice rings out from behind the bar. She's already moving, her heavy boots thumping against the wood floor as she closes the distance between us.

Before I can speak, she's pulling me into a tight hug that smells of vanilla and whiskey, a blend as familiar as the steady beat of her pulse against mine. Her arms lock around me, firm but not smothering, and for a moment, I feel like I might not fall apart.

"We've been calling you about the store," Goldie says, her concerned voice floating over my shoulder like the brush of a feather. She steps up next to Rap, her worry etched in the furrow of her brow. "Are you. . ." Her words falter, her gaze roaming over my face. "Are you okay?"

Snow appears beside her. "Of course, she's not okay," she says, as if stating the obvious. "Look at her."

"I'm so sorry," Ariel says quietly from nearby.

Despite the bar being full of people drinking and laughing, the music thumping through the floor and into my tired empty bones, I let them guide me to the back and into Rap's office. The edges of my vision are still hazy from exhaustion and the cold. Rap shoves a mug of something hot into my hands, her tone leaving no room for argument. "Drink this." Goldie wraps a blanket around me that she seems to have procured from out of nowhere.

I take a sip, the warmth of the tea spreading through me, but it does nothing to ease the broken edges inside me. My fingers tighten around the cup as I force out the words.

"He left me," I whisper, the sound barely audible over the low murmur of the bar.

Rap's brows knit together. "What do you mean, left you?"

"Dominic," I say, my voice breaking. "He. . .He ended it. Our marriage. The contract. Everything."

Snow mutters a curse under her breath across the bar while Goldie's hand flies to her mouth in shock. Rap rocks back on her heels slightly, her expression unreadable for a moment before she speaks.

"Contract?" Rap asks in a voice far too controlled. She sits on the edge of her desk, crossing her arms. "Alright, Belle. You're here now. Start at the beginning."

I SPEND the night at Rap's. Goldie lent me some extra clothes, and after sharing what bits I could bring myself to voice, I passed out for fourteen straight hours. Whether it was the aftereffects of the hex or the bone-deep weight of grief dragging me down, I can't tell.

Chapter Three is gone. Dominic betrayed me and left—rejected me without hesitation. I don't have an apartment to go back to (I'm not calling Tock), and my father still needs collecting.

But I can't stay in bed forever. My stomach makes its discontent clear with a loud rumble, and the dull ache in my head reminds me I haven't had coffee since. . .Well, before everything burned. Maybe before the gala.

I groan, dragging my sad, sorry ass out of bed and into Goldie's borrowed clothes, which hang awkwardly on me like a second layer of despair. I don't bother looking in the mirror. I know I look terrible—my hair is a tangled mess, my face is pale and puffy from crying and too much sleep.

Coffee. Just coffee. That's the only goal I can muster as I shuffle downstairs and out the door, crossing the alley to Poison Apple. The bitter cold snaps at my cheeks and wakes me up just enough to make me regret leaving the cocoon of blankets, but it's too late now. I push through the heavy door and step into the bar's warmth and dim light.

By the time I'm inside, the sun is well past its zenith, its muted light filtering through the frosted windows. The air carries the faint smell of polish and wood, layered over a lingering trace of last night's whiskey and laughter. It's that rare quiet hour before opening when the world feels like it's holding its breath.

Rap is behind the bar, her laptop open, fingers moving with steady purpose. The Lost Girls are tucked into their usual booth, their chatter familiar. Goldie shows something on her phone to Snow and Ariel—probably wedding plans—and Ted hovers nearby like her shadow.

The moment they notice me, their conversation halts. Goldie starts to rise, concern etched across her face, but Rap shakes her head once, sharp and decisive, calling them off. They hesitate, torn between their compassion and Rap's silent command, but eventually, they settle back, their chatter subdued. I know it's not indifference. Last night, they doted on me, offering encouraging words and steady hands when my grief threatened to drown me. I'm not sure I can bear another wave of kindness without falling apart.

I sit across from Rap on my favorite stool. She doesn't say anything, just pours fresh coffee into a chipped but beloved mug and slides it across the counter along with a donut on a plate.

I sit, my fingers curling around the warmth of the mug, and glance at her. "Why do you always know exactly what I need?"

"Call it a gift," she says, leaning her elbows on the counter.

The back door swings open, and I glance over my shoulder. Red steps inside, glowing with that serene energy of someone nearing motherhood. The former Lost Girl is pregnant with twins. Her fiancé, Brexley, is at her side, his hand steady on her back. Behind them, another former Lost Girl

—Cinder—strides in, her gothic elegance softened by Kai's easy smile. His hand brushes hers, their movements synchronized like they're two halves of the same whole.

Red doesn't hesitate. She crosses the room and wraps me in a gentle hug, murmuring soft condolences for Chapter Three. The silver-haired werewolf offers a quiet, "Let us know if you need anything."

Cinder joins them, pulling me into a quick, uncharacteristically tender hug before stepping back. Kai lifts my hand and presses a courtly kiss to the back of it. "My deepest sympathies," he says, his voice smooth as velvet.

I manage a weak smile, but my throat tightens as the attention weighs on me. It's Cinder who senses it first, pulling Kai gently toward the booth. "Let's leave her to Rap," she murmurs, her hand resting on his arm. The group drifts toward Goldie's corner.

I take a long swallow from the mug, but it's not the same. I can't help but miss the hazelnut coffee from home —or I guess—not my home anymore.

I miss sitting at the kitchen counter as Mrs. P bakes while we chat, my dad reading or writing in the breakfast nook. I miss the library, being surrounded by all of those books I now consider to be some of my closest friends. The flutterbuns that flap around the house, and come to me for snuggles throughout the day as I slip them different types of fruit. I miss Dominic's voice, low and gravelly as he challenges me, teases me and excites me. I even miss the nights spent in Dominic's company when we just enjoy our respective activities. And then I miss our. . .other activities.

I chug the rest of my coffee, needing to drown out the feelings. There's no going back. None of this can be undone.

Rap watches me carefully as she refills my cup. I go

about doctoring this one with cream and sugar. "Did you know I consider you the original Lost Girl?"

I meet Rap's hard green gaze. She pours a cup of coffee for herself. "My Lost Girls. . ." she starts, and then shakes her head as if deciding to take a different tact. "I find girls who have lost their direction, who are running from something, or don't know their own worth—usually because someone tried to convince them they were worthless, and I make this their new home." She waves a hand at the bar.

Rap likely has a point, so I wait.

"This is where they can be safe. A place where no one will fuck with them, or if someone does, there will be immediate retribution." Her teeth are bared now like a mama bear pissed off anyone would even think to lay a finger on one of her cubs.

And I'd seen it. Patrons who think they can mess with the staff in any capacity are immediately shown that won't be tolerated. I've worked in enough places to know not every employer empowers their employees to strike back so swiftly and without hesitation if boundaries are crossed or disrespect is shown the way that is done here.

Not to mention, if you try to hurt one girl, you bring down the wrath and power of all Poison Apple on your head from the bartenders, to the bouncers, to the emcee. Even the regulars.

Something stings the back of my eyes when I remember how Rap showed up on Dominic's doorstep with the other girls that day to make sure I was okay.

Forget the Wolves. Forget Roman and Adrian. My family is right here. Though the hole gaping in my heart tells me I'm losing the rest of my found family who resides in that gothic mansion I've come to love so much.

"It's a place where they can rebuild their confidence, and earn some cash, obviously," Rap goes on.

"We helped each other when we were both starting out in our businesses," I point out quietly. Five years of friendship seem like both an eternity and not nearly any time at all. "Granted, you helped me more—changing my name, scrubbing my past. But I'm not lost. I haven't been for a long time."

She shakes her head. "When we met. . ." She stops, her voice thick with emotion as she looks down at her coffee. "You helped me more than you could possibly know."

I can't say that I do know. Rap always holds things tight to the chest. All I know is when I met her, she was filled with the kind of rage and anger that had to be caused by the deepest of pains.

Rap rests her arms on the bar, folding her fingers together as she leans toward me. Her face softens, and it's there I find a layer of my friend I've never witnessed before. Her expression is full of a kind of longing mixed with pain. "This is also a place where girls can finally admit what they want. A place for you to realize what *you* want."

"What I want?" I shake my head, still not understanding.

"Belle. Babes. Since I met you, you've told me love is a sham. It's not real, and people only create relationships to use each other. I don't know what absolute douche nozzle taught you that, but I also know that you use that excuse to protect yourself. I know because you and I have a friendship that is based on more than need. And as far as romantic love, you and I see that real love here." She digs a finger into the bar. "All the time." She turns to the group in the booth. I follow her gaze.

Lost Girls, past and present, are crowded in. Red seems

softened by motherhood, and her scary, scarred-face fiancé keeps his hand steady on her rounded belly. Cinder leans into Kai, her gothic coolness melting as he pulls her closer, their matching vampiric grins a quiet testament to their bond. Ted's fingers absently thread through Goldie's hair as he tries to follow her whirlwind wedding planning. Goldie chats with Ariel, while Snow eggs Kai on to mess with Cinder.

Their laughter and quiet touches form a picture of love that feels almost too bright to look at.

I swallow hard.

"Love is real," Rap says quietly. "And you've wanted it desperately for as long as I've known you."

My nose tickles and the sharp heat behind my eyes kicks up again even as I continue to watch the group.

"It may not be exactly like it is in your books, but it's real. The passion, the devotion, the loyalty, exists in our actual world Belle, not just in your fantasy ones. And you deserve to have all of it."

"Do I?"

The words slipped by without consciously letting them out.

I feel rather than see Rap smile a little. "You deserve it because you want it. And what I need all my lost girls to realize is if there is a desire in their heart, it was put there because it was meant for them."

Her hand covers mine, forcing me to look up. "You've wanted love so badly, even if you didn't want to admit it, that I've had no doubt that one day it would waltz right in and find you. Even if you resisted." A wry chuckle escapes her. "I didn't exactly realize how literally that would manifest, but that Beast of Boston is literal putty in your hands. You shouldn't be afraid to give him a squeeze."

A wet burst of laughter escapes me even as I realize the tears are traveling down my cheeks.

"He doesn't really care about me. He needed me. It's different."

Rap shakes her head. "No, it's not. He wants you as much as he needs you. The issue isn't him loving you. The issue is, you have to *let* him love you. Everything you want is just on the other side of allowing it to come to you."

The realization that what she's saying is true doesn't hit me with the violence of a bombshell; it comes as gently as a wave lapping the shore. It swirls in me, percolating.

"And what do *you* want, Rapunzel?" I ask, using her full name. "What do you desire?"

She's always helping and mentoring everyone else. But no one asks her what she needs.

Rap's gaze flickers to mine with surprise. Cogs and gears grind behind her eyes, but it doesn't take long for her mind to churn out an answer.

"To be well."

The words come out softly and more vulnerable than I've known her to be capable of. I catch a flicker of fear in a woman who I thought possessed none.

Then she straightens and returns to her laptop to immerse herself in work.

The conversation is over, but I'm happy to sit across from my friend in misery for a while longer.

When the bar opens and a crowd begins to gather, I decide to retreat back to Rap's apartment.

Snow crunches under my boots as I step outside, my breath puffing out in quick clouds. The sun has already set and the streetlamps illuminate the many people walking along, absorbed by wherever they are headed.

I barely register the shadow moving in my periphery

before a rough hand grabs my arm, yanking me sideways. My yelp is muffled as something sharp pricks my neck—a needle, cold and unyielding. My vision blurs as the ground tilts beneath me.

I blink, trying to focus, but the edges of my sight are already going dark. The last thing I see is the red neon glow of Poison Apple's sign, flickering like a distant beacon, as the world goes black.

CHAPTER 40

A BEAST ON BORROWED TIME

THE BEAST OF BOSTON

Pain radiates through me, relentless, as my body tears itself apart at the seams.

My claws twitch, half-formed and aching, as I press a hand to the edge of my desk to steady myself. The wood groans under the pressure, my claws scraping deep gouges into its surface. A sharp crack splits the air as the desk buckles, collapsing under my weight. Splinters scatter across the floor like shrapnel, embedding in my palms and the soles of my feet as I stagger back.

Around me, the wreckage tells the story of my torment. Bookshelves lie upended, their contents strewn like the entrails of something gutted. Shredded papers cling to jagged edges of broken glass where picture frames once hung. The air reeks of split varnish and old ink, a sickly combination that churns my stomach.

I glance down at my hands, blood smearing my knuckles, a testament to my inability to hold myself together—or anything else. My claws flex involuntarily, catching on the ragged edge of a chair leg I don't even remember destroying. The study was supposed to be a sanctuary, but now it's as broken as I am.

I locked myself away in here, afraid to be anywhere else. This house is full of ghosts and I don't want to disturb their resting places. Even Isabelle's imprint is on the library, the kitchen, my own bedroom, and I couldn't stand to destroy those echoes.

And yet, isn't that what I've done? I let her go, and now she's become another haunting presence I can't escape. She isn't dead, but this. . .this feels like a death. Hers. Mine. Ours.

Agony surges again, ripping through muscle and bone, the visceral war raging beneath my skin. I double over, the air searing in my lungs, and roar—an inhuman, broken sound that shatters the silence and leaves my throat raw. My claws lash out, tearing through the leather of the armchair beside me, the stuffing spilling out like entrails. The shredded fabric tangles in my fingers as my vision blurs, and the edges of the room dissolve into a haze of fury and pain.

I deserve this.

The thought settles deep into my chest. I deserve every ounce of this agony.

Because I let her go.

My fist crashes against the desk before I can stop myself, splintering the surface. I've always been able to control my anger, to direct it outward, but now it's turned inward, feeding on my regrets like a ravenous beast.

Belle.

She trusted me. Somehow, despite all the lies, the blackmail, and the violence that followed me like a shadow, she let herself believe in me. And I repaid her faith by shattering her.

I never should have blackmailed her into marrying me. I see that now—how I forced her into my world, my war, and left her with nothing but ruins. Chapter Three is gone, her sanctuary reduced to ash and rubble, and it's all because of me.

The image of her standing in the snow, clutching that broken sign to her chest, burns behind my eyes. I told her I'd rebuild it, that I'd make it better than before. But how can I? How can I ever give her back the freedom and the peace I stole from her?

I sink into the last mostly intact chair, my head dropping into my hands as the pain in my body sharpens, flaring hot and wild. This isn't just physical—it's the weight of my failures, the guilt of knowing I've destroyed the one person I swore to protect.

And in turn, it's speeding up the war of cells in my body. Man versus beast.

I thought I was doing the right thing by letting her go. Telling her she deserved better, that I'd take care of her father, that I'd keep her safe from a distance. But I can't even convince myself it was the right call. It wasn't noble; it was cowardly.

I was too scared to admit the truth—to admit that I need her. Not just because she's my wife or because she's tied to my survival, but because she's the only thing that's ever made me feel whole. And now she's gone.

My claws bite into the edge of the chair, and I force myself to breathe through the searing pain. It doesn't matter what I want. I've done enough damage.

The beast in me roars against that thought, furious and unrelenting. It doesn't care about right or wrong, only that she's gone. And for the first time, I wonder if the beast is right.

Should I try to get her back?

The ache in my chest sharpens, twisting through my ribs like barbed wire. I press a hand there as if I can hold my body together by sheer force of will, but it's a losing battle.

I'm dying.

The realization settles over me with brutal clarity. I've known for a while now, in the way my body strains to maintain control, in the way the half-shift breaks down my insides like a curse I can't escape. But there is no Petal for this. The beast inside me is tearing me apart, slowly and agonizingly.

And there's nothing left to stop it.

Forming a pack was supposed to save me. That was the plan—to forge bonds strong enough to anchor me and make me whole again. But I failed. The very foundation of that plan—Belle—is gone. And I can't even blame her.

At least when I die, she'll truly be free. She deserves that much.

Everything I've built, all the power and wealth I've hoarded, will belong to her. The lawyers will see to it. Provisions have been made for Mrs. P and the staff, but the rest? It's hers. She can burn it all to the ground if she wants.

I exhale slowly, the air rattling in my chest like a dying ember. The beast snarls within me, but it's quieter now, almost resigned.

I meant what I said. There would be only one way out of this marriage.

Death. Mine, specifically. If Belle and I didn't form a pack, she wouldn't be forever bound to me because I was already on borrowed time.

The buzz of my phone from somewhere on the floor disrupts the silence, grating against my frayed nerves. I almost don't answer, too weighed down by exhaustion and regret. But something pulls me out of the chair to locate it, some gut instinct I can't ignore. I don't recognize the number.

Hitting the answer button, I don't speak.

"Dominic," comes the slick, venomous tone of Roman. His voice slithers through the receiver like a snake. "Can't say I'm pleased to be talking to you again, but thanks for saving my cousin from the fate meant for you. And wouldn't you know, the little lost lamb was out wandering by Poison Apple on her own. Tsk, tsk. You really should have kept a closer watch."

The air leaves my lungs in a vicious rush, my vision narrowing to a pinpoint.

He has Isabelle.

It takes all my control not to give into another mindless rage.

"What do you want?" My patience is nonexistent, my body trembles from the effort it takes to keep still and listen to this despicable fuck.

"You," Roman drawls, the amusement in his voice enough to make my claws dig into the desk.

I remember standing here not all that long ago, having the exact conversation with Isabelle.

Perhaps Isabelle was right. Maybe Roman and I aren't so very different after all.

The thought more than disgusts me.

"She's not part of this," I snarl, my voice raw with fury. "If you touch her—"

"She'll be fine. For now," Roman interrupts, his smirk practically audible. "That depends entirely on you, though. You can come to me and exchange yourself for her. Or don't, and I'll make sure the next time you see her. . .Well, let's just say you'll need a strong stomach."

The line goes dead before I can respond, leaving the threat hanging in the air.

He really has absolutely no loyalty to family. He'd kill his own cousin just to get to me.

My entire body trembles—not with fear, but with rage. The beast inside me surges forward, roaring to life with a violent demand for blood. My vision blurs again, but this time it's not from weakness.

It's fury.

I push myself to my feet, every nerve in my body screaming in protest. It doesn't matter. The pain doesn't matter. My body tearing itself apart doesn't matter. Only one thing matters now.

Belle.

She's in danger, and I'm going to find her even if it's the last thing I do.

Which it very well might be.

CHAPTER 41

KILL THE BEAST

BELLE

The room is dim and smells of damp earth and iron. The walls are made of crumbling brick, streaked with soot and time, their jagged edges softened by decades of neglect. Once, this building might have been part of Boston's industrial backbone, a factory churning out textiles or machinery. Now, it's a hollowed out shell, its purpose twisted into something far darker.

Roman's base of operations is nothing like the polished veneer of his public persona—it's a place drained of the humanity it once served—just like Roman, who has no qualms about stripping away the bonds of family if it means seizing more power.

A shiver crawls down my spine, and I can't tell if it's from the cold or the danger coiled around me.

I've been stashed away with two Wolves guarding the door, to make sure I don't go anywhere. The cold of this place bites through my borrowed clothes. I pace the room, rubbing my hands over my arms to generate any warmth I can, though it does nothing for the icy realization that I'm under Roman's control. Again.

My cousin saunters into the room, his tailored suit a jarring contrast to the gritty surroundings. "I trust your accommodations are to your liking." His voice oozes false charm.

"Cut the crap, Roman." My voice is steadier than I feel. "What do you want?" My stomach churns, bile rising in my throat, but I force it down. I can't afford to show fear. Not to him.

He smirks, circling me like a predator toying with its prey. "You always were the ballsy one in the family. Shame you wasted that ambition playing house with Dominic Blackwell."

At the mention of Dominic, something sharp twists in my chest—an ache I've been trying to bury since the moment he walked away. But I don't give Roman the satisfaction of a reaction. "This isn't about me," I say. "It's about power, isn't it? It's always about power with you."

"Of course it is," Roman snaps, the charm slipping from his tone. "Power is the only thing that matters. And I learned long ago that the Beast of Boston and the members of his empire were, in fact, true beasts. Shifters, Isabelle. Real, powerful, untouchable. It all makes sense now, doesn't it? How they've ruled Boston for so long. Why they had everything I've ever wanted."

I glare at him, my hands clenching into fists. "So you killed them. His entire family. Little kids?"

Roman rubs his lips. "Admittedly things got out of hand. I hired a local anti-fae group to handle my problem, but they were. . .messy."

My blood turns to ice. Messy. That's what he calls the slaughter of an entire family? Dominic's family. The weight of his casual indifference presses against my chest, and it's all I can do to keep breathing.

He's not even sorry. I expected as much, but the sheer lack of remorse still feels like a slap. The room feels smaller, the air thicker, but I straighten in my chair, meeting his gaze. He won't see me break—not yet.

"You're disgusting, Roman. Is this why you pushed the wolf pack dynamic so hard? You thought it would make you like Dominic? You're nothing like him. You're barely even a gnat to him."

He stops pacing, his eyes narrowing as he leans in. "You think I don't know that?" His voice drops to a venomous hiss. "That's why your father was so important. Basil was supposed to create the answer. A curse that would elevate our people, make us equals to Dominic's kind—No, their superiors."

"You pushed my father too far," I whisper. "You're the reason he lost his mind."

Roman's smile is razor-sharp. "Uncle Basil wasn't strong enough. He cracked under the pressure, and when his own potion failed, I made him drink it. I thought maybe it would give him a needed nudge to focus. But I suppose that backfired. . ."

"You poisoned him," I spit, the words tasting like ash. I knew it. I felt it in my bones that Roman had been directly responsible all these years, and now I know. The depths of my hatred has no bottom. "You're nothing but a bottom-feeding parasite. You destroy everything you touch."

His laugh is low, curling with menace. "Oh, spare me the sanctimony, Belle. Dominic isn't some noble figure. He's driven by power, just like me."

"No, he's not," I snap, my voice trembling with fury.

Dominic might be ruthless, but his strength comes from protecting those he cares about, not discarding them when they're no longer useful.

The clarity of it nearly stops me mid-thought, and I realize—Dominic's strength isn't in his power alone. It's in how he uses it, not for himself, but for others. I've seen it in the way he fights for Basil, even when it hurts him. I've felt it in the way he looks at me, as though I'm more than just a tool to be used.

Saying it out loud solidifies something I hadn't dared admit to myself before. I was wrong about Dominic. He isn't like Roman. He never was.

"Dominic doesn't succeed because he's a shifter. He succeeds because he's smarter than you. Because he knows how to lead without ruining everyone around him. You wouldn't know the first thing about that."

Roman's smile falters, his eyes narrowing. "Is that what you think? That your Beast of Boston is some noble king? He built his empire on blood, just like me."

The room feels colder, the air thickening as his meaning settles in. Roman doesn't just want to defeat Dominic. He wants to be him.

"Maybe," I say, my voice sharp and unwavering. "But it's not the blood of the innocent. He doesn't throw his own away as if they were trash. My husband knows how to build loyalty and respect."

The kind of loyalty Roman can't buy or bully his way into. Dominic's people don't follow him because they're afraid—they follow him because they believe in him. He saved Chip with no agenda. The deference he gives to his own housekeeper shows respect most wouldn't give their own staff. Even I've seen it, felt it, in ways I didn't expect.

"That's the difference, Roman. That's why you'll never be as powerful. You're just a bottom feeder sucking on the underside of his boots."

Roman's smile falters, his eyes narrowing into slits of

cold calculation. "You think that loyalty will save him?" He steps closer, the heat of his breath curling against my skin. "He's coming for you, Isabelle. And when he does, we'll be ready. My Wolves will meet him on his level."

A sick wave of dread crashes over me, but I don't flinch. Roman feeds on fear, and I refuse to let him see mine. Still, his words stick, their venom seeping deep into my chest. Dominic is coming. I know that as surely as I know my own heartbeat. But Roman's gloating isn't just for show—he has a plan.

"What are you going to do?" The question lodges in my throat like a stone.

Roman's grin spreads slow and triumphant, malice dripping from every corner of his expression. "Just because Uncle Basil couldn't crack the code on a Thorn that would turn me into the very thing your husband is, doesn't mean someone else didn't."

"You're going to force the Wolves to drink Thorns?" My throat tightens as I struggle to understand what my cousin hopes to achieve.

"Of course. They're mine to order, Isabelle. They pledged their lives to me, and now they'll serve their purpose."

Roman steps toward the nearest guard and claps him on the shoulder with a grin that oozes mock camaraderie. "Loyal to the end, aren't you?" he says, his voice dripping with smug satisfaction. The guard doesn't flinch, his expression stoic, but there's a brief, almost imperceptible lift of his chin as if accepting the twisted honor Roman bestows on him.

"You see, the Thorn doesn't just level the playing field. It will make them stronger. Better. Real predators. We'll be real wolf shifters but better than the natural-born kind. Because we took the power and made it our own."

My chest tightens, a mix of fury and terror roaring through me. Roman doesn't see people—only pawns.

I look at the two guards by the door, searching for even a shred of doubt, some sign they understand the cost of what he's planning. But they remain stone-faced, their gazes fixed forward, unwilling or unable to meet mine.

His Wolves aren't his allies. They're sacrifices, and he'll feed them to his ambitions without a second thought.

"And when Dominic comes running to save his precious little wife. . ." Roman leans in, his voice dropping to a deadly whisper. "He'll face a pack of true monsters."

The bile rises in my throat with the horror of it. Roman isn't just setting a trap—he's creating a massacre. Either he kills his own crew with an unstable curse, or he'll unleash twisted monsters to destroy Dominic and claim the city for himself.

"You're insane. You'll destroy them. Your own people."

Roman throws his head back, laughing, the sound bouncing off the stone walls like a harbinger of doom. "Destroy them? No, Isabelle. I'm going to reshape them. Break them down and rebuild them into something no shifter could ever hope to match. Power like Dominic's, instincts sharper than any wolf, and most importantly, my control. And when your husband comes to save you, the Beast of Boston will face a pack of true monsters."

I swallow hard, fear curling in my gut like a living thing.

"Dominic will come," I whisper, the words quaking in the cold air. I wish he wouldn't—for his sake—but I know better. He'll come, because he's never let me forget: I am his.

CHAPTER 42

BECOMING THE BEAST
THE BEAST OF BOSTON

We crouch in the shadows. The building where Roman holds Belle looms, a jagged monstrosity of concrete and iron that seems to pulse with malevolence. The snow around us is filthy, streaked with ash and oil, but I barely notice. My senses are trained on the Wolves patrolling the perimeter, their movements sluggish and predictable. Their guns are no doubt loaded with silver bullets.

"Boss, you're sweatin' like a sinner in church," Lucien mutters under his breath, the faintest edge of amusement in his tone. A flicker of flames dances across his fingertips, restrained but itching for release. His eyes cut toward me, sharp with concern despite the jest.

"I'm fine," I growl, low and tight. The lie tastes bitter on my tongue. My body betrays me in ways I can't ignore—my breaths come shallow and uneven, each one burning as if I've been inhaling smoke. My muscles twitch uncontrollably, the lion within clawing at the edges of my control, straining for release. Pain radiates through my ribs, spreading like wildfire with every beat of my heart.

Tock adjusts the lapel of his sharply tailored coat, the movement precise and deliberate, his gaze as cold as the frost biting at my skin. "If this is what 'fine' looks like, I'd hate to see you on an off day," he says. His voice carries that cool British detachment, but his grim expression betrays him. Tock's hand is wrapped around a well-polished Glock, and I'm sure there is another somewhere on him. It's not often he does the dirty work, but he refused to stay behind.

"I'm sure about this," I grind out, my claws twitching involuntarily. I curl my fingers into fists to steady them, the effort costing me more than I'd like to admit. I know what they're thinking. They've been watching me unravel over the past year and a half, watching my strength bleed out of me bit by bit.

Lucien leans in slightly. "You sure you ain't gonna keel over halfway in there? Look, we get it—You're hellbent on gettin' her back, but if you go down, we're screwed. Belle's screwed."

I snap my head toward him, narrowing my eyes in a silent warning. The look alone is enough to make him press his lips into a thin line, his flames flickering lower.

Tock raises a brow but speaks barely above a whisper. "Not the time for arguments. Let's keep moving."

The tension between us is thick enough to choke on, but I force myself to focus on the Wolves ahead.

A soft crunch of snow behind us has all three of us spinning, weapons at the ready. Chip emerges from the darkness, hands raised. "Easy, easy! It's me."

"What the hell are you doing here?" I snarl, my claws itching to rip into something, anything.

Chip straightens, a defiant edge to their stance despite the tension radiating off them. "I couldn't sit this one out. Belle's my friend too."

"This isn't your fight, *mon ami*," Lucien says, his flames flaring brighter in his frustration.

"It is now," Chip retorts, pulling a small handgun from their belt. The weapon is a cheap, scratched piece of metal —probably picked up from a pawn shop. It looks wrong in their hands, too small and jittery against the tremor of their fingers.

Tock mutters a curse under his breath. "This isn't a rescue mission for rookies."

Just then, a black and white flutterbun lands on Chip's shoulder.

Witchtits. I knew some of them had escaped the house. Who knows how many have already gotten to reproducing and nesting in the city.

Unphased, Chip doesn't even seem to notice the awkward way the gun slips slightly in their grip as they reach up to stroke the flutterbun's ear. "I overheard two of the Wolves talking. Roman's got them guarding the east side heavier than anywhere else—it's a dead giveaway that something important's over there."

I exchange a glance with Tock, whose brow furrows in thought. Lucien curses softly under his breath.

"It's a trap," I point out the obvious. "But it doesn't matter. Isabelle's in there."

Chip hesitates, the flutterbun nuzzling against their cheek like a comforting presence. "I'm not leaving until she's safe," they say firmly, their other hand steady on the pistol.

I glare at them. "No. You're going back to the house. If Roman sent Wolves out to guard this place, who's to say he hasn't sent more to circle back? Basil and Mrs. P need you. You're the only one I trust to keep them safe."

Chip falters, their grip tightening on the weapon. "But—"

"No," I cut in, leaving no room for argument. "You've done your part. If Basil or Mrs. P are hurt while you're out here playing hero, Isabelle will never forgive us."

Chip's shoulders sag slightly, the fight draining out of them. They glance at the flutterbun on their shoulder as though seeking reassurance, then nod reluctantly. "Fine. But you'd better bring her back."

Lucien huffs, shaking his head. "This is already a suicide run, and we're sending the kid home to babysit."

"Exactly," I say, baring my teeth in something that's more snarl than smile. "This isn't their fight. Let's keep it that way."

Chip gives one last glance toward the building before retreating into the shadows. The flutterbun takes flight into the night sky. I exhale slowly, forcing my body to focus despite the pain ripping through it. Isabelle is in there. None of this matters. Not my pain, not their doubts. Nothing.

The words hang in the frigid air, a vow more solid than stone. My body protests with every step as we move toward the building, but my determination burns hotter than the pain.

MY MONSTROUS FOOT slams into the door, and the warped metal groans before giving way with a resounding crack. The flickering fluorescent lights inside cast jagged shadows across the walls, emphasizing the grime and disrepair.

"We're heeere," Lucien mutters, dragging the words out in a low, singsong tone that sets my teeth on edge. His flames flare to life in both hands, their glow dancing off the cracked concrete walls. The acrid smell of oil and decay hangs in the air.

Tock steps in next, scanning the room with precise movements, his Glocks at the ready.

I follow.

Every step sends jolts of pain through my body, but I force it down. Isabelle is here. Pain is irrelevant.

We move in formation, boots crunching over shattered glass and debris. The sound grates against my nerves. Every step is a reminder that stealth is irrelevant.

The moment we round the corner into a wider room, the trap springs. A dozen humans emerge from the shadows, half-hidden by the dim light.

"You came," one of the Wolves sneers. I recognize him from the alley. Curt. His grin is feral, his teeth gleaming unnaturally in the flickering light. "We've been expecting you." Then he pulls a vial of viscous, dark liquid from his pocket. He holds it up like a trophy. "Roman said you'd come. He made sure we'd be ready."

Then they all quickly uncork their vials and drink. Curt smirks as he downs his own, tossing the empty container aside.

The transformation is immediate—and horrifying. Bones snap and reform, limbs elongate unnaturally, fur sprouts in patches.

One of the Wolves collapses, their body bubbling and dissolving into a heap of mangled flesh, fur, and bones. Another lets out a strangled cry as their limbs twist and lock at impossible angles before falling silent, their remains little more than a steaming pile of gore.

The room fills with guttural screams, a cacophony of agony and rage.

Tock doesn't flinch. "Bloody hell," he mutters, raising both guns at the horror twisting in front of us.

At the end of it, only six of the original group remain standing, their forms warped into something that defies nature. They aren't wolves—not even close. Their bodies are amalgamations of fur and muscle, with limbs too long and twisted, jaws that unhinge unnaturally, and eyes glowing with a feral, maddening light.

They charge forward with reckless fury.

Lucien's flames roar to life, cutting through the dark like a blade, while Tock's pistols bark with sharp precision.

I meet one head-on. My claws tear into its malformed chest, and the sickening crack of bones reverberates through the room. Blood sprays across the concrete as the thing that's no longer human lets out a guttural scream before falling lifeless to the ground.

Fire, bullets, and fangs collide in a chaos of violence. The room erupts into a cacophony of destruction as we crash into the oncoming monsters.

CHAPTER 43

DISSENT AMONGST THE RANKS

BELLE

The sounds of violence echo through the walls—screams that twist into snarls, the deafening crack of gunfire, and the low, guttural roars of something not entirely human. The building trembles with each explosion of noise, the chaos outside drawing closer.

I can't sit down even though there is a broken down couch in the corner. My heart pounds with every terrifying sound. Dominic is here, and hell has broken loose.

I recognize one of my new guards, Levi. The one who recognized me in that alleyway. He stands by the door, arms crossed. The younger guard beside him is rigid, stoic, and completely unmoved by the chaos rattling the building.

Another roar shakes the walls, followed by the wet, sickening crunch of bone. A muffled yelp cuts through the chaos, the kind that makes my stomach lurch. The fight isn't just close—it's coming straight for us.

My stomach twists, but the younger guard doesn't so much as glance at the door. His grip on his gun is steady, his face unreadable.

"You don't have to do this. You guys can walk out this door and just leave."

Neither of them responds.

"You know this isn't right," I focus on Levi, forcing my voice to steady. "Roman doesn't care about you. He doesn't care about anyone but himself. You're just a means to an end for him."

Levi doesn't look at me, his jaw tightening slightly, but his expression remains impassive.

"Shut your mouth," the younger guard snaps, his voice low but cutting.

"Don't tell me you actually trust him," I press, ignoring the younger guard and keeping my focus on Levi. "You've seen what he's done to people on the streets with those dirty hexes. What he's done to his own family. Do you really want to be his tool? Do you trust you'll be fine drinking that shit?" Roman gave both of them a vial of the shifting Thorn before he left them with instructions to put a bullet in my head if Dominic gets a chance to set eyes on me again.

Levi's gaze shutters, just for a moment, but it's enough.

Something slams into the dirty window. Quickly crossing the room, I open it to find a black and white flutterbun. It's one of my little buddies from the house, though how it got here totally leaves me confused. It flies into my arms, nuzzling me.

Dominic was right. Once they get loose, they get into all kinds of places.

Another shake of the building and a gurgling scream come from too close by.

The flutterbun takes flight again, darting back out the window. Whatever is happening, it's not natural. A loud crash erupts just outside the door, followed by a guttural roar so deep it feels like it vibrates through my chest.

I glance at Levi, hoping for some flicker of reassurance, but his face is a mask of tension.

The fight sounds like it's at the doorstep.

The younger guard pulls out his vial. "It's time."

"You're going to kill yourself," I say sadly.

Levi shifts subtly, his stance widening slightly as he glances at the younger guard.

"No," Levi says quietly, his voice steady.

The younger guard frowns, his head turning toward Levi. "What?"

"I said no," Levi repeats.

The guard's expression hardens, his grip on the rifle tightening. But Levi moves first. His hand shoots out, grabbing the barrel of the rifle and yanking it downward. The guard stumbles, his composure breaking as Levi strikes him across the temple with the butt of his pistol.

The guard collapses to the ground, his weapon clattering beside him.

Levi opens the door, his expression grim. "Go."

"Thank you," I whisper, my voice barely audible over the chaos outside.

We barely get two steps into the hallway before the sickening stench of death hits us—a mix of burnt hair and rotting flesh. The pile of remains sprawled across the cracked floor is unrecognizable as anything human or wolf. Bone juts out at impossible angles, splintered and sharp, while patches of fur cling to twisted muscle like moss on a decaying log.

One of the bodies twitches, a spasm running through what's left of its limbs before going still. The sight churns my stomach. Whatever this Thorn is doing, it isn't just unstable—it's monstrous.

Levi pauses, his jaw tightening as he scans the grotesque heap. "Sweet baby witchtits."

I swallow hard, the bile rising in my throat.

The Thorn is unstable. It's mutating and killing Roman's people.

A roar tears through the chaos, deep and guttural, so warped it sends a shiver down my spine. It's not Dominic.

I guess the Thorn isn't killing all of them. I don't want to meet Roman's new super race, but I have to find Dominic. We've got to get out of here.

Another crash reverberates through the hallway, followed by what sounds like a blowtorch igniting. Levi doesn't wait—he takes off down the corridor without so much as a glance back.

I stumble after him, but he's faster, his figure vanishing around a corner as the noise behind us grows louder. I don't know where I'm going, only that I need to keep moving.

A jagged hole gapes in the wall to my right, a window shattered inward. Wind howls through the opening, carrying the scent of rain and smoke. Shards of glass littering the floor crunch under my boots.

My pace slows as instinct tells me danger is near.

And then—a presence.

A hulking shadow detaches from the darkness ahead, its breath steaming in the cold. Not human. Not fully wolf. Bone pierces the slick, patchy fur, ribs pushing against too-tight skin like they're trying to break free. Its yellow eyes lock onto me, and for a breath, I know—I am prey. My muscles seize. My body knows what my mind refuses to process. Death is here.

It lunges.

Something small and fast streaks past my face. A blur of

black and white. Then another. Then three more. The flutterbuns.

They descend like winged demons, their tiny fangs sinking into exposed flesh. The beast snarls in fury, shaking its head as more of them pour through the shattered window, exploding into the hall like a furry-gothic plague. Claws scratch. Fangs tear. The monster shrieks, snapping wildly as the swarm overtakes it.

I don't waste my chance. I run.

My lungs burn as I blindly sprint, still having no sense of where I am or how to escape this place. I round a corner and slam into something solid. "Belle," a low, familiar voice says, sharp and breathless.

Adrian.

His face is pale and slick with sweat under the dim hallway light, eyes darting nervously.

"Roman's lost it," he blurts, grabbing my hand and pulling me along. "He's gone too far. We need to get out of here."

"I'm not going anywhere with you." I stop, wrenching my wrist away from him. "I've got to find Dominic."

Adrian stops and grabs my shoulders. "Forget him. Forget Roman. We were good once. We could be good again. Once the bodies are buried, we can start over. We'll pick up the pieces and rebuild."

Before I can say anything, his lips crush against mine in a frantic, twisted imitation of affection.

And then he's gone.

Adrian flies across the room, slamming into the wall with a sickening thud. Dominic stands there covered in blood. His chest heaving. His claws extended. His green eyes glow with murderous intent.

"What did I tell you," Dominic growls, low and lethal, "about touching my wife?"

Adrian scrambles to his feet, but he doesn't get far. Dominic is on him in a flash, claws ripping through flesh in a brutal, precise strike. Adrian's body crumples to the floor, lifeless.

My knees are suddenly gelatin, I can't breathe.

Dominic turns to me. "Are you hurt?"

Relief sweeps through me so hard I almost collapse on the spot. Dominic's alive. The relief is fleeting. He's covered in blood, and I'm not sure if it's his or someone else's. The sounds of snarling and yelps near.

I start to run to him when the metallic click of a hammer being drawn halts me mid-step. Roman stands to the side, a gun trained on me. A menacing growl rips from Dominic's throat.

My cousin holds up a bottle of dark liquid in his other hand. "You think you've won, Dominic?" he sneers. "Let's see how you handle the strength of a beast more powerful than you."

"Roman, don't do it. It could kill you or worse. It's not stable. You've seen it for yourself."

Roman's lip curls. "They aren't all as strong as me. Welcome to the new age, *cousin*." His last words are a taunt. Then he downs the vial in one swift motion.

His body jerks violently, like a puppet with its strings pulled too hard. His spine arches with a sickening crack and his limbs convulse, elongating at uneven angles. Bones splinter beneath his skin, pressing outward in jagged ridges, some tearing through muscle as if his body is rejecting its own transformation.

Fur sprouts in uneven patches, thin and wiry, leaving sections of raw, mottled flesh exposed. His face elongates unnaturally, the jaw unhinging with a wet, snapping sound as fangs erupt in chaotic rows. One of his legs twists entirely backward, dragging as he struggles to stay upright, his movements jerky and disjointed.

His glowing eyes meet mine for a fraction of a second, and in them, I see terror. Roman might have thought he could control this, but the Thorn has taken over, reshaping him into something monstrous—a creature of pain and rage.

He collapses to all fours, his chest heaving as his malformed claws scrape against the blood-slick floor.

Dominic squares his shoulders, his body quaking with visible exhaustion, but his claws remain extended. He doesn't move, not yet. He watches my cousin writhe in piteous agony. I want to look away from the horror, but I can't.

Dominic seems to revel in watching Roman snarl and gurgle as he writhes in pain. I can only imagine the satisfaction he feels at watching the man who slaughtered his entire family suffer what looks to be unimaginable pain and torment.

My cousin has destroyed himself and is now trapped in a malformed body, harmless to do anyone harm again.

"Belle," Dominic finally rasps, his voice heavy. "Your call."

My throat tightens as I meet his gaze, the weight of the decision pressing down on me. Roman is no longer human, no longer even a man. He's a thing, a consciousness trapped in torment.

I swallow hard, torn but resolute. "End it," I whisper.

Dominic nods, his movements slow but deliberate as he approaches Roman. The crack is brief, violent, and final.

Then Dominic stumbles away to lean heavily against a

wall, his claws retracting with an audible click as he struggles to catch his breath. His shoulders tremble with the weight of his exhaustion, his broad frame sagging like a fortress on the verge of collapse.

"Dominic?" My voice wavers as I take a cautious step toward him. His face is pale, his green eyes dull, and the ferocity that had driven him moments ago has drained away like water slipping through cracks in stone. "What's wrong?"

He shakes his head slightly as though he can't afford the energy to respond. Slowly, he slides down the wall until he's sitting, his back pressed against it for support. The sight sends a jolt of fear through me. Dominic never looks weak—not like this.

"Dom, talk to me," I plead, kneeling beside him. "You're scaring me."

A faint smile tugs at the corner of his lips, but it's brittle and fleeting. "I told you. . .this marriage was always going to end one way," he says, his voice hoarse and barely above a whisper. "In death."

CHAPTER 44

TOO LATE TO MATE

BELLE

My stomach plummets. "No," I whisper, shaking my head in disbelief. "No. You're going to be fine."

A bitter laugh escapes his lips, accompanied by a pained exhale. His eyes flutter closed for a moment, and I see the lines of agony etched into his features. This can't be happening. Not to him.

"Isabelle. . ." He trails off, and the use of my full name sends hot spikes of desperation through me. He's always been the only one who refuses to call me by the nickname everyone else uses. "We tried. We tried to form a pack, but it didn't work. That's okay."

Shifters die without a pack. It hits me so suddenly, so intensely, I instantly hate myself for not connecting the dots earlier. I knew half-shifted Dominic was in pain, but I never guessed it was killing him. How could I have been so stupid?

"I meant what I said, Isabelle. You'll get your freedom. Everything I have will be yours—except for what I've left for Lucien and the others. You can live your life however you want."

"Stop," I plead, cradling his face as if I can physically stop him from leaving this world. "Just stop."

His eyes flicker open, softer now, filled with something I can't bear to name. "Belle. . .you'll be better off without me."

The words hit me like a physical blow and the fear I'd been holding at bay surges forward, consuming me whole. I press my palms to his chest, feeling the sluggish thrum of his heartbeat beneath my hands. "You don't get to decide that," I snap, tears blurring my vision. "You don't get to give up on me—on us."

"I'm not giving up," he murmurs, his voice faltering. "I've just. . .run out of time."

Dominic's breathing slows, the weight of his body sagging further against the wall. His pallor is ashen, his once-vivid green eyes now dim.

"If I could stay, I'd show you how much I love you. I'm sorry I didn't tell you before now."

Hot tears trail down my face as I scooch forward, trying to get as close as possible without hurting him. "You did, though. Remember? When you opened the library for me, and then I fell off the ladder? After you caught me, you kissed me before telling me you loved me. And then we did it right there against the ladder. The thing nearly broke, remember? It was perfect."

A smile appears on his face before it twists as if a tidal wave of pain has hit him.

A terrible, soul-crushing realization slams into me with the force of a tidal wave.

I'm losing him.

My body locks up, a scream curling in my throat,

clawing for release. This isn't happening. This can't happen.

My chest tightens as I realize I've spent so long guarding my heart that I never truly let him in. But I was wrong. I'm passionately, over the cliff insanely in love with Dominic. Not because I need anything from him, but because when he is simply near I feel whole, complete, safe, and loved. I know to the marrow of my bones what it is like to be thoroughly and selflessly loved and the idea of losing that, of losing him, makes me want to die.

"Dominic," I whisper, leaning my forehead against his. "I love you too. And you're right. I'm yours. I'll always be yours." Then I drop a kiss onto his lips. They are cold and unresponsive.

His body slackens in my arms.

"Dominic?" I cry, shaking him gently. "No. No, no, no. You can't leave me!"

A guttural sound echoes from the doorway, shattering the fragile stillness. I whip around, my pulse pounding in my ears. One of Roman's creations stands there, its twisted form barely recognizable as a wolf. Its matted fur glistens with blood, and its muzzle drips with saliva as it snarls, fixing its red, feral eyes on Dominic.

Panic floods my veins, but something deeper stirs—a need to protect my husband.

I grab a gun that is lying forgotten on the ground nearby.

I stand, trembling, but my resolve is firm. "You won't touch him," I growl, my voice fierce and unwavering as I lift the firearm. I haven't picked up one of these in years, but I haven't forgotten a thing.

The beast stalks forward, its jagged claws scraping

against the floor, but I refuse to back down. Not now. Not ever.

The gun barks and kicks back in my grip.

The beast lurches but takes another step forward. Two more loud cracks from the gun before it clicks, empty of bullets.

The monstrous wolf's guttural snarl rips through the air as its claws swipe toward me. My heart seizes, but before the blow lands, a golden blur streaks past me.

A massive lion slams into the mutated werewolf with bone-crunching force. The room echoes with a sickening thud as the beast is thrown to the ground, its grotesque limbs flailing. The lion's roar is deafening. The air vibrates with the raw power of its cry.

"Dominic?" I whisper as I stumble back.

The lion is magnificent, his golden mane gleaming in the dim light. His massive form ripples with strength, claws digging into the abomination beneath him. With a swift and lethal swipe, Dominic tears into the werewolf's neck, silencing it forever. Blood pools beneath the corpse as Dominic rises, his massive frame towering over the carnage.

I freeze as the lion stalks toward me, his glowing green eyes locking onto mine. The feral intensity in his gaze softens as he approaches. My breath hitches when his massive head dips, his muzzle brushing against my shoulder. The gentle touch sends warmth flooding through me, a stark contrast to the violence moments before.

"Dominic," I whisper again, my hand shaking as I reach out. My fingers graze his mane, the coarse yet soft texture grounding me. He rumbles low in his chest, a sound of reassurance, of comfort. I can hardly believe what I'm seeing.

Fresh tears fall down my face from joy this time. Dominic shifted. We formed a bond. We're mates. And I can feel it. It's right there—a second pulsing sensation right beside my heart, tethering me to Dominic no matter what form he's in. I drop to my knees and bury myself in his body, hugging him as tightly as I can, allowing his warmth to seep into me.

The sound of bickering breaks the moment.

"You bloody idiot," Tock grumbles as he strides into the room, his polished boots crunching over debris. "Do you have any idea how much this jacket cost? You scorched my sleeve!" He gestures at the singed fabric, his British accent sharper than usual.

Lucien saunters in behind him, his drawl dripping with mischief. "Oh, c'mon, *mon ami*. You're still alive, ain't ya? Call it a little character for your fancy threads."

Tock glares, adjusting his cuff. "Character? I'll show you character when I—" His words cut off as his eyes land on Dominic. "Well, I'll be damned."

Lucien's playful smirk breaks into a full-on grin. "Looking good, boss."

Dominic steps away from me, his lion form graceful and imposing as he moves toward the two men. He lets out a low, rumbling growl.

"The Wolves have all been disposed of," Tock says, "But not without some cost." He shoots an accusatory glare at Lucien again.

"Yeah, yeah," Lucien says. "But how about we get out of here because this is like," his head swivels around, "a lot of corpses. And I'd much rather be at home with some tea courtesy of Mrs. P. Maybe a little celebratory whiskey." He waggles his eyebrows.

I nod. When Tock extends a hand to help me off the

floor, Dominic lets out a warning growl. Tock lifts his hands in surrender, backing away.

"So you can shift now, but you still haven't lost that grumpy impossible attitude," I say, getting up off the floor on shaking legs, but never letting go of Dominic.

My husband's low rumble vibrates through me, steady and real. "Let's go home," I say softly, no longer afraid of believing in love.

I once thought love was a fantasy—something spun only in the pages of a book— beautiful, completely unattainable. But this? This is flesh and blood, unshakable and true.

It fills the center of my being, satisfying the deepest, truest part of me. Despite trying to deny my need, it's just like Rap said. It feels like the secret desire in my heart was there because it was always meant for me.

CHAPTER 45

PROVOKING MY HUSBAND

BELLE

My husband is *hot.*

There's no two ways about it.

Because there are at least three.

First off, I had never seen pictures of Dominic from before he got stuck between two forms, so I had no idea what to expect. Not that I hadn't imagined it, but my imagination—which is incredibly healthy considering what I sell for a living—did not come close to the mark.

Dominic as a lion is magnificent—powerful, commanding—but as a man? He's *devastating.*

Broad shoulders that seem carved from marble, a beard rough and unkempt, framing a face that's all hard edges and raw power—and green eyes that still burn with the feral intensity that drew me to him in the first place.

His presence is magnetic, a force that makes it hard to think straight. But it's not just his looks—it's the way he carries himself with a confidence that doesn't demand attention but commands it anyway. He's still dangerous, still wild, and he still makes me feel like I'm the only person in the world when he looks at me.

And when he smiled for the first time—an actual, genuine smile—it felt like the sun breaking through storm clouds. My husband is hot. In every possible way. I am, without question, the luckiest woman alive.

Not only because he's a smokeshow of a man who occasionally shifts into a lion—though that makes for excellent fireside cuddling with a good book. When he gets incredibly amped up, either agitated or insanely aroused, his body finds that spot between forms again.

I'll lick and suck, agitating his cock and then pull away right before he comes. His already generous muscles thicken and lengthen, claws sprout, fangs lengthen, and his pupils turn to slits. Barbs lift against my tongue, and that's when I know he's about to pull me by my hair and piston down my throat, or throw me over the nearest piece of furniture and rail me within an inch of my life.

So yeah. There's three ways about it, and I'm addicted to all versions.

~

THE GOLDEN LIGHT streaming through the solarium filters across the room, touching everything with a soft glow. My dad sits by the window in a sturdy armchair, the light making the silver streaks in his hair glimmer. His posture is relaxed, and the teacup in his hands remains steady as he sips carefully—something I can't remember seeing in years.

I stop in the doorway, the sight making my chest feel tight. When was the last time I saw my dad so...at ease?

After coming home from Roman's massacre, Dominic and I stayed in bed for two straight days before we got back to any sense of normalcy. Even coming down to the kitchen without him, I feel the pull on our connection. The need to always be near him is impossibly strong, but I don't mind.

Though for the last week, Dominic insisted on spending two hours a night in the basement.

He'd come to bed smelling faintly of magic and burnt ozone, and when I pressed my mouth to his, I tasted something almost *electric* lingering on his tongue.

But we still spend every evening together in the library. So when Dominic asked me to get us a snack from the kitchen instead of calling for Mrs. P, I suspected something was up.

"Dad?" My voice is barely above a whisper as I step forward.

My dad sets the cup down gently and looks up, his eyes meeting mine. They're different now—clear, sharp, no longer clouded by the fog that had consumed him for so long. His lips tremble as they curve into a smile. "Isabelle."

The sound of my name from his lips, spoken with such clarity, nearly undoes me. I cross the room quickly, sinking to my knees in front of him. "How are you feeling? Are you. . .Is this real?"

"It's real," he says, his voice steady but thick with emotion. His hands—those same hands I had held through his worst episodes—reach out to cup my face. "Mr. Blackwell, your husband. He helped me make a Petal."

My chest collapses in on itself as I throw my arms around him, burying my face in his chest as the tears spill over. "I missed you," I whisper, my words muffled by the fabric of his shirt. "I missed you so much."

He holds me tight. "Oh, my sweet girl," he murmurs, his voice shaking. "You've spent your whole life taking care of me, and I didn't deserve a moment of it. I'm so sorry."

I pull back just enough to look at him, and shake my

head fiercely. "Don't say that. You're my dad. There was never a question."

His eyes mist over, and he wipes at them before taking a deep breath. "Seeing you all grown up and so capable—it makes me miss your mother. I wish she could see you like this."

The words hit me like a jolt. "Mom?" I blink in confusion. "I thought you didn't care that she left."

Basil winces, his face crumpling with regret. "I was heartbroken when she left. I loved her deeply, but I couldn't give her what she needed. We were two very selfish people who needed to live life on their own terms. I was so consumed by work, by everything else, that I couldn't make her believe how much I loved her."

His voice breaks, and he exhales shakily. "You suffered for my mistakes. When she left, I told myself I had to stay strong for you. But I didn't. I buried myself in science and potions to shut out the pain. And you—you were the one who stayed strong for me."

My throat tightens as I process his words. "You actually loved her?"

"Very much," he says, his voice soft but certain. "Not perfectly, but deeply. And you. . .you are the best part of both of us. You have her passion, her heart. But you're the most selfless person I've ever known. You didn't get that from either of us. And you did it all while building your dream from nothing, Isabelle. I'm so proud of you."

Tears blur my vision again, but this time, they don't feel as heavy. "I used your money— the blood money from the Wolves—to open it. I didn't even get your consent."

I jerk in surprise at the laugh that explodes from my dad. "My sweet Belle. You did nothing wrong. You took care of yourself and me at the same time. Again, I'm not sure where you learned how to do these things, but I am so impressed, and honestly, I need to be more like you."

"Thank you, Dad," I whisper, my voice shaking. A heavy pressure lifts from my chest. It had been there so long I almost didn't understand how I could feel so light and unburdened. I didn't even know it was possible to be absolved of the sins I'd pinned on myself.

Mrs. P's laugh rings through the hall, followed by the unmistakable click of her heels. She appears in the doorway, hands on her hips and a twinkle in her eye. "Basil, you promised to help me with that new recipe, and I don't accept broken promises. Don't worry, Belle, you can taste test."

My father chuckles—a warm, rich sound I haven't heard in years. "I wouldn't dream of breaking my promise, Agatha."

Agatha?

As he stands and takes her hand, I see the spring in his step, the lightness in his movements. He throws me a wink before joining her in the pantry to gather ingredients.

"You know baking isn't all that different from alchemy," he says, obviously trying to impress the housekeeper.

"Then we'll just have to see what we can conjure up between the two of us, shall we?" Mrs. P says in a tight but knowing voice.

Wow.

What?

Okay.

CHAPTER 46

REBINDING THE DREAM

BELLE

Later, Dominic insists on taking me out. He doesn't say where, just that it's important. We drive through Boston, the familiar streets giving way to ones I'd avoided since the fire. My stomach twists as we turn a corner, and I recognize the block.

I clench my fists in my lap. *Why would he bring me here?*

The car slows to a stop. I hesitate, my heart pounding in my chest, before stepping out. And then, I see it.

The ruins of Chapter Three remain, and my heart sinks. Despite feeling the intense satisfaction of allowing love in, there is still a hole inside me. A desperate clawing of some unnamable force scratches fiercely, widening that hole as I take in the wreckage where my bookstore once stood.

"Why are we here?" I ask, my words coming out strangled with grief.

I still want, I *need*, to make an impact. I miss the cozy space I'd created, the people who became a fixture there like the Lust & Lit Book Club, and Chip. I miss seeing the awe and joy of new readers discovering my shop. My throat is dry. My feet turn to lead.

Dominic wraps his arm around me and directs me to walk down the block, away from the burnt remains and the limo. His hair and beard are mussed in that impossibly attractive way, a somehow compelling juxtaposition to the designer suit he's wearing. Instead of a tie he keeps the collar unbuttoned, revealing a bit of carved clavicle and dusting of chest hair.

"Remember when I said you were perfect because you would read and keep to yourself in my company? And you told me that you were so much more than that? That I didn't bother to consider your ambition, but it's just as much a part of you?"

"Where are you going with this?" My anticipation rises, though I'm not sure why. I have no idea what he's driving at, even as we reach the end of the block.

He grips my shoulders, pulling me in for a deep, lingering kiss that leaves me lightheaded and thoroughly melted.

"You were right. But then you became perfect for that too. And I couldn't stand the idea of having you lose that part of yourself." He turns me around.

The large corner shop gleams in the afternoon sunlight, its two-story storefront framed by wide windows and a lavender door. Embedded in the wood, a stained-glass panel depicts a pink rose wrapped in thorns. Above the entrance, a sign in elegant script reads: *Chapter Three: Where Love is the Best Plot Twist.*

I can't breathe.

I might be having a stroke.

"What. . .How—" Words fail me as I turn to Dominic, who has his hands shoved in his pockets. His green eyes watch me with a mixture of amusement and something deeper—something that steals my breath.

"It's not just a bookstore anymore," he says, stepping closer. "It has a café and a bigger community space to easily host book signings, events, whatever you want."

I blink rapidly, tears blurring my vision. "Dominic, I told you before. You can't just buy me off."

I'm only saying that because I am fully bought and paid for with this gesture.

Any moment a receipt will emerge from my mouth to give him proof of sale.

"I know," he says, his voice quiet but firm. "And I'm not trying to. This isn't about money. It's about giving you back something you lost because of me, because of the Wolves. While it's half penance, it's also because I watched you from the limo for weeks on end. I fell in love with the way you smiled and went about tidying up the store. I've never seen Chip so relaxed or excited as when they were working here for you, and I know they've missed it. Mainly because they text me about it almost constantly. I even fell in love with the look on customers' faces as they left with bags of your books clutched to their hearts. You make a difference, Isabelle."

The words settle inside me, light and warm. I step closer, resting a hand on his chest. "This almost feels like you're trying to blackmail me again."

Dominic scoffs in mock shock. "Blackmail? Please. This is a strategic negotiation. If anything, it's a bribe wrapped in a heartfelt, romantic gesture—with, you know, a side of real estate."

I arch a brow. "So, I should just use you for your money, your kindness, your thoughtfulness. . ." I let my hand drift lower, tracing the hard lines of his torso, "and your very generous, very sexy body?"

His lips twitch. "That does seem like the reasonable thing to do."

I hum, pretending to consider. "Well, when you put it that way, refusing would be fiscally irresponsible."

Dominic's laugh rumbles deep in his chest as he pulls me into his arms. "You once told me you were a realist. But here you are, letting a grand gesture sweep you off your feet." He presses his lips to my temple. "Don't worry, wife. I won't tell anyone what a romantic you are."

"I'd appreciate that," I say before throwing my arms around him and kissing him with all the enthusiasm and gratitude I possess. A low growl emits from his chest, vibrating into mine, and pleasure coils in my brain and body at the possessive way he tilts my head so he can claim my mouth more deeply.

When we finally break apart, he gestures toward the building. "Come on. You need to see inside, and if you kiss me like that again I might end up taking you right here on the street. We're both far too busy to be arrested today."

I laugh and follow him to the door which opens with a cheery jingle of a bell. "Yeah, like we'd get arrested." I snort.

"Okay then, I'm in no mood to schmooze or threaten cops."

Before I can answer, a group of women jump in front of me.

"Surprise!"

It's the Lust & Lit Book Club. Yanette, Rachel Anne, Gingie, Hannah, and even Jessie and Nikki crowd around me in a flurry of hugs and laughter, all talking at once—gushing about how gorgeous the place is and how *hot* and *helpful* my husband is.

Dominic stands back, arms crossed, his brow slightly

furrowed as his already darkly blushing complexion turns a shade redder.

I bite my lip to keep from laughing. He can handle mercenaries, criminals, and entire packs of territorial shifters, but six romance readers openly admiring his biceps? Apparently, *that's* his weakness.

Mrs. P and my father emerge from the background, giving me hugs and congratulations. My father's eyes shine brightly with pride and Mrs. P asks me a few surreptitious questions about a historical romance book that caught her eye before they head to the bar to pick up glasses of champagne.

Across the room, Lucien has somehow wedged himself between Yanette and Rachel Anne, all effortless charm and lazy smirks.

"Now tell me, *cher*, what's a man gotta do to get himself a spot in this fine book club?" he asks, voice as smooth as the champagne in his hand.

Yanette gives him a once-over. "Actually read romance novels."

Lucien leans in slightly. "Oh, I *love* romance. Passion, tension, steamy climaxes—"

A few feet away, Tock stands by a shelf, completely unaware of the disaster happening behind him as he discusses narrative structure with Hannah.

"The key to any great book is the climax," Tock says, adjusting his glasses. "Everything builds to that one pivotal moment—"

"Oh, I agree," Nikki earnestly nods her head as Gingie tries to suppress her smile. "I think the building up part is most important. In fact, I think most of the time in a book should be about building up to the . . .climax."

Completely missing the double entendre, Tock smiles

with delight at what he believes to be a very cerebral conversation.

The space is everything I never dared to dream of. The café on one side is warm and inviting, with plush chairs and shelves stacked with well-loved books, spilling onto a small back patio strung with fairy lights. Inside, rows of towering bookshelves create a maze of stories, their spines forming a vibrant mosaic of color and possibility. The scent of fresh wood and coffee weaves through the air, as intoxicating as the moment itself.

Behind the bar, Chip stands grinning, already sporting an apron that reads *Brewed Awakening: Monster Smut Edition*. Their smile is so wide it's a miracle their face doesn't crack.

I blink at the wall behind them, where a row of neatly hung tee shirts are displayed for sale. *Tentacles & Tea* features curling tentacles wrapping around a floral teapot. Next to it, *Read Between the Lattes* is printed in a bold, bookish script, set against an open book with steam rising from its pages like a freshly brewed story. And at the very end, *Cream & Creatures*—a gothic-style pitcher of cream, smooth and overflowing, a monstrous, clawed hand gripping the handle. A single drop of cream slides down, dangerously close to looking obscene.

My lips twitch. "You're really leaning into the brand here."

Chip throws their arms in the air. "Belle, it was my artistic duty. Also, I may have ordered most of the stock, so I *really* hope I did okay." Their eyes widen almost comically. "But honestly? This is the best day ever."

I shake my head, warmth curling through my chest. "You did perfect."

Chip beams, but instead of clapping their hands

together, they snatch another bottle of champagne from behind the bar and start pouring into more flutes that are already lined up. "To new beginnings! To monster smut! To me, for single-handedly managing all the newbie hires!"

I blink. "You hired people already?"

Chip lifts a brow, giving me a look like I just asked if books require words. "Belle. Did you think the two of us could run this entire operation alone? No, no, I'll be training a whole squad of caffeine-fueled, book-loving recruits. Minimum qualifications include speed, sass, and a deep respect for their new overlord—me."

Dominic sighs, rubbing a hand over his face. "I told you, you can't make them call you 'overlord.'"

Chip hands him a flute of champagne and clinks it against their own as they continue to argue about appropriate titles.

The door swings open again, ushering in another wave of chaos. Rap strides in first, a bottle of vodka raised high like a battle trophy, the Lost Girls flooding in behind her. Ted follows close behind, balancing a heart-shaped pink cake that's so perfectly frosted it could only be Goldie's work.

Rap and Dominic end up locked in a low conversation, a silent standoff that ends when she rolls her eyes and hands him a shot, which he downs without question.

Ariel is already taking photos for Poison Apple's socials, capturing a moment of Ted standing beside Goldie, looking deceptively patient as she excitedly flips through a romance novel. His expression is neutral, but the way his fingers subtly trace the spine of another book on the display betrays his interest. Meanwhile, Red and Brexley are in a deep debate over whether the section should be renamed *Absolute Filth and Therefore Perfect*.

Snow is convincing Kai to test the sturdiness of a rolling ladder, and Cinder—far too entertained—leans against a bookshelf, waiting for the inevitable crash.

And, of course, Dame Kiki Eleganza—full Fairy Godmother mode engaged, complete with shimmering heels and a feathered fan—takes one dramatic look around before declaring, "Gorgeous! But this place could use more glitter. Or at least a disco ball."

The store hums with life, a beautiful, chaotic mess of laughter, overlapping voices, and too many champagne bottles being opened at once. I step back a bit, letting it all wash over me, feeling both entirely in it and just outside of it at the same time.

I shake my head, overwhelmed and full in a way I can't explain.

As I stand by the door of Chapter Three, Dominic steps in behind me, his arms sliding around my waist, pulling me flush against him. He leans down, his breath warm against my ear. "What do you think?"

I can't even pretend to fight the smile. "It's *perfect*."

He presses a slow kiss to my neck, holding me tighter.

This isn't just a bookstore. It's a home. A family. Proof that love—messy, imperfect, real love—exists. That it was always real. That I was never foolish for wanting it.

And now? It's mine.

Love. Family. Friends. Purpose. And romance books.

For the first time, I'm not just reading the story—I'm living it. And I wouldn't change a single page.

EPILOGUE
THE BEAST OF BOSTON

If you had told me I would lose my entire pack only to make a new one, I would have called you crazy. But here I am, outside the hospital, pacing like a caged animal, every instinct screaming at me to be inside that room.

My mate. My wife. My Isabelle. She's in there, doing the impossible. And I—an apex predator, a beast who has torn through enemies, ruled over shifters, and faced down death itself—am completely, utterly powerless.

I flex my hands, my claws itching to break free. It's unnatural to be kept from her, but apparently, I was 'too much.'

Which is *bullshit*.

I mean I broke a couple pieces of hospital furniture, so what? I'll pay for the damage.

And that thing I said to the doctor could barely even be considered a threat.

That's just me being *supportive* and *attentive*.

And I was *completely justified* in growling at that nurse.

But apparently, threatening to shift and "take over if

they couldn't do their jobs faster" was where the staff drew the line.

Mrs. P was the one who ultimately came in to drag me out. Said I'd done enough hovering, and that Belle didn't need me *snarling* through her contractions.

Which. Fine.

But I've spent hours outside this room, every second stretching unbearably long.

And then—the door swings open.

Mrs. P's eyes are bright with excitement.

"It's time."

Everything in me stills.

Time.

I move before I can think, flying past her and Basil toward Isabelle's room.

The scent of my wife—her sweat, her pain, her strength—hits me like a punch.

She's tired. My beautiful, impossible woman is utterly spent, her dark hair wild against the pillow. But when she sees me, her lips curve into a weak, breathless smile.

And then I hear it.

The tiniest, angriest little wail.

My chest caves in.

Isabelle laughs—hoarse, exhausted—but I've never heard anything so goddamn beautiful.

"Dominic," she whispers. "Come meet our son."

I stumble forward, my legs not working right, my heart hammering.

And then— he's there.

A bundle of warmth. A scent that is somehow both hers and mine. A heartbeat that already owns me.

I reach out, my hands massive compared to his tiny body.

Mine.

His eyes crack open—deep, wild green. Just like mine.

I swallow hard, looking at Belle. "I should have been here."

She gives me a knowing look, fingers threading weakly through mine. "You are now."

And just like that, I am forgiven.

I bow my head, pressing my lips to her knuckles, then to the soft, downy crown of my son's head.

I may always be the Beast of Boston, but I'll never be a beast to them. My family. My pack. My everything.

Go to **https://hollyroberds.com** for a bonus epilogue featuring Rap and a Lost Girl problem!

TASTING RED

Want more of the Lost Girls? Enjoy this peek into book 1 of Tasting Red

"Why did you call me here?" I ask, though I know perfectly well why the grizzled old son of a bitch sent for me. I spin the titanium ring around my forefinger with my thumb.

He frowns under his thick beard, across from me at the wooden table. He pushes a pint of ale over before grabbing his own. I don't pick up the mug, but the man shrugs and takes a swig.

How did I end up here? For most of my life, I've lived on my terms with no consideration for anyone else. Not even the women I sometimes let in my bed. I follow the jobs that bring the most money and that has served me perfectly well until now.

"It's been a long time, Brexley," he says.

Nineteen years, if one were counting. And for nineteen years, I've felt the ghostly shackle, tying me to someone else. Nearly two-thirds of my life, waiting for the shoe to drop.

"Not long enough," I say gruffly, finally grabbing the mug and taking a healthy swallow of the stuff. I hate to admit the shit is good. So I don't.

I've done everything I could to be free of social ties. There is no place for me among mage, man, or fae. But today is the day my only marker is called.

I owe one being a favor in this entire world and he has summoned me here to the musty backroom of his tavern. Boxes pile high around the room, surrounding us. He named the joint *Sam's*, though his name is Jameson. I never asked who he named it after, and I still won't ask.

The drizzle kicks up a heavy mist that clings to the windows. The cold seeps its way into my bones despite my knit sweater and leather jacket. On a shitty day like this, I'd normally be at home by the fire with a book. But this old son of a bitch has me by the balls.

"You owe me, Brexley," Jameson starts, as if he expects a fight.

I wipe my mouth with the back of my hand. "I'm aware, you old bastard. Just tell me what you want so we can get this over with."

His calloused fingers drum on the manilla folder next to him before sliding it over. "I need you to take care of her."

His tone tells me he doesn't mean take her out for lunch and shopping. He must have been keeping tabs on me to know what kind of business I'm in now. Or maybe he's just a sadistic son of a bitch, and I could be a florist and he'd still give me the same mission.

I push the mug away, despite wanting more. Drinking won't make this problem disappear. But once my only debt is paid, I won't have anything hanging over me. I'll truly be free.

I flip the folder open to a picture and a single page of

details: name, occupation, home addresses. But I didn't need any of that info. I instantly recognize the older woman in the photo. I've seen her many times—on billboards, commercials, packages of food, enamel pins that people stick on their jackets.

A dry snort escapes me. "You've got to be joking."

The old bastard doesn't crack a smile, doesn't move a muscle.

Fuck me.

I run a hand through my already unruly silver hair. "Grandma. You want me to go after Grandma from 'Grandma's House?' The face of the most popular household brand, and one of the most powerful witches known to the world?"

Jameson repeats himself in slow, steady words. "You owe me." Coiled tension is locked up behind his dark eyes and in the set of his broad shoulders. Blood lust shines out from his face. This is business from his past. But I don't ask questions, and I'm not about to start now.

I study him, observing how he's changed since I last saw him. Even more gray strands pepper his black hair and beard. His scowl has only deepened with the years, multiplying the lines at the corners of his eyes. He must be nearing his fifties, but under his flannel shirt vest is a body still packed with the sturdy muscles of a heavyweight boxer.

Once upon a time, I considered this man to be like a father to me. He quickly dispelled me of that notion with an unholy vengeance. He taught me the truth. Dependence is death. Don't buy into the lie. You don't need others to survive in this world. It is a gilded lie that ends with getting stabbed in the back.

Or, in my case, a set of claws raked across my face.

But finally, I'm given the opportunity to dissolve my last tie to another being, and this is my chance. As one of the most beloved celebrity icons, this also may be my chance to get killed.

My fingers wrap around the cold handle of the mug, suddenly thirsty. "She won't be easy to get to. And afterward, I'll be hunted like an animal."

His chair creaks with a loud groan as he leans back with a smirk. I've already accepted his terms. "Good thing you're used to it."

So he does know my business.

I shoot him a cutting look over the edge of the mug as I swallow the rest of the amber liquid.

"After all," he folds his arms across his chest, "you are the Big Bad Wolf."

My grin is half-grimace. "And that is very bad news for grandmas right now."

~

Read *Tasting Red* now to find out what happens when Red and the Big Bad collide at grandma's house

FEEDING BEAUTY

Preorder the next Lost Girls book now, and we'll return to
Poison Apple in Fall of 2025.
Reserve Your Copy Now!

Available for preorders on Amazon and hollyroberds.com

A FREE LOST GIRLS NOVELLA

HOOKING TINK

A cursed pirate. A furious fairy. Every tattoo unlocks more than just his magic—it unravels them both.

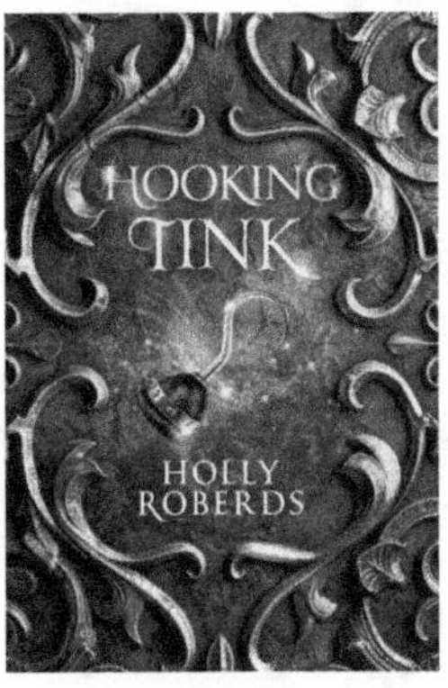

Download this Lost Girl's Novella and 52+ Fairytale Retellings for FREE at hollyroberds.com

LOVE THIS BOOK?

Enjoy more by this author

Vivien woke up with no memories and a terrible thirst for blood.

The Grim Reaper must destroy all blood suckers.

The reaper dogs just want to get pets and loves in between fetching the souls for the Afterlife.

Read this COMPLETE trilogy and you'll laugh, you'll cry, you'll absolutely die.

ACKNOWLEDGMENTS

Thank you to my assistants, Leah Crowell and Tara Volpenhein for keeping all the machines running and the lights on even when I disappear into my writing hidey hole. I would be seriously unwell without you two.

Thank you to Sarah Urquhart for laughing at me as I cried and raged my way through a particularly challenging phase of life and then again when I had to go through the dreaded editing process. Thanks for giving me my turn to be fussy. Your turn!

Thank you to my editors Theresa Paolo, Havoc Archives & Athena Franks for making sure I don't launch a pile of garbage at my beloved readers. Thanks for making me seem smarter and dealing with the mess of my nonlinear writings.

To my special reader fan group, *Holly's Hellions* – thank you for all the gifs and comments of support! That really got me through this one! Especially when I was afraid of living up to the hype of Beauty and the Beast, you reminded me I have your fealty. Yay! We're like a cult!

To my Patrons – thank you for sharing a space that feeds my soul and voting on so many aspects that went into this book. Your interaction brings the fun.

Thank you to l'husbun, for pouring me the good tequila while I raged my way through edits. And for being the absolutely love of my life without being a beast. You are the beauty. Wait that makes me the. . . dammit.

A Letter from the Author

A Letter from the Author

Dear Reader,

Thank you for reading!

There is more to come! Ariel, Snow, Rap, and a Sleeping Beauty retelling are all in the works, and I can't wait to continue sharing this world with you. You're enthusiasm, DMs, reviews, and support is what keeps this series going and I hope to deliver your wildest, spiciest fantasies.

Want to make sure you never miss a release or any bonus content I have coming down the pipeline? Make sure to join my Patreon: Holly Roberds Books

And definitely sign up for Holly's Hotspot, my newsletter, and I'll send you a FREE ebook right away!

You can also find me on my website www.hollyroberds.com and I hang out on social media.

Instagram: http://instagram.com/authorhollyroberds

Facebook: www.facebook.com/hollyroberdsauthorpage/

And closest to my black heart is my reader fan group,

Holly's Hellions. Become a Hellion. Raise Hell. www.facebook.com/groups/hollyshellions/
Cheers!
Holly Roberds

ABOUT THE AUTHOR

Holly Roberds is an Amazon Top 40 Bestselling Author of the Vegas Immortals and Lost Girls series, known for badass heroines, gut-busting laughs, and spicy romance. Holly lives in Denver but is only outdoorsy in that she drinks on patios—with a prosecco in one hand and an espresso in the other. When not writing, she's playing D&D, sharpening her banter skills, or sinking her teeth into her husband's very bitable arm.

For more sample chapters, news, and more, visit www. hollyroberds.com